S0-ALG-661

NO LONGER PROPERTY OF
SEATTLE PUBLIC LIBRARY

Also by Porochista Khakpour

Brown Album: Essays on Exile and Identity

Sick: A Memoir

The Last Illusion

Sons and Other Flammable Objects

Tehrangeles

Tehrangeles

Porochista Khakpour

PANTHEON BOOKS
New York

This is a work of fiction. Names, characters, places, and incidents either are the product of the author's imagination or are used fictitiously. Any resemblance to actual persons, living or dead, events, or locales is entirely coincidental.

Copyright © 2024 by Porochista Khakpour

All rights reserved. Published in the United States by Pantheon Books, a division of Penguin Random House LLC, New York, and distributed in Canada by Penguin Random House Canada Limited, Toronto.

Pantheon Books and colophon are registered trademarks of Penguin Random House LLC.

Library of Congress Cataloging-in-Publication Data
Name: Khakpour, Porochista, author.
Title: Tehrangeles : a novel / Porochista Khakpour.
Description: First edition. | New York : Pantheon Books, 2024.
Identifiers: LCCN 2023040059 (print) | LCCN 2023040060 (ebook) |
ISBN 9781524747909 (hardcover) | ISBN 9781524747916 (ebook)
Subjects: LCGFT: Domestic fiction. | Novels.
Classification: LCC PS3611.H32 T44 2024 (print) |
LCC PS3611.H32 (ebook) | DDC 813/.6—dc23/eng/20231006
LC record available at https://lccn.loc.gov/2023040059
LC ebook record available at
https://lccn.loc.gov/2023040060

www.pantheonbooks.com

Jacket design and illustration by Philip Pascuzzo

Printed in the United States of America
First Edition
1st Printing

For Hushi ⚝
dearest friend ◉
muse & musemaker 💝
& emperor of Persian party girls 🍂

"My biggest fear is to die. Because I have no idea what happens after. And I'm really scared that there is nothing because that would be . . . beyond boring."

—Paris Hilton, *The American Meme*

GQ: Didn't you always feel like a freak growing up?
Tom Ford: I thought I was fabulous and everyone else was stupid.

—Lisa Eisner, "Tom Ford: The Ultimate Interview," *GQ Australia* (2012)

"Fear is the cheapest room in the house."

—Hafiz

a note to our viewers

"tehrangeles" was not invented by any of us. we've used the
word our whole lives,
and it was used before us, and before that too.
how do you introduce a people, a place?
tehrangeles is, as my sister roxi likes to call it, a *poor-man-toe*
(i promised her i would put that here), or: a *portmanteau*.
two words smashed up, two worlds mashed together.
i wrote a state report on california once, and did you know
the name california
comes from a 16th century spanish novel involving a fic-
tional island called california,
populated by all black women with a pagan warrior queen
named califia in charge?
califia comes from the arabic word *khalifia* or caliph.
so it's closer to us than we ever knew.
if i had to describe our world, i'd say it's hell dressed like
heaven or the opposite,
depending on who you're asking.
it's boulevards and avenues and drives and canyons and pla-
yas and paseos and palisades.
it's pale yellow-gray skies and hot pink sunsets and bad air
and dirty water.

it's long driveways, it's those weird branchy ficus-lined residential streets,
it's the palm trees that were never from here, transplants
like most everyone else.
it's spanish colonial revival, craftsman, mid-century modern, victorian, art deco.
it's fendi and gucci and chanel and versace and cartier and
rolex and
bentley and rolls royce and maserati and white bmws.
it's swarovski and diamonds; gold and fake, and gold and real.
it's jumping over the fire, throwing rice at weddings, knife
dances,
praying five times a day, and praying never.
it's saffron butter rice, it's rosewater ice cream, it's *khask* &
tahdig.
it's jewish and muslim and christian and bahá'í and zoroas-
trian and nothing at all.
it's *joon* and *aziz* and all the *dears* and *darlings* your aunts and
cousins surround you with.
it's nosejobs and botox and sugaring and highlights and
lowlights and gel manicures.
it's chanel no. 5 and baccarat rouge 540 and le labo santal
33 and the obscure stuff i don't know,
but it's also the basic stuff, the way girls even my age smell
like vanilla if vanilla was *money.*
it's all of our valley girl vocal fries. (dear god, make mine
die one day.)
it's california girls and . . . california guys? it's *california girls.*
it's a homeland far far far away that we will never see.
it's this place, i am supposed to tell you, that made us, but
we hear we were born made.
it's the world's largest community of iranians outside iran.
tehrangeles, california.
honestly, i hate it here.

we can't speak for them, we can barely speak for us. we're young and I worry we'll be forever young. you know how they put a spotlight on a people? ta-da, here they are? well, this was our year, they told us; but this is the year the spotlight left us.

—Mina Milani

Book I

The Show

1

Roxanna

One Paradise Crescent Place,
Bella Rosa Vista, Los Angeles, California

It was a perfect eighty-three-degree December morning and Roxanna had decisions to make. "I think it's called 'zodiac reassignment something something,'" she was muttering into the perfumed pages of a magazine, knowing well that her sisters were half listening at best. She was sure she had seen it somewhere in those pages, and so she tugged at her Cavalli Havana-frame shades dramatically as if they were the culprits behind the day's compromised reading comprehension. "It's just a legal thing, really. Court documents. I would be interested if I were you, bitches. Cursed energy is not just me here!"

It had been a while since all four sisters found themselves gathered together by the Grecian infinity pool, their favorite spot for morning family meetings. This time, Violet's charity brunch had been rescheduled for another Saturday, Haylee hadn't made it off the wait list for her Barbie barre class, and Mina—who was usually on her computer or sleeping in from a late night on the computer—had set extra alarms to avoid her sister's wrath. Roxanna hated being up early, but she needed her sisters gathered together in the name of their future fame.

But instead of discussing the show, there was Roxanna's pressing issue at hand: changing her birthdate.

"11:11—make a wish!!" Her iPhone went off in a custom tone she considered angel chimes and so off she went as well, interrupting her own train of thought. She had learned about the power of 11:11 through so many socialites, models, and influencers who loved to post it to their social media. Only recently, with so much at stake, she began programming it into her phone.

Nobody made a wish. Just Roxanna, who wished for the obvious. (*Score-pee-ho,* she mentally whispered into where she imagined her brain and conscience met.)

"Wait, can I just ask . . . ?" Haylee said, as she had many times that day. Roxanna kept grunting as if to say, *Go ahead,* and Haylee again blurted, "Why are you doing this again?"

Roxanna threw down her magazine and looked her youngest sister in the eye. "We all have things we need to figure out! You know, this is going to be *big*. We gotta get it together."

"I'm confused—are you trying to move your birthday to be older or younger?" Mina asked, also not for the first time. She was trying to hold her tongue, like she had weeks ago, as *zodiac reassignment* sounded absurd at best and transphobic-adjacent at worst. But it had been hopeless with Roxanna then, and it was hopeless with Roxanna now.

"Jesus fucking fuck!" Roxanna belted out. She was regretting this whole thing: the meeting mostly, kinda the show, and basically her life. Was this what the show was going to be like? She hoped not—she would of course have to carry the thing, regardless; that she knew. Her gaze slid over to Violet, who looked to be calmly listening, although it was hard to tell with her eyes obscured by her oversize red-acetate Balenciaga heart-shaped sunglasses. She was likely asleep, not having said a word the whole time, but Roxanna preferred her silence to the reactions of her two younger sisters. Mina and Haylee could not be more different, but they were unified in not understanding her one bit.

"I just—I just cannot go down as a Gemini—it's not, like, good for me!" she said. "Not the vibe. It's that fucking simple."

Mina tried not to groan. "Right. But do you really believe

that? Does anyone even care about astrology that much any-more? It's almost 2020."

Roxanna rolled her eyes. "It doesn't matter, babe," she said in her snarliest snarl. "Everyone knows. Trump, Kanye. Both are Geminis. It's not good."

Haylee was nodding. "But then, like, wouldn't *all* Geminis do that? Or, like, Aquariuses? I mean, seriously, is it that easy to just switch?"

Roxanna smiled big. Sometimes it felt like Haylee was the sole sister who did speak her language. "With money it is, bitch." Their family lawyers were their friends, the *real* kind, who came to the holiday parties, and Roxanna already had a tentative okay to go with her zodiac reassignment from her father. "It's just not done that often. There was that one case of the creepy old dude who just wanted to be younger for dating profiles. But we're not changing my age. We're just claiming my birth certificate is, like, wrong."

This did not add up for Mina, but she had learned a long time ago to stay out of Roxanna's hijinks. Plus, Roxanna had Haylee, who would eventually go along with anything Roxanna wanted.

"You are such a Gemini, though." Violet spoke up slowly, yawning into the sun. The pool hadn't been cleaned in some time—dead leaves, a variety of crispy flower petals, and strug-gling insects floated on the surface—or else she would have dipped in. "In the good way, Roxi."

"I am actually *very much* Scorpionic," Roxanna snapped at her older sister. "And, like, everyone knows that."

Violet (Pisces) offered a tight smile and exchanged a quick glance with Haylee (Libra). Mina (Capricorn) was the only earth sign in the family, with Homa a Cancer and Al an Aries. Roxanna, of air and now water, everyone knew, was the most invested in all kinds of convenient magical thinking, especially of the painfully trendy variety.

There had been so much to do and so many decisions to

make now that the show was really happening, and Roxanna had decided this winter that they were going to settle it all. There were their names, for instance. "Roxanna," her real name, had always been fine—well, her *real* real name was fine too: "Roxanna-Vanna," Americanized from the start. Violet had been born "Banafsheh," but started using "Violet," the translation, when she opted for homeschooling, and only recently had she considered switching back. There was a supermodel named Violet she didn't want to be confused with as her own career took off, she had said at first, but privately, Roxanna wondered if Violet didn't simply want to appear more Iranian. Haylee, meanwhile, had been "Haylee" since kindergarten, as no one could pronounce "Haleh," or so she insisted. And Mina, like Roxanna, had been born "Mina," the perfect, nondescript name for the least flashy of the sisters. Their parents, Homa and Al— even as "Ali"—were to use their real names.

The producers had encouraged the family to keep everything as real as possible. *Reality TV is all about keeping it really real,* Roxanna remembered the main producer saying more than once over the phone.

Roxanna had assured them everything would be real. "Oh, well, we like put the *keep it real* in *keep it real*," she had quipped in a bemused half-cringe, to the producer's delight. *This one's the one,* she had heard the producer say to his assistant, her body filling with a weird warmth that she knew was just a dusting of stardom over a wash of absolute embarrassment.

The only thing Roxanna had left to worry about was her astrological sign. After all, identity was *in,* she had heard someone important say. The business of changing the birthdate on her documents had to be cheaper than the gender reassignment some of her classmates were opting for, she had argued to her parents, who were less worried about the cost than the state of Roxanna's mental health.

And then there was the Secret. Only Mina knew. Violet was

out of school now. She had been homeschooled, had finally graduated, and was still unready to commit to higher education. Haylee was a few months into high school, but she would eventually know. Roxanna could reason with her. Mina was more the issue, so practical and grounded—and, well, always around. She would ignore the issue mostly, but occasionally it would smack right into her, when someone asked her about her heritage. At first Mina had thought it was because of their dad's company, but as she entered tenth grade that year, Roxanna told her the truth.

Oh, well, we put the keep it real in keep it real . . . Her sister's words buzzed shoddily like a dying neon sign in Mina's mind.

Roxanna, in a measured hyperventilating Mina knew too well, had begged her not to tell. It had been a big secret for her, the biggest of her life. Roxanna did not have many secrets she could keep and Mina felt like it was a miracle she could keep this one, especially from Violet—who tended to know everything—and Haylee, who would be the most upset. In an ideal world, Mina should have been the last to know, and more than once she had considered telling their parents. But what would that do—Al would maybe find it funny, Homa would use it as just another reason to remain depressed. It was bad enough that Roxanna's very Roxanna-ness had resulted in the reality TV deal anyway.

Unfuckingreal, Mina had said over and over. *Unfuckingreality.*

When the producers wanted to meet, when something of the nothing was actually set in stone . . . *well, then, we could decide!* was how Roxanna had spun it. Mina, of course, had eyed Roxanna suspiciously, her silence tense and measured. Mina, who spent her time between Twitter and TikTok and Instagram and Snapchat, and kept her notifications on when she was supposed to be sleeping, was what they called *extremely online,* and for that reason she had been the first to speak up and announce that reality TV was totally over.

"What are you talking about, bitch?" Roxanna had nearly screamed.

"There are rumors this season is the Kardashians' last," Mina said plainly. "Who else is there? No one cares anymore. It's very ten years ago."

Roxanna was furious, but she did the only thing she could: ignore her. Fine with Mina—she wasn't going to be a main character, anyway. Haylee, meanwhile, was elated. She was new to being a teenager and she was ready for the world to see her. Homa had finally allowed her to dye her hair white-blond— she was born with lighter hair than the rest but certainly not platinum—and she was trying to figure out how to look like her new favorite celebrity, always rotating among models and actresses and pop stars and influencers. She imagined that, as reality TV stars, they'd get all sorts of perks—even better clothes, maybe even some lip filler, which she'd been dying to get after Roxanna and Violet had had theirs done at the height of Kylie Jenner Lip Kit mania. That was where Haylee's mind was: the extravagant possibilities of fame.

Violet had been calm, as usual. As long as Tens, her modeling agency, was okay with the show, and as long as it amplified, not minimized, her modeling, then it was fine. Who knew, maybe it could really help, but the truth was Violet, like Mina, was more introverted. Her shoots were enough attention for her. She prayed that their dad, Roxanna, and Haylee could hog all the attention and Violet, Mina, and Homa could linger on the sidelines in peace. The show, of course, would be Roxanna's.

Everyone agreed except Al, who said the show was really his. Roxanna was his favorite, and he was hers, though they were the two who competed the most against each other. Homa and Violet played the quieter matriarchs, and Mina and Haylee didn't have much say in anything.

The best part for Roxanna was that the whole endeavor hadn't taken too much convincing for Al. The bottom line, the producers said, was that it would be good for business. In the entire history of reality TV, there was not a case of a business not growing due to heightened profile offered by this sort of opportunity. Look at *The Real Housewives*—Bethenny Frankel's Skinnygirl Margaritas, they had said. Or *Love & Hip Hop*—Cardi B's entire career. Al was in, regardless. It was almost as if he had imagined it. He was the man behind Pizzabomme, and he was more than fine with introducing America to him and his beautiful family. He knew it was Homa who needed the nudging.

Homa had been suffering from clinical depression since the day they met but she made sure it rarely showed, if ever. She didn't want to be seen, but she tolerated it. She was also beautiful but not in a showy way—hers was not the sultry full moon–like beauty of her oldest, Violet, or the wild, trendy gorgeousness of her electric stunner Roxanna, not the angular, elite crisp of Haylee either. The one who resembled her the most was Mina, the only daughter who had settled into herself in a composed way. She had never even dyed her hair, and had kept it in a chic but fairly boring smooth, brown bob her whole life, much like Homa had.

When the producers finished their pitch and Al declared his unequivocal interest to Roxanna's elated applause and all the other daughters displayed their varying degree of excited-to-polite smiles, all eyes fell on Homa, who, in her low, deeply accented, rich tenor, said, in barely a whisper, "Well, it will have to be okay with me, it seems."

What Homa really meant to say was that it was clear it was somehow decided already without much input from her. One of her few friends had once told her Roxanna reminded her a bit of Ivanka Trump, as it felt like she was the real lady of the house, Al's perfect counterpart. She was not just a scene-stealer, but the real dealmaker. Homa knew there was little she could say to get out of it, but she felt most consoled hearing from the producers that they should not count on this having a long life, that shows like this rarely aired for longer than a season. It would likely be a one-off and they could not expect much network support either. Of course they hoped for success, but the real secret to making it in Hollywood was to never bank on anything.

"Well, my wife is great at pessimism!" Al immediately announced, though he, like Roxanna, was thinking ahead to a lifetime of seasons, a few more sports cars and jets and villas—all the essential extras his considerable wealth could *almost* still not afford.

"We are the heiresses of the world's most popular junk food— you can count on us to be *a lot,*" Roxanna had said at the end of the meeting, after the producers mentioned that the dynamics between the sisters would probably carry much of the show. "Right, sissies?"

Violet had flashed a shy but still model-y smile, Haylee had put on her most overenthusiastic beam, not realizing how child-like it came off, and Mina had lifted her eyes from the ground and tried to smize her way into gratitude. Just one season—if her mother could do it, so could she, she reasoned.

And so there they were: four parallel planes, little intersection, all reflection, by the lambent luster of the seldom-used pool. December 2019: before. Before so much, nobody thought at the time.

"If I were you I'd be less worried about lying about your star sign and more worried about things that matter," Mina muttered to Roxanna privately after their pool gathering. "Like the Secret. How exactly is everyone supposed to play along with that?"

Roxanna hated when Mina spoke about the Secret, just as much as she hated not having figured out what to do about it. She would, though. Eventually. There was time. Maybe exiting Geminidom would change her world somehow. But she didn't say that to Mina. To Mina she just nodded and smiled sweetly. "Don't you worry about a thing. It's all in the works. Trust, bitch!"

Nobody considered that if their Persian cat, Pari—classic, flat face with full cheeks, marble-round blue eyes, and 9.75 pounds of pristine-white glossy fluff—could have a word, maybe it would be something no one would expect. Perhaps she would have a few things to say about the Show, the Secret, everything that was to come. She had that quality so many cats possess: conveniently lovable but never too reluctant to unnerve. Her age was unknown but she maintained a vaguely ancient air crossed with the only-(pet)child convention: being the forever baby of the family. Some of the sisters loved her more than others—Pari knew this—but she didn't care. She watched her human family with increasing concern as the last days of 2019 ran out. There was something wrong with the picture and the only thing that put her little feline heart at ease was not knowing what something right would look like with the Milanis.

2

Violet

Violet was the first sister to reach any level of fame. And it wasn't just because she was the oldest. It was because at a young age, her talent had become obvious—everyone saw it, from schoolteachers to classmates to strangers at the mall to Roxanna. Roxanna, who lived for nineties nostalgia, especially via fashion sites on Instagram and style-influencer TikTok, was always the one hoarding old fashion magazines she would find on eBay. She would cut out photos of all-American cover girls Niki and Krissy Taylor and insist the two girls playact at being them. When Violet finally gently told Roxanna that in that scenario she, as the younger one, would be Krissy—the one who died a very tragic premature death—Roxanna transformed her momentary fluster into an exaggerated groan. *So basic.* Who would think to bring that up when you could instead be captivated by the tube tops and the cutoffs and the forever-wet hair and the bronze body shimmer and the perfect pearls of white teeth? She used Violet's vibe-killing as proof of a simple-mindedness that was yet another great reason for her to consider modeling.

It was not an obvious sell to Violet. She was reserved. As the oldest, she felt some responsibility over the others, especially when Homa was checking out, in her deep depressive funks, sometimes for days at a time. Violet had looked after her sisters for as long as she could remember—she had been the one to direct the family's team of housekeepers and nannies, sending them off with lists and reporting back to her parents on their progress.

Everyone knew Violet was the favorite. Violet, with her near-mythic beauty—she had never, not even for a fraction of a season, known an awkward phase. Violet, with her soft voice that had the feel of cotton candy and whipped honey and shredded silk. Violet, who was the Persian rose, everyone agreed, like the ingenue of a classical Persian miniature tableau, with her huge black eyes and long, silky black hair, always giving a bit of Persian princess dipped in a Ferdowsi goddess mood. Violet, the surrogate mother; Violet, the first daughter; Violet, the soft and loving and sweet heroine of a better story.

Sweet! Diabetic-coma sweet, Roxanna would snicker, because of course Violet had to have a flaw or at least an Achilles' heel. Roxanna loved to play up her spidery frame and deep distrust of everything edible against her sister's food anxieties. What marred Violet's perfect record, after all, was something as American as it was Persian: Violet was addicted to sugar.

Violet's palate ran sweet *only.* And so for most of her life—Homa really could not remember a time when this was not the case, her milk formula even requiring date syrup to be tolerable for her as an infant—Violet had been hooked on sweets. This was no exaggeration and a source of great wonder to everyone. How did Violet survive on sweets alone?

A typical day of food consumption for Violet would be a breakfast of sugary frosted cereal with strawberry milk, a handful of Cadbury Creme Eggs as a snack, a large caramel iced coffee with extra vanilla syrup, cinnamon bagel with pineapple cream cheese drizzled with orange blossom syrup for lunch, a large chai coffee with extra almond syrup, half a pint of peppermint ice cream with coconut-cream topping, a handful of Red Vines or Twizzlers, sweet grits with candied yams and honey-glazed coconut shrimp for dinner, some variety of pie for dessert, Jordan almonds or Junior Mints as a final dessert. Roxanna would watch her in awe; Roxanna, who was likely naturally thin, though no one could be sure, since she had been rabidly dieting since she was a toddler; Roxanna, whose diet was carrot and celery sticks dipped in soy sauce and bowls of iceberg lettuce with a few splashes of apple cider vinegar and cayenne pepper. If Roxanna was not "very underweight" on the BMI chart, she did not feel herself, she would argue; her thinness was a mindset, she argued, a crocheted Kate Moss–ism NOTHING TASTES AS GOOD AS SKINNY FEELS banner hovering in black silk over her vanity.

Violet wasn't one to gain weight easily anyway, though in recent months, she had noticed her curves announcing themselves rather insistently. She began to wonder if Haylee's warnings that "things will catch up with you, Vivi" were finally coming true. Haylee was unabashedly orthorexic, the family's home gym entirely her labor of love, full of Pilates gear, weights, yoga mats, plus a steam room and a sauna. Violet's agent had mentioned that plus-size modeling was becoming a promising new option for a lot of models, as beauty standards were shifting and influencers were suddenly being applauded for bravely showing cellulite and stomach rolls. The agency sent these reminders to Violet because they were well aware of her eating habits—on set, her agent had gone as far as to call it *special needs,* her manager explaining that she required sweets for energy. The usual spreads of hummus and vegetables would just not do; Violet needed milkshakes, cupcakes, sour candy, chocolate bark, gummy animals.

Of course it concerned those around her, but it also amused and delighted them. The world loves nothing more than a thin, beautiful woman who eats with abandon, someone had to have said. And so Violet, in having a dessert-only diet, was doing what few ever entertained—it seemed nearly impossible to survive this way. But she did, and there were no sugar highs and crashes, no mania or dips, just Violet serene, and in fact as sweet as the foods she consumed.

It disgusted Roxanna sometimes, though other times she felt she was living vicariously through her. Roxanna wasn't sure she had ever consumed a candy bar in her entire life, only recalling a Hershey's Kiss or two at the holidays or on Valentine's Day, perhaps. She had embarked on her first diet when she was four.

Though Violet was known as one of the better-adjusted sisters if not the best, people tended to blame her addiction on isolation. She had been homeschooled for most of her student life, with a few years of jumping back in just to jump back out. She had always felt too introverted to participate in normal school but it wasn't the usual shyness; she was extraordinarily beautiful from the moment she was born, which for any K–12 kid spells constant bullying, and she needed only a season of kindergarten to spark the envy of every three-and-a-half-foot little girl around her. She grew out of her extreme introversion but not out of her need to have time to herself, to sequester and recharge, which required she be in her bedroom as often as possible—her bedroom all roses and marble accents and pink vintage lace and lilac scents, whereas Roxanna's was minimal gold-and-black marble, smelling like the sort of exclusive boutique you'd find in Paris, aggressive and sexy, what Roxanna hoped gave off power vibes. The soft femininity and floral serenity of Violet's space revolted her—plus, the smell gave off powdered-sugar clouds and she worried that just breathing in there would make her gain weight.

A trip to the mall as a teenager changed Violet's life. Of course it happened in the food court. *Of all the clichés, the model being discovered at the mall is just so, like, nineties at best,* Roxanna said, driving a spike into her model sister's enchanting origin story. Violet had found peace sitting in the food court sipping on a root beer float, slicing into a cinnamon pretzel, and trying to very slowly pick at her bag of mostly Swedish Fish and Sour

Patch Kids and Smarties. A scout had brazenly taken the empty seat opposite her, her eyes locked on Violet's, and had struck up an innocent conversation. She had a thick European accent, and Violet assumed she was a tourist looking for directions, but after a few minutes of uncomfortable small talk, the Dutch woman in the navy blazer took a card out from her breast pocket and pushed it toward Violet with two nude stiletto-manicured fingers. Violet absently rested her root beer float on it like it was a coaster, smiled, and nodded.

"Thanks?" she had said politely.

"Young girl, do you know what this is about?" the scout said in a hissy villain tone, which mostly came from amusement over Violet's obliviousness. Young women usually shrieked from excitement at the prospect of this dream opportunity. "Where are your parents?" she asked.

Violet shyly shook her head.

The scout looked so frustrated. "This is the real thing, girl. I think you have what it takes. No promises, but call us up and make an appointment. I could be wrong, but I think I see something special in you—just not sure of your attitude."

Violet had looked at the card with the slight head tilt of a lapdog when it all finally computed for her. "Oh my goodness. Modeling? Wow." She was about to pull out her phone and suggest the scout take a look at her sister's Instagram when it really hit her. This could really be a path for her. The kind of path that Al encouraged each of the sisters to find, even when they were small.

"Ulrika," Violet sounded out. "Thank you."

The scout moved her eyes to Violet's snack spread. "Just don't tell me you have that problem," she said, waving her hand at the mess of sugary forbiddens.

"What problem?" This was a modest spread compared to her usual.

Ulrika grew flustered. She had forgotten the name for the

disease, but it was a common one among her girls. She waved her hand at the snacks again and then her long pointer finger hovered at her mouth, while her body rippled in an exaggerated heave.

Head tilt from Violet.

Ulrika waved her hand at the bathroom across from them and made vomiting sounds, a bit too loudly, until Violet seemed to get it.

"Oh, barf. Barf?"

Violet was sixteen, a young sixteen. And because she was homeschooled, she had not been around too many kids her age. *Bulimia* was not yet in her vocabulary.

The scout assumed Violet did not want to admit her problem, so she let it go and decided to just forget what she saw at this young potential's table. Instead she focused on Violet, a tall girl, with curves, her heavily moisturized honey-brown skin, iridescent lavender tube top and pink gingham pencil skirt, and silky black hair French-braided down her back. She looked like she had walked off a teen-romance movie set, a universal love interest.

The only meaningful question she had asked Violet was her age—she would need parental consent—and the rest of the time, the agent talked. Violet had taken in what she could, but a combination of her shyness and queasiness had made it all feel like a dream. The next day, not believing that what had happened was real, she let Roxanna finally make the call for her.

"Yes, Violet M-I-L-A-N-I," Roxanna said over the phone, with a thumbs-up sign to Violet, who sat next to her trying to make out Ulrika's voice on the other end. "I am the mall girl you spoke to. And I am so thrilled you found me. . . ."

She went on and on, and plans were made. "I have a sister you might want to meet too," Roxanna added, winking at Violet. "She's a bit younger, but she was made for this stuff. She's, like, a lot thinner than me too, much more into fashion—

should I bring her?" The scout reluctantly agreed, and a week later, Homa was driving her two oldest daughters to a modeling agency appointment.

Violet wore a misleadingly simple calico dress with a sweetheart cut—a vintage Betsey Johnson—with gold Vivienne Westwood Mary Janes that belonged to Roxanna. Roxanna had done her sister's hair too, which was sprayed stiff and swept to one side. She had done Violet's makeup according to a tutorial she saw on YouTube for "unicorn girls," all blurry pastels and iridescent shimmer with muted rainbow tones, confection references, and an all-around manic-pixie cloudscape ambience. Violet felt as uncomfortable as ever, but when she saw her thirteen-year-old sister in a medley of mismatching but gutsy metallics—Daisy Dukes, a halter top, a choker, a beret, and platform clogs, all in a haze of silver, gold, and bronze—she felt relieved. Maybe the attention would fall on Roxanna instead of her. The entire car ride, as Homa glumly listened to Roxanna's directions, Violet silently popped chocolate-covered espresso beans and prayed for the best.

The interview had been more like a casting—or so she thought, as she barely understood what castings or even interviews were like in the first place. Ulrika and two of her coworkers looked Violet up and down while Homa and Roxanna waited in the adjacent reception area. Roxanna had tried to come in with Violet, but Ulrika stopped her.

"I am the little sister she mentioned on the phone." Roxanna flashed a huge smile. "The thinner, fashionier one. I wasn't at the mall that day but I'm here now!"

Ulrika had looked at her, this strange, glittering girl who looked made of coins.

"We will call you if we need you," Ulrika muttered. "Violet's mom, can you come in?"

A half hour later, when Violet walked outside, her face flushed, her hands wrapped around her body as if she had been violated, Roxanna assumed it was all over. Violet looked sad, a unicorn with no chance of horn, and so she thought it was best not to rub it in. Roxanna put her arm around her sister to console her.

By the time they pulled into the long driveway at home, Violet knew she had to say something.

"Well," she said as the Audi doors declared themselves unlocked and she stepped into the almost annoyingly perfect Southern California midday sun, "I guess I am a model now, whatever that means."

It took Violet turning twenty to finally embrace her calling and learn to "level up," as Roxanna put it. For one thing, she needed to be more open to risqué shoots, she told herself. Just a year before, when her agent had asked if she was open to shoots that showed more skin, Violet had blurted out, "Maybe when I'm not a teenager anymore?" She of course knew well the world of teens and nudes—Roxanna had sent her first nude to a friend at twelve, she boasted—but going there before twenty was not right, Violet thought. Never mind that Homa would find her too young to do that at forty, but luckily, as with most things, their mother was absent. And so she decided twenty it was.

Roxanna had been shooting Violet since way before Violet had gone the professional route. It was decided at a very young age that Violet was going to be the Pretty One—even as Roxanna maintained she was sexier, edgier, and, did she mention, *naturally* (maybe not so naturally) thinner? Violet could have the Persian rose status. Roxanna would do her makeup and hair and style her for hours. *The Violet Milani Swimsuit Calendar!* she loved to shout with the same bravado of a lion tamer at a circus. It usually went well until the incident when Roxanna posted one of Violet's bikini shots as hers—beheaded her sister in the photo, chose an angle that looked suitably thin, and, voilà, there it was, posted and tagged as hers, never mind that anyone with eyes could tell you that Roxanna, to this day, could not fill out a bikini top like that. Violet had somehow been less mad than Roxanna had expected—she had calmly grabbed the phone, opened Instagram, and, with a world-weary sigh, hit delete, arguing that the day would come when her swimsuit photos would be out there in a major way, and certainly her audience would take note of every mole.

Still, showing more skin was not automatically in Violet's comfort zone. But as Roxanna pointed out, it was where the money was.

"Well, we're not exactly hurting for money" was always Violet's response. She had said it all through their teenage shoots and she had no problem reminding Roxanna of it last year, when she had brought it up again.

"Do you really think Linda Angelwhatevervista *was* when she said she wouldn't get out of bed for under ten thousand a day?" Roxanna yelled at her. "Plus, you're getting old, Vivi. Who is gonna want to see, like, a forty-year-old fossil?!"

So this year Violet reluctantly updated her online profile to indicate that she was open to swimsuit shoots. She assumed she wouldn't get asked to shoot swimsuits anyway. Violet was promoted less as a supermodel and more as a cover girl, cute and sweet and girl-next-doorish. To her surprise, the requests came pouring in. But somehow she had already sold herself on the logic of doing them, and so she did.

Around this time, Violet faced yet another big decision. Her name. She loved how "Violet" was a translation of the word for the flower in Persian, but her true name, "Banafsheh," always haunted her. She had held on to that name into elementary school, but it was definitely one of the catalysts that made her want to be homeschooled. She was called "Banana" and something that sounded like "BananaShit" and even "BananaFish" by a third-grade teacher, which ultimately was what sent her back to some years of homeschooling. (It took Mina years later to gently break down BananaFish as a Salinger reference to her sisters, who refused to read the short story.) Violet hated her name so much that she felt embarrassed by the yellow fruit, living in absolute fear of hearing her name be butchered into sheer, contagious ridicule. Al had noted this and had pushed for what he had wanted to do even when she was in the womb—he had wanted her to have the English name. But Homa insisted they honor her great-grandmother, so it had stuck. Al imagined Violet might opt out of that name later in life. To his great satisfaction, it happened.

She had whispered, "Violet," to herself, wondering if she truly was a Violet. She questioned it. It sounded a bit British, like she was a timid girl with a secret garden or something, or else it made her think of the ill-fated, gum-chewing Willy Wonka character. She wasn't sure it was her. But "BananaShit"? *Violet*, it was.

Somewhere around her twentieth birthday, whatever had clicked for her about "Violet" became unclicked. She no longer wanted an Americanized name, which had incidentally become her legal name—Al with his team of lawyers on hand for every whim. Violet was retreating from the world and into her phone. She loved any and all social media, searching hashtags that featured identity and social justice discourse. She had begun to see more and more women of her age reclaiming who they were. She realized, thanks to Al's affinity for all things American, that they barely registered as Iranian to the public. A lone American flag flew outside next to their tennis court; they only spoke English, except for occasional calls to relatives or when Al was upset about something and needed to speak in code to Homa. Otherwise, their public presence was scrubbed of anything "ethnic."

Roxanna: "Are you crazy? Or should I say Bananas, Banana-Shits? Why on earth would you think this was a good idea? Did you tell your agent?"

Violet sighed—she had expected this. "No, of course not. I wanted to try it on you all first, though honestly I knew you and Dad would be against it. And Haylee too. I guess Mina and Mom are into it, or at least they'll respect my decision."

Roxanna raised a finger to point at her ear and rotated it. "Psycho!" As if that word had cleansed her, she promptly switched gears: "Please, like, promise me, sissy, you absolutely cannot do this. Think of me! You can't do this to me."

Of course Violet did not think to question what Roxanna meant there, she was so used to her sister making everything about her. This time, the stakes were way higher than Violet knew.

"Have you run this by Roxi? It's not gonna be that simple," Mina told her when Violet raised the subject with her. "There are stakes." *Like the Secret,* she wanted to say, but couldn't.

Violet's face fell—she had no idea what Mina meant exactly, but the idea of there being stakes made her realize that changing her name back was not going to work.

Homa: "It's a beautiful name. But please do not involve me. Al will have thoughts."

Al: "Don't you think 'Violet' is working out pretty good, baby?"

Haylee: "You're just much more a 'Violet.' Even more than that other model Violet Something. It's just you. Just like I am much more 'Haylee' than 'Haleh.' Anyway, I don't want to look like the only one who Americanized, especially these days and with everything that is going on. Just keep 'Violet'?"

"So you know what I am talking about!" Violet immediately snapped. "You know what I mean about it being like activism these days?"

Haylee shrugged. "Trends are trends."

But Violet didn't feel like this was a trend. She wanted to announce her Iranianness and longed to declare her roots. It felt important, like the beginning of something.

In the end, Violet's agent advised she hold off—*they're just beginning to know you!*—and Violet finally agreed. Roxanna seemed the most relieved, explaining that it was because of the show.

"American audiences can barely say 'Milani'! They're gonna call us, like, 'Mulan' or 'My-lan.' You want them to say 'Banafsheh'? Please. Just something else for them to mock us for!" She paused, staring into the mirror past her own reflection to her older sister's teary eyes. "Besides, Vivs, you *are* being so Iranian. Remember what Dahlia said when I dyed my hair?"

Dahlia was Roxanna's stylist and it had been a whole ordeal last year when she transitioned from blond highlights to a much more all-over golden-blond look, using photos of heavily maned lions as her inspiration. *Shirrrrrrzan,* Dahlia had purred, "lioness" being her favorite Persian word. (*The maned ones are the males,* Mina had tried to correct her sister and Dahlia, only to get a mocking word-salad lecture on gender that Mina had chosen to immediately forget.)

Violet did not remember any of this, but Roxanna already knew that. "She said, 'What is more Persian than dyeing your hair blond? Persian is not natural, baby!' And that's what I say to you. What is more Persian than Americanizing your name, if that's really what you are worried about?"

Out of all the arguments, this one made the most sense, Violet had to admit. But the idea of changing her name back never quite left her head and she let it run around there, both an option and a threat. It felt liberating to have the option; it also felt like a panic button.

So Violet left it alone and focused on her modeling, especially now that she was expanding her repertoire toward the risqué.

The first gig she got was from a photographer who was looking to broaden his portfolio. This guy was apparently starting to get big in London and was shooting L.A. girls here and there. He was going for a "diverse array" that "reflects the city's rainbow of heritages," he told her. That seemed close or at least a bit closer to the activism that had seduced Violet that season, and so she agreed. It was probably going to be as meaningful as a first swimsuit shoot experience could get, she thought.

In the car ride there, with their driver, Randy, at the helm, Violet remembered what Roxanna had told her: it was gonna be just like how it was when she had been coached by her sister, she in some skimpy designer getup, ready for the surf and sun, soaking in the perfect air and light. Violet told herself she should just imagine Roxanna behind the camera, cracking jokes and shuffling the playlist as she writhed on the carpet trying to evoke some sort of sexiness she admittedly knew little about even at twenty.

Randy wished her well as he parked and waited as usual. It was all classic Violet, in her usual off-duty model look—hoodie with matching sweatpants, pink Uggs, Swarovski-studded thermos full of her favorite syrupy iced coffee—though he noticed her shaking a bit as she stepped out onto a mostly deserted street in L.A.'s Diamond District.

As instructed, when she arrived at the warehouse's entrance, she sent a text announcing she was downstairs. A pale British man probably a decade older than her at most greeted her with a big smile. She assumed he was the assistant, but once he flung open the door to the large studio, she realized it was just going to be the two of them. He was the photographer.

"Where is everyone?" she muttered, not seeing the hair and makeup crew.

He laughed. "We're keeping this really natural so it's all about you, your body, and the message we want to send. There's no need for you to be anything but yourself, Violet." He tried to expand his smile and meet her slightly nervous-looking eyes, now that her sunglasses were seated on top of her head. "Is 'Violet' a Persian name too?"

She paused. The sisters used "Persian" and "Iranian" interchangeably, though Al had once discussed with them that the terms were "political." He was a "Persian" guy; Homa usually said "Iranian." But there was something about other people choosing one or the other that sometimes made her pause. The way the photographer said "Persian" made it sound somehow fancier than it was, and not in a good way. That, plus the dreaded sore subject of her name, made her immediately feel like she didn't want to be there.

"My real name is different, actually," she said, and she wondered if this was the instance to try it. "My agency and everyone in the business knows me as 'Violet.' But my real name, my Persian name, is different."

He widened his already too-wide smile even more and raised his eyebrows expectantly. "And that is?"

Violet barely noticed her face flushing, she was so focused on reading his eyes and the import of this very moment, even if it were to be entirely private. "'Banafsheh Milani.'" She said it three times just so she could watch him.

"Oh, wow!" The man's face was going to split into two if he smiled any wider, she thought. "'Bana-shay Milano'?"

She shook her head, then quickly nodded. "Close enough." She looked around and saw a table where a few sets of bikinis were laid out. "These are for me, I take it?"

He nodded. "Yeah, well, they sent a few over. All reds, whites, and blues. You see, the point of this shoot is to celebrate America and its many diverse faces. And bodies!" The smile: widening more.

"How many of us are in this whole thing?"

"Well, right now my portfolio is set for a dozen of you girls," he said. "A Ghanaian, a Japanese, a Cambodian, a Colombian, a Sri Lankan, a Croatian, a German . . . so on. And you! A Persian!"

She nodded slowly. "We will all be wearing the same thing? This?" She waved at the nearly identical bikinis, all red-and-white-striped tops and blue bottoms with white stars.

"Yep," he said and suddenly reddened a bit. "Well, why don't you try it on first?"

She took the bikinis in her hands and followed his gesture to where the bathrooms were. It was odd, she thought—the first time she was being asked to dress herself at a shoot. She wondered if the agency knew about this and why they had not told her. It all felt very unusual and she felt a bit embarrassed fumbling with the ties on her bikini.

The agency had certainly gotten her measurements right, as the first set she tried on fit like it was made for her. She glanced in the bathroom mirror and wondered if she looked a bit trashy—who in this country wore patriotic bikinis, anyway? But she tried to imagine all those women from different backgrounds wearing them and her representing Iran. She wasn't sure how he had landed on her ethnicity at all.

On the set, the photographer was fiddling with his camera and readying the lighting and various lenses. He seemed to mostly ignore her, as if something were bothering him, but at this point in her career, Violet had learned to never internalize the anxieties from anyone on set. Assistants freaked out, photographers had fits of frustration, models near-fainted from exhaustion, and hair and makeup feuded, but Violet knew she had one job and it was to be in service of the shot.

"Banshia," the photographer finally muttered, still engaged with fiddling behind his lens.

Violet didn't bother correcting him, thinking this butchering was the best reason so far not to revert to her original name.

"I have one more item for you. . . ." He pointed at the table again.

There didn't seem to be anything on the table. "Where?" she asked.

He pointed at it again and Violet walked over to see it was still empty. Just a black tablecloth and nothing.

"I don't . . ." she announced awkwardly.

He turned around. "Oh, of course, you grew up here—you probably are not as used to it, like me!" There was the ghost of a chuckle hovering on his breath.

He walked over and plucked up the tablecloth, which was apparently not a tablecloth but a prop: a large black runner of fabric, somehow for her.

"Sorry to be dumb—I just don't understand," she said, taking it from the photographer, the material nicer than she expected.

He gestured for her the way you would if you were miming putting on a shawl but draped over your head.

"What do they call them, not 'burka,' but you know . . ." He was laughing, the laughter unable to hide itself.

Violet this time felt herself grow very red, her cheeks burning suddenly. Her voice came out in a deep rasp: *"Chador?"*

This time the miming was applause. "Sure! It's been bothering me for the past many minutes! I didn't want to get it wrong and, you know, offend!"

She nodded slowly, smoothing the cloth with her hands, eyeing it suspiciously, as a talisman of the enemy. "I've never worn one."

He nodded vigorously. "Yes, of course, I imagined you are from here, but each of our models is wearing a symbol of their culture. This seemed the right one and plus with the bikini peeking out under, it's quite a statement!" His face looked like it was cracking from the pressures of his smile, applied a few too many times that day.

Violet, meanwhile, could not shake the red off her face. She wasn't even sure why she felt so humiliated. Yet she did. Her first swimsuit shoot. In a chador. Or was it a hijab? She wasn't even sure what the difference was. (*A chador,* Mina later corrected her.) In this era, when her mind was on social justice. It felt insulting but in ways she could barely comprehend. She wanted badly to walk out but it felt too late somehow.

Before she knew it, he was putting the black sheet on top of her head, letting it drop down her shoulders. For a second it seemed like he was letting it cover the front of her body, but his hands stopped short of that. Respect, she imagined. The stylist's duty, anyway. Here was this clueless British man, with a mostly naked Iranian girl in front of him, and he had given himself the task of covering her up just so.

She got in front of the camera and the shoot got under way in earnest. It went like they all did, much to her surprise. She tried to get everything right so it wouldn't drag and she could leave faster. She wondered if she was the first woman in a veil that was barely on her, exposing a red-white-and-blue American bikini. Was this activism? The statement she'd hoped for?

"Brilliant, Bashina!"

"You can call me 'Violet,'" she said at the end of the shoot, when she wrapped the black cloth around her like a towel, no longer wanting his sharp photographer's eyes on her.

By the door they made small talk, a bit tense on her end, though she received his card graciously, and nodded at his many compliments. It was almost over.

"And, you know, given that we are probably gonna be at war with your country later this month," he said with a laugh. "I can't imagine a better image for the shoot, Bashra!"

She nodded. War. "'Violet,'" she repeated. "My name is 'Violet' in English." She waved at him without looking back and left the studio.

In the car with Randy, she burst into tears, and Randy kept

asking if she was okay. "Please, Randy, ignore me, like I don't exist. Please!"

Once home, Violet realized she had accidentally left the shoot wearing the blue-starred bikini bottom that suddenly felt almost thong-y on her. Were they this revealing all along? She imagined the photographer telling her she could keep it but she knew one thing for sure—she wanted no memory of what happened there. Later that day, she wrapped the bikini bottom in a brown paper bag and threw it in the trash. She told her agent in a text that whatever happened with the shoot—*and it was fine, don't worry, it was fine, it's always fine, please do not ask*—she would just rather never see the photos.

"They're gonna call you 'Violet,' okay?" Roxanna said many weeks after that, the white glow of her phone lighting up her face like a blockbuster villain, which made its own sense, given everything.

Violet pretended not to hear and buried herself in her own phone. They were lazing on opposite ends of a restored antique Howard & Sons Chesterfield chaise longue.

"I am serious, Violet," Roxanna repeated. "No 'Banafsheh' business. It's gonna, like, complicate things for all of us. The show, the war. It's all a yikes for me. So, promise—okay?"

Violet nodded absently. It bothered her that Roxanna wanted her to keep her name in the first place. One time Al had said to them, in a bit of a fight, that because of how much money they had, they could be absolutely anyone they wanted. There would be no shame in this house, he said, or any house any Milanis entered.

But she remembered the photographer, his gelled hay-colored hair and overeager blue eyes, that smile, the weight of that black cloth over her also long-black hair, as if she were doubly protected by something undeniably hers, the smell of the warehouse and the smell of his body odor the few times he adjusted her a bit too close—steel and concrete and a sport deodorant and potato chips—and how he had scrambled her name over and over. She felt like her Persian name had been molested by him, like it would be molested by any outsider from then on. It was better to just stay herself. Some things, she had realized in her twenty years, were just like that.

She dropped a few Good & Plentys in her mouth like she was Homa with the Advil and Xanax, and said extra loud and extra clear so that Roxanna would not ask again, " 'Violet Milani.' I am 'Violet' and only 'Violet.'"

And then, once again, she tuned out the world and went deep into the images on her phone, ignoring her always-abrasive and, somehow, unlike her, completely indestructible younger sister.

3

Mina

Mina had concerns. She was the third-born sister but at times she felt like she knew more than everyone combined. She was the practical one, the stable one, the one who was always home, the very informed one, the "conscience of the family," as Violet had once called her. It was not lost on Mina, and in fact maybe lost on everyone but her, that she was the most plain of the sisters. This had been hard at one point, when the concept of the "Milani sisters" became a thing—or, rather, when Al began pushing them to do more promotional activities after that one Pizzabomme commercial they all appeared in turned out to be a hit. Roxanna would point out that in many cultures, such as certain white cultures, being less obviously beautiful was something chic. Mina was like Miranda of *Sex & the City*, Roxanna often said. She wasn't really the favorite, but no one would ever call her anything but essential. Instead, Mina liked to say she was the youngest in the Milani Sanity Line, together with Violet and their mother. But secretly she feared being boring.

To be sure, there were things about Mina that were highly un-boring. For example, she had been, since a wee toddler, chronically ill. That was all she called it, what she had finally learned to call it as she grew older. No one knew what she had, and luckily her mental health was stable enough that the phase when people assumed hypochondriasis and somatization had been short-lived. Mina was shyer and quieter than her sisters, and slightly more tortured the way precocious children often are. She had been born quite underweight and colicky. As she grew up, she remained sickly—thin but not Roxanna-thin. No one thought Mina's narrow hips and small bones and flat chest looked model-y, nor did they think her pale skin looked elegant like Violet's. By the time she turned ten, others noticed that her hair would never grow longer than a bob—a brown bowl, not unlike Homa's, though even her mother's was toned to a gold luster. Mina's nails were fragile and her skin prone to hives and acne. Her appearance was one thing, but the constant gastric unease—SIBO, GERD, IBS—plus the joint pains and muscle aches, the chronic migraines that would put her out for days, and the tendency toward pneumonia and bronchitis, well, that was something else. She always carried a note that allowed her to skip gym class and had rarely ever in her life broken a true sweat. Homa and Al had taken her to the best specialists in the world. Mina had been seen at clinics in upstate New York, Switzerland, Japan, Australia, all to no end. No one knew what was wrong with her. Anemia, ME/CFS, fibromyalgia, hypoglycemia, tachycardia, mitral valve prolapse, POTS? There was no one diagnosis.

It all added up to Mina spending lots of time at home by herself. She sometimes found her sisters too stimulating, or too often just plain exhausting. Mina took days off school, skipped holidays, at times. She liked to stay in her room with the white-noise machine on blast, the blackout curtains drawn, an eye mask on, and earplugs in, just trying to not move for as long as possible until whatever ailment passed.

The homebodiness that had come from all this made her an internet addict. She wasn't active on social media in the way Roxanna and Violet and Haylee were—they had large follower counts, as if they were celebrities. Mina's was different: she was anonymous. Anonymity gave her pleasure in her day-to-day life, and she realized she could be that way online too. These days, she interacted with the world online as her main means of interacting with the world at all—most of her days were sick days, after all.

But her life had changed when she discovered stan culture, first through Tumblr and soon via Twitter (she had only studied LiveJournal secondhand, too young to be seduced by its peak). It fascinated her, these anonymous armies of fans, with avatars that reflected the artists they stanned. No one had any desire to know who these stans were, and the stans seemed to have no desire to reveal their identities. Individuality was meaningless. Their existence had to do with their service to the superstar they obsessed over. Mina found it so pure. Music was not her main obsession, but she fell for the sense of belonging this international, faceless tribe offered.

Out of all her sisters, Mina was the least obsessed with being known.

She started joining all sorts of stan groups. First she got with the Britney Spears stans. They seemed older, devoted, and there was even a #FreeBritney movement that felt high stakes and a thrill to be a part of. Then she found Ariana Grande stan Twitter, which was very united and aggressive. She moved to Lana Del Rey stan Twitter. They fought, but also had an admirable work ethic. This went on and on until she became most enchanted by K-pop stan Twitter. Mina was not even listening to that much music on her headphones. She enjoyed meditation apps designed to quiet her body and mind, so the fact that she had seemingly, in just a few months, become some kind of expert in Korean pop music fascinated her. She did like the music, but more than that she loved the fellowship of the fans. It was a global collective and of all ages, from teens to senior citizens. There was no way to know who anyone was, really, because their avatars were all Jungkook, Baekhyun, Jisoo, IU, and so on. Mina would rotate hers—she was a "multi-stan," she decided, hashtagging as many stan groups as she could. And so Mina somehow ended up having more followers than each of her sisters, which Roxanna and Haylee, especially, found infuriating, given how much they had devoted to cultivating their followings.

There was another reason that Mina was drawn to stan Twitter, and especially K-pop stan Twitter, and it worried her. It worried her just as much as Roxanna was worried about her secret being revealed. Mina's anxiety about Roxanna's secret coming out bubbled up not just for Roxanna—maybe not for Roxanna at all—but for herself and her own little secret.

No one knew Mina's secret, not even Roxanna. Maybe Violet had a clue, but only because Violet was as close to a real mother as she had. But Mina never spoke of it with any of her sisters directly.

Mina knew that there was one thing people needed to understand about the Milani sisters, and it was that you absolutely could not trust them.

Including her. Maybe especially her, Mina thought. She wondered how it would go if she told them. Haylee was only ten months younger—Haylee would just roll her eyes and say, *Duh.* Violet would probably be extremely sympathetic and give her a nice, long, warm hug and tell her she was glad she had told her and that it would get better, that she was born this way, and so on, that it was fine and she loved her. Roxanna, on the other hand—who knew. She had no reason to think Roxanna would be against it, but she felt certain it would weird her out and she would make it known. She would probably poke and prod. Then, if she took it well, she might suggest some style changes; if she, for whatever reason, did not take it well, perhaps thinking her secret was wrong, then she would ignore Mina for enough of a while and then finally begrudgingly accept it.

That her parents might find out somehow bothered her less, especially because it seemed like they had given up a bit on her and Haylee.

Haylee and Mina had largely been raised by the housekeeping family who lived in the back house: Rose and Randy, the driver, who were in their late fifties. They had daughters in their twenties and thirties, Melissa and Jess and Abby and Schuy. By the time the Milanis were gearing up for the show, the daughters had basically moved out, but occasionally they came to visit. It was unusual to employ a whole family as staff, but Al had thought it was a beautiful idea. Their families mirrored each other, each with four sisters of similar ages apart. Maybe that was where the similarities ended, but Mina also recalled once, as a child, overhearing Al go on to Homa about how it was essential the staff be white.

"I had an uncle in Tehran who dreamed of exactly the life I am living now," he had said. "That he'd be in America and be very, very rich. A rich Persian prince among the American trash! And the detail I always remember is him saying how he would have white servants, all *moo boor,* you know, just loving that blond hair. I thought it was genius. And then I got here to America and it seemed no one did that. But again, I am always one step ahead. In great Amu Reza's memory, let's get them as white as possible!" A colleague had once said Al's cackles were rehearsed to sound like gold coins clanging against one another.

Mina couldn't work out if the move was racist or the opposite of racist, but shortly after, the family had hired their white staff and had kept them for the past eleven years.

They were all close in various ways, but Haylee and Mina felt the deepest connection to Rose and Randy. They had lived with them the longest. And so Mina imagined trying out her secret on them first—maybe their cultural and class backgrounds could make them more amenable, or maybe not. It was so hard to tell.

Mina had tried to tell Schuy once, and it had gone horribly wrong. *Ew, gross, I would never be friends with "one"* was what she had said when Mina had mentioned the possibility of even befriending someone with the same secret at school, much less being "one." Schuy had walked away but she always felt Schuy looked at her differently since then and she regretted telling her and not telling Abby, who, as time went by, revealed herself to be more tolerant. The real mystery was their religious affiliation, if they had any at all, and if that could be a factor, although Mina never recalled them leaving on a Sunday to go to church.

Mina decided in the end it would be best to keep that part of her online only, since she had many alts that even her sisters were not aware of. More than a few of those alts had tried it out: a rainbow flag in the Twitter bio; one even said "QUEER" in all caps in the bio. No one had treated her very differently, but she was not totally sure—she was turning fifteen and trying to figure it out. Somehow it felt better to spell it out boldly: "QUEER" plus rainbow flag, even. She had tried "BI" for a few months, but it didn't seem to get any type of attention at all. She noticed a lot of stan Twitter, and mysteriously a lot of K-pop stan Twitter, was queer or at least so queer-friendly that they seemed queer too. She started to learn more and more through her exchanges with others in the communities, and, given that she felt little sexual interest in anyone, she wondered if she could be asexual too, though she shelved that thought. By the end of her experiment online, she settled on a rainbow flag and "queer" in all lowercase, plus the initials "NB," as in "nonbinary," which seemed to her to be strongly the case.

But all of this just seemed so very impossible to express to anyone, much less her sisters or her parents. Plus, why did she suddenly think she needed to tell them? What was the urgency? Well, the show, of course, she told herself. But then it was possible that she wouldn't have to make it public at all or maybe just not at first. Maybe she could just see how it would go.

For now, she had not even decided if she was a "they/them." She left "she/her" even if she felt "she/they" was probably more honest.

For whatever reason, she still felt she had to come out to her world, and that meant, with this show on the line, the whole world. It seemed to her to be a golden opportunity that a higher power had sent her. If she missed this, she would be closeted for life.

Of all possible bad endings she imagined for herself, none seemed worse than being closeted for life.

So Mina felt plagued as the talks for the show grew heated. Everyone assumed she was angsty because of her looming birthday or the talk of war brewing with Iran. Of course, Mina also considered herself an activist and quite political, so while Haylee and Roxanna could be oblivious and bury their heads in fashion and celebrity and nightlife news, and Violet could swallow her feelings in a pint of ice cream or a jar of Jelly Bellies, Mina was reading every news alert, worrying about one half of her identity being at war with the other half.

"You're gonna be okay, Mini," Violet whispered into her shoulder, when she had yet another illness flare with the show nearing—of course, a war nearing, possibly, too.

"Am I?" Mina asked, her head bound in ice packs, her eyes back in the eye mask, her skin slathered with Tiger Balm, her heat pack strapped to her back like a corset.

Violet gave her another gentle, mostly symbolic hug—only Violet knew to barely touch her when she hugged; her skin so often felt neuropathic—and said, like a mother bird cooing at her baby chick, "You *will* be okay, Mini, I promise. People like us always are."

From somewhere neither sister could pinpoint, Pari, unprompted by anything they could perceive, uttered a robust cry that sounded just a bit formidable.

Mina was glad her eyes were behind a mask so Violet could not see them fill with tears. She'd wonder with great alarm why Mina was crying, and she would be forced into some platitudinous speech about how not even she, her favorite sister, could say who she was as a person. All this time—well, at least since she'd hit puberty, which was not that long ago, so maybe a bit before, but who even knew how these awakenings worked—she, sweet, innocent, sickly Mina, had been living a lie, that all her worry was not about what really mattered. Her worlds colliding and exploding. The truth of her very existence, without which there would not even be consciousness, *her* consciousness, to even have the dilemma of war or peace, didn't she understand—

"And if we're not okay," Violet went on this time, almost as if she could hear Mina's thoughts, "then it just might be too late to know that. . . ."

4

Haylee

It was true that Haylee cried a lot, but what the family and even her friends did not seem to grasp was that she could cry on command. One could say she was a pro at faking tears, and for what? Attention, manipulation, whatever, but sometimes it was simply because the situation called for it, and for whatever reason she was not very good at being natural, the way she assumed most people were. She had to force the emotion, nudge the instinct out of herself. For example, she'd had no interest in Violet's beloved silken windhound, Anastasia, who had died prematurely at age five of unknown reasons, but at the very elaborate funeral, pink marble tombstone and all, at the celebrity pet cemetery, Haylee knew better than to have a dry eye. Violet was too pure to suspect anything, but that was also another reason why Haylee, the youngest, didn't gel all that well with the oldest. They were too different.

Haylee, the joke went, was Mina's evil twin and Roxanna's child. She thought of herself as the Pretty One, though she was sure Roxanna thought of herself the same way. They were both born to be Main Characters. And of course it was very possible that Violet, given that she was a model, was actually the Pretty One, but she would be the type who would say, *Oh, come on now—we are all pretty.* And Mina, bless her, Mina her older sister by less than a year, well, she was too realistic for that—Mina was plain, always had been, and she liked it that way. Mina would prefer to disappear, while Haylee lived to be seen and heard.

Haylee was popular at school. Middle school had been brutal, and the fact that Haylee had spent every middle school year being the most popular girl had to count for a lot. She was the baby and special. She was the only natural blonde in the family. Must have been from some stray relatives on Homa's side, went the family story. When she was ten, Haylee accompanied her sisters to the hair salon and she asked for hair as "white as snow." (*Snow White's skin was white as snow,* Mina reminded her, but Haylee retorted that she already had that.) She started wearing color contacts too, rotating green and blue until settling on purple. Haylee was devoted to the idea of her own uniqueness.

Unlike the rest of her family or even any of the popular girls, Haylee was something of an athlete too, the fastest runner in her class all elementary school, and always excelling at tennis or karate or ballet or swimming lessons. She loved to compete. By the time she had hit her preteen years, this became less an interest in school sports and more being into a very strict, orthorexic health-and-wellness culture. Given that both her oldest sisters had eating issues—Violet with all the bingeing and Roxanna with the constant deprivation, though Mina's chronic illness also kept her quite anxious about food—Haylee all the more devoted herself to fitness. Al let her have an extra room off the family gym, which could be her special space. For her twelfth birthday, they hired a designer to paint it her favorite color, "mimosa-pudica pink." She was elated, and to Homa's consternation, she spent more time there than with her homework or at the art classes in which she had initially shown interest and talent but now discarded.

Haylee, like Roxanna, had prepared for fame for quite some time. Before Roxanna had brought reality TV to their actual reality, Haylee and Roxanna both dreamed about it—at times, together. Haylee rehearsed reality TV confessionals for hours in front of her vanity, and would often invite Roxanna, whose fluidity seemed to reveal she did this a lot too. Haylee would oscillate between imagining herself in a *Real Housewives* sequin-studded jumpsuit and a Kardashian stretchy strapless maxi dress, all just to look into some imaginary camera and coo, *It's not easy being the youngest in a family like this. But easy was never my thing.*

When the question of them *actually* becoming the stars of a reality TV show came up, Haylee was very demonstrative about her allegiance to it. She was extremely screen-ready, she decided, an old soul at fourteen going on twenty-four. Haylee made sure Roxanna was watching as she closed her eyes and commanded an impressive reserve of tears to gather and overflow through her tinted lashes. This was the best news of her life, and she had her favorite sister, Roxanna, to thank for it.

"Can we be ourselves? That's just the one issue for me. I've worked my whole life at this—I just want to be *me*."

More tears were coming. There were two possible major obstacles threatening their plan, Roxanna announced shortly after that initial get-together at the pool. The sisters now reconvened for an emergency meeting in one of their dens, the one Violet swore was haunted. Roxanna had to make it all the more ominous by lighting candles and placing a few apologetic crudités on a tray.

"Sissies, it pains me to say it, but our show is in jeopardy," Roxanna began.

"How? Before we've even filmed?" Mina asked.

Haylee could see Violet was biting her lip in that particular way so relief wouldn't trickle out.

"I doubt any of you have been on top of the news—maybe Mina?" Roxanna went on wearily, seeing a quick nod from Mina. "There's a lot going on. The U.S. could be at, like, war. And you know with where. There's also this weird plague they're talking about on the news—who knows what will happen there. This could, like, mess us up. Like just one of these bad things would spell disaster for this show. That's what the producer's assistant emailed me about the other night, and while nothing is final, we just need to think on this and whatever it means." Roxanna was getting flustered as she spoke about it, clearly not in her element as her sisters' glazed eyes seemed to confirm.

"We could just not do it," Violet murmured.

"No one asked for your opinion, babes," Roxanna said, snarling almost. "Constructive comments only."

Haylee started to feel her eyes grow wet, against her will, even. Real tears? She didn't realize how badly she'd wanted this.

"Roxi, we gotta do this," she blurted out. "It's really important we think positive and think that it's going to happen. Even if there is war or some disease, that's not gonna last forever, right? The world has experience with those, right? I want to do this."

Mina groaned. "Not everything is about you, Hayles."

Violet got up, quietly went to the corner behind the lavender Fendi Casa loveseat, where Pari the cat liked to hide, found her hissing under a cushion, scooped her up, and cradled her all the way back to her own room. That was that.

Haylee also went to her room and had a deep satisfying cry. She hated her life, she thought, but then the lie of it made her pause in her despair. Her life was great, at least mostly great, at least better than most people's, that much she knew for sure. What was it that she hated? She hated her sisters, maybe? She'd considered this many times before and while it felt somewhat true-ish, it really wasn't the whole story. Roxanna was her idol in life, the Paris Hilton to her Nicky, she had long ago decided; they were a duo. Violet, well, Violet was a matriarch—she was dependable, since Roxi certainly wasn't, and who could resent that? And there was Mina, the good sister, who always made her look bad; well, Mina was almost her twin, and luckily they were so different, they would never compete and could even complement each other, though they rarely did. Her parents were fine—they were as problematic as everyone's parents were, but at least they were rich, and that was what counted. And there were of course the many kids in her grade who worshipped her—Haylee the prettiest, Haylee the fastest, Haylee from the richest family. What was wrong with her? Violet had mentioned once that teenagers cry a lot, relieved she was no longer a teen—was that it? She couldn't even remember what the matter was, honestly.

The door flew open and a sulking Mina appeared in front of her.

"What happened to the knock-first rule?" Haylee scowled at her sister. She looked from her sister to her sister's reflection in the vanity mirror, somehow an entire world away despite being next to her. She was amazed at how little they looked alike in that moment. Haylee in tears but icy somehow, her white-blond hair strikingly slick, her face chalky in its depleted pallor. Mina, even with her sickliness, still looked flushed in an almost good way. She didn't raise her voice—Haylee could barely hear her when she wasn't upset, but when she was, it was as if Haylee could smell her outrage, like her body odor emanated anger.

"First of all, you don't know what you are talking about."

"What on earth do you mean? I am too tired for this, Mini."

"There is something you don't know. While Roxi was talking about global crises, there is another reason that it might be best if the show doesn't happen." Mina was shaking, as if the pressure of some fact were forcing her to a boil.

Haylee blinked at her blankly. "What is it?"

Mina sighed. "I can't tell you, Haylee. Only Rox and I know."

"She told you some secret before me?" Haylee's purple eyes narrowed much like Pari's when she hunted.

"No, no, listen, I know because, we've, you know, shared a school. You just got to us."

"The school knows?!"

"No," Mina almost shouted. She was tired of this already. "Listen, I just know, because I had to know, but she can't know that you even know there is anything to know—got it?"

Haylee's face crumpled in pure disgust. "What does that even mean, Mina?"

Mina paused. She hated this. "I am just gonna say this—Roxi is your fave and you want to watch out for her, so follow her lead and know that if she lets something pass, it's for a good reason. Some things are more trouble than they are worth, you know?"

Haylee shook her head. "I'm supposed to say yes to something that makes no sense? You guys all love to leave me out. Whatever." She paused. "But the show is not just her show or your show or Violet's. It's also mine. And it matters to me. You can't just take away my dreams. Maybe I can go join the show without you all!"

Mina closed her eyes. "Listen, everyone has everyone's best interest here. Try not to get too involved. Just trust us for now and you will see."

"You all are in something and I am left out—this is so gross!" Haylee's eyes refilled themselves.

"Haylee, that's not it," Mina said, almost feeling bad now. "Anyway, let's just keep things on the rails, okay? I started feeling dizzy again in there—probably from all the stress—and I can't have another flare and miss more school so I am going to lie down. Just don't give Rox a hard time." With that, Mina was gone.

Haylee opened her mouth to send some strong parting words after Mina, but as her sister exited, she wondered what even was the point. Something for sure was up. So typical. She decided to not care, to forget the whole thing as long as she could, as she had other things to look forward to. Plus, if for some reason the show didn't happen, she would find her own way to the limelight. Haylee was fourteen now. She was no longer going to be ignored. She would find her way, that was for sure.

5

Al

"Of course it's going to happen," Al said in his loudest voice, often reserved for his jokes, but sometimes he liked to put it on to show extreme alpha confidence. He looked at his second-oldest daughter, usually so well postured, now splayed like a discarded doll atop his favorite white leather Bentley Home couch, looking like a poster girl for some hideous failure he could not imagine. "What is wrong with my Roxi? What are we all upset about now?"

"There's just so many factors they are throwing at us," Roxanna blurted out. "I'm just, like, worried!"

It was not like her to be anxious—it was not like *him* to be anxious, and Roxi took the most after him. He liked the Roxi who was all *sheitan*, a little devil, a handful, the hellion of the family. She was, after all, going to be the centerpiece of the show—next to him, of course. Without Al Milani, there could be no show. This was the house that Al built—*we really want to show the House of Milani, not just the Milani house, if that makes sense,* one producer had said, and of course it did, all too well. This household of wild women was his invention—as much as he complained at times about being the only man (well, not counting Randy), he loved it. He was their core, the alpha and omega, and in his mind everything revolved around him.

No politics, please, Al said, and he repeated it all the time,

whether to an assistant or a colleague or to his wife or occasionally his daughter Mina. His entire life had been marred by politics as it was. He was nearly sixty-one—the Revolution was four
decades in the past. It was hard to say what it had not touched,
but he liked to dwell on the good news: that it had brought
him to America and ultimately made him wealthy. Contrary to
what many Iranians believed, Al and Homa had not been born
rich. Homa came from slightly more money than he did, but
Al? Nothing. His parents worked in restaurants, dishwashers and
waiters, and his grandparents before them were farmers. When
the Revolution hit, Al had just dropped out of Tehran University. He knew he did not have the grades to graduate. He was a
proud *laat,* a troublemaker, and he liked to party. He wondered
if he was meant to be a farmer himself, if his parents were meant
to have gone that route themselves—country kids at heart who
had made the mistake of coming to the city for a better life that
never came, their whole lives shadowing chefs and line cooks
and angry bar owners in the boiling-hot kitchens of mediocre
restaurants in Iran's capital, for pitiful wages.

Al was just about to consider a move to the countryside, and
he was about to tell his adviser he was done with school for
good, when the Revolution hit. Then, shortly after that, the
war. It was time to leave. Al was the only child his parents had
the means to send abroad, the only out of six. His parents col-
lected what little they had and urged Al to go to America, where
all the more fortunate Iranians were going. Al had nothing but
them to leave behind—he had no real job, no real home, no real
goals, no sweetheart, just a bunch of unruly friends. Life had
been party after party and never very good ones either. The kind
of girls who liked Al were unremarkable and bored him, and the
kind of girls he liked would look at him only to roll their eyes
or laugh. Iran had become a joke with no punchline, a mistake.

Al purchased the cheapest plane ticket he could and ended
up in Los Angeles, like most Iranians he knew. But the Iranians

he had known from school barely stayed in touch, all too busy figuring out how to make their way in this new country, with limited skills, with little grasp of the language and culture, and little idea of when they were going to return home. Nothing made sense. Everything felt glittering and expensive and beautiful, but out of reach. Al soon traded the downtown motel he had made his home for a low-income apartment on the Eastside, where there were no Iranians. He would frequent a pizza stand down the street and eventually, when he realized he could barely afford the slices he was getting, he decided to ask for a job. The owner realized he didn't know the language and stuck him in the back of the kitchen, with the dishwashing and garbage. But Al excelled at grating cheese, and eventually he assisted the cooks, helping them roll out the dough, placing little flat circles of plastic-looking meat on top of pie after pie. He dreamed of a life outside this place, perhaps even a return to a repaired Iran, where he could tell his parents America was not that much to brag about in the end, anyway.

He never returned to Iran, not even once for a trip, not even when his parents died, six weeks apart, in a spacious condominium in the nicest part of town, which he had bought for them in the last decade of their lives. It had been something of a miracle for them, their mostly delinquent son, Al, in America, over the span of a few years going from a nobody to a stable man to, dare they say it, a major success.

Al had gone from nothing, literally, to becoming one of the richest men in California. *Only the eBay guy and another tech dude,* he grumbled often, had him beat, but for his age group plus given his life story, he had to measure up as the greatest success.

It was almost too good to be true, but Al discovered what would be the secret to his success in all those years in that very dingy kitchen at Mario's in Alhambra. Al had been assembling his dinner after his shift, a foam container full of discarded odds and ends: burnt dough, battered peppers, unappealing-looking sausages, moldy mushrooms, bruised pineapple, balls of slimy cheese. He would take these containers home and sit on his used couch, and stick a plastic fork in the contents. Sometimes he would shape them into something and pretend he worked in an avant-garde fine-dining establishment, assembling their most coveted creation, the essence of a pizzeria mashed up into some high-concept chaos. Or something. He often would roll the whole thing up in his hands and just eat it like *koofteh*— a Persian meatball—and tell himself this was actually something someone somewhere could consider delicious.

One evening as he ate, his mind wandered and he fantasized that this was a new American fast food.

Americans loved efficiency, and everything was always on the go. He often saw people cradle their slice like a taco, as if it were a sling, as they walked to their cars, their face and fingers a mess of grease and crumbs, before taking the wheel. He imagined his ball of discarded pizza ingredients wrapped in wax paper and sold in its own case alongside the pizzas. Maybe something smaller for kids? Something certainly more fun? The center would be full of hot, oozing cheese wrapped in a dry, cratered crust smoothed out into a globe. This idea amused him for some time. Eventually he decided to suggest it to his boss and ask for a raise for contributing a new delicacy to their menu. Doing something with all these scraps would help save them money too, after all.

The next day when Al told his manager, Carlos, his idea, Carlos shrugged. Al's coworkers, seeing his discouraged face, convinced Carlos to put a few on the lunch menu. They were scrappier calzones—what could they lose? Carlos didn't enjoy the one Al made him much at all and argued that if a real Italian came in, they wouldn't know what to do with it. But everything they made was so different from what real Italians cooked, Al's coworkers retorted—was there even pineapple-and-ham pizza in Italy? Al called his invention a "pizzaball," and that day they sold a dozen. One young man had even bought a second after eating one in his booth. After a month Mario's came to be known for its pizzaballs. After a few months, Al even got to make a sign that read: AL'S FAMOUS PIZZABALLS ARE HERE.

The pizzaball didn't make Al, Carlos, or the owners of the pizza shop millionaires, at least not at first. It created a bit of neighborhood buzz at best. But it was enough for Al to decide that he had talent. When, a year later, a man in a suit approached Al with his card, Al smelled opportunity. The man had walked in and asked for Al, who thought to hide at first, worried that his immigration status was what had brought this man here. It turned out he worked for a packaged frozen foods company and he was here because they were interested in the pizzaball. Soon after, the man invited Al to a meeting where they made him an offer in exchange for the rights to produce the pizzaball. Al rejected it. He was not ready to let it go. But the experience made him think. He had something here, and just three years later, the pizzaballs became a reality in grocery stores nationwide.

They were called "Pizzabomme." Apparently "Pizzaballs" already existed, and so did his second choice for a name, "Pizzabon." Al had been doing "field research" when he discovered the Cinnabon at Northridge Fashion Center. It was just a cinnamon roll, but people were crazy for them, and when he got his, he was surprised by how good the warm, gooey dough was. And like his pizzaball, it was efficient. You could carry a Cinnabon with you, dig a plastic spoon into the pastry, and go about your day, no plate or seat necessary. It also had a good ring to it: "Cinnabon." When he asked a friend of his from the pizzeria what it meant, his friend shrugged. *Not everything in America has to mean something, Al.* Al thought about that a lot. And then he turned to his friend and asked the question that would shape the rest of his life:

"What if I called it 'Pizzabomb'?"

"*It's a bomb?!* Is that what you said?"

Al revised. " 'Pizzabaulm'? 'Pizzabombe'? 'Pizzabomme'?"

His friend looked confused. "The pizzaballs?"

Al nodded, excited. He knew he had it—he didn't even need his friend's validation. "Yeah, like Cinnabon but Pizza. Pizza-bom."

"You don't want, as a guy from Iran, to bring up 'bomb.' No offense."

"No, like *bomme*. Like the French word—isn't it French?"

"What is it supposed to mean?" his friend asked a few times.

Al shot right back to him, "Not everything in America has to mean something, my friend."

And the rest was, indeed, as they say, history.

The thing was, Al didn't even like pizza that much. In Iran, pizza involved ketchup, which was an abomination to him, and at Mario's the pizza was subpar, at best. Everything at Mario's had a tinge of burnt plastic flavor. But Al had suffered through eating the pizza scraps and leftovers because it was his job and it was free and he was buying himself time. Still in less time than he could have imagined, he was convincing the country that the greatest food in the world was pizza—and not just any pizza, but a highly portable, extremely playful, extra-special type of pizza, the Pizzabomme.

He had never had a plan in his life before, and then there he was: Al Milani, Iranian American fast-food mogul. What a life.

Of course, he worried the press would highlight his Iranian-ness. Iran had never stopped being in the news since he had arrived; it seemed to always be on every American's tongue. And not in a good way. Iran was not a place you wanted to be from, and Al only hoped that what happened at Mario's would happen elsewhere too: people would just assume he was some other brown. None of the customers at Mario's asked where he was from, no one questioned his accent, no one seemed to care. Most of the other employees were from Mexico. Maybe they assumed he was Mexican too. Or even better, Italian. Al loved that "Milani" sounded like "Milan"—surely, if people knew of Milan, they could assume he was named for it. Plus, he had learned in his first months in America that while "Ali" was easy enough for Americans to pronounce, "Al" was preferable. Als came in a variety of colors, ethnicities, races. "Al Milani" offered endless possibilities. *Al Capone, Al Pacino, very authentic.*

Luckily, no one in the press had much to say about Al's background. There was one time, at a benefit, when an older white woman in a sequined gown who looked a lot like Nancy Reagan turned to him and asked where his "gorgeous accent" was from. Al had stumbled out with "Europe-Asia . . ." He really had no practice with this one. "Eurasia, is that what you said?" the old lady, hard of hearing, muttered back. He nodded and she smiled blankly. Another advantage for him was that many Americans were not worldly, and just because they had heard of Iran in the news, it didn't mean they knew where or what it was.

At home, Al was determined not to drape their rooms in Persian flags, portraits of the monarchy, murals of Persepolis, and all the usual, almost kitschy, crud you found on the walls of the homes of most Iranian refugees. He knew where he was from, and there was no need, frankly, for others to know too. So his daughters grew up without the full force of their parents' pride. They were taught Persian on and off, half-heartedly. Al even planted an American flag, perched atop a gold flagpole, outside their home, right on the sloping private driveway, high enough that neighbors could note that, yes, Americans lived there, proud Americans.

And so when Roxanna was faced with *Where are you from?* which quickly became *No, where are you really from?* she never even thought to say Iran. It was as if her consciousness hit delete on the whole Middle East. Her brain went right to where her dad's had: Milan.

She was Italian, of course. How dare anyone question it?

Being Italian didn't just make sense to Roxanna because of

her last name, but also because of what had put her family on the map: Pizzabomme. It wasn't an obvious European delicacy—more American than anything—but it was a take on an Italian food and therefore it was Italian, or Italian American enough (and a little bit French—why not!). Plus, they all just looked it, anyway: the naturally dark hair (except for Haylee), the golden-brown skin, the nose, the cheekbones—it was all there.

When they had rented the first *Godfather* movie on DVD and screened it in the Milani mansion movie room, Al mumbled over and over, *Look, they could be Iranian, all of them.*

You mean, we could be Italian! Roxanna had snapped back. It was the first time he had heard that from her.

It would be years until he realized what she had done, his daughter, with shimmery eye shadow smudged all over her crying face, waving her gold iPhone in the air, as she bawled incoherently in his office.

He knew better than to stop or even comfort her. Roxanna, like himself, was not one for hugs.

"I mean, how the hell did you even avoid this issue?" she kept crying.

"Avoid it?" He laughed. "You think you could hide Iran back then? I didn't avoid it. No one asked. I was lucky. Pizzabomme was bigger than me."

"Well, I need it to be bigger than us! I need the show to be bigger than us! It's the 2020s! Identity's, like, back *in*!" She fell into the buttery Bentley leather couch, which he had always said was off-limits to the girls, given how much self-tanner and moisturizer and body glitter they all—but Mina—wore. But this time, he let it slide. Roxanna was in deep distress.

And she wasn't wrong. Identity was everywhere these days. So much so that even he worried.

"So what do we do, Roxi—what do you suggest?" he said. "The show is part of that. Identity. Americans have always been obsessed. It's showing us as the first Iranian reality TV family. How can this be avoided?"

She sounded like a choking animal, her sobs were so loud. "I know, I know, I've went over everything a million times. I thought we could just not do it! I thought we could lie! I thought we could pretend like we are half—like Mom is the Italian one, you know? Honestly, I have thought of it all and all I can hope for is, like, a miracle or a time machine to go back in time!"

"And do what? Say no to the show? Or not lie to your class-mates about being Iranian?" He didn't want to put it so bluntly, but there was no other way to put it. He fought the impulse to take a tissue to the white leather, which was already taking on the bronze shimmer of her thigh.

Roxanna suddenly stopped and sniffled. For a second it looked like she was turning to God, praying, but he had never known his girl to do such a thing. The thought almost made him laugh.

"Dad, I don't know," she whimpered. "I know a lot about a lot but, like, has it ever occurred to you I am, like, just a teenager?"

The thought was actually shocking. Al had always seen her at this age, whatever it was. When they'd be out together, people would regularly mistake her for his girlfriend or spouse, and that definitely had to do with more than his occasional adventures in cosmetic surgery. Roxanna had a way of being very old and young at the same time. In a way, all his daughters had that quality.

"We'll figure it out, Rox," he said, eyeing the door. "We always do. We've already done so many impossibles, haven't we? We've made it here. I did that. We can do far more. A show is nothing for us."

Roxanna's tears had made it so it looked like the couch— the only Bentley item he owned so far, though he knew the vehicles were in his future—was soiled, a mess of brown droplets and gold smudges. She didn't notice. Instead, she took her cue, straightened her silk Saint Laurent minidress as she got up, and, as usual, stamped her exit with words she hoped were iconic. "Reality is like a whole other game."

"Maybe they can use that as our tagline. Not bad, Roxi," he tried to joke, but she was already out, stomping down the marble halls in her gold heels, his perfect little girl, looking for the next loved one to terrorize.

6

Homa

The bang on the door was followed by the clicking of nails, a signature knock. *Not my Roxi every time I dare find my peace!* Homa thought about not answering, but she knew Roxanna would barge in anyway. She was struggling to fall into her usual afternoon nap, her habit for decades now in this country, the only time she really got to herself, in her beloved Guest Bedroom Five, with its hand-painted de Gournay chinoiserie wallpaper in a tranquil cornflower blue. It also doubled as her own bedroom when she needed time away from Al, which was more and more often these days. As her nap hour began stretching to nap hours, the more dizzying her life became, the more her daughters also seemed increasingly intent on needing her exactly *then*.

The door flung open and Homa peeled off her silk paisley eye mask. There was Roxanna, poised for high drama, her face smeared in tears that were so polluted with cosmetics it had the effect of an oil spill—dirty and beautiful all at once, a wounded, wobbling mess of iridescence and filth.

"What is it, *aziz*?" She sighed, knowing it was unlikely to be anything alarming, but still playing the part with her most difficult daughter, the Mainest Character of the house.

"I just—I just think we should quit!"

Quit. Homa let the word turn over in her head, over and over. What could she possibly mean? Homa had been a quitter her whole life. She often even dreamed about quitting life, so she wasn't sure what to make of what Roxanna was saying.

"The show," she went on, as if she could read Homa's mind. She was pacing the bedroom in those new gold Louboutins that sounded like horse clompers. Homa wished her children had gotten one thing from Persian custom, that they'd remove their shoes in the home, but that habit had been abandoned once they started going on playdates as kids. "I think the show is no good!"

Homa sat up, resisting darting up, as if Roxanna had said some magic words. Roxanna had to know—she was a manipulative one—that Homa dreaded the whole prospect of a reality show. She had to be saying it for her sake—Roxi was tied with Al for most enthusiastic about this whole fiasco. It had to be a trap. Homa wearily put on the silver Cartier frames that often carelessly dangled on a pearl chain from her neck, so as to get a better look at her daughter.

"Roxi, baby, this doesn't seem like you," she said. "Let's not get too worked up. You slept okay?"

Stomp and screech—that question did not go well. "I hate how before you don't even listen to me, you're, like, already not listening to me!"

Teenage logic. Homa blinked absently and got up to open the window a crack. Roxi had introduced a lot of heat into the room and she felt suffocated by the smells—a mix of bad perfume and body cream and hair product. Roxanna always smelled like a mall—an upscale mall (Dubai or Singapore or Monaco, maybe?), but a mall, nonetheless. Homa's room smelled like fresh laundry and tuberose and rain, a formula a scent designer had concocted especially for her a few birthdays ago.

"Forgive me, baby, but you wanted this show so bad and now you are suddenly here very upset because you don't want the show," Homa said. "What am I missing?"

Roxanna put on a look of outrage and then just froze, as still as she could ever get, as if she were about to say it all, say something very revelatory and profound, that could just maybe win over her mother once and for all, but she couldn't. If she told Homa, what would stop Homa from telling her sisters? Only Mina knew, or at least she thought only Mina knew. If the show went on, they would all find out that way, and then what? For a second, she considered if Al had perhaps told her mother, but she remembered that she had properly threatened Al. If he said a word, she swore she would tell Homa and the girls about the model he took out on his boat last summer. Al and Roxi had all kinds of secrets like that and Roxanna never hesitated to use them at opportune times. Al prayed it was a teenage phase and she would grow out of it, though he definitely erred on her good side just in case. Al would never risk that much. Plus, Al didn't seem to think her secret was such a big deal. The consequences were largely hers—it was all about her school and her peers and the gossip, after all. The only way they would all be implicated was by being related to her—by having a daughter and sister so crazy that for years and years she had convinced teachers and students alike, her whole scholastic society, that she was an ethnicity she was not.

The thing was, Homa, who had struggled with mental illness since her teens, could perhaps understand it. This could have been one of those confessions that Homa understood: the self-hatred, the xenophobia and racism that manifested as depression and suicidal ideation, the deceit out of sheer desperation, the torture of living a lie. Homa could wrap her head around all of that, but Roxanna had never quite trusted her mother. This was not the time to start.

"Mommy, I am sorry to have woken you—I made a mistake," she suddenly said, coolly. It was almost like she was imitating some aristocratic character in a period drama, the way she spun on her heels and looked at the sparkling Lalique Rinceaux mirror and wiped her tears and smoothed her hair. Composure came over her with an alarming abruptness.

"Are you sure, Roxi? You are worrying me a bit," her mother said.

But Roxi's eyes were somewhere well past the reflection and into the future, some scheme a horizon away—perhaps the whole episode had triggered an idea in her. Who could know? But the storm had subsided for now.

"I am totally sure," she said, leaning into her Valley lilt, plastering on an almost disturbingly saccharine smile. "I just have thinking to do. And the show will be fine. I don't know why I was all like that—I think I am just studying too hard or something."

Homa nodded weakly. Roxanna never studied—or the most she studied was the bare minimum. Other than Mina, her children were just not academic. That was from Al. And Roxanna loved a lie—she'd spin any narrative any which way that suited her. So she was tired from studying and it got to her and made her cry and demand to her parents that the show be stopped. That was all nothing, apparently.

"Well, I am glad to see you are okay," Homa said, collapsing back into her repose. "Lock the door on your way out and please stop stomping in those—why are you wearing those heels, anyway?"

"Breaking them in," Roxanna said, with a defiant, loud stomp. "Can't be off my mark!"

Homa rolled her eyes into her eye mask as the door shut, with a loud click of Roxanna's gold red-bottomed hooves.

The exhaustion she felt those days was not a new thing. It had never been easy to be the Milani matriarch, but lately it felt impossible. She would dream of an escape if she were less depressed, but depression had been a constant for Homa, ever since she arrived in America. During the Iran-Iraq War, her parents told her they were all going on a long vacation to the U.S. Then, with a war brewing, she was told they just had to ride it out in America. Homa in Iran had been nothing like what she would become in America: she had been happy. And happy not in a manic way the way Roxi and Haylee sometimes were. She had been content, a middle-class Tehran kid, the oldest of four, with a stable, comfortable family. She had dreamed of being an art history teacher. She had never thought of leaving Iran, and so when her family landed in Los Angeles, Homa was horrified. She had brown skin and very curly black hair, and suddenly, within weeks of being there, her hair uncurled itself. *The water doesn't agree with you,* her mother would say. Her skin began to fade and freckles appeared. Her body grew sunken and sallow. It was as if all the life force were taken out of her. She went from being a good student to a poor one—the English language was unreasonably challenging. She had had minimal English tutoring, and suddenly language was just one of many impossible barriers. She stopped being interested in art—the American and European artists she had read so much about had lost their allure for her now that she was in the West. She tried to look to Persian miniatures and other art from the East, but even the idea of art seemed frivolous and silly and almost obnoxious. Most things did. She had begun to feel what would be the defining characteristic of her adult life: clinical depression, without friction, sans any struggle, expressed always in the register of the purest pessimism.

Depression and pessimism seemed so out of place in California. Everything was so gold and neon, lavish and ecstatic, fluff and froth in the L.A. of the eighties. But in the worst ways, she always emphasized. There were palm trees everywhere, which she soon learned were not even native to California but fakes that had been imported. The sky was always a bit smoky and soiled, the smog of that era a constant; she soon forgot she had grown up under a blue, not yellow-gray, sky. The buildings were a mess of multicolored calamities, flamingo pinks and moldy greens and toilet-water blues alongside dead beiges and brutalist grays; glassy skyscrapers next to slabs of sticky stucco melting into the earth like Play-Doh cakes, everything commercial or residential plastered with signage, exclamation points and non-sense slogans, all trying to sell themselves or sell you. So much *lo* and *diet* and *hey* and *yay*. The food, even: dull, gooey, and bland, if not fizzy and chemical-y. All the white children were beaming and giggling, running and skipping and galloping blond things in French braids and side ponytails that smelled like cheap apple shampoo and fake tans the color of canned pumpkin bought from drugstore bottles, and everywhere hairless, waxy limbs that seemed born of Barbies, belonging to their forever-young mothers, girl and woman alike all in those cheap polyester fringey and frilly and ruffly and eyeletty clothes that barely covered anything in that climate. Dry and yet wet seemed to sum it up. You had mountain and valley and ocean and desert impossibly in one, and none seemed too real. The only thing that seemed authentic were the endless, illuminated serpents of gridlocked traffic, the low-flying police helicopters, and the noxious, carnivorous sunsets that had to come at a price. No one was bothered by all the many disturbing aspects of life there. Wildfires, earthquakes, droughts, landslides, extreme heat, acid rain. No one wanted to be anywhere else.

This land was repulsive to Homa, the exact opposite of the grace and simplicity she had grown up with in Iran. She longed to go back home, but every year her parents told her, *Next year.* Next year never came.

And then she met Al. She was twenty-four and he was thirty, a young CEO, with a business called Pizzabomme. Her English was still not perfect, so she thought it was an American word. She had applied for an administrative job at his company and flunked the typing test. The supervisor was reviewing her results when Al happened to walk through the Sherman Oaks office building's break room.

"You misspelled every word, Miss Aibadee," the supervisor in her stern beige suit said, fumbling over her surname, Abadi.

Homa shrugged.

"That's it? That's all you have to say for this?" The supervisor acted as if she wanted a fight, but Homa just wasn't interested. She had gone on this job interview mostly at the prompting of her mother, who was worried that without a proper college education Homa would get nowhere.

"What I was supposed to say?" Homa muttered. She hated the way her accent sounded in English—she was hyperaware of the mechanical twists and turns around the vowels and consonants of this forever-foreign tongue of theirs. If Farsi was curvy and spirally and ornate, English was boxy and rectangular and flat. She resented knowing all she did know of it; she resented sounding like she was bad at it.

It was just then that Al took note of her accent. He was months into his first year at accent-elimination classes in Beverly Hills. He had seen a sign on the street and he had finally taken the plunge. As a result he had become sensitive to accents, and this one he knew well. It was how he used to sound, or how he hoped he didn't sound like at all anymore.

He looked up from the stacks of paperwork he was carrying idly and took a good look at the woman with the clearly Iranian accent.

She was medium-size and olive-skinned, with a flat brown bob, and she wore a simple navy-blue tennis dress and white pumps. She looked unremarkable to him. She wasn't wearing much makeup either. Iranian women, particularly in Southern California, wore a lot of makeup. Perhaps she was trying to look American. But usually Iranians veered toward excess, and so he could always spot them by their thick mascara, heavily drawn eyebrows, excessive, bruisey blush, and aggressively lined lips that were either blood-red or a frosted metallic. That, plus big, feathered hair, often blond, defined their aesthetic. But this woman wore only a bit of lip gloss, at most. He couldn't even place her age. She stood out for not standing out.

"Ma'am, this is a job interview," the supervisor was scolding her, no doubt a show for Al. "You applied for this. The idea, when you apply, is that you want the job. You've had nothing but attitude since you got here, so I have to question your interest in this role. I don't appreciate having my time wasted."

Homa squinted her way through the words, to make sure she understood, and smirked. These American women, they sure did not have confidence. The insecurity that made them bully others was something Homa had noticed before. Pathetic.

"I did fine for someone not from here," she said quietly, grabbing her purse and getting up, ready to leave.

"Yes, well, you don't have to be here," the supervisor snapped. "We don't require you be in our country. You are free to leave just like you are free to leave our office!"

Al froze. He did not like that tone one bit. And the implication—it sounded all too much like a racist expression he had learned all too well by then: *Go back to your country.* They would resort to that whenever they could not win in another way. It seemed they were always ready to send Iranians away, always ready to imagine them on a plane. He had heard it at the gas station, on the supermarket line, once at the DMV, and even once from a vendor whom he had argued with over the phone. In accent-elimination class, in fact, he had announced to the other students on the first day that that was part of his impetus for taking the course: *to show racists we too belong here and that we can fit in easily, with just a few shifts in our speech.* The teacher had applauded while most of the class had looked mortified—there were several Iranians in there who looked especially ashamed, as if the xenophobia were just something you did not bring up. Especially not in a setting like that.

Al had to do something.

"Excuse me." He spoke up quickly. He had forgotten the supervisor's name. "What is happening here?"

"Oh, nothing, sir. Mr. Milani, this person applied for this job and failed in a big way and now wants to talk back," she said loudly, glaring at Homa for extra effect. "We'll be getting rid of her soon—I just have not encountered this behavior, not in our offices, at least!"

Homa rolled her eyes. It was funny that this short, tan man in his too-tight suit was Mr. Milani, the founder of the company. It made sense why her mother thought this would be good for her—it was rumored that an Iranian had founded this company and she assumed her odds here could be a bit better because of it. But once she got there, she was surprised to see no Iranians were employed—at least no one she could immediately identify as Iranian. It was as surprising as the big boss being there himself and pausing to take her in.

Nonetheless, Homa was eager to leave. She avoided meeting Al's eyes, which were evaluating her carefully. She wanted to be gone, to forget it all except maybe to use it for a dinner anecdote with her family, evidence that she had at least tried. It wasn't that she didn't want a job—jobs just did not want her.

"Miss, where are you from?" Al's own accent was unmistakable, accent-elimination class or not.

Homa's eyes darted to his. If this had been just some American, maybe she would have lied. She assumed he had heard her speak and that he knew where she was from too. Their accents aligned—the odd one out was the supervisor in that room, and for a moment Homa relished the idea of making her feel like the one left out.

"Iran," she said simply. She was tempted to say, *Like you?* but that felt dicey in front of these racist white Americans, especially. She had no doubt the supervisor did not like Iranians. She probably saw Mr. Milani as the exception or maybe she didn't know his background at all.

She later swore she heard the supervisor snort, but who could tell what number her imagination did on her memory. She was always on such high alert. Insults were hard to predict and even harder to dodge.

"Ah, I thought so!" he said, with a big smile. "Like me!"

She looked away from his performative joy shyly and nodded with little enthusiasm.

"So nice to see one of my own!" he said, laying on the delight thick. "So we speak nicely to my people, okay?" That last part was for the supervisor, who was pretending to go through some files.

"Nice for you, but not her," Homa said with a smile. She had dared to go there; somehow his pleasure had given her courage.

"Excuse me? I'm just doing my job," the supervisor said. "Mr. Milani, she failed everything. I was just seeing her out but if you need to speak—"

"Seeing her out? That is so rude," he said. "Please, my name is Al. Ali. And you are . . . ?"

"Abadi," Homa said. "Homa Abadi." She paused awkwardly. "I should go. She is right. I failed."

This was the second thing Al found notable about her, after her plain appearance. She admitted doing poorly on the test. This, like the lack of makeup and ornamentation, made her seem so unlike an Iranian. What culture was so self-defeating in this way?

"It's perfectly fine," he said. "Please, I can get you some tea. It is not common we have an Iranian here. Perhaps you can tell me about why you wanted this job?"

Homa was touched but also assumed he was lonely. So many Iranians in America suffered from that affliction. Here he was, a man who had made it, at least to some degree, trying to win over a low-level employee candidate, and for what?

But Homa could feel the supervisor's eyes on her. "I should go," she said. She didn't really want the job, anyway—she had known that before she got there. Al's kindness was touching, but

it also embarrassed her. She wanted to get back to the few people she interacted with regularly: her family. This whole ordeal
was too much for her.

Al tried to win her over a few more times, but she walked
over to the door and promptly disappeared.

Al had taken her seat and gone over the whole encounter in
his head, ignoring the supervisor, who beamed with the satisfaction of a cat who had caught a mouse.

"We have four more candidates interviewing this week, sir,"
she said. "Don't worry—they are all much better qualified than
she is. I can already tell from their résumés. Her interview was
just very bad. You didn't see the worst—"

Al was furious. "I don't care," he said. "I want her to have
the job."

"She failed everything," the supervisor said. "You can look at
the test yourself. It was a mess. You would not have—"

"Please give me her phone number," he said. He suddenly
realized how that sounded. "I will be calling her to apologize."

The supervisor was perplexed, but did as she was told. She
scribbled the number on a pink Post-it and handed it to him.

"And I need you to watch it with the people you interview,"
he said. "I need you to be not rude. No matter what. Especially
to my people."

The supervisor looked confused.

"We have been through a lot, you know," he said to her, his
voice shaking a bit.

That night, as he ate a microwaved Pizzabomme in front of
the television, he went to wipe his hands and suddenly the pink
Post-it appeared on his lap, as if a higher power were sending
him a message. It must have fallen out of his pocket.

HOMA ABADI, it said. A nice name, he thought. Or nice because
it was familiar. In this land of Jennifers and Melissas and Jessicas
and Ashleys and Amys, it was nice to see a Homa.

He looked at the clock on his wall—it was not too late. He

wished he had her résumé in front of him so he could figure out how old she was. She had to be around his age, he imagined. But to have had no job at all? Nobody with a real job would be coming to him, he thought. She must have not gone to school. He pushed these thoughts out of his head—the Revolution did all kinds of things to their people.

He dialed the number, with little idea what he was doing. *An apology, right,* he said to himself—even though he knew that, even for an Iranian, that was absurd. He prayed her husband would not answer, and he found himself praying there was no husband.

What on earth was going through his head? Al was often unknowable to himself.

And there it was: the hello that was more *Allo?* The Persian hello. It was her.

"Homa Abadi?" he asked. He was amazed at how nervous he sounded.

"Who is this?" Immediately suspicion. This was the most Iranian thing about her yet.

"This is Al—Ali, I mean, Milani," he said. And then he switched to Persian: *I hope I am not interrupting you.*

There was a long pause.

Homa remembered that conversation well. Why on earth was this businessman calling her? His employee, the supervisor, had humiliated her and asked her to leave. She had refused his multiple requests for tea. Why on earth would he be calling her now? Was this some American custom she did not yet understand? And talking to her in Persian now too?

"Mr. Milani, a nice surprise to hear you," she said, answering in English, for some reason. "How can I help you?" She truly had no idea what this could be about. Had she left something behind? But then why would *he* call?

"I am calling to apologize," he said in English. "I did not like how things went today. It is not like our company."

She chuckled. "It's no matter. I did not want your job so much." She knew it was the wrong thing to say, but at this point, the situation being so bizarre, she thought, *Why not?*

"Yes, but it was a poor reflection on my part," he said. He paused. He knew what he had to say but he could not quite believe it. In all these years in Los Angeles, he had not approached any woman quite like this. He had not gone on a date since he lived in Iran. The Iranian women he saw in L.A. were out of his league—way more American than he was, somehow already rich and part of the fabric of the place. He was not there yet. But why he suddenly wanted to ask out this plain woman, this woman who had applied for the lowest-level role at his company, failed at that, who had been a disaster of an interview, who had rejected his request for tea at the office—it was all beyond him. He felt like his life was a movie and things were about to take a turn. He could have sworn he heard her hold her breath.

She indeed held her breath in the space of their awkward pause, as the whole operation began to dawn on her. In her years in America, not a single time, did a man, Iranian or American, take an interest in her. She wasn't like the American women or the Iranian women here and she was fine with that. But this feeling—this strange sensation—was something she had not felt since her days as a schoolgirl in Tehran.

Maybe she was wrong but she felt it coming.

Maybe he was making a mistake but he felt there was no way but forward.

"Well, I wonder, can I perhaps have a dinner with you?" he said, still in stilted English, sounding like his old teenage self before a neighborhood girl, but with English dubbing. "You know, to make up for things, I would like to do this."

He heard her breath lightly skim the surface of their tension.

She didn't know what to say, but somehow this was much harder to refuse than tea had been that afternoon. It was hard to believe it was happening, she thought, but there she was. She knew it would be too painful—somehow—to refuse.

"Okay," she said, in Farsi suddenly, it pouring out of her, as if she really were that neighborhood girl in the movie of Al's life. She felt a blush wash over her face.

Al was relieved. "I am so glad," he said in English, and then repeated it in Farsi.

A week later, he pulled up in his leased white BMW, which he had forgotten to get washed, and appeared at the door of Homa's run-down apartment in the other Valley, a bland, suburban area called Monrovia. He could immediately tell no Iranians lived there and certainly not in that shabby apartment building. It was relatable, nothing like the world of the rich Iranians who were every day setting up all kinds of shop all over town, with everyone clueless as to where their wealth came from. He had a good feeling she was not rich, and definitely not rich like them. It was a good thing: he was at the beginning of his career and he was not convinced he would make it. Going back to Iran was not entirely out of the question.

She answered the door, again to his relief, though he could hear two older voices in the background chatting against the hum of the television on a commercial break. She was wearing the same navy dress she'd worn to the job interview, this time with navy pumps, but he swore her lips had on a wash of light-pink lipstick. Her hair looked nice too.

She did not offer to let him inside, but quietly walked with him to the car. She noted that his dinner jacket and pants were a class above her outfit, but she had only the one nice dress, and she had no idea what the plan was. He had said dinner, but who knew what that meant to a man who was a company CEO.

In the car, the smell of vanilla air freshener and cologne overwhelmed her. She rolled down her window and took in the scene-scape she rarely got to appreciate. She didn't often leave the house. She had no real friends.

"I thought we could have Persian food," he said, again in English. He wasn't sure why he chose English—perhaps it sounded less intimate, and that seemed like a good first step.

She nodded quietly. It sounded nice to her. The Persian restaurants in Los Angeles were surprisingly good. It was as if Iranian restaurateurs from Tehran had simply picked up and reinstalled their homeland kitchens here seamlessly, much like the rug merchants. Americans seemed to forget their racism when their stomachs were calling or their homes needed furnishing.

They pulled up to Shamshiri Grill, and at dinner, without asking her, he ordered a bottle of red wine. They shared a kashk bademjan for an appetizer and a mast moosir, and then they shared a kabob soltani as well. The sharing felt so much like a date to her—she did not expect it and further did not expect it to feel natural. She had not been on a date in years.

She barely sipped her wine, but she ate ravenously.

He loved that she ate well—another thing he found to be unlike the forever-dieting Iranian women of L.A.

At dinner, he forgot to ask her much about her. He went on and on about his company.

At one point, she asked him about Iran, and he was amazed how uncomfortable it felt to talk about it.

Because of the waiters and the Persian menu, they spoke entirely in Persian, with little formality. It was like the chatter of friends, not lovers. At one point, she let out a burp, and if she was embarrassed, she did not show it.

She was honestly surprised her little burp did not mortify her more. She wondered if they were friends, just *doost*. She thought that would be okay. Her first friend in America.

He thought, on the drive home, with some horror, that she could easily be a friend. Al made friends easily, even in America, and he did not want another. He didn't feel especially attracted to Homa, but she was the first girl he had gone out with here—of course things would seem strange.

By the time he pulled up to her garage, they were both ready for the date to be over. It was too much and yet not enough.

"Well, thank you," she said, suddenly in English, with her head turned to avoid showing him how she really felt. She could not say she was attracted to him.

But without her permission, he took her hand and put a kiss on it. A dry kiss, a simple kiss, one she thought was harsh, almost, a bit sandpapery, only vaguely romantic.

She heard herself thanking him, strangely.

She heard him thanking her back, also strangely.

They did not belong here and yet here they were.

At their engagement dinner they would recall this night for their family and friends, the punch line being over and over that as lonely as it was in America then, they both really and truly felt very little for each other that night, almost nothing.

It was to be their pearl anniversary in 2020: thirty years of marriage for Al and Homa Milani. Al had suggested it as a show storyline—perhaps they could do a big party and Homa, as usual, expressed little interest. *It's okay—as you can see, it's part of her character,* he insisted to one of the producers (the younger, feminist-seeming one, who was perpetually worried Homa was being lured into something she did not want). *My wife is just a bit like this—we call it* yakh, *like ice.* Sard: *cold. It's just—what do you call it—an affect, really.*

Homa had shrugged helplessly and so they had begun arrangements for a party. One of the producers wondered if it would be good for the show for their daughters to throw the party, but Al and Homa didn't even bother to suggest it.

They were unsure how their daughters felt about any of it, if they had to be honest. When it had appeared as if they were getting divorced a few years ago, the girls' reactions were not what they had expected. Roxanna had seemed relieved and assured Al she was sticking to him no matter how the custody agreements broke down officially; Violet had decided to just stay out of it but had wished them both well and stayed focused on school and her modeling; Mina at first seemed most upset but when she and her therapist talked about the prospect, it seemed much happier for all involved and she knew that so many American families were divorced these days, anyway; and Haylee had decided to make a big dramatic show of it, blaming everything on this, from her poor grades to her getting in trouble at school to not getting the lead role in her elementary school's production of *Funny Girl,* but secretly even she knew a divorce was for the best.

They all bought the reason, for the most part—that the arguing had become too much and that they had grown apart. But Al and Homa had never shared the real reason. When Al confessed it to a male producer, he made sure he understood not to mention it again. It had been a traumatic episode in their lives, one that Homa still dangled before him like a weapon, a costly one for Al in every sense of the word. He had spent the intervening years trying so hard to win her forgiveness—with everything from lavish gifts to a promise of counseling.

In a sense, Homa was not that surprised he had cheated. She was not even that bothered by it. To her, Al always seemed like the kind of guy who would cheat, and Iranians were prone to all sorts of romantic transgressions, she felt. It was in the poetry, the pop music, every bit of lore, and she remembered it from her own father and her family's suspicions about his tendencies. She had imagined this day would come, that her husband would fall in this manner. And she predicted what would happen too, of course: she would stick by him. That was the difference between her people and Americans, she thought. They left and families broke up. She was frankly surprised by how close they had gotten to that, but that was all Al. He had become so much more American than she was. Plus, it had seemed he was eager to move on. And so the real surprise was that they actually stayed together through it all. But then, who but her could stand Al really in the end—all that money was barely worth that kind of trouble.

She recalled their fourth date, when he finally asked her to be his girlfriend—at that restaurant by one of the nicer L.A. beaches, one of the Malibu ones. Homa was then still barely invested in this man. But she had noticed when she was returning from the bathroom that he and their waitress were sharing a rather intimate exchange. By the bar, Homa had frozen. She thought by then she had learned all of Al's expressions, but apparently she had not. He was glowing, beside himself in a very particular kind of laughter. With her he had smiled and laughed and all that, but this look was something else. The waitress, quite young and rather Persian-looking (though Homa didn't think she was in fact Persian), was a very petite, curvy brunette with that deep tan the girls in L.A. favored. Her hair fell down to her waist, and for some reason she and Al were discussing it. It seemed like perhaps her hair had dipped into his plate or something and this had caused them both so much delight.

Homa hovered there and watched this man, who just twenty minutes before had asked her to be with him—she had said yes, because why not, these were dates after all—suddenly lose himself in the face and curves and hair of this young woman. It had been the first time she had watched him in action without her—really observed Al when he did not know he was being observed. She was astounded by how long it went on—was the waitress really allowed to linger at tables like that, when the restaurant was so packed that evening? It seemed he was asking her questions about herself and she was answering and then turning the questions on him, and they were just locked in an endless loop of flirtation. Homa could not relate. She waited for them to stop, but they didn't and so she just marched back to the bathroom, and when she came out again, the waitress was at another table, but Al's eyes were still on her. And Homa could tell he was on the waitress's mind too, as she very deliberately smiled at him while brushing past to another table. Al chuckled silently. In the span of her bathroom visit, he had found a woman and now they had jokes.

Homa had coolly taken her seat and watched him shift modes entirely, suddenly very serious and somber. She watched his eyes closely, but not once did they wander back to the waitress. He was a pro, she thought. She wondered at what point in their relationship he would get caught.

And so she did not imagine it would happen again many lives later. But when it turned out that Aurora, a relatively new assistant of his, was doing way more than assisting, she was not surprised.

Aurora had that same look as the waitress had: short, voluptuous, little but also bursting at the seams, glowy, sweet and fun and silly and flirty. She was everything that Homa was not. She was just a handful of years older than Violet but her presence was always very *present*. The way the house would fill with the scent of Victoria's Secret freesia whenever she'd linger, the cosmetics-counter aura of her, the trails of makeup Homa could never quite find but *felt*. She was always too much. She wore these little T-shirt dresses that seemed unapologetically cheap to Homa, as if to say it didn't matter what she draped on her impressive body—everyone would be imagining what was underneath anyway.

Homa marveled at how these women Al went for were the opposite of her, but isn't that how it was with these cheating men? Most people considered Homa tall for an Iranian woman—five-eight—but she was built in all angles, not much in the way of waist or hips or breasts. Her long legs were one of her main charms but she rarely showed them off. Her skin was nice enough—mainly bare but for some French moisturizer she special-ordered. She kept her hair dyed a rich, expensive, and mostly natural brown, always cut in a clean bob, a look Mina had basically adopted since childhood too. She rotated many glasses but her thin tortoiseshell Ralph Lauren optical frames were her favorite for how they delicately framed her dark eyes and gave her the look of someone official or important—a woman who would have been friends with Princess Di and had senators on speed dial. There was nothing flirty or frivolous about her. She looked serious and she took pride in that. Her wardrobe consisted of sensible creams, grays, navies, and blacks—a cold-winter palette that almost read exotic in L.A. She had expensive accents, gold and pearls and very small diamonds, all over her, but again it all read as someone you reported to, not someone you lost your heart to. Whether Homa was thirty or fifty seemed to make no difference—there was something solid about her. She felt it was a timeless elegance, which certainly these waitress and assistant types, who reeked of bad retail jobs and community college degrees at best, could not compete with. Or could they?

It was Rose, the housekeeper, who had told her. Rose was loyal to Homa. She was also not one for frilly presentation, though for her it was religious—Homa thought of Rose as a devout Christian but she wasn't all that sure what it meant in America. But this made her discovery of Al's infidelity all the more upsetting, Homa imagined. She had gone into his office to clean up during off-hours when she knew he would not be there, and there he was—with Aurora in a compromising position on the couch beside the desk. At first Rose was confused, she said—Aurora was still only a couple months into the job and for a second Rose mistook her for one of the daughters' friends. But then the curves and the peach T-shirt dress hiked up to her waist and that raspy voice gave it away. Rose quickly shut the door and shuffled out, praying they had not seen her—it certainly seemed possible, they were so engrossed.

Later that evening, as Rose was tidying up after dinner, Al asked to speak to her. It was almost intimate how he did it—he walked up to her and in the lowest of tones, as close to a whisper as possible, he requested she come to his office in five minutes. She of course knew what it was going to be about but when she walked in those five minutes later, she did her best not to eye the couch and revisit the episode. Al himself was seated at his desk, as if to bring professional formality back to the room. He looked anxious—Al never looked anxious—and he met her eyes pleadingly.

"Rose, I know you saw something," he began softly. "And I am sorry for that."

She was frozen, but his stare implied he expected a response, so she nodded back, a nod that she hoped included forgiveness in addition to acknowledgment.

"Does anyone know?" he went on. "Did anyone send you? And have you told anyone?"

She shook her head vigorously.

"How can we keep it this way, Rose?" His eyes had not broken from hers once. He tapped his breast pocket, his wallet, she guessed.

"Oh, no, Mr. Milani, I don't need you to do anything," Rose said. "It's not my place to say a thing and I certainly will not."

Al had seemed unsatisfied with that answer. The anxiety was not leaving him. "This is not good for my family life. I am sure you can understand." He paused. "White people . . . are they more or less discreet, I wonder?"

There was a silence that lasted a lifetime between them.

"Well, I barely saw a thing and I can tell you for sure I have nothing to report!" She wanted the discussion to be over so badly.

He seemed to as well. He smiled at her, that same big smile that the world saw on the Pizzabomme commercials, the one that guaranteed satisfaction for the whole family. "Thanks, Rose. I won't be forgetting this." He patted his breast pocket again. She imagined she'd have some extra padding in her Christmas bonus that year.

Still, the whole thing bothered her profoundly, and she imagined what would have happened if the tables had been turned: if her Randy had been caught by Homa. What would she want? She would want to know, of course. After all, she thought, there were sexually transmitted diseases to worry about, for example. But most of all, her heart would want to know. She struggled with this scenario—Randy would never lust after those Aurora-type girls. Randy liked country girls, much like she had been, before life had aged her. Randy's girls were simple, but they were also Christian.

White people. She couldn't get that out of her head.

Rose carried all this with her and avoided Al and Aurora as much as she could for months. Instead she stuck by Homa's side. She searched her face for signs of stress, suspicion, envy, upset. But nothing. Homa had no idea.

It wasn't until that Christmas season, when she saw Homa agonizing over a golf equipment catalog, searching for a present for Al, that the enormity of it all hit her. Rose was a good Christian woman and infidelity was a sin. How could she not tell Homa? Plus, Al had never asked her to promise to him or to swear to God or anything—maybe he knew her too well, knew too well her allegiance to God would prohibit that. That very moment she decided it was not just an obligation but her duty to tell Homa.

Rose studied Homa, looking exhausted, her eyebrows furrowed over the catalog. Homa was not big on physical affection but she really did shine when it came to gifts. She would no doubt buy something amazing for Al, something he definitely did not deserve from her that year.

Homa could feel Rose's eyes on her and she met them with some curiosity. "Are you okay, Rose?"

Rose nodded quickly and, never one to lie, she then replaced it rapidly with a headshake.

"What is it?" Homa was worried, as Rose rarely complained. It had to be bad.

Rose felt her face grow red. She was so bad at this, she already knew it. She had never had to deal with this kind of thing before, but she just knew this was something she would be terrible at. She tried to calm herself down by reminding herself this was his mess and not hers and she was merely doing the right thing.

"It's about Al," Rose said, but it came out strangely, coated in a gasp.

Homa immediately looked alarmed. "Is he okay? Where is he? Upstairs?"

"Oh, he's fine," Rose said. "He just did something."

Homa's left eyebrow lifted tensely.

"To someone. With someone." She paused. She had not rehearsed this. "Not with me," she added awkwardly.

The catalog dropped from Homa's hand. "Please tell me now."

Rose could barely recall how it came out but it came out fast, and all she remembered later was Homa's expression: pure ice. Her jaw was clenched under her skin and she muttered something in Persian. Rose could not bear to ask what it meant.

"I am so sorry," Rose said, with tears in her eyes. She could only imagine how hurtful it all was.

Homa just shook her head tensely. "You have nothing to be sorry about. I should thank you, rather."

"Oh, please, I was just—it was just a bad accident that I saw," Rose fumbled.

Homa rose out of her chair. "Well, God has his ways." It was the one and only time Rose heard Homa refer to God.

Rose comforted herself with that sentiment. And then it seemed to her that it wasn't until several weeks went by that Homa confronted Al. She remembered the day perfectly. There was something off in the air of the house, the sisters ducking in and out of their rooms, quieter than usual.

Then, just before dinner, the screaming began. She heard Homa unlike she had ever heard her, in her own language, of course, but she knew it was cursing. And then she heard Al's roar, somehow weak, a wounded lion.

That was the last day she saw Aurora.

And that was the beginning of a few months of tension, until Homa told her, shortly after she told the girls, that they were getting separated and maybe even divorced.

Rose immediately felt awful, as if this were all her fault. Homa predicted that. "Why don't you take a vacation, Rose? You deserve it." She produced a bulging envelope from her purse. She imagined this was from the breast pocket Al had tapped.

But Rose never took a vacation. Instead Homa did, with the girls. They went to some Polynesian resort Rose had never heard of, while Al went to London to see old friends, or so he claimed. Rose never quite trusted Al again.

When everyone returned and were back together again, it was like nothing had ever happened, like they had all stepped out of some time machine. The Milanis were restored. Al hired a new assistant, a young man with glasses, and Homa and Al started couples therapy together. There was a sudden lightness in the house. Things were better than ever before.

Rose never dared ask what had happened. Life just went on. It seemed in the end that every conflict could be solved for the Milanis because of the one thing they had that many others did not: money. A few trips, a few expensive therapists, some gifts, time off work, new people to hire, and, voilà: problem solved. Rose knew that nothing comforted Al like checking his bank accounts every night—it was always the last thing he did, and without fail, it sent him a very clear message: everything would be okay. There was nothing money could not solve for the Milanis, everyone knew that.

So when the producers of the show began working with them to figure out the concept for Homa and Al's thirtieth-anniversary party, both of them just pointed to the obvious: *mehmooni,* the Persian word for party. But the producers couldn't seem to understand what the Persian concept of a party was. Not to mention that this was going to be a party thrown by the Milanis. They could have a three-day party, one day for each decade, several live bands, a magician or two or three, dinner and brunch banquets, ballroom dancing, and fireworks. Oh, and a zoo?

The producers watched Homa's expression for enthusiasm as they listed it all—the expense was wild, but since Al was covering it, their budget was limitless.

"Does this sound good? Like something you too would like?" the feminist producer asked Homa.

"Why would it not be?" Homa snapped.

"Well, it just seems very much like your husband's show," she said.

"My husband is the only man here, outnumbered by women," Homa said firmly. "We are not oppressed. And don't think for a second we need saving. Or that we don't like all this mess. We are in it for the money too."

The feminist producer looked confused for a second and then almost sad, and then suddenly her eyes lit up. "Do you think we can get you on camera saying that?"

"Saying that? I am living that!" she said. She almost sounded like Al, like she was doing an impression of her husband, in earnestness or in jest, no one could tell. "But sure—who even cares. If I had concerns like that, I wouldn't be here."

"Well, we're so happy to have you here, on the show—"

Homa snorted. She couldn't believe that, except she could. "I don't mean the show. I don't think about the show. I mean, here. All this. I wouldn't be here if I didn't want it."

7

The Persians/Iranians

Roxanna could not stop fixating on the two potential obstacles to the show—two outside of her own personal dilemma, the ever-nagging Secret, that is—war and virus, *ew and double ew.* It was astounding to her that her old childhood fear that America could find itself in a war with Iran was actually inching closer to reality, but here they were. A general had been assassinated and the tide had turned among people in Iran. American sanctions had been crippling, for one thing. Then the mullahs seemed tired of denying plans for nuclear weapons and everyone was tired of the mullahs and talk of nuclear weapons. Some careless threats were made to Israel and then, instead of backing off from the U.S.'s rebukes, Iran did what it had never done before: posed an incredibly clear, dreadfully noncryptic challenge of war against the U.S. and Israel. Commentators on the news were very clear that this time it could really happen. All eyes were on the president to decide, and he had made it clear in a recent speech that he would not be shy about using force.

(*Big drama,* Roxanna captioned an Instagram draft that had her wearing a Victoria Beckham red, white, and blue slip dress in one slide, and then a Missoni red, white, and green halter dress in another. Nothing felt right. She changed the caption to *Fuck this shit* before deleting it once and for all.)

Interestingly, it was that second obstacle that had the chance of helping put a stop to the first: suddenly everyone was talking virus. At first it began in East Asia, and Americans did what Americans do: they ignored it. Roxanna felt like she always heard about outbreaks over there, and they seemed to just magically go away on their own. But this one started competing for space on the evening news. The number of those afflicted was growing rapidly, and China was taking strict measures. Entire cities were under what they called a lockdown to stop the spread. No one understood where it had come from, though theories abounded. It could have been a lab leak, and it could have started from exotic animals—or perhaps just bats, someone somewhere had mentioned—at a wet market, whatever that was. It all felt surreal to Roxanna (*bats?!*); it only grew more real when the news suddenly had the virus popping up in Italy. Roxanna, never mind her ethnic and cultural ancestry lie, had always felt an affinity for Italy—since she was a child, they'd taken family trips to Rome, Florence, Milan, Naples. It was a country she liked to call a second home. It was beyond her how a plague in China could spread to Italy. (Mina: *Ever heard of tourists?!*) And now there was the possibility of it coming to the U.S.

Apparently, wars have difficulty starting when there are plagues to contend with.

It was unclear to Roxanna what was going on, but it seemed unclear to everyone what was going on too. There was a cultural confusion that somehow felt correct. The president, at a press conference, was going on about deliberations with Iran one moment; the next moment, he was suddenly trying to assess what the nature of this pandemic—the word *pandemic!*—was. Roxanna wondered whether her med dosages were suddenly off, but for once everyone around her seemed to feel the same.

And as if this weren't all too much already, Iran then developed the third-worst outbreak. Roxanna could not believe it—first Italy, her adopted motherland, and now Iran, her real one? What was happening?

"It's, like, so *Black Mirror,*" she had heard an older influencer say on an Instagram Live and so she repeated it at dinner one night. She had never seen the show but Mina had nodded: a success.

These new obstacles, war and virus and whatever else was coming, were bad news for the show, of course. The producers warned them that everything could be delayed to next season or even indefinitely. Nothing was ever certain in Hollywood—they could be waiting years. Their contracts did not account for wars or pandemics. Not a soul could predict how things would pan out, so they had to sit tight. It was recommended that they all record their own video journals—little confessionals they could tape right on their cell phones.

Roxanna was a mix of mortified and relieved. Video journals? It felt so unprofessional, so school project, so therapy home-work, so unlike a thing that might really turn into a reality tele-vision show. It was easy enough, but what if it was too easy? And then the relief: she could buy some time to avoid the issue of her Secret. She could figure out what to do with it all. She had no clue what. But it was definitely a blessing and a curse—annoying in both ways.

Roxanna did not do well with waiting in uncertainty, and this was apparently what was being asked of her and all the other Milanis. This was a nightmare for Geminis—and, she had to assume, Scorpios. Who did well with this? Maybe Mina—it seemed to snap her into some adult responsibility. Now that there was no school, she had started to use her free time to make sure everyone was informed. She was routinely popping up on the family group chat, debriefing them on every news develop-ment, adding hand sanitizers and high-tech masks and all sorts of sundries to something Mina was calling their "preparation stash."

Violet seemed utterly confused—some photographers were keen on arranging remote sessions with her, which sounded like a scam. It meant she had to invest in better ring lights and maybe even convert one of the guest bedrooms into a photo studio. She had no idea what she was doing, but she frantically ordered boxes of her favorite candies, those she certainly could not live without. *This is not what they are talking about when they talk about survival essentials,* Homa said with disgust as yet another jumbo package of tiny gummy creatures appeared at their door. Everything was arriving late at prices that made no sense—for the first time in her adult life, she began to really linger on the price of things, as she heard people complain about it more and more—as it all felt like something to do.

Haylee was an absolute mess. This had been her first year in high school, and already she had received so much attention from the upperclassmen, who, she was sure, thought she was special somehow. She was getting invited to all the right parties and had even planned to throw a big spring break bash for her new, cooler friends. But instead, March was the beginning of it all—war talk had made way for plague talk, and all her friends were a mix of scattered and frazzled. Haylee became actively involved in five group chats—all circles of popular kids—and they shared their worries and fears every few hours, it seemed: mostly that this would never end and somehow their rule as the coolest of the school would be compromised. Someone would interrupt the anxieties with a meme and the dread would dissipate until someone else brought it up again. Meme, worry, meme, worry, meme. She wasn't cut out for this.

Al was also irked—he did not like the feeling of tense stagnancy. This was like Roxanna's feeling of restless uncertainty—things not happening were even worse than the unknown happening. He wanted action. He spent his days wondering what new companies to invest in—what could he fund that might bring the world back to normal and what could he profit from while it was so heavily abnormal? Al had traveled the world, flying somewhere almost every month. Now he was stuck at home—a big home but never big enough, if you considered that this was a home of all women, very intense and demanding and all-over-the-place women. He didn't know if war was preferable or this plague—perhaps it would be war *and* plague! He tried his absolute best to channel any patience he could muster. *It will pass, babies,* he told his daughters with his usual Stable Happy Dad smile, but he was really trying to console himself. When he caught glimpses of his face in a passing mirror, he flinched: his smile looked like the Joker's.

Homa felt nothing—that was her line, at least. In a sense, very secretly, she could admit to herself that maybe she felt a tiny smidge better than she had before. Suddenly the world was on her level: depression, isolation, immobility, nihilism. *The apocalypse,* Roxanna was calling it, but if this was the apocalypse, well, then it was awfully boring. Now the whole world had to get used to all the nothingness that she knew all too well. Hope for a future? It was iffy, but she'd known that since she arrived from Iran. Dreams for safety and well-being? No one could say, but that was fine with her, because what was life but waiting out one's days till death, anyway? She had done her duty: married and married well and given life to four women, and now there was just time stretched out ahead of her. And time was more wobbly and gelatinous and flaccid and slippery than ever. As the days ran into each other and everyone went from zombielike shock to frustration to depression, she wanted to welcome them to her mind state. It was awfully chilly in there, no? Yes, she had grown used to it. Plenty of practice. And there they were. She would have laughed if she laughed.

The producers had the Milanis record a spot that was to air at some point soon. They were to all wear yellow—*a hopeful color,* the email said—and they would film on the front lawn, as if they were having a picnic.

The script was simple:

AL: A wise man once said the best things come to those who wait.

MINA: Wait, was that a ketchup commercial?

AL: And if there is something we Milanis know well, it's waiting. If we've waited this long to arrive, well?

HOMA: We can certainly wait longer.

ROXANNA: This is not us ducking out or saying bye, but simply taking a rain check.

VIOLET: We are extremely excited to join you next season.

HAYLEE: It's gotta be—right, everyone?

ROXANNA: Of course.

VIOLET: Hopefully!

MINA: Don't be too sure.

AL: Think positive!

ROXANNA: Anyway, America, we are excited to see you soon. Consider this just a time-out.

AL: We'll be scheming up lots of great content for you in the meanwhile, so you can be properly introduced to . . .

EVERYONE: The Milanis!

"I look terrible in yellow," Haylee complained the minute they cut. "All to say four words."

"You said five," Mina corrected her.

Homa watched her youngest wearily—they were increasingly at each other's throats, a phase she thought they had gotten over years ago. But with the lockdown, all of them were home all the time—this was not going to be peaceful.

Meanwhile, as the press release for the show circulated through all kinds of channels, word had finally traveled to Iran. The Milanis still had their close relatives left there—most of the affluent set had fled during the Revolution—but it was always a bit of a surprise who kept in touch and who did not and how the cycles of correspondence worked with this world that they often forgot existed.

The first to call was Homa's cousin Marjan, who generally only reached out during Persian holidays, mainly to make sure the family had not abandoned their roots, now that they were in the West indefinitely.

"Oh, Homa-*jaan,* everyone knows!" She laughed nervously, as Homa questioned her. "You know, news always travels here fast. Fast for us, of course! The aunts and cousins—they all called me. That's why I wanted to call. Is this such a good idea, Homa? Of course you know best, but I just wonder—"

"No, it is not," Homa said flatly. She didn't hesitate. "It's a terrible idea, but you tell Ali. You tell Roxi. These two are obsessed. Haleh is a bit too. Mina and I want out, but we have no choice. If they don't record us, then it looks like the family has broken up, and we can't have that either."

"Of course not, of course not. I think you did the right thing. What could you do?" Marjan did not sound reassuring. "Anyway, maybe these things are more normal in America."

"Being on reality television is not normal anywhere. It's a disaster. Very bad taste. But they say it will be only one season—or so I hope. I will be rid of it soon. Anyway . . . how are things in Tehran? We hear this virus has hit bad."

Marjan sighed. "Oh, it's so awful. But you know this regime. We barely know how bad it is. And then you have the religious people who say it's Allah's will and their belief in Allah will keep them safe—have you seen them licking the gates of mosques?"

Homa actually had—of course, American news loved to showcase Iran's most unflattering spectacles. "Hopefully, it will pass soon," Homa muttered, frustrated by her own generic sentiment. "Please make sure you take precautions. Stay inside, wash everything, all that. Hopefully this country, with all its wealth, will help you."

Marjan let out a laugh as dry as a prehistoric husk. "Your country has sanctions on us! Help how? I guess the help is not blasting us with a war. At least for now!" Homa could sense her bitter smile from the phone.

"You know, Ali knows a lot of people in government—he said he would talk to them. He has some influence."

"Money cannot solve something that God cannot, Homa-jaan," Marjan said more softly. "We are stuck. All we can do is do our best and pray. We will pray for you all too."

"Pray for us? The numbers are okay in America. We got a start on this—we shall be okay. This country doesn't fall apart from things like this."

"No, no, I mean the show," Marjan corrected. "Hopefully it will be better than we think and reflect flatteringly on us all."

"Us?"

"Iranians."

There was a tense silence.

Marjan comparing their reality television debut to the pandemic was too much for Homa to stomach. They said their usual goodbyes, and it wasn't until the next call, a few days later, from Fereshteh, Al's niece, that Homa really began to reconsider her ties to Iran.

"Oh, big congratulations to family!" Fereshteh said, giggling in her broken English, which she loved to practice.

Al was out on errands. "Hello, Fereshteh, *aziz*. Ali is out right now. How are you?" Homa's head was already hurting from Fereshteh's high-pitched voice, a familiar experience whenever Fereshteh called.

"Oh, no problem—you can just pass on congratulations! Everyone is so excited!"

Homa wondered who "everyone" was. Most of Al's side was like Homa's: very average, unflashy people, *comfortable* enough, but people who had not profited one bit from the family's—Al's—wealth in America. Maybe they hoped to, but Homa had little idea why they bothered to keep in touch. Al personally hated having any ties in Iran. Not only did he no longer feel connected to his homeland but he also worried it would look sketchy to authorities, all the calls and emails and letters.

"Everyone is gushing that now you have really made it—not that you didn't make it with the pizza thing, of course, that was what got you here, but this is such a big deal, to be television stars. Well, now you are Hollywood celebrities—all the sisters must be so excited! I'll bet you will all go to the Oscars!"

Homa groaned. "No, dear, there will be no Oscars. This is not the movies—this is barely TV. Reality TV is not the same thing—it's not such a big deal."

"You are too modest, Aunt Homa!" Fereshteh cried, in giggles again. "I wonder if you will meet Angelina Jolie soon! Maybe Madonna!"

Homa didn't know what to say. She was just so exhausted, and she swore to herself that she wouldn't take any more calls from Iran in the next few days. "It's being delayed anyway, because of the virus. Speaking of that, how are things in Tehran? We hear things are not so good; we are praying for you all."

"Oh, Aunt Homa, what can I say? It's not good but it could be worse. The Chinese, you know!"

Homa sighed with an extravagant audibility. In the past few weeks, there had been subtle waves of anti-Chinese sentiment on so many people's tongues, though few were coming right out and saying it. It stressed her out, as it reminded her of the hate that had been in the air for them in their early years in America.

"The lab in China," Fereshteh was saying. "They say it was from there. Don't believe the bats story! We are in Asia too and so we hear more directly. Just avoid Chinese people if you can!"

Homa tensed up, appalled. "What on earth do you mean? It's in Italy too. Shall I avoid Italians?"

"Oh, Aunt Homa, please do not take offense. And anyway, it did not come from Italy. Certainly it was Chinese people who traveled to Italy. They are so many and so rich. Did you know, in ten years, more than half the world population will be Chinese?"

"No, and I don't think that is correct." Homa turned her attention to the dusty gold of her usually pristine Cartier Panthère watch. Fereshteh was always doing her own research, reading into things, and it was always a mess. "Anyway, please stay safe—we are so worried for you all."

"My friend Ruhi makes a special balm that is antibacterial and kills everything. I apply it every day. With this I am sure I will be safe! But you are so lucky—you have your good president to protect you all! Long live the U.S. president!"

Homa tried her best to stifle a groan. "He's not gonna do a thing, Fereshteh," she said, holding back stronger words.

"Oh, he will! Look how good and kind he was not to start a war with us! Everyone loves him in Iran!"

Homa knew that was not true but she didn't think the point was worth arguing. "Okay, well, Fereshteh-*jaan,* it was so nice talking to you. I have to go . . . lie down now."

"Yes, please rest and take good care, I know the risks are worse for the elders!"

She always managed to say something like that. Fereshteh was not Homa's favorite.

"Anyway, we love you, and we are so excited for the show! Cannot wait till you are on all the talk shows, sitting next to Beyoncé!"

Homa mumbled a few half-hearted Persian blessings at her and hung up.

"God, does all of Iran know?" Mina asked later that day. She had apparently overheard her mother on the phone.

"It seems that way. Meanwhile, their numbers are horrifying. But they are more concerned with us. Imagine there being this new awful plague and them wanting to talk about reality TV with us!"

"Maybe it will entertain them," Mina said. "They'll download it illegally and I am sure it will be a nice distraction. Though, who knows, maybe it will only air after this whole thing is over."

"I think it will be sooner rather than later. This is America. It won't get too bad here," Homa said.

Mina nodded uncertainly. She had her doubts, but she hoped she was wrong. In any case, there were too many other things to worry about.

They were just barely in it. What was to come was so unimaginable, they would long remember those days when speculation had more weight than the reality of adversity, their imaginations filling the space the horrors were bound to take up.

The Milanis could never quite escape their fellow Persians/ Iranians. Luckily, they were largely out of touch with those distant relatives in L.A. who, once in a while, popped up for no apparent reason. But their so-called community they too often forgot—conveniently.

When Violet had been at St. Michael's Academy, there were a handful of Iranians in her year, but in Roxanna's senior class, there were only two. Or really only one. The other had taken some sort of leave—she went back and forth to Iran, and was a person no one really got to know. Most of the Iranians Roxanna was familiar with, whether from Instagram or because they were friends of friends, went to Beverly High. Even some of the other rich ones. Beverly High had clout for a public school, but everyone knew Southern California's real one percent went to St. Michael's.

The one other Iranian in Roxanna's grade was a girl named Ladan. She was still relatively new to America and lived with distant relatives, her family all still in Iran. She came from some sort of rug dynasty. Ladan was what they called "FOB." *"Fresh off the boat,"* a *slur,* Mina always reminded Roxanna, which was why Roxanna avoided it. But she also avoided Ladan: her thick accent, her terrible clothes, her strange clinginess, her nerdy obsession with academics, and her just overall "off" vibes made it so Roxanna preferred to pretend as if she did not exist. At first, when Ladan arrived at the school in tenth grade, she sought Roxanna out, but Roxanna was cold and made it very clear they were not going to be friends. Roxanna was always just doing the bare minimum to pass, whereas Ladan was a top student, so they never had class together and it was easy for Roxanna to ghost her completely.

Until now, when, out of nowhere, Roxanna got an Instagram message from a Ladaninlalaland. It took her a second to realize this was Ladan, although the photos were far less catfish-y than they ought to have been: lots of shots of Ladan as she was, little makeup and boring, conservative clothes, winning at state math tournaments and knowledge bowls and all that. She had 86 followers whereas Roxanna had 224,000.

Roxanna immediately had a bad feeling. Ladan had never sought her out before like this. But there it was:

Hello Roxanna-Vanna Milani,

I hope you are doing well in this crazy time! What a weird world we are in! I wanted to write to congratulate you on the show—my relatives in Iran had heard from some talk show. How exciting for you—and for all of us, as this is a big moment for our representation. This reminded me, though: I was just in a group project with Damon and he mentioned you were Italian. I told him I had thought you were Iranian like me and he said, no, you are Italian. I guess I am confused, especially with the show and all. No worries if you don't want to respond but just wanted to reach out and say cheers to you!

Ghorbanat (affectionate Persian sign-off),
Ladan Esfehani

Roxanna nearly choked. Where to begin? It was horrifying. First of all, few people in 2020 called her "Roxanna-Vanna" anymore—sure, it was her full name, but who even knew that? And "representation"?! Then to follow it with how Roxanna's on-again, off-again boyfriend since ninth grade, Damon, had denied she was Iranian. And then explaining "ghorbanat" to play along with her alleged non-Iranianness. Or maybe she assumed Roxanna knew even less Persian than she did? In any case, there was no message that could have messed up Roxanna more.

I don't get how you've managed to pull this off, Mina once said to her. *I don't get how the jig is never up. It's like a miracle no one is questioning you. Maybe no one can imagine someone being this crazy, except for, like, the transracial weirdos? It's just unreal, Roxi. I am almost impressed. I guess you're lucky you're in this family. The only person really as in-the-spotlight as you is Dad, and he would do anything to dodge being from Iran too. It's a mess, but just know one day . . .*

Roxanna was sweating. She quickly blocked Ladan. There was no way she was going to respond, and it was clear Ladan knew that. And luckily, now with the pandemic, she did not have to run into her, though she never had before, anyway. Their worlds did not overlap and it would definitely have to stay that way.

Her first thought was to call Damon, but they were in an off-period. Everyone knew them as an item, but they took long breaks, sometimes an entire month or the bulk of a summer. Roxanna had grown to appreciate the rhythm—Damon could be so exhausting, and there was a way in which the idea of a boyfriend was better than the reality. They were together for things that mattered, anyway: the winter formal, homecoming, their junior prom. Any day now, they'd be back together, she thought—she truly could not recall what had split them up the last time. They had so many fights. But she didn't need to get back in touch with him because of Ladan. It would open so many new conversations she could not risk. Damon would have to be one of the first to know, but she had to think it through. It didn't help that Damon was Italian American himself—Damon Damiano's grandparents were immigrants from the Venice not in California. Damon had never once doubted her, especially since he had never been to Italy himself and Roxanna had three times. But their background was just not something that came up, and so she really had to think carefully about how to break the news to Damon.

For a second, she thought about quitting Instagram. All those followers, though many bought bots—she couldn't risk it. But the idea that Ladan was thinking of her, that Ladan was watching her, that Ladan was waiting for a response—it all gave her chills.

How could she escape Iran when she was about to become the face of it? They were talking about it all the way in Iran proper. The clock was ticking, and all she had on her side was that the world was just maybe going to end.

Ever since the announcement of their show had hit the airwaves, Haylee had been glued to social media. She wanted to know what people were saying about her. *It's okay to be self-absorbed when you are young, because it builds confidence,* her most popular TikTok went, featuring her sweating and beaming as she rode the exercise bike in her gym. Beyoncé's "Halo" played in the background and she made a peace sign. The video had gotten her eight thousand likes, which was way more than usual for her. She had made the saying up on the spot, but she felt it represented her well. But with the announcement she felt sure there would be a lot of commentary on her: the world revolved around the youngest, didn't it?

They had all looked amazing in the video: Homa in a canary Chanel suit, Al in a vintage Bijan "Bijan yellow" suit, Roxanna in a gold-and-yellow strapless Versace minidress, Violet in a frothy buttercup Chloé peasant dress, Mina in a lemon Supreme tracksuit, and Haylee in her beloved amber leopard Dolce & Gabbana bustier dress that she'd had to beg Homa to sign off on, as she knew it was a bit much for her age. She knew she looked immaculate and she expected the reaction online to reflect that plus her favorite usual: the comparison to Hailey Bieber. It was more than the name. There was something about their face shape and their style and, well, their entire aura, she had decided, even though Hailey was way older. Of course Haylee had studied the model more carefully than any math homework for years. She liked it when people noticed the resemblance, and when someone would invariably ask if she was named after Hailey Bieber, she somehow felt seen.

But as Haylee searched her name on Twitter, she wasn't finding much. A couple mentions of her dress, one asking how old she was, another saying she looked like some Russian actress she had never heard of, one calling her Roxanna by mistake. Then she saw her name mentioned with Mina's—"the two youngest"—with a few wondering who was older and if they were twins (*ew*, Haylee thought—*even Mina knows I am the Pretty One. Are they blind?*), and then she saw there were not just dozens but it seemed hundreds of tweets about Mina.

The stylist who had worked with their yellow theme had been quite stuck on what to put Mina in—she was not quite a tomboy and she was not quite austere either. Her lack of style felt like a style in itself. It was hard to describe. She'd brought a few basic dresses to Mina but the only thing Mina really liked was this tracksuit that the stylist said was inspired by Sporty Spice, the Spice Girl. The stylist was surprised Mina knew who that was, but that seemed to seal it. Mina was pretty thin, with few curves, so she kept the top all the way zipped up, the way boys would fit into it, and she thought it was good enough. The rest of the crew offered plenty of pizzazz, so it would be fine for Mina to fade into the background a bit.

But the tweets not only fawned over Mina in her tracksuit, they fawned over Mina herself. One was using her commercial quip as a hashtag, even: #waitwasthataketchupcommercial; and there was a memed GIF of Mina smirking and saying, "Don't be too sure." Where was all this coming from? She searched her sisters' names, and while Roxanna was a close second—there seemed to be consensus she would be the lead of the show, and she had the most followers on social media, anyway—no one had as many mentions as Mina. Haylee was shocked, and she kept digging. When she figured it out, a tidal wave of emotions swept over her.

Oh god.

It was so obvious, but also how? They should have known. And it was 2020—it made so much sense. How could they not have seen this coming? Or maybe Mina had and never said anything—you never did know with Mina and what she knew and didn't. Mina kept a lot to herself and she was more online than any of them, so she had to know.

Haylee went down the hall and knocked on her sister's door, extra-loud so Mina would hear her even with her headphones on.

Mina flung open the door and went back to her chair at the computer, with a casual "What's up, Hayles?"

Haylee gulped, trying so hard to hide her anger—and her jealousy, although she was not at a point where she could really explore all that. She just thought this was so supremely unfair— the one person who cared the least was getting all of the attention, and for a reason like that. It was appalling, and of course it was bound to affect the whole family. It could even become a plotline.

"Mina, have you seen what they are saying on social media?" She had no time for small talk.

Mina took off her headphones slowly. Haylee looked seriously upset. "I mean, yes? No? I don't know. You mean from the special spot we did about the delay? I saw a few things the other day. What do you mean—what are you seeing?"

Haylee had her phone clutched tightly in her hands, screenshots ready. She had made a whole folder: MINA TWEETS. But she didn't even know where to begin. She was worried this would turn into a Conversation and she just didn't have it in her to have a heart-to-heart with Mina right now, when really what she was fixated on was the hideous injustice of there being barely any tweets about her.

For the first time in her life, Mina had completely overshadowed her. In a way that mattered, that is.

In school, of course Mina was better. Mina was neater, more responsible, all that. But this time Mina had beaten Haylee on her own turf. Mina was the talk of Twitter, and no one had seen it coming.

"Well, where to begin?" Haylee tried to sound calm. She glanced down at her phone. "There's a lot of tweets."

"Well, yeah, we knew that—Roxi has always been big on social media and with Violet doing these bigger modeling things and Dad being who he is . . . you know, it makes sense. Wait until it airs—there will be a ton then! Why would this bother you?"

Haylee felt sick imagining the tweets once the show was out. More tweets about Mina? Would she be getting less and less attention meantime, and would she eventually just become invisible? What was even the point? She realized Mina had no clue where she was going with this.

"Mina, have you searched your name?"

Mina shook her head. "I try not to do that anymore. I don't like what I see when I get mentioned—it's too weird. Someone compared me to an ostrich once in a photo with Roxi a few months ago. That was enough for me." She was sure this would make Haylee laugh, but no such luck. Her sister looked glum in an almost worrying way.

"Well, maybe you should look it up now," Haylee mumbled.

"There are a lot. About you. Much more about you than me, or really any of us."

Mina looked confused. "What? No. There's no way—you probably didn't search it all. No one cares about me."

Haylee rolled her eyes. "I know how to search on Twitter," she groaned. "Trust me. They are fixated. I took screenshots. Do you want to see?"

Their eyes locked and everything was suddenly very still. Neither sister moved a muscle. It was as if they knew that something was shifting between them. Haylee was ice, all tension, and Mina felt herself burn up. She wasn't sure she wanted to know. She wanted to rewind on this whole exchange. She wished she hadn't answered the door when Haylee knocked, but it was too late now.

Haylee unlocked her phone and flipped to the screenshots. She met her sister's eyes and passed it over.

Mina grabbed the phone and started zooming in, screenshot after screenshot. It took less than thirty seconds, and then, as if she could not fathom how they were real, she turned to her computer and began looking it all up there. There they were, all over Twitter.

Haylee did not see any change in her sister's face. A part of her wondered if Mina would cry—Haylee would have cried. Instead Mina seemed eerily calm as she scrolled. Eventually, she saw it all, everything Haylee had in her phone, and then she turned away from the computer and looked back at Haylee.

Haylee's eyes were pumped full of tears. She didn't want to get into why—that it was because she was disappointed no one was talking about her. It was such a frivolous concern compared to what was being said about her sister. But there she was—she was always herself with Mina.

Mina remained calm, her expression more surprised than anything. She seemed at a loss for words.

"I just never saw this coming," Haylee said softly, meaning the tweets being more about Mina than her, but it seemed possible to Mina that she could be referring to something else.

Mina nodded slowly. "It is kind of weird." She paused, turning to the computer. "Often it starts with one account and then it just spreads. I don't know—it just is weird. It's definitely a new thing . . . a new speculation. I used to be ignored. They were all into Roxi."

Haylee nodded. "I had barely anything about me. Like three tweets, maybe four. That was it. But you are everywhere. All over. A lot from Iran too. It's all about you and you know . . ."

Long pause.

"Well, we could just say it," Mina replied. "Me and me being queer." She paused and backtracked. "Speculated queer."

Haylee tried not to roll her eyes. It was of course, not the first time anyone had thought Mina was a lesbian. When the girls were very young, some people even thought Mina was a boy. Homa liked to treat Mina and Haylee like twins, dressing them up in coordinating sets. Haylee would get the very girly, frilly stuff and Mina would be in whatever looked most like boys' clothes. According to Homa, Mina had insisted on short hair when she could barely speak, while Haylee had asked for "Princess Pony hair." It was true that Mina was the blue to Haylee's pink, the Legos to her Barbies, the playing doctor to her playing house, and so on. That had always been her role, and so more than once it had come up, usually playfully but sometimes mockingly, that Mina could be a lesbian. Kids on the playground, a relative or two, a neighbor once. There was just something about Mina. *It's hard to say why, but she gives a young Persian Jodie Foster vibe,* a producer had even told Homa as they were going over plans for the season. Homa had asked why, but Mina had interjected, *Mom, she literally said it's hard to say why.* They had dropped it, but Mina, of course, knew why. And while Haylee had never heard of Jodie Foster, she had a feeling.

Was she gay? Haylee couldn't quite say. Neither of them had had *experiences*. No first kisses yet. Crushes, sure. Haylee liked to discuss hers, but Mina's were more abstract—someone on TV, a K-pop star, a dead poet. But of course Haylee thought it could be possible. It was just worrying, as she had read that gayness could run in the family. She hoped it was just Mina if it was true. She worried it might spread, like chicken pox. She hoped her own proximity to Mina did not make her more susceptible, even though Mina never said anything about it. As usual, her concerns spiraled right back to her. Haylee had very little to add to the speculation around Mina's sexuality.

Mina guessed this. She still felt too young to give the question of her sexuality much thought and it made her uncomfortable to discuss it. Also, she had never been close to a gay person in her life. She knew of the celebrities and public figures, mostly, but it was pretty much zero IRL. She thought that some of her teachers might be, and there was that one goth girl in her history class who people said was trans, and of course a bunch of possible bisexuals, but the *really* queer kids usually went to the art school nearby or the public school over the canyons, it was said. It all felt out of Mina's reach.

Maybe Mina kept it that way.

Haylee's eyes were on her lap. She was clearly uncomfortable.

Mina doubted that Haylee wanted to talk about it. She doubted she could handle the talk either.

"Hey, I know," Mina suddenly said. "Why don't you go tell Roxi to post a photo with you on IG? With both of you in your yellow outfits? Like it was an outtake. Then I'll bet you'll get more tweets on Twitter. I can even have one of my alts post about it."

The idea appealed to Haylee, of course. But it also seemed kind of pathetic. Why would it come to that?

It was almost like Mina could hear her thoughts. "Look,

Twitter loves drama," she said. "If there was something they could make all juicy about you, you'd be discussed too. That rumor about me got them going. Plus, Twitter is very, you know, queer."

Haylee nodded. She was much more of an Instagram girl. "Well, I just wanted to tell you," she said, getting up. "I don't need anyone's help with tweets and views. When the show gets rolling, I'll have my own fans. Maybe before. There's plenty about me that can be juicy."

Mina sighed, and she just nodded. Haylee had seemed so hurt, and it was not worth it to upset her even more. Plus, Mina considered that there might be more dimensions to her hurt than even she understood. It would be a lot for all of them when it was truly time.

"That's right, Hayles, you got this," Mina said, walking her to the door so that she could lock it behind her. "And when the time comes, we will all support you so much! It will be great. Trust me, I don't want this stuff on me one bit. I'd much rather all the attention be on all of you and how cool you are."

Haylee sniffled, nodding. "So many of the Twitter people— the Twitter girls—think you are cool."

Mina tried to hide a smile. It was hard to not be flattered. But who knew what to say to that? "Well, they may be very disappointed."

It's okay to be self-absorbed when you are young, because it builds confidence: the words ran through Haylee's brain like one of those paid banners airplanes drag across the sky. She thought about saying it to Mina, but what was the point? She could not relate to Mina's dilemma; she wasn't sure confidence was going to help her. But Haylee had other work to do. She had to make sure she wasn't going to be "Mina's sister." She had spent her whole life as "Roxanna's little sister" and sometimes "Violet's little sister" but she would never let herself just be Mina's little sister. The whole world would be watching. And Mina had a head start no one could have predicted.

As she walked away, she could not shake off the image of the smile she saw Mina try to hide.

Mina wasn't the only one people were talking about online. They talked about Roxanna too, but they always did—she was what they already called a "microcelebrity," show or not. Violet didn't have as many tweets about her, but there were a good number of fashion and beauty sites talking about her. Including ones in Iran.

Violet had been trying to improve her Persian but it was going worse than poorly. It was a nightmare. Al had already fired her Persian tutor, an older Iranian man named Farshad, who had been very flirtatious and was caught by Randy going through their cabinets. The online course Al had found instead ended up being far too advanced for her. So Violet took a slower approach. She was teaching herself. She spent hours in their library poring over the few books her parents had brought from Iran, dictionary at hand. Eventually nothing taught her better than the internet—she found YouTubers, Instagram accounts, even Persian TikTok.

She did not expect to run into herself there. But there she was, on this guy Maany's TikTok as "Iranian American of the Day." The algorithm had presented it to her without any prompting— she did not follow that guy—but as she scrolled, she saw herself in one of her old glamour shots: on a staircase, in a tight red Jessica Rabbit–looking dress and Louboutins. He spoke in a rapid-fire Farsi she had to play back a few times to fully understand: "This is Violet Milani of Los Angeles, a supermodel, and I want to guess that she might have a bit of Persian in her, no? We don't know too much about her except her sister is socialite influencer Roxanna-Vanna. She is signed with Tens Models and she seems to be about twenty. She is also going to be, along with her family, on the new reality television show *The Milanis.* Comment below what you want to know about Violet and I will see what I can dig up about this beauty!"

Violet winced. The guy seemed a decade older than her. He was overeager as he spoke, frantic, almost. Maybe it was excitement. Modeling images online were one thing—she was used to those—but people commenting on her as a celebrity? And "supermodel"? She was far from that.

She felt so embarrassed. She knew this would get worse and worse as the show hit the airwaves, and a part of her just hoped it would never happen. Who wanted this? Roxanna and her father. Well, maybe Haylee too.

Did you see what the comments were like on Twitter? Haylee wrote to the group chat, with Mina blocked.

Um no we have lives, Roxanna retorted.

I can't say I have looked, Violet responded.

Well, you should because it's bad and not what you think!

This had made Violet curious but not curious enough that she bothered to search. She had deleted her Twitter account a while ago—it was way too volatile for her there.

Oh god, please just tell us, Hayles.

Haylee let the screenshots go.

There was a pause. As she expected.

WHAT, Violet wrote.

Hahha this is something! Roxanna wrote. *I mean, we all thought it. I wonder what started it online.*

She was wearing a sports suit while we were all wearing dresses, Violet pointed out. *That's probably all it took.*

Roxanna had more to say on this. *I mean, she's very active on Twitter! You two aren't but she is. And what does she tweet about? Like social justice and kpop right?*

Pretty much, Haylee wrote back. *I don't know it's so weird. There was barely anything about me* ☹

Violet was quick to be reassuring. *Oh, Haylee, just wait til the show, I am sure they will say more. Plus, you're so young, people probably don't want to be creepy. (Is she blocked on this?)*

Yes, ofc. Anyway I am just barely younger than Mina, and they are out here speculating on her sexuality! As if she's having sex! Mina's like a nun. She has the most virgin-vibes of all of us.

Well, that's probably part of it. I wouldn't give it too much thought, Hayles. And then, of course, Roxanna pivoted to her favorite subject. *Wow, look at all the cute things they are saying about me—"step on me, Versace queen" lol we love to see it . . .*

And that was that.

Violet started looking at social media more closely, examining the comments more than she used to. Usually people said very nice things about her—complimented her looks, said hyperbolic things about her face and body, the usual internet worship stuff. It was flattering but Violet worked hard not to internalize it. She imagined that things would not end well for her if she took it in as much as Roxanna did. Roxanna was built for this stuff—she was definitely not.

But on this one man Maany's post there were hundreds of comments. Apparently he was popular. Almost all the comments were in Persian, with a few in English. Violet could barely read in Persian—she was working on it—so she cut and pasted the comments into her translation app. After seeing the tweets about Mina, she was curious.

There were, as expected, lots of comments about her appearance. The usual, though in Persian they sounded more seductive and syrupy. She skimmed those. Then she saw other comments, ones that would piggyback over one another, ones that were not so nice.

For all that plastic surgery, you'd think she could have sucked in her body too.

Hopefully she will get a trainer and a weight-loss plan before the show!

Tell sis to cut down on the kabob and polo!
Model? Is this for a plus-size catalog?

It went on and on. Violet sighed hard. It was not the first time she had heard such things. She was by no means large—but perhaps relative to other models, she was on the thicker side of the thin spectrum. Compared to her sisters too, she was curvy—Roxanna and Mina were sticks, and Haylee was still too young to grow into her curves and she was also too athletic to let them properly develop. Violet definitely had a *shape*. She was mostly happy with how she looked but once in a while, *this* would happen.

Every model she'd ever met seemed to have a version of this story. She remembered an agent once telling her she needed to lose fifteen pounds, at least, to get real work. That was back when she was thinner too. The agent, a tiny man in a plaid suit with a bow tie, had looked her up and down, and shaken his head. "Well, there is always plus-size modeling. That industry is booming! We are in the dawn of body positivity."

She knew that at times she was on the edge of the plus-size-modeling category. One of her dear friends, Calista, was a plus-size model, and she weighed just ten pounds more than Violet—she also made a lot more money. Violet, meanwhile, even with the sweets, had to watch her weight. If there were cookies or cake, that would be a meal; a box of candy was the only snack she might get in a day; a milkshake was something she'd have to remember to work off. She had the Lose It! app on her phone, and it always astounded her how easy it was to get to her allotted 1,376 calories. Plus, she hated exercise—and she had a tendency to tune out Haylee's many offers to design some basic regimens for her. In many ways, she did not think modeling life suited her, but as Al often put it, *You do this for a few years, make some money, and you never have to work again.* That seemed to be his answer for everything he thought his daughters should do—it was certainly his perspective on reality TV—but it became painful for Violet to consider doing modeling work for much longer. She looked forward to aging out.

Moreover, sweets were emotional for Violet. She couldn't imagine what she would eat if that were taken away, thinking with horror at Roxanna's lifeless, dressing-less salads and Haylee's Blue Majik superfood smoothies. She truly had no idea what Mina ate, though her doctors occasionally put her on special diets to combat allergies and other issues. Still, she was the only one of her sisters who partook in desserts too, with the exception of her parents, who seemed to mainly show interest in desserts ordered directly from the best Persian bakeries in Westwood.

Then there was one week during the pandemic when questions about her weight really hit her hard. Her agency required that the models update their profiles monthly, and that also meant updating their stats. It was the only time Violet would get on the scale, which always felt like bad news was just looming. Not by much, but the numbers did go up every month. Now, at twenty-one, she could no longer claim she was a growing girl. This time her weight had spiked more dramatically—she wanted to blame "pandemic pounds," something she had begun hearing online, though she didn't think she was eating differently— and it hit her that she had to do something. She went over to the gym, only to spy Haylee stomping away on the treadmill as if she were being chased by a monster, sweat raining down her body, her tiny frame, in a hot-pink bra and shorts, shaking to some motivating soundtrack. She must have been in there for hours. Haylee could easily model, she thought, though she was too short, and, like Roxanna, she preferred the life of the influencer—those two didn't like answering to anyone. And, to them, there was something old-fashioned about being a professional model. Violet stood there for a few more minutes, trying to gather any motivation, but it was hopeless.

She went back to her bedroom, where an open box of doughnut holes sat. There were cupcake tins and empty candy wrappers and rainbow sprinkles strewn across her desk. Where there
used to at least be some pens and paper for homework there
was now Colombia-imported candy cigarettes and Tootsie Pops
and licorice sticks. She could imagine how repulsive this would
be to some people. This was probably what the people who
commented on Maany's video thought she was like: a sugar-
obsessed, trashy American model who could not be helped. She
wished she could bully herself out of it, but instead she reached
for a glazed doughnut hole at the bottom of the box and ate it
glumly. What could she do?

Her reflection gazed back at her from the giant floor-length
mirror, a special edition from Tiffany's her mother had bought
her for her birthday. There she was, in her frilly, strawberry-
patterned vintage Stella McCartney baby-doll dress and lace
tights, her hair in a French braid, wearing little makeup, chewing
away at sugary dough like it was nothing. Roxanna and Haylee
wouldn't eat in a year or two or three what she had mindlessly
just thrown back. For her it was no big deal.

Maybe it was time it was.

She eyed herself guiltily and thought about trashing all the
treats in her room, but that wasn't a proper fix. She needed a
strategy. Her little attempt at the gym that day had been a failure,
though she knew she would have to go back. Still, she recalled
reading a study that said exercise didn't really help with weight
loss, anyway; nothing was more effective than just eating less. It
was hard for Violet to imagine cutting down—besides, it was
less how much she ate and more *what* she ate. There had to be
another way.

She remembered what another model taught her at a lake-
front shoot in Northern California. She was a very skinny and
somewhat older Eastern European girl who gawked at all the

other models picking at their plates during their lunch break and offered her two cents about sustenance:

Stupid girls, there is only two choice. You choose. The first there is one way, the second you have two choice. Out of theses—she pointed to her filler-puff-lipped mouth—*or out of thats*—she pointed to her flat ass. She had burst into laughter as if it were all a big joke, though none of the other girls joined in. They knew what she meant and they must have resented the reminder.

Back then, Violet believed that some women were just built for this, that some girls just never gained weight. Until the past year or two, that was mainly true for her. Sure, the scale inched up, but she was suited for this, and certainly so were the rest of the girls. She remembered how they all pretended not to hear the Eastern European model girl as she laughed and laughed.

But what she said had stayed with Violet. The options were there, elephants in the room in every shoot. Was a model anorexic or bulimic or the rare unicorn with a miraculous metabolism they all wanted so badly to believe existed?

Not eating seemed impossible to Violet; anorexia just seemed to take a willpower she could never muster. *But bulimia?* she wondered. She had rarely thrown up in her life—unlike poor, sickly Mina, she, like most of the family, had a stomach of steel. It seemed gross to her to go there, but it also seemed more doable than depriving herself of food altogether. And maybe it was safer? Obviously, forcing food up and out like that couldn't be good for you, but it had to be a bit better than starving yourself.

Violet popped another doughnut hole as she gathered herself. She Googled it first: "How to make yourself throw up." She was amazed by how much she found: *How to Make Yourself Throw Up with a Finger, How to Induce Vomiting with Salt Water, How to Make Yourself Throw Up Without a Finger, How to Vomit with a Toothbrush, Gargling with Egg Whites, How to Use Baking Soda to*

Induce Throwing Up, How to Make a Mustard Solution That Will Make You Gag, How to Ingest Bloodroot Herb to Vomit, Things to Imagine to Make Yourself Sick to Your Stomach. There was so much there. For a second she considered that laxatives might be a less challenging approach, but then she thought that somehow this seemed quicker, easier to control, something that could be done as an occasional thing and perhaps easily forgotten. In any case, she could do a trial run. Why not?

She wondered which approach could work best, and her eye landed on her toothbrush. It seemed the quickest way. She couldn't imagine eating something disgusting like mustard or egg whites.

> *The toothbrush technique follows a similar approach to using your fingers, but certain individuals might prefer not to employ their fingers for this task. Here are the steps for using a toothbrush:*
> * *Dampen the toothbrush.*
> * *Insert it into your mouth and begin gently brushing the rear part of your tongue.*
> * *If you experience a gag reflex, withdraw the toothbrush.*
> * *If there's no progress, you might need to perform the process again.*

It seemed easy enough. She grabbed her toothbrush and, without overthinking it, she wet it and started brushing, as instructed. She went to the back of her tongue and tried to trigger gagging. When nothing happened, she did it even more aggressively. Still, it didn't work. She had tears in her eyes from the gagging, or so she told herself.

She looked up another site.

If inducing a nauseating sensation using your toothbrush's bristles is your aim, the procedure involves first moistening the toothbrush with water. Subsequently, guide the toothbrush to the back of your tongue, ensuring it remains oriented toward the throat. Employ a back-and-forth motion with the bristles as you wait for the activation of your gag reflex. Once triggered, sustain the action until you experience vomiting. Throughout this process, maintain the toothbrush within your mouth. Upon completion of the vomit, proceed to cleanse both your mouth and the toothbrush meticulously.

An alternative approach involves provoking vomiting through the use of the toothbrush's handle. Dampen the end of the toothbrush handle and guide it down your throat. Initiating a reflexive gagging response is anticipated. Persistently engage in a reciprocating motion with the toothbrush's handle, ensuring a continuous motion. This process is designed to culminate in vomiting. It's important to retain the toothbrush within your mouth during the vomiting phase. Following the expulsion, carry out thorough oral hygiene and be certain to thoroughly clean the toothbrush as well.

She decided to try this—it seemed more direct and more violent. She pushed it down and tried and tried.

It was so hard. She kept reading:

Regardless of which technique you choose, once the vomiting is completed, rinse your mouth with a warm-water solution containing a tablespoon of baking soda. This step is crucial in neutralizing the gastric acids present in your mouth before proceeding to brush your teeth, floss, or use antiseptic mouthwash.

The more she read about it, the more she wanted to throw up. It was as if reading through all these websites, one after another, were giving her body courage. She felt her stomach gurgle in anticipation. *You can do this, Violet,* she whispered to her heart, to her uvula, to her guts, to her cellulite.

This time she jammed in the end of her brush so aggressively she thought she had bruised the roof of her mouth. She felt herself cough at first and then the heaving began, and it was unstoppable. There it came, like cement, the creamy and yet crumby gray-brown mounds of doughnut and candy mixed with her bile, so horribly sour and metallic. Her stomach couldn't seem to stop—once the first push came, others followed, and she imagined just riding each wave with grace, as she gripped the counter and the toilet paper dispenser, praying she was not causing a mess on the floor or on her dress. She tried to soothe her mind, frantic at the novelty of this violence, by telling herself that generations of women—millions, if not billions—had been here before.

When she finished, it felt like years had gone by, and as she wiped her mouth and began to rinse, she realized the sound of heaving had been replaced by the sound of her sobbing. Her face was so red, blotchy, tear-streaked. She had forgotten to wipe off the red lip gloss, which now looked like a terrible syrup drizzled across her face, with saliva and the cakey residue of food and bile on her cheeks and chin. She had never looked worse.

It was easy. And it was less awful than she had thought it would be. She was surprised by her tears—she had no idea why she had been triggered in this way, but she could not stop. She left the bathroom and rolled up in a ball on her bed and continued to cry softly into her pillow.

Suddenly there was a knock on the door. She darted up. What if her parents had heard? How could she explain this? But the repeated knocks started to sound like Roxanna's.

"It's me, bitch!" Roxanna yelled. "Let me in."

Violet groaned, partially in relief, and used her cell phone to undo the lock. In came Roxanna, with the biggest smile. A smile that Violet knew well—it was Roxanna's knowing smile, a bit mischievous and a tad wise but a smile that definitely said, *I know what you were doing.*

Like clockwork: "I know what you were doing, Vivi."

Violet resumed her fetal position in bed while trying to wipe away her tears. "Yeah, I'm crying—leave me alone. Did you just come here to torture me?"

"No, silly, I came to, like, comfort my big sis after a barf sesh." She laughed, moving her gaze from her sister to her own reflection in Violet's mirror. "I mean, you're like a model, duh. This can't be the first time, right?"

"It actually was," Violet said, sniffling, shoving her phone with all the websites and instructions at Roxanna, as if to prove it.

Roxanne looked at the sites and began cackling. "What amateurs! Personally I do the salt water, but I guess you are too sweet-toothed—what got you in this mess in the first place!" She eyed the wrappers on Violet's desk judgmentally. "I mean, I don't really do any of this. The Limia Life is not for me. I'm more of an Ana girl."

Violet was astounded by how cheerfully her sister could just announce that. Of course it was no secret to anyone that she was eating-disordered, but how liberating it must be to just accept it, she suddenly thought.

"Yeah, well, it's not for me either. I don't think I can do this. It made me cry so hard."

"It's just, like, a beginner thing!" Roxanna shrugged. "You could get used to it. Or you could, you know, just diet properly. All models but you diet."

"Or I could go plus-size," Violet said softly.

Roxanna looked horrified. "Oh god, not that. I know everyone's into body positive, but I don't think I can handle you eating more. You'd have to, like, gain weight, you know? What could you do next, eat entire cakes for every meal? It would be too gross. You'd have to have, like, your own fatty fridge." She paused, shuddering. "Honestly, it wouldn't be healthy. You don't want to die of, like, a heart attack, do you? Like that one plus-size model? You know the one?"

Violet shook her head. Roxanna must be lying.

"She was, like, twenty-two and all her arteries were clogged to the max," Roxanna claimed. Violet was sure she had made this up. She got up and headed to the door. "Anyway, I don't want to welcome you to this club, and frankly, model or not, you'll never be as skinny as this bitch, but I think a part of me is proud of you."

Violet's eyes were still full of tears. She looked at her sister, still in her fetal ball. "What on earth do you mean?"

"Making changes! Thinking bigger! Self-improvement! Pandemic projects!" She gestured into the air like a magician blessing his magician's girl. "We're all gonna have to get to our best selves, especially when we begin taping. The world will be watching, and the Milanis cannot, like, let them down, babe!"

Violet went to the door and waited for her sister to walk away. There was no out anymore. She knew what she was going to do. That was the worst part of it all.

8

Pandemic Projects

Mina's fixations kept her occupied—sudoku, chess, martial arts, video games, anime, crocheting, calligraphy, learning foreign languages like Japanese and Portuguese—but K-pop had started moving up in her priorities. Her family ignored this interest of hers, but she had become enchanted at a young age, around the third-generation wave, and now it was well into the heyday of the fourth generation. She was obsessed with BLACKPINK, BTS, NCT, EXO, TXT, Stray Kids, Aespa, LOONA, TWICE, Red Velvet, GOT7, SHINee, THE BOYZ—you name it. K-pop was the reason she was on Twitter so often. Her family assumed it was because of how closely she followed the news and her social justice activism, but they didn't know any better. In a lot of ways she felt she was addicted.

It was hard to say what it was that had sparked her interest in that way. It was maybe the visuals: the over-the-top fashion, the neon, candy-colored, pastel dreamscapes, the Technicolor imagery, the out-of-this-world magic these groups projected. It was maybe the fact that even though these groups were from so far away, there was no real language barrier—it felt like a miracle to be able to bond with something so foreign, when there was such a cultural chasm. There was the way in which the fan groups would go about their fan service—the video calls, the signing events, the Instagram Lives, the constant updates on Twitter and Instagram and TikTok, all the many comebacks. She felt so involved. She even began making her own fancams, which got several of her online alts very large followings. She grasped the aesthetic and she was good at it. And there was something so safe about it. It was all very cool and exciting, but in a way that did not make her feel anxious or left out or alienated. She had crushes on every single one of these stars but none of them felt gross to her. Her crushes were cool and composed and casual and fun. It was all part of the game, fan worship as a form of therapy.

And so Mina had gone along with it. She had kept her notifications and updates on, bought all the hoodies and caps and lightsticks and photocards she could and went to as many concerts as she could, often alone. Last fall, she had convinced Haylee to go with her to a SuperM show—Haylee had agreed one of the rappers was kind of cute—but ultimately Haylee had hated the music and stayed glued to her phone the whole time. Her sisters found the whole thing perplexing—Violet maybe took the most interest. *What's their budget that they can afford only designer clothes? And the plastic surgery is so good, how do they make it so subtle? And those K-pop diets, how do they keep up with them— they are so brutal?* Mina loved that this was something that was only hers in the end. In a household where so much was so shared, it was nice to have something that no one else could touch. She cherished her obsession in solitude.

There was also the queer-coding. At first, she worried she was imposing this on the fandom and these groups and that maybe it was inappropriate. But then she discovered that so many others had written about this online. Mina was still not sure how she fit into all of it. *Was she queer? A lesbian? Bi? Nonbinary?* She had begun toying with making several of her alts reflect her "they/ them" inclinations. She didn't fully grasp what that meant, but it felt like a gateway. K-pop was helping her, she realized. It wasn't that she bought into rumors of the K-pop stars' queerness, just that the very atmosphere of it all somehow felt "queer."

Gay vibes was the first thing Roxanna had said when Mina had shown her a classic K-pop hit video, and actually she was right. It was in everything. She didn't want to effeminize the boys but she related so deeply to their gender-nonconforming aesthetic. The confection-colored mullets and shags, the glittery eye shadow and flower-colored lips and rainbow clothes— they weren't queer uniforms, exactly, but they just somehow screamed non-hetero. Mina didn't buy the aggressive male-female love anthems; they seemed almost too campy in their convictions. And she, like so many fans, latched on to the many "ships," the sexual tensions between same-sex stars, the innuendos and allusions in the choreography and the lyrics and even in their somewhat-scripted interviews. It was as if they were winking, and those who knew, *knew.*

Mina knew.

She had thought about going to therapy to think through the questions she was mulling about her sexuality, now that she was well into her teens and without any real romantic prospects, but maybe K-pop offered all the help she needed. She spent hours and hours a day with her obsession, to the point that she started learning some Korean without even trying—*yeorcobun, saranghae, hajima, jeoneun, annyeonghaseyo.* She dreamed of visiting Seoul, and was so touched to stumble on the fact that there was a Tehran Road on the most elite street in the Gangnam district, and there was a Seoul Road in Tehran—they were sister cities. She made do with ordering Korean food as often as she could and she ordered beginner language books in Korean that she could study. She had even made some K-pop friends in Korea, and she kept in touch with them regularly.

It was important to her now that the world felt small. The pandemic was making it feel small in the wrong ways, so Mina held on all the more tightly to the ways its smallness felt right. Or less wrong, at least.

No one at home understood her, and that was fine. Mina

had learned long ago she was going to be the black sheep in this family. The joke was that every one of her sisters claimed that role, something they all unwillingly shared.

Haylee realized early in the pandemic that she was well equipped to survive it. *This is one hell I was born to handle,* she had heard Homa say at dinner one day, and she understood. For Haylee it was a perfect opportunity to hone her fitness regimen. She was already fit, but she imagined toning up to her ideal, getting her body fat down to a minimum, finally being marathon-ready, as bendy and flexible and strong as her favorite fitness gurus. And there were so many to follow: Tracy Anderson, Taryn Toomey, Kayla Itsines, Gunnar Peterson, Jen Selter, Jeanette Jenkins, Natalie Uhling, Kaisa Keranen, Anna Victoria, Massy Arias, Amanda Bisk, Jen Sinkler, Tanya Poppett, Cassey Ho, Ricky Warren, Nude Yoga Girl, and more. She even loved watching the old Jane Fonda workouts—as hokey as the women in the videos were in their metallic leotards and fluffy leg warmers and kitschy old soundtracks, their power were no joke. She took this all in like she was studying it. This was an investment in her future. She imagined one day she might be Haylee Milani: Fitness Guru to the Stars, or something like that.

A text along these lines had come in the other day: *Hayles, you might want to take on your first client soon? For real?* She was confused. Who was Roxanna talking about? *Violet. I know I know but seriously. Don't tell anyone, but I caught her throwing up. I think finally all the eating-like-a-fatty shit has caught up with her and so I saw her making herself upchuck—she's getting desperate. Anyway, I think I convinced her not to take a turn on Limia Way. Bitch really eats all the bullshit she wants all day and never breaks a sweat. Maybe design a beginner's workout for her? Offer to take her to our gym and like sit with her? Idk if anyone can help with this one, it's you!* Haylee nodded

absently at the phone, never wrote back, and never followed up.
A model throwing up? Please.

Before the pandemic Haylee had worked with three different
fitness instructors. One was Kym, the family personal trainer.
Another was Allic, her own personal trainer, who she sort of
shadowed and interned for. The other was Iona, a yoga and
Pilates and barre instructor Roxanna had befriended at some
benefit. She gave the two of them weekly sessions. Now that she
couldn't use the lessons, Haylee tried to spend anywhere from
two to four hours a day in their gym, doing interval training,
cardio, yoga, Pilates, dance, or a combination.

"And I really think everyone should start spending more
time there, as it's very good for immunity," Haylee said to the
others at dinner one night. That had been her new thing. She
was determined not to get the virus and she was sure that she was
the least likely to get it because of her physical strength. It was
proven, in some study somewhere, she added, that staying fit
staved off illness.

"A very good point, darling," Al said. He too spent a great
deal of time in the gym.

"Oh, I never get sick—this virus is not getting me," Roxanna
declared. "Plus, I work out always too. And I barely eat! I think
Violet is most at risk. Mom doesn't eat much, so that's great too."

Violet and Homa exchanged helpless glances.

"Well, I'm obviously immunocompromised, so yeah, I'd
appreciate everyone taking care not just for themselves but for
me," Mina said. "I am sure there will be a vaccine soon and
that will be a big help to getting numbers down. I am already
astounded the U.S. is doing so bad. I assume you all saw the
headlines today?"

There were some mutters and head nods, but it was clear to
Mina that no one else was following this as closely as she was.

The word *vaccine* triggered Haylee to no end, and she was
not sure why. First of all, she did not love shots. Secondly, a lot

of the fitness gurus she followed were warning people about vaccines—there was apparently one being developed and it was important that people knew the truth. Haylee didn't fully understand it, but her body was her everything. She would do everything it took to stay well and in good shape.

"Luckily, we live in the age of fitness and organic foods and wellness culture, so we have so many natural options," Haylee said loudly. "Luckily we don't live in Iran or whatever."

"We ate much better in Iran than we do here," Homa said, her usual sentiment whenever anyone slandered Iran.

"Okay, Bride of Pizzabomme!" Roxanna shrieked. "Anyway! I support you getting us all on the fitness track! More gym time for everyone! Maybe we should make a schedule! Don't you think you'd like some special sessions with your lil sis the fitness guru, Violet?"

The oldest eyed the youngest warily. "I think I'm fine."

"I think you are *not*—you know what I, like, mean," Roxanna said emphatically. "You want to make sure your eating doesn't cost you your job, Violet. Haylee has offered before!"

Violet sighed and turned to Haylee, whose eyes were right on her. "I'll consider it some more. I probably should do something, maybe some light barre?"

"Not a problem!" Haylee smiled. "I'll make you a list of Instagram accounts to follow and then we can talk about some seshes."

"Look at us all, living our best lives!" Roxanna was delighted. "It's like *so us* to survive the apocalypse!"

That night, as Haylee went through Instagram to make Violet her workout routine, she stumbled on an account called Fit-Faxxx2020. She thought it would be more of the same, but on it she saw a whole slew of posts dedicated to the virus. "If you try to connect the dots from the virus (a made-up illness to explain the side effects of the 5G rollout) to 5G, the media will tell you it is a conspiracy theory." Haylee eyed her cell phone nervously.

She had heard some things about 5G on some other wellness site, but she didn't know very much. She scrolled down farther and found herself on a blog that told her more about the virus and vaccines and all sort of terrifying stuff:

Unraveling the Enigma of Vaccine Dilemmas

Within the depths of a veiled narrative, an intricate story unfurls, entwining itself with the enigmatic Y____ scheme. By the year 2019, a mysterious depopulation strategy appears to have peaked, leading to an unprecedented plummet in birth rates. The traditional nuclear family teeters on the verge of fading into obscurity. Startling statistics from the CDC expose a remarkable shift, where nearly 40% of American infants entered the world under the care of single mothers in 2018—a stark contrast to the mere 12% recorded in 1980. Similarly, within the same timeframe, a disconcerting 70% of black infants and 30% of white infants shared similar beginnings, marking a disquieting transformation from the meager 3% in 1960 and 12% in 1980. Amidst this era of transformation, societal norms find themselves reshaped into an eerie lexicon. Even masculinity and femininity take on new dimensions, with individuals redefining themselves as "trans," while dissenters risk the label of "bigot" for not embracing these linguistic shifts.

As the curtains rise on the tumultuous events of 2020, a chilling climax emerges in the overarching narrative that engulfs not only the United States but the world at large. The enigmatic Y____ scheme, previously suggestive of voluntary sterilization, finds its foreboding echoes in the aftermath of the tragic events of 9/11, which seem to have paved the way for a grander design. The concept appears simple—instill fear in the hearts of the populace, and obedience shall follow. Back in 2001, "terrorists" and "Muslims" played the roles of bogeymen. In 2020, an unseen and ostensibly lethal adversary—a capricious virus—took on this mantle. The United States underwent an unprecedented shift, halting its activities in March 2020. Iconic events like the NCAA basketball tournament and the NBA season ground to a halt, with citizens urged to stay within the confines of their homes for their own safety. This abrupt transformation reverberated as an electrifying shock, leaving the population bewildered and unnerved.

In the domain of manipulated perceptions, a stark narrative takes root—the notion that succumbing to the Virus equates to swift demise. Despite the ready availability of CDC data indicating a survival rate well above 99% for individuals under 70, the masses embrace this narrative fervently. A curious choreography unfolds, where masks become emblematic of the times, worn without question, even as an expanding body of evidence suggests an intriguing connection between mask mandates and the rise of virus cases.

We will soon be plunged into the "vaccine" chapter, strategically positioned to capitalize on the groundwork laid in the preceding era. Projected statistics indicate that the majority of Americans will embrace full vaccination status. Amidst this backdrop, a maze of uncertainties emerges, hinting that these inoculations might yield unforeseen consequences. A shadowy specter lurks—whispers suggest that these injections might prompt spontaneous abortions and stillbirths, their influence potentially extending even through breastfeeding, from mother to child. An elusive layer of evidence surfaces, hinting at the capacity of these vaccines to interfere with placenta development, casting shadows on women's fertility. But here's the twist—all these somber predictions materialize only for those who navigate through the ordeal unscathed. . . .

Haylee gulped. She knew what her parents would say, what her friends and sisters would say—that this was nonsense and that the internet was full of all sorts of crazy things. But she couldn't stop reading. Somewhere deep in her heart she felt it was true.

Depopulation. What a concept. She wondered who she could talk to about this. Not Roxanna, because most of the links on the page took her to MAGA sites, and possibly no one in their home hated conservatives more than Roxanna. Violet was a possibility just because she was looking at a lot of influencers who had fashion overlaps—Violet tended to be impressionable but Haylee wasn't sure she could handle this much darkness. Al seemed to love the right wing, though he always said, *Listen, it's a rich person thing—all us riches go that way in the end.* Homa: no way. And definitely not Mina.

She thought about whether she had any friends who she could talk to, but she had just barely begun high school. And now they were all separated and left to only Zoom classes. All of her friend dynamics had shifted. Haylee could understand this because she understood that to achieve a peak form in your body meant you also had to reach enlightenment in your mind. Most people just weren't cut out for that.

She remembered when she first became vegan a few years ago and began introducing raw and paleo diets to the family. It was actually Roxanna who accused her of being "culty," which had made her cry. But these days she didn't care what anyone called her. What did it matter, compared to being a survivor when there were so many victims.

It was the first night of many that Haylee stayed up all night. She started to fall asleep an hour into dawn, mentally rehearsing the suggested line for nonbelievers that she had heard on an influencer's vlog: *Sorry, if you don't mind, I'm gonna be doing my own research, thanks; sorry, if you don't mind, I'm gonna be doing my own research, thanks; sorry, if you don't mind, I'm gonna be doing my own research, thanks . . .*

If I'm gonna help any of you do bodily self-improvement stuff then I also have to talk to you about your minds. I have a lot of new info. We could all do it together. Before the gym. It's like meditation stuff but with really important info about what's really going on. It's not just Violet who needs it—we all do! But we have to be open, k?

Roxanna couldn't make much sense of Haylee's text. *Sure whatever, Hayles?*

The truth was this pandemic period was changing all of them and not in ways they could have foreseen. They had been worried about war, and in a sense what they'd gotten was the opposite. Not quite peace but a real absence of everything: a vacuum. They were living with a very quiet, tense fear in the air, a sense that they had no idea what was going on or what was going to happen, an endless waiting. Sure, there was death but the death felt so remote, so abstract. The Milanis didn't know a single person who had gotten sick. It was a theoretical danger.

Well, we'll look back on this as a time we really made history! Al kept saying, ever the optimist, trying to put a spin on things. He had been hassling his marketing team to put out special ads for the Pizzabomme, Pandemic Edition—special pandemic Pizzabommes of some kind. He had a vision of an endless slumber party with a big family, the microwave going off and off and off, and more and more plates of steaming Pizzabommes coming out, to the delight of the kids. *You needed to bring some fun into this. Maybe Pizzabomme is sort of a food for—what is that American saying—tent flu?* It took the director a second, but she finally got it: *Cabin fever?* That was it.

At home no one ate Pizzabomme at all. None of them had had one in years. Randy and Rose occasionally had made some on their breaks—they had a free lifetime supply—but even the thought of it made them sick now. That was a secret, of course.

Still, the prospect of an endless party, an endless night where people were making the most of the pandemic, went from Al's cackles to Roxanna's ears. That was what was missing. A party. Plus, when the show aired, she had to be on everyone's good side if she was going to make it through the Secret. She needed to round up her allies, really know who her friends were, to survive the world after all this.

And if she threw a party, she thought, maybe the producers would want to film it? A sort of exception to the usual lockdown? A way to make the best of things? A tribute to Al and Homa's pearl anniversary, after all?

"Are you out of your mind, my dear?" Homa snapped, when Roxanna announced the idea to the family at dinner one night. "The world is locked down, everyone is killing germs all day and hiding, and you want to have a huge party. Who does that?"

Roxanna was prepared for this. She handed over her phone. "Just scroll through my pics. You'll see. Those are just, like, from this week. All the influencers, not just in our city but in New York and I think one in, like, Chicago and maybe, like, one in Atlanta? There's a Paris one too! People *are* having parties! They're just, like, doing it differently. Like you can only post about it *after.*"

"Yeah, so it doesn't get shut down because people know it's nuts," Mina said. "This is honestly the worst idea you have ever had, Roxanna. Honestly."

Roxanna rolled her eyes. "Ugh, live a little! With the show on pause too, it's just been, like, such a downer. You know mental health is really important too? It can mess with your immune system!"

"Actually," Haylee immediately spoke up, this being her new area, "Roxi is totally right. I was just reading today that more people are dying of the virus's mental health effects than the virus itself."

"What? How?" Al asked.

"That's bullshit, Haylee," Mina instantly interjected.

"No, and you don't know what I was reading," Haylee said with a forced strength that made up for her fourteen-year-old lilt. "A scientist in Canada wrote about it. It's killing people, just not in the ways we think. You hear the numbers on the news but those people's bodies were fine. Their minds, though? Another story. There is a mind-body connection. Plus . . . *suicide*."

Everyone went quiet. This was different. Haylee didn't seem to go for weird theories like this.

"In any case, I am all for Roxanna's plan," Haylee said. "I think a party would make us feel so good, boost immunity, and help create nice bonds. Also, we can share info with our community, which is so important. I really wouldn't worry about the virus—it's barely real."

Homa looked disgusted. "Haleh, now what is wrong with your brain these days?" She shook her head.

"I don't know about this," Violet spoke up. "My agency has been real strict about social distancing. If they saw me at a party or, even worse, if they knew that I threw a party, they would not like it. They need us back to work, not engaging in high-risk behaviors."

"Okay, wait, what if that was, like, part of the theme? No cell phones? Like, people còuld attend but they could not record it? Honestly, that's low-key revolutionary. Like a party you have to really live, not one you just post. No one does that!" Roxanna was so proud of herself.

"That doesn't take away the risk!" Mina was so frustrated. "I can't believe we are even debating this. It's beyond unsafe. And I don't care what influencers are doing it. Plenty are getting canceled for it too. America is having worse and worse numbers because of all this. China's cases are almost under control."

"Don't even get me started on China," Haylee mumbled. She had learned a lot about the Wuhan lab, the possibility of the leak, and what they had been researching there. "Or WHO and Bill Gates."

"What the hell, Haylee—this is insanity!" Mina could not take it.

"Insanity?" Haylee smiled. "Ableism much?"

Mina shook her head. Haylee's comebacks were always too good.

"Okay, can we all just stop for the night?" Al said. "Let's think about this later. This whole thing just began, you know! Maybe we can all enjoy spending some more time together? Usually, I would not be having dinner with you all every night, you know. Maybe we can make the best of it all." Al and his optimism again. What he could barely admit to even Homa was that after the first couple months, staying home this much had begun to drive him a bit crazy. He was never so aware of just how *extra* his four daughters were as he was now, when there was no escaping them.

It was clear to Roxanna that no one but Haylee would have her back for this—and, honestly, for reasons she did not understand. Her idea was a flop and there was little chance of making it happen—and yet. Roxanna did not give up easily, so she decided she would keep bringing it up every few weeks. They'd all go through their own cycles of loneliness and abandonment and isolation. Inevitably they would crack and agree that having a few friends over to celebrate their survival through this grim, never-ending experience could be nice. Clearly they were not there yet, but, as usual, Roxanna was ahead of the game.

What Roxanna-Vanna Milani could not stand was being bored, and she was starting to get bored. Violet had her modeling, Mina had her internet causes and her K-pop and her video games, and Haylee had her fitness goals and whatever this other stuff she was into was. As an influencer, Roxanna did not have much going on and she was starting to lose followers because of it. She could post only so many selfies, and she had a rule that she posted just one a day.

There was nowhere to go, nothing to do. Roxanna was losing herself.

And then, of course, she missed Damon, but it surprised her just how little time she spent thinking about him. Maybe it was because they had been together so long, but it was just weird to her how other girls obsessed over the guys in their lives and Roxanna barely gave him a thought anymore. She recalled how it had been different in the early days—it had been a big deal to her, after all—but every year that went by, she panicked, thinking that maybe they'd always be together. They never fought quite enough to fully break it off. And that was no thanks to Roxanna. Damon was one of the most agreeable people on earth, she swore. He made it so easy—too easy.

Thinking about him made her realize he was actually one person who *would* agree with her party idea. She was sure he'd think it was great and offer to DJ and pick up decorations and help her with the list. He was just that great.

She picked up the phone to text him and looked at the logs. She realized it had been almost three months. Sigh. Their off-periods were so off. Thanks to her too. She knew he wanted to hear from her. He was only giving her space, as she had asked. But she realized there was another reason she was so hesitant to reach out to him, why she'd been so avoidant these past few months.

She felt she had something to confess—well, one thing, really.

It always came back to the Secret (she thought of Ladan and her message and shuddered).

She had lied to Damon ever since they had met. But as the clock clicked closer to showtime, she felt that time was running out. He really did need to be the first to know. Aside from the family, of course. She'd have to just give it to him straight and deal with his response.

She knew it had to be something like that but the very off chance that it was not kept her up at night. She had seen Damon mad only once, and it was not pretty. They were in Algebra 2 together that day and his frenemy, this awful kid Eddie, had framed him as being the owner of a cheat sheet when it was really Eddie's all along. But Eddie was the second or third cousin of their teacher, Mrs. Clemmons, and so she believed him. Roxanna had watched the whole thing sitting behind Damon. She massaged his shoulders and whispered, *Fuck that rat—you can get this cleared up.* He hadn't said a word but his jaw had done that one clenching thing it did when he didn't know what to say and was holding a lot back, like his lower jaw was coming unhooked. It was so movie villain of him. Roxanna dreaded the ring of the bell for class to be over, because she had no idea what to say to him—she had never been good at consoling, the only time words really escaped her. But he had other things on his mind. He was first out, which was rare, because he usually walked in that very slow saunter gentle-giant types in high school assume. But this time he was out and waiting, as if for someone. That someone was not Roxanna, but she rushed to his side.

Baby, what are you doing? She had to know, not trusting the red that had washed over his face.

Split, Roxanna, he said simply. He rarely gave her commands like that and never that tersely.

What the hell? Like, I can't just pretend you don't look all crazy, Damon.

In a moment his victim was right in front of him. Eddie had been pushing past the crowd to get out of the way as fast as possible—he must have sensed it—when Damon's large hand pounded down on his shoulder. Damon was one of the tallest guys in his class, a basketball player—very few people dared mess with him, if any. Roxanna had to admit his wrath was a little bit sexy.

Hey, man, I'm sorry, I just panicked, didn't know what to do . . . Eddie was stammering, his eyes darting back and forth.

Oh, yeah, well, now you're gonna know what to do, you bitch, and that's cry to your mom. 'Cause I haven't even begun with you. Damon put his hand on Eddie's collar just strategically below his neck, as if to point out just how close he was to ending him.

Roxanna was astounded. This was like an anti-bullying ad climax, except the bully was the good guy here.

Eddie: *Hey, Damon, I'm so sorry, please let me go, I'll explain—*

Damon was nearly growling with animal rage. There was a composure to his fury but he also looked like he was going to explode.

Roxanna had to stop herself from clapping. *You piece of fucking shit,* she hissed, as if she were backing her man up properly.

Damon shot her a quick glance to stop and then turned again to Eddie, who had tears in his eyes. He was nearly a whole foot shorter. *Meet me on the courts right after school. Don't be late. Write a will, asshole.*

He let Eddie run off. Damon turned to Roxanna and made her promise she wouldn't follow them later. She promised, flustered but into it. She gave him a kiss on the cheek. She was surprised by how hot his skin felt. There was a group of students standing and watching; Roxanna felt so proud, like she and Damon ruled the school.

She never saw Eddie again. He was absent the next day and they heard he transferred to the private school in the neighboring district. That was that. There was no discussion of what had happened, and Damon never got in trouble for allegedly cheating on the test. Damon earned his C+ all on his own.

When Roxanna remembered all of that, she realized there was a lot more to Damon and his emotions than she could ever fathom. He'd of course never lay a hand on her, but she wondered what it would look like if he actually got *mad* mad. At her.

She looked down at her phone again. It had been so long. But what else could she do? She decided to call him—why not? She could put this off only so long.

He answered immediately. Of course.

"Hey, Rox." His voice sounded so soft.

"Hi, baby." Already she didn't know what to say.

"Wow, I've missed your voice. It's been a minute."

"I know, Damon, I know. I shouldn't have waited. It's just been, like, crazy, you know?"

"Yeah, the plague. It's nuts. I was worried about you. For a second, I thought, what if you had the virus?"

"Oh god, I would have called. But yeah, no. People like me—like us—we don't get the virus." She caught herself laughing in a way that sounded very unwell.

"Yeah—I guess. My aunt in Maine got it."

"Oh. I'm sorry. Is she okay?"

"No. She's . . . on a ventilator."

"Oh god. That's so awful." She had no idea what a ventilator was. "Wow, get well soon to her. What a mess this all is."

"Yeah, it is."

She couldn't read his emotions.

"Anyway, there's just been so much on my mind. So much I want to talk to you about . . ." she began, with a deep sigh. Was she even ready for this? She had to be. This had gone on so long.

"Sure, babe, anything. I miss you. I almost called you the other day."

"Why didn't you?" She welcomed the opportunity to stall.

"I don't know. You said you needed space. It's always you needing space. I get it. I'm happy to give it to you." He paused. "Well, not happy, but you know. I'll do it for you."

"Oh, baby, you are so sweet. Yeah, I want to tell you so much. . . ."

"Shoot, Rox, anything. I'm all yours."

He really was all hers. She found the thought a bit startling.

All sorts of thoughts roamed through her head, like particles of neon light, the kind that strobe on your bedroom ceiling from one of those cheap spinning-light generators. What to say? It was so rare for her to lose her words.

"Okay, well, don't judge me too much, because it's a lot . . ." she began, losing all sight of where she was going the minute she started.

"Never, Rox, I got you. . . ."

She wondered if he thought she was going to break up with him and she nearly laughed at the absurdity of it all.

"Okay, well, I sort of . . ." She paused, the air in her throat feeling toxic suddenly. She took another pause and before she knew it, the words were tumbling out of her. "I sort of wonder what you'd think if I had a party in the next weeks?"

He gave a funny snort that was maybe a laugh into the weird silence.

"I think it's a terrible idea," he said. "I mean, my aunt's dying."

She tried to conjure up his big, goofy Great Dane grin and failed.

"Yeah," she sighed, the tension in her body melting into his voice. She was a coward. It just wasn't the time. "No one thinks it's a good idea."

"It's one of your worst!" he said with something that sounded like a chuckle. "But that's why we love you. But you and I, we can have our own party—we can see each other again?"

He could be so corny.

A part of her dreaded reuniting with him but another part couldn't wait. At least something was finally happening.

9

The Pandemic Hits Home

Violet had decided that one thing she could do during the pandemic was to get into baking. It was something that she thought might help combat her newly developed inclination to disordered eating. These were for enjoying and sharing, not for puking. Rose had agreed to give her lessons in cake-making whenever she had spare time. Violet had rarely ever stepped into the part of the kitchen that was all hardware: pots and pans and utensils and appliances. She went in there—a whole wing—with a sense of wonder and imagined if she could really do this. The joke of spring 2020 was that there were two kinds of people during the pandemic: those who shaved their heads and those who got into baking. Not one of the Milanis was going to shave their head and none of the sisters had any culinary talents, so it was going to be up to her to bake.

On her first big day, she was surprised to find Mina in there too, going through the pots and pans.

"What are you doing?"

Mina looked up, startled and bit embarrassed. "Just checking out what we have . . . in terms of pans. You know what people have been doing, right?"

She nodded. "Baking."

Mina looked confused. "No, I mean, I am sure, but no, I am

talking about a much more important thing. Seven o'clock ring a bell?"

Violet was so confused.

"Oh, Violet!" Mina really felt if any of her sisters would know, it was Violet, but like everyone else in their household, she was oblivious, it seemed, which was even more reason why they needed to do it. "People all over the country—all over the world, actually—at seven each evening go outside banging pots and pans, cheering and stuff. For the essential workers, people on the frontline. To say thanks. You can see videos online."

Violet's eyes had grown very big. She had no idea. "For who? How can they hear?"

Mina sighed. "It's like in places where people have real neighborhoods. Everyone just goes out at that exact same time and it's like a whole thing. You can hear everyone. Everyone's distancing but they come together for this. It's nice." She paused, realizing it made no sense. "I mean, we live far from the people next door and we have no real neighborhood. . . ."

Violet instantly looked annoyed. "We do too have a neighborhood!"

"What neighborhood would that be? Please."

"Tehrangeles!" Violet announced, with all the sincerity in the world.

Mina had nothing to say. "I don't totally identify as a Tehrangeleno, Violet."

"Well, I do. And you are, whether you like it or not. It's not like a mentality or something you can put on and take off. It chooses you, you don't choose it. This is how they see us. This is who we are."

Mina shrugged. "Anyway, our neighborhood Tehrangeles doesn't quite work like that. If I go on the mezzanine balcony and start banging on things, only you all are gonna hear it. Maybe, just maybe, if someone in a convertible drives by somehow just slow enough to catch it . . . But we're sort of stuck by ourselves. Which is why I initially thought it made no sense. But then I thought, we are each other's communities too, on top of family. We should do it anyway. For ourselves. A gratitude ritual!"

Violet was biting the head off a Swedish Fish. In her other hand was a bowl of Cadbury Mini Eggs. "I mean, I will do it if it matters to you a lot, but I just don't see how this will help the rescue workers. Plus, if other people are doing it, why does it matter if we do too?"

Mina sighed. "I mean, there's a lot of talk about the power of prayer. Who knows. I just think the whole world is doing it and we don't know about it because, well, we're rich and out of touch. I wish we lived in a real neighborhood and had a real community, but we don't. We barely know who our neighbors are."

"You wish we were poor?"

"Not all neighborhoods are poor," Mina said. But she wasn't totally sure. She had never spent time in one.

"Those poor people, in their overstuffed, overcrowded project housing things, all dying on top of each other—it's horrifying. And you're telling me, as they waste away in all that, they are the ones banging pans and cheering every day at seven?" It sounded nuts to Violet.

Mina nodded. "Yes, actually. Anyway, you don't have to do it. I figured I'd be doing it alone. But don't get weirded out if you hear all that from the main balcony. I'm gonna just take a pan or two and a mallet and I'll probably just play some YouTube audio of people cheering. Just for a minute or two at seven. Maybe I'll skip weekends, though I doubt the rescue workers get those days off."

Violet gave her little sister a soft hug. It was clicking. Mina was always trying to do good—she had to give her that. "Maybe

I'll try to join you one day, okay? If I remember. Anyway, please don't take the pretty pink one you have there, because I want to use that for some baking project."

Mina did a cartoonish double-take and her eyes landed on the Le Creuset berry-pink Dutch oven that her sister was waving at.

"Yeah, I want to try baking. That's my pandemic thing now."

"Nice," Mina said. "Persian Princesses of Tehrangeles, Pandemic Edition, I guess."

Violet laughed, laughed so hard that for a moment Mina was not sure if she was laughing or crying.

At Roxanna's urging a few months before the pandemic, Al had started exploring medical marijuana to help with the lingering pain from his golf injuries. He had begun with CBD but quickly advanced to the real thing. He had little lozenges, gummies, tinctures, and lotions he used, but once the pandemic hit, he started ordering weed from dealers and smoking in the house—especially in his bedroom, as he was definitely not comfortable enough to do it around his daughters yet.

Homa was mortified.

"This is disgusting." She would spray the air around him with her favorite ARQUISTE room spray: Caroline's Four Hundred, the St. Regis Hotel's signature scent. It was supposed to smell like the domestic gardens of the Gilded Age, but it stood no chance against the stale funky musk of Al's vapes, joints, and bongs. "If I had ever had any idea you would smoke—and smoke *this*—I would have never married you. Can you not keep to the candies? This is awful."

"You should try—just a puff," he said, laughing. He always laughed so much when he was high. "It really does take the edge off. I should have listened to Roxi ages ago on this one."

"You are an Iranian old guy, not some American rapper!"

"Oh, please, our grandmas smoked opium in Iran!" He laughed even harder. "They have cannabis in Iran too. Life is hard these days, my love, Homa—we need to let loose a bit!"

They suddenly heard a clanging, like the sound of a cheap gong, a jarring cacophony of stainless steel and aluminum and copper.

"Do you hear people screaming in the distance?" Homa asked, alarmed.

"I think they are chanting?" Al said. Just like her to hear screams when he heard chants.

Al had the shades drawn, as he preferred to smoke in the dark, but he pulled them up to see what the commotion was. It was coming from the heavens. It took him a second to realize it was directly above him: his third daughter, little Mina, on the main balcony, holding various pots and pans and banging them against each other. She'd take a break and then look to her cell phone and apparently play a soundtrack of people cheering. She did this for a few minutes.

"These girls must be losing their minds." He chuckled.

Later at dinner, Al asked her what she was doing and Mina explained with her usual tense patience.

"Please, that is so crazy!" Roxanna laughed. "What in the flop era, Mini!"

"Who's gonna hear it?" Haylee asked.

"I think it's nice for Mina to be so thoughtful," Violet piped up.

Mina smiled at her. "It's symbolic," Mina said. "We don't live in a neighborhood for people to really hear us."

"What—yes we do!" Roxanna shouted. "We do too live in a neighborhood, and the best one."

"Tehrangeles!" Al immediately declared.

"It's not a real place," Mina mumbled.

"It's unfortunately too real," Homa grumbled.

"How can it be realer, baby?" Al laughed. "We run this town!" He was still very stoned.

"Not we running this town!" Roxanna cackled back.

Mina looked unconvinced but she shrugged. "Is this scripted for the show? Anyway, you're all free to join me. Seven. Daily. On weekdays."

Violet ended up joining her once—the very next day—but she felt it was too weird. No one got it but Mina. Homa cringed every day at seven. She hated the commotion. Haylee and Roxanna ignored it. Randy and Rose occasionally joined in, but it was Mina alone who carried the tradition. At night she'd watch videos of neighborhoods in Italy and China and Iran and France where people did the same, and she consoled herself. While her family barely cared, there was a world out there that did. And even if she couldn't really depend on her community—or Tehrangeles—to put an end to all this, maybe the people of the world she was in sync with could will it. She had a very bad feeling about it all, and her family's varying degrees of obliviousness worried her even more.

As summer began to close in, everything changed: the virus came to them. Randy tested positive.

Rose broke it to them right before dinner one night, double-masked and in gloves, her eyes full of tears, looking and sounding both ashamed and apologetic.

"Mr. and Mrs. Milani, girls, I'm so sorry to say this but the virus has come to our family. So far it's just Randy but the girls and I are all gonna get tested. We can leave if you want. My cousin in Temecula said we can stay in her back house."

Homa and Al looked at each other tensely, shocked. The girls were silent.

"I am so very sorry," Mina said, the first to speak up. "What's Randy's status? How can we help him?"

"And you don't have to leave—you can just stay there," Homa

said. "Unless you want to? I don't know—my, this is so bad." Homa had barely realized Rose and Randy's daughters were back; their family was always in a sort of flux. But it made sense that in the pandemic everyone went back to where they were from, and in this case, the Milani home was also their help's home.

"We are so sorry to hear this," Al said, in his most rehearsed politician voice. "Please send Randy prayers and love from us all."

"Does this mean we all have it?" Haylee whispered to Violet, looking frantic.

Violet shook her head.

"It was bound to happen. It's worse than people thought. No one is wearing masks, distancing, or washing hands enough," Mina said. "Yes, Rose, we are so sorry to hear this. Please let me know what we can do. I'll be there every day at seven, of course, still."

"Oh, thank you, everyone," Rose said. "We don't know what's going to happen. The doctors say there are no guarantees, of course. And Randy is very . . . at risk."

"Why?" Haylee immediately blurted out.

Everyone looked embarrassed. Haylee looked confused.

"His weight, of course, Haylee," Rose said softly. "But, well, we'll work on that."

"Oh! Well, when he's all clear, I can help you all in the gym! Do you need some workouts?" Haylee eagerly interjected. "I'm designing some for Violet, not that she's using them!"

Violet closed her eyes and inhaled deeply.

"Well, this is very scary," Homa said. "I feel like we should call Dr. Beheshti and have him figure out a plan for Randy and test us all too."

"Dr. B. sees *sefids*?" Roxanna asked. She turned to Rose. "Whites, sorry."

Rose forced a small smile.

"Is Randy going to . . . be okay? Or . . . ?" They all knew what Haylee meant but hated that she said it.

"Oh, honey, he'll be fine, I am sure," Rose said, tears now spilling. "Plenty of people get better. We just need to stay on top of it. I think prayer can also help."

They all nodded lukewarmly.

"Well, we will make sure you are all in isolation for the next weeks and we will just keep the house ourselves. Maybe we can cook the food too, I guess?" Al suggested.

"I mean, I am okay, I can do it, but I get if you feel we should all be isolated," Rose said.

"Let's think about it," Homa said, horrified at the thought of being in the kitchen again, especially for this household, everyone with their special preferences. "Let's see what Dr. Beheshti says. He's very good."

For many years, the Milanis barely ever left their house to go to a doctor. Their personal doctor, Abbas Beheshti, would make house calls for them every time. He was one of the best doctors in the L.A. area.

Rose excused herself, and they just all stared at one another glumly.

"I can't believe it is finally here," Mina said. "Like, at our household. We need to be prepared. We might all go down."

"Go down? Are we gonna die?" Haylee asked, her face twitching with anxiety.

"No, no, dear," Homa said, but she looked worried. "This is very troubling, but we will be okay."

"Of course we will! Nothing bad happens to the Milanis!" Al said, but even his voice sounded a bit weak.

"He needs to, like, lose weight," Roxanna muttered. "That's why he got it. Fat people have it way worse. Couldn't be me!"

"Roxi, stop it," Violet snapped.

"Yeah, skinny people are dying too," Mina said. "It doesn't discriminate."

"I just don't want it to get in the way of my party," Roxanna said.

"Who's having a party?" Homa asked.

"No one," Mina snapped. "You're a monster, Roxi."

"Eventually!" Roxanna insisted. "I am still planning. We need this. Our immune systems are, like, a wreck from all this worry."

"Jesus Christ," Mina muttered.

"One day, Roxanna," Al said. "We will have things to look forward to again. For now, let's think how to help Randy."

They all sat in silence.

"There's not a lot we can do." Mina broke the silence with common sense.

"Please don't make us live without a housekeeper. We can't do all their work!" Roxanna said.

"But also, we shouldn't have them around?" Haylee said.

"We should give them more money," Violet suggested.

"We should create a system where we check in on Randy hourly or something from a distance," Mina offered.

"We should get Dr. Beheshti here," Homa again said.

"Well, sounds like we have a lot to do! Isn't that nice? We have things to do! Someone but ourselves to live for!" Al exclaimed, as he got up from the table and went off to his office, to spend the next few hours smoking the rest of his weed in blissful isolation.

Violet was baking her first proper cake for Randy—a simple vanilla one, but in a soothing pink, she had decided. She had been tempted to use one of the mixes in the pantry but she found the recipe was not so hard—and the batter was worth the effort alone! Admittedly, she'd had to repeat the buttercream three times. Who knew buttercream was a thing you could "break," but that was what kept happening. She couldn't get the balance and temperatures right. She was sure Randy would be too sick to tell, anyway. The good gesture would register and that was enough—and Rose had warned her that it seemed

Randy was losing his sense of smell and taste but she wasn't quite sure, as the fevers had him so delirious.

Just as she was putting a few drops of pitaya food coloring into the finally correct buttercream, Dr. Beheshti breezed in through the kitchen as if he lived there. He quickly gave Violet a too-wet kiss on the cheek and they exchanged formal Persian greetings.

"I hope you girls are all keeping healthy! And your boyfriends too!" He always, without fail, mentioned boyfriends. There was something vaguely pervy about the guy, Mina always thought, but they all tolerated him anyway.

Abbas Beheshti was Al's age—they had been born just weeks apart, it turned out—and he was a wealthy doctor who really did not need to work. He had had three wives and no kids, and he dressed way too flashily to be taken for just any doctor: Hawaiian shirts, Gucci and LV logo sweatshirts, leather pleated pants, metallic loafers, fedoras in gem tones, and one time he had even come in a chinchilla coat he claimed a client had gifted him. Occasionally he would join Al for golf, but Al said he was terrible at it and talked too much.

"Okay, we are testing everyone, and then we go to the gardener, is that it?" Dr. Beheshti boomed.

"He's more than a gardener—they are our housekeepers but they're like family," Mina said, popping in out of nowhere. "Hi, Dr. Beheshti. Nice pashmina." He was wearing a fuchsia paisley wrap over his navy linen suit—a strange but slightly charming touch.

"Scarf! Wife Number Two left it behind!" He laughed, exposing those horrible fluorescent-white teeth of his. He was always trying to get Al and Homa to do their teeth, telling them he had a Persian guy who could give them a deal, but the entire family agreed his own creepily glowing white teeth were not enticing advertising.

Roxanna and Haylee came in, and once again Dr. Beheshti:

"Here they are! What's wrong—have you been fighting with your boyfriends, babies?!" No one laughed but him.

"Abbas-*jaan,* Randy is in the house in the back—we can't be exposed to him—will you go there?" Homa asked.

"Yes, of course, after I am done with you all." He saw them one by one, giving each an antibody blood test and a nasal swab. Only Haylee made a slight fuss about the awful tickle in her nasal cavity, but that was that.

"Aren't you supposed to be wearing a surgical mask or something?" Mina asked.

"Of course I am supposed to be!" Dr. Beheshti, for some reason, began laughing. "I will with the gardener!" He tapped his side pocket to imply a mask that he had neglected to pack.

"Speaking of that, Abbas!" Al patted him on the back and began to lead him through the back garden to the back house.

"Oh, Ali, I forgot to say! I've been hearing about the show—congrats! And what a genius stunt, the Italy thing—I was, like, that is my Ali, all brains!" He was beaming so aggressively.

Al was confused. "Italy? What do you mean?"

Dr. Beheshti stopped in his tracks and rolled his eyes dramatically. "Ali-*jaan,* come on, why play the part with me now? I have been taking care of you and your wife and kids forever! Are there cameras following us now—is that why?"

Al was perplexed. "Abbas, you're acting like you have the virus in your brain! I don't know what you are talking about. And no, filming is delayed. We don't know when it will start."

Dr. Beheshti reevaluated, reminding himself to take care not to anger Al, who was of course one of his favorite celebrity clients. "I understand. I know you can't talk about it all. And I won't say anything but I just heard and I thought it was so smart—a great touch! You in pizza-foods business and Italy! A great way out!"

Al truly had no idea what he was talking about. "Abbas, I

wish I could understand a word you are saying. There is nothing
Italy happening. No idea what you mean."

Dr. Beheshti squinted at Al—it was unlike his friend to be
that tight-lipped. What was the point, especially with taping
delayed? What was he worried about? True that Dr. Beheshti
knew all of Tehrangeles, but why would he gossip about a
patient? During a pandemic too? He had a heart. He decided
to let it go but just said one thing more. "You know, my first
wife and I, in the early days here, we had to pretend we were
Italian. Every Iranian I know discovers that for themselves. But
your connection is particularly good. Plus, 'Milan' and 'Milani.'
It could not be more perfect. So congrats. You win again!"

Al just looked blankly at the sun. After a long pause, he slowly
turned his eyes to the doctor. "Zegna?" he asked, gesturing to
his linen blazer.

"Cucinelli, of course!" Dr. Beheshti smiled widely. He tried
to think of something to say back but Al was in a T-shirt and
cargos—expensive ones, certainly, but still not Cucinelli.

"Always nice to see what I pay for." Al winked at him, a bit
too dryly.

Longer pause.

Dr. Beheshti took that as the final sign to move on. "Okay,
let's go fix up this gardener-mechanic-plumber-whatever he is
of yours!"

"Did he say anything about Italy to you?" Al asked Homa later
at dinner.

Roxanna started coughing.

"Italy? What?" Homa was confused.

Roxanna's coughing grew louder and louder. In between her
fake coughs, she gasped, "Not the virus—don't worry!"

"Yes, my reaction too," he said. "He kept saying it was smart

of me, the Italy thing, something about the taping, and told me
a story about how he and all Persians say they are Italian."

Homa raised an eyebrow and shook her head. "Abbas is a
little nutty. Did he say Randy is okay?"

Roxanna nearly choked on her arugula. Dr. Beheshti? How
was that even possible? Why on earth would he know, and why
would he bring it up?

"Wait, what did he say?" Roxanna asked, her voice cracking
weirdly.

"Oh, nothing, just some nonsense I could not figure out—
maybe implying I have said I am Italian!"

Mina's eyes suddenly darted like laser beams at Roxanna, who
avoided her stare.

"Did he say why he said that?" Mina asked. "Like, where did
he hear that?"

"How do I know? I didn't even understand what he meant,"
Al said. "The guy is getting crazy—maybe time to look for a
new doctor."

"He, like, skeeves me out," Haylee said.

"I second that," Violet said.

"Well, let's wait to get our results and let's wait till this pandemic blows over. They say it will be over in a few months. Let's
not change up too much until then," Homa said.

They all nodded, and everyone but Roxanna and Mina forgot
all about it.

Roxanna muted Mina's number and social media accounts.
She knew Mina was going to grill her and went to her room
holding back tears. What was she going to do? How was it possible their family doctor knew? Who was telling? Who knew?

She looked to her phone and realized time really was running
out. She had meant to tell Damon ages ago, but every time she
tried, she couldn't quite get it out. Now that they were back in
touch, things seemed more harmonious than ever. She didn't
want to introduce anything this crazy now.

She hated this, all of this.

She'd begun dipping into her Adderall stash again—she still had her old prescription, even though she had promised the whole family she would never again do it—her rages had become so awful. She took a pill and crushed it with a nail file until it was a perfect powder. She rolled up a blotting paper pad and snorted it. It burned—it felt like the most caustic, punishing, weird sadness. She had done this to herself. No one could get her out but her. And here she was—the liar, the fake, not trusting others. It was too much.

It was around this point in the pandemic that Roxanna started to wish she did not exist—a familiar feeling she'd had quite a few times in her short life. She knew this story would have to be sorted. At least while she was alive, she could make up another lie to make up for the lie she had told.

In the end, after two weeks, Randy was stable again. The whole family, Rose and her daughters too, tested negative for the virus. Randy still got weird headaches sometimes, but he began working again. He thanked Violet for the cake he never ate. He'd had no appetite, but his family had enjoyed it, even though it was undercooked and much too sweet. Overall the Milanis had been so kind and Randy and Rose felt lucky to have such good employers.

"You're one of the good ones!" Al would say with a wink. And they'd go with it because it wasn't worth not going with it. Not with the Milanis.

Randy and Rose had been childhood sweethearts in Lawrence, Kansas. Instead of enrolling in college, they had moved to Los Angeles to pursue acting—something neither of them had any talent for, they always said. They did not fit in in Los Angeles. They were both pale, freckled Midwesterners with no fashion sense and little idea of how Hollywood worked. They cleaned motels and washed dishes at diners while going on auditions and taking acting classes, but it was all one big waste. They ended up being housekeepers for a very famous pop star they could never name (they had signed an NDA) until he died very mysteriously (a drug overdose, although that was never confirmed). Because of that, they were out of work when Al Milani put an ad out many years ago, when the kids were just kids. In Iran, housekeepers often lived with the family, and so Al wanted to re-create that dynamic. He could not find Persian servants for the job. They were just too well off.

And that's when I realized what a gas it would be to have an all-white staff. My uncle's old dream! Can you imagine? They did all that racist stuff to us, said all that awful stuff about go back to your country *and made us feel like brown shit, and then now we can buy them? Can you imagine? I got so big I got to own white people? Can you imagine: in my story the only white people are the help!*

Al talked about that over and over for years until he worried it was getting back to Randy and Rose and their kids. But it was such a big source of pride for him. It took more convincing for Homa. She was sure white people lied and stole too much and that they would envy her and the girls. *How can we trust these random white people, Ali? Where is Kansas, even? Is that the Dorothy place? Did these white people even go to school? Do they have guns?* Al soon realized Homa had never even had a white friend before. And so, for the first year, he always had to be in the room when she was speaking to them. She could not stand being alone with them. She hated how they looked, these white people. She could not stand their terrible clothes. She even floated the idea of them wearing uniforms.

Oh my god, like a maid costume? A butler costume? Come on, Homa—who does that anymore? They didn't even do it in Iran! I won't suggest it—you go ahead, though! You see what they say!

In the end, Homa did not dare. She was convinced they had

a dark side. She kept telling herself it was only temporary—they would eventually find a Persian staff. But once Al really got her signed on to the idea of them owning white people as an act of empowerment, she acquiesced. She wasn't into those kinds of things like Al; she just wanted an easy life. Maybe it would be easier with these white people. The difference between them was so big, after all, maybe they would never have to worry about understanding each other. That felt very nice to Homa. She just had one big rule for them and that was to never ask about Iran. The show would change that, to some extent, she realized. But even so, she controlled the narrative. In Al's story, the only white people they knew were the help; in her story, there was no knowing anyone, no knowing at all.

10

The Canceling

There was one particularly horrible day that the whole family agreed marked the start of the worst patch of the pandemic period. It began with a terrible omen: Pari, the Persian cat of the house, had run away. It was shocking because Pari rarely moved. She was often perched on one of Homa's Afghan cushions in the library, old and grumpy and aloof, or she would hide in Homa and Al's bedroom if there was too much activity about the house. Occasionally she curled up with her favorite Milani daughter, Violet, in Violet's room.

One morning Mina noticed she had not been around for some time.

"Are people not worried? Pari has literally vanished—I had Rose look everywhere too!" Mina said as half the family was milling about the kitchen at breakfast.

"Don't cats just go away a lot and come back?" Haylee asked. She almost never took care of Pari. They mostly ignored each other.

Violet shook her head. "I mean, some do, but not Pari. Pari's an indoor cat. I don't know who let her out or if she somehow crawled out the balcony. She's so old!"

"Is Roxi up yet?" Mina asked. "Maybe she knows."

"Should I call the neighbors?" Homa wondered.

"Yes!" Mina said. "Good idea. I can put up posters around the area too. I just hate that we didn't notice and we can't say exactly when she left."

"Well, she's an old cat who never goes anywhere," Violet murmured. "What did we know?"

Violet suddenly burst into tears and Mina rushed to her side to comfort her.

"Hey, Violet, it's okay. Pari will probably show up soon," Mina said. "We've barely started looking."

"My friend Marci's stepdad is a pet psychic," Haylee offered. "If we need, there's that. He's just up in Laurel Canyon and I think he does everything by Zoom."

They all looked at Haylee blankly. She cradled her large protein smoothie and moved out of the kitchen and up the staircase to lose herself in the gym for the next few hours.

"I need to take a nap," Violet said, sniffling. "I am so upset. I'll keep searching when I'm up again. Is that okay?"

Homa gave her a squeeze and a kiss.

"Yes, of course, we got this. I'll go check on Rox," Mina said. "She might have seen something—who even knows—but just text me when you're up and we can figure out the search later."

It was nearly noon. It was not unusual for Roxanna to still be asleep at this hour during those pandemic weekdays, but something told Mina she needed to visit her older sister anyway. All night she had heard pacing and loud music from her wing. Roxanna and Mina were often up the latest, but Roxanna was usually more careful about not blasting music well into the morning hours. Mina had crashed earlier than usual but she could not get the energy to walk to the door and yell to Roxanna to please keep it down. She had simply fallen asleep. By her estimation, Roxanna had not gotten to sleep before dawn. She'd probably be upset to be woken up, but Pari's absence was an emergency.

As expected, Roxanna did not answer the door when she

knocked. "Come on, Roxi, this is important! It's past noon! We need you!" She knocked even harder.

Eventually, the door swung open. A very disheveled Roxanna stumbled back to her bed. She was wearing a tiny slip and her face was heavily streaked with makeup. Out of all the sisters, she was by far the messiest—Mina could barely stand being in her room, strewn with shoes and underwear and pill bottles and plates of half-eaten food and makeup.

Today it smelled like perfume and lotion and cigarettes and weird incense and a touch of burning plastic, somehow.

She took a seat on the edge of Roxanna's California king bed. At her bedside table an alarm was going off—who knows how long it had been buzzing away—and a corked, quarter-filled bottle of red wine lay on its side next to a porcelain plate filled with some powder and rolled-up bills. Mina sighed, but reminded herself she was here for a reason: Pari.

Roxanna was almost asleep again as Mina said, "Roxi, Pari is missing. We need your help."

"Who the hell is Perry?" Roxanna groaned, barely forming words.

"Pari."

"Okay, who, like, even is that?" Roxanna squinted at her as if she were the sun.

Mina sighed. "Our cat, Roxanna."

Roxanna squinted even harder and then, suddenly, as if she remembered, started giggling. "Oh, right. God, I hate that cat."

"Yeah, well, she's missing. Violet is very upset. We all are," Mina said. "Can you help us find her?"

Roxanna tried to sit up on her elbows. "What the hell? This is why you woke me?"

Mina nodded.

Roxanna aggressively rubbed her face as she tapped the alarm off. "Jesus Christ. Like, I've barely ever even touched that cat. . . . Besides, isn't that cat too old to, like, even get out the door?"

"She's very old. We don't know what happened. But please look out?" Mina asked. Then she added, "God, Roxi, your room is so awful. Can I call Rose to help? How can you live like this?"

"Absolutely no way." Roxanna was suddenly alert. "There are things here that—anyway, no. And last night was special— I was up FaceTiming with the girls and we were doing dance party makeup and photo shoots. It was so fun. Did you see the pics I put on Insta?"

Mina shook her head. She avoided Roxanna's Instagram as much as she could. Looking at her older sister's thirst traps was not her thing. "I'll look later."

"No, no, let me show you," Roxanna said, smiling. Somehow she was able to fish out her phone from under her covers. But the minute she turned her phone on, something was off.

"What's wrong?" Mina asked, hoping it was related to Pari.

"I just have all these messages and texts—what the hell . . ." Roxanna looked upset.

Mina watched her sister scroll frantically and her face go from confused to shocked to angered to sad and then back to confused. "Is there news about Pari?"

Roxanna shook her head angrily. "It's so crazy . . . I'm being, I don't know, like, kind of accused of something!"

Mina was confused now. She scooted up to Roxanna's phone and saw the spectacle of notifications Roxanna was wading through.

" 'Blackfishing'?" Mina kept seeing the term.

"Yeah, what even is that?" Roxanna asked. She sort of knew, but she hoped she was wrong.

"I think that's when someone acts Black for clout," Mina said, trying to put it as mildly as possible. It was bad. She knew it well, an accusation she had encountered on stan Twitter along with discussions of cultural appropriation.

"I think it's my new photos! What the hell—there's been a

mistake. . . ." Roxanna hopped onto her Instagram, where her recent post was flooded with comments. "Oh, fuck. Fuckity fuck."

Mina took a look. It was the usual Roxanna selfie photo dump, ring light–lit and filtered and all, but there *was* something a bit different. Roxanna was straddling the windowsill in a neon-green bikini, with her skin very tan. Her lips were lined weird, way outside their usual lines, and her face was also powdered darker. "I guess I see what they mean." But she had seen her sister do this before. Why was this happening now?

"Is it that different than usual?" Roxanna cried. Her face was red. "What the fuck? How is this Black? We were just messing with makeup! Is it the lighting? I just don't see it."

Mina tried to see who the bulk of the comments were from, if they were bots or not. "I'd have to look more closely, but I can figure out where the source is later, if you want. I guess I wouldn't worry? Isn't this just part of being an influencer?"

"Being accused of acting Black?! Are you crazy?" Roxanna was livid, raging now. "Black people are, like, my best friends!"

"I don't know. I don't keep up with this stuff. Just delete the photos."

"Imagine people thinking I'm Blackfishing when all these years I've been . . ." Roxanna adopted her best Italian exaggerated hand gesture pose, which only looked all the more Iranian.

Mina started to laugh. "Whitefishing." If only these people knew the only thing Roxanna had pretended at was being Italian, of all things.

For a second, she thought Roxanna was going to laugh too.

"I almost want to say it, but it'll make me look more nuts!" Roxanna groaned.

"Yeah, best not to do that," Mina said.

Meanwhile, Roxanna was reading even deeper into the recesses of her social media. Something even worse was wrong.

People were commenting: *So Blackfishing and using the n-word too?* and *Is the n-word part of your brand?* and *Not the n-word, dirty bitch.*

"When the hell is all this? When did I say the N-word?!" Roxanna was nearly howling.

Mina refrained from pointing out that Roxanna said it constantly when quoting her beloved hip-hop songs, but that was another story. "Is someone saying that now?"

"Hundreds are, if not more! Where did this come from? Blackfishing and the N-word? This is so random! Someone is just after me!"

Mina actually thought that had to be it. On stan Twitter she'd seen it many times—a particular type of cyberbullying that fixated on social justice issues. The stans would decide they did not like someone, they would dig into their profile, which included their posting history, they'd flag whatever problematic things they could find, and they'd riff on that, whether it meant hyperbolized accusations or doctored quotes. It was, in effect, what the right wing called "cancel culture."

And, like clockwork, Roxanna said it too: "Like, who the fuck is, like, trying to, like, cancel me?"

It was not the first time Roxanna had gotten into trouble online. She'd had her Instagram suspended before for nudity. Another time, she'd been nearly canceled for starting a fight with a Brazilian model over something no one could recall. The worst was when she wore a real fur bikini and animal rights activists flooded her social media with insults. Instead of backing down, Roxanna had called them *grass-nibbler uglies, hippie choad turdbirds,* and *bunnyfucking virgin bedwetters.* Al made her apologize the next day—he argued it would be bad for his brand—and then she'd gotten in trouble for how half-hearted her apology was. In the end, she didn't care, because she didn't lose many followers and Al forgot about it, but Mina wondered what Al would think of all this now. He'd probably hear about it from his PR firm if Roxanna didn't tell him first.

"Just apologize," Mina said. It was her go-to solution. "That's what you do. And a good apology. There are templates online now—search 'celebrity damage control scripts' or something like that. But we all make mistakes and apologizing is—"

"What the fuck, Mina?! I did nothing! Why are you, like, on their side?!" Roxanna was shrieking.

Mina got up. She was so exhausted by Roxanna, and none of this had gotten her any closer to finding Pari. "You can figure it out. If you need my help later, I can contact cybersec and figure out where this all started. But for now, we have a real emergency—"

"Oh my god, like this isn't a real emergency? I have more social media followers than all you bitches combined!"

Mina bit her lip hard to make sure she wouldn't say anything more. "I have to go. Please text the group chat if you hear or see Pari. Thanks."

As she closed the door behind her, Mina heard glass breaking and the sound of Roxi's too-familiar *FUCK EVERYTHING*.

Dinner was particularly glum. There were no new developments. Roxanna showed up in her oversize Tom Ford mirror aviators as if she'd been crying all day—*or drugging*, Mina thought—her eyes still glued to her phone.

"Is this the new fashion, eating with your sunglasses on indoors?" Homa looked appalled.

Roxanna didn't even look up. "Yes. It is."

"I still think we should call the pet psychic," Haylee offered. "I trust him. Their family were major Republican donors and—"

"And that's a good thing?" Mina said, horrified. Something

had been happening to her little sister. She noticed Haylee was following more than a few Twitter accounts with MAGA in their bios. She couldn't figure out what had prompted it.

Haylee scowled at Mina—so predictable Mina would come at her. "I mean, they're legit, and people of, you know . . . real American values."

"Pari's a cat—what does it matter," Al grumbled. Al's whole day had been derailed by the women of the house freaking out about a cat they barely paid attention to most of the time.

"I just think it's good to support people who are, you know, up against a lot these days." Haylee paused—she was a bit unsure what she even meant. It was true her politics—if you could even call them that—had taken a more conservative turn this season, but the virus just brought that out. You had to be on the right side of things if you wanted to survive, she thought.

"Up against what?" Violet was perplexed.

"There's a lot of information being kept from us. Our own Randy was struck with a bioweapon. We need truth tellers." Haylee's eyes were closed—it looked like prayer, almost. "Anyway, it's a free consult, I think, and then the session is around four hundred and fifty dollars. A deal. He's only not found one pet in his decade of doing this and that was a monkey. His specialty is cats."

Homa and Al eyed each other wearily.

"Maybe we should wait a few more days? We won't rule it out," Homa said gently.

"I'm just worried with the sky like that and all," Haylee muttered and realized immediately she shouldn't have said anything.

"Not that again," Mina said, moaning.

She had brought up chemtrails before and a huge fight had broken out between her and Mina. Haylee had pointed a few out as they lounged poolside one early evening and Mina had snapped back that those were normal condensation trails from airplanes and that water-based contrails were simply an everyday phenomenon left by high-flying aircrafts in certain atmospheric conditions. Haylee had insisted these lingered the way "cloud-seeding weather modification agents" did and that this was "human population control" and "chemical warfare." Mina had found it so disturbing. They had gone back and forth for nearly an hour until Violet broke up the fight.

"I've been getting those migraines again—they only come when the sky is streaked like that," Haylee said. "And, Mina, with all your illnesses, you've probably been poisoned worse than all of us. I'd try one of my detox shakes, honestly, with what we're being exposed to."

"Spare me. Let's stay focused on Pari, please," Mina said. She felt almost embarrassed for Haylee.

"Mina-the-woke doesn't like that I've *woken* up," Haylee said, getting up abruptly. If it sounded rehearsed, she didn't care. It was. "And it's fine. I don't love having a radical, communist, agendered or whatever sister, so I guess we're even. Anyway, I'll text the fam group chat the pet psychic number again. But I have to go clear my head—the toxic negativity in this house is getting to me, and to be honest, that's probably what happened to Pari too."

Haylee got up, disappointed Roxanna didn't even attempt to defend her. But Roxanna was too deeply immersed in her phone, her hair falling like a veil over her face and her sunglasses. It was hard to know where she was.

"Is Hayles getting this stuff online? From social media?" Violet asked, alarmed.

Mina shrugged. "It's everywhere. It's just weird to see one of us Gen Zers go that way."

"This is why I can barely stand social media these days," Violet said.

That comment seemed to snap Roxanna back to the table. "Good job, sissy. It's disgusting out there. Like, the worst. The lies, the hate, it's all just, like, absolute hell."

"Are you okay, Roxanna?" Al asked her.

She got up, knowing she had way more calls and texts to make that evening. "Nope!"

And that was that.

Mina was still mad about Haylee when she went back to her room. She didn't know what was going on with her sisters these days. Only Violet seemed herself and even she appeared to be in the middle of a hopefully short-lived eating disorder.

She put on her headset and debated what to spend her time on first: finding Pari or helping Roxi. Roxanna was clearly in bad shape, and while she was a social media master of sorts, she'd never had to un-cancel herself before. Mina was a bit worried she and her sisters would get called out too. She knew there was little she could do for Pari—though she was tempted to research Haylee's pet psychic just to rule him out for everyone. But she decided to focus on Roxanna. The first thing to do was to find out where all this came from.

Whenever Mina mentioned contacting "cybersec," she was really talking about her friend Ian. She had never met him—he was an ex-hacker noise musician who lived in Ohio, and they had bonded over obscure alternative K-pop groups sometime in 2019. On average, they texted around fiftysomething times a day. Ian was sort of like her best friend. She had never had many friends and so having a long-distance one like this was just fine for her. They hadn't even Skyped or FaceTimed, and she preferred it that way. There was a purity to their connection. They talked about tech and social media and K-pop and electronic music and video games, and lots about memes. It occurred to her Ian might figure out what happened with Roxanna. He didn't know too much about her sisters, and this was a terrible

intro. It stressed her out—him finding out and her very associa-
tion with Roxanna. Still, she texted him for help:

Hey Ian what's up

Minaaaaaaaa hi

I need your help, I hate to say it

Shoot

*It's my sister. Roxanna. Not sure you know too much about her, but
she's kind of an influencer and she's in trouble and I want to help*

Lol omfg

She couldn't tell if that meant he knew.

Yeah. She's being canceled

Jfc. For what?

She took a breath.

Saying the n-word. Blackfishing.

There was a pause. Typing.

Did she

Idk. No.

She hated that she lied.

Um ok

*Yeah anyway can you help me figure out who these accounts are and
where this started*

Yeah ok what's her IG and Twitter handles

Both of them are roxannavannatime

Roxannavanna?! Is that her name

*Roxanna-Vanna is her full first name, yeah. She goes by Roxanna
mostly or Roxi.*

Lol ok. Looking it up. Whoa I see.

Yeah, it's bad.

Gimme a sec let me look at something

Mina sent him a gold-star emoji and waited.

*Ok this is not that easy. It's not all bots It seems almost like some
people know her. Does she have enemies?*

No idea. I mean, she's a rich skinny influencer so yes?

Yeah ok. This will take me some time. But wow I plugged in some keywords into her social media and yikes. She's definitely been risky— I guess she only got a lot of followers in the last few years, but in her early days eeeeeek

What do you mean?

Well, it looks like she joined Twitter seven years ago, 2013. Five years ago, she seemed to use the r-word a lot and also she seems very . . . homophobic? lol

That lol. Mina froze. Ian didn't know anything about her sexuality. They never discussed stuff like that and she made sure to keep it that way. She didn't know that much about Ian's life either—but they were politically aligned, that was for sure. She was pretty sure he had no idea how hard this hit her. Ian even knew several of her alts—she wondered if he'd noticed her switch to "they/them" pronouns.

What do you mean, homophobic? Can you give me some examples? I don't remember Roxi ever being like that.

Yeah, here you go.

And there it was. One tweet after another.

Too much gay shiz on Twitter.

No homo means NO, HOMO.

Have we decided if Shawn Mendes is gay or not

Ew lesbianic to the max no thank you. Take that shit back to dykeslandia please!!

I am way too selfhating to ever be a lesbian lolz

Oh great now everyone is gay? Is that what we're doing now? Ew

Swing that way? Babes, I'd rather not swing thxxxx

There was probably more. Mina felt so sick reading it all. But it felt true—it sounded like her sister. Even though she hadn't been explicitly homophobic to her, Mina could suddenly see it in her. She was low-key bigoted: fat-phobic, elitist, snobby, all of it. And other than a few gay men at clubs, she'd rarely seen Roxanna with gay friends. Certainly no lesbians. Her vibe was aggressively heterosexual, and so this display of unsolicited hate made sense in a sad way.

Of course, Roxanna hadn't known then, and likely still didn't know, that her little sister probably swung that way.

Mina was depressed and angry. Here she was, trying to help her older sister, and this was who she was. The tweets were all from 2015 to 2017, but that wasn't so long ago. Roxanna would have been in middle and high school and old enough to know better. Mina wondered what else she could have said. She thought if this was what Roxanna put out publicly back then, then . . .

Fuck I feel so sick. I hate this.

Yeah, sorry to find all this. Your sister seems . . . um messy?

Yep. I don't know what to do.

Well, there's nothing you can do. Maybe flag these for her to delete and just tell her to do an apology? Send her the boilerplate ones famous people use?

Mina had no energy to explain she'd offered that. *It's just very hard to excuse all this.*

Definitely. Weird to see homophobia this blatant.

I gotta go, Ian. Thanks so much.

Np. Do you want me to keep sending you stuff I find? For her to delete? They're definitely gonna find these and it looks like she got rid of whatever n-word one they were talking about, if that's not doctored.

She felt sick.

I feel sick. I just want to forget about all this. K anyway talk soon xxoxo

Bye pal x

But of course Mina could not forget all of this. She rolled into bed early and turned on her galaxy nightlight. She tried to lose herself in the sparkle of the fake Milky Way as it rotated peacefully around her.

She kept trying but failing to text Roxanna to delete those posts. She'd grab her phone, write the text, and then delete. She was just too angry. She hated being Roxanna's accomplice. A homophobe's assistant. The disgust she felt was so intense, she was feverish. The worst feeling was how helpless she felt. She fell asleep uncharacteristically early that night, her face streaked with tears, and her body shaking from nightmares, as the galaxy spun onward.

When she woke up the next morning, she knew exactly what to do. She logged onto Twitter under her least-used alt: kittyxkittyxbangxbangx007. This was the account she used for her worst dirty work. "Kitty" was located in "Scandinavia" and she was twenty-four years old. The only tweets she liked were about Wicca and black metal. Her avi was a generic anime girl with purple hair and facial piercings, her eyes looking possessed. She was shocked by the courage Kitty always gave her, and today she knew exactly what to do. She hated having to do it, but she hated the helplessness she had felt even more. She typed:

Uh-oh, I guess Twitter hasn't found the worst of Roxanna-Vanna. What about her homophobia to add to her racism? Quite a collection here and I'll bet there's more! So yuck. #roxannavanna #roxannavannamilani #roxannavannaracist #roxannavannahomophobe #roxannavannabigot #fuckroxannavanna

She attached a cropped screenshot of the tweets Ian had sent her. That would do it. She hit send without hesitation and logged off.

Fuckroxannavanna. It should have been the hardest bit to type, but as Kitty in this merciless and yet equitable world online, it was the most satisfying.

Amazingly, Roxanna never said a word. At least not to her or any-one on the internet. Mina guessed it had less to do with shame and more because of the barrage of hate she was receiving—it probably all just blended in. Kitty had only about eighty-five followers, anyway.

But it haunted Mina. That she had done what she did, that Roxanna had made those tweets. It all felt cursed. It was not her style to attack her sisters in such a sneaky and cruel way, but it also seemed like the right thing to do at the time. She could not bear to confront Roxanna. There would be no point and it would never fix things. At least she'd taken some real step in pushing back.

Still, she was surprised to get a text from Roxanna suddenly, in the group chat she shared with her sisters only, addressed rather impersonally to them all.

Hey, sissies, I need a meeting with you all. Can we do like after din-ner by the pool? It won't take long. I just have to tell you all something important. I've done some soul-searching. I want to do the right thing. Anyway it will all make sense! Don't tell anyone & just be there? Xx

Mina debated going. She had not once said a word to Rox-anna since she discovered those tweets. She couldn't stand the thought of being near her.

Dinner was a blur, and afterward, each sister rather dutifully filed into the garden and over to the pool. They all took their usual seats. Everyone looked a bit shaken. This was not like Roxanna.

Roxanna seemed the most rattled, still in her giant sunglasses, her hair ratty and piled in a disheveled bun on top of her head. She was wearing her usual all-black but this time the sweatpants and crop top gave off a certain solemnity. She had on barely any makeup or else her makeup made it look that way.

"I wish I could say this is about Perry but it's not," she said.

"Pari," Violet corrected, exasperated. "Roxi, lord, that's our cat."

Roxanna looked flustered. "Pari, sorry. I'm sorry the cat is still missing." She paused. "I really am sorry. For, like, a lot. Seriously."

Her sisters nervously glanced at one another.

"As you know," Roxanna said after a very dramatic deep breath, "they've come for me."

"Who's they?" Haylee whispered to Violet, a bit too loud.

"*They* is the internet," Roxanna answered. "*They* is social media. Twitter, probably Instagram and TikTok too, at this point. I can't, like, keep up. But they are trying to take me down and I have no idea who they even are or why." She paused and faced Mina. "We don't know, right?"

Mina turned so red she was nearly purple. Until this moment, she hadn't realized just how scared she was of Roxanna finding out what she had done. "I asked a friend. He's working on it. Nothing yet. Could be . . . anyone."

Roxanna nodded. "It's bad, though. I was trending the other night. I couldn't bring it up—I was just too upset. I've been crying for days. My biggest fear has always been being canceled, and I have to say it's worse than I imagined."

"Can't you just call Dad's publicist to fix it?" Haylee suggested. Even at her age, she sounded like a pro.

Roxanna waved her hands dismissively. "It is just very complicated. I've been working on my apology. I just want it to be really good. But first I thought I should apologize to you all—my team, I mean, my sissies."

They all, in their own way, tried to hide their smirks at the word *team*. They kept quiet, though—Roxanna looked on the verge of tears.

"I lied to all of you too," she said. "Well, not to Mina, really, because she knew. But the rest of you. In different ways, but the basic lie is the same. I wanted to begin with all of you."

"You're scaring me—just say it!" Haylee cried.

Roxanna closed her eyes, as if she were praying. When she opened them, she was still, her head tilted, seemingly asking something of the heavens. And then she turned to them, made eye contact with each and every one, as if she could imagine the cameras.

"Okay, here goes, babes," she said. It had all sounded better in her head. "Well, I've been lying about being Iranian, being Persian, whatever. I've said something else. For a long time."

Mina couldn't stand to look at her, it was so embarrassing. She felt like a slight accomplice for not stopping this back when she'd first heard of it.

Violet angled her head, confused, and Haylee's eyes went super wide.

"So what did you say you are? Or we are, I guess?" Haylee asked.

Roxanna sighed again to the clouds. "I said I—we—are, am, whatever, Italian." She paused. "Not even Damon knows."

"Wait, isn't Damon Italian?" Haylee cried.

The silence was so tense.

"I guess people sometimes think we are anyway and our last name and Pizzabomme," Violet murmured slowly.

"So this whole time everyone thinks I am Italian? Like, when school is in session and I'll be back at the high school they will all be, like, that's Haylee Milani, the Italian sister of Italian Roxanna-Vanna Milani? Is that it?" Haylee looked a bit out-raged, as the magnitude of it all hit her.

"That's why I know, because school, but the good thing is people don't tend to ask too much," Mina blurted out. Even though she was so mad at Roxanna still, she couldn't help but feel sorry for her sister. "We were gonna tell you, Haylee—we just didn't get a chance."

"It's crazy and I'm nuts and I'm so sorry," Roxanna said, her tears suddenly overflowing. "Obviously, I have to fix this with the show. I'll fix it all."

"They might make it a storyline in the show," Haylee said, her eyes still wide.

"I just want it to go away," Roxanna said. "Right now, it's all so nuts. I'm also being accused of Blackfishing when I've been basically whitefishing all these years."

"Persians are basically white," Haylee said. "Persians are white, right?"

Mina rolled her eyes, wondering if this was part of Haylee's MAGA conversion.

"I feel so stupid," Roxanna cried. "I am so sorry to cause this mess and, like, so many other messes. I have to really work on myself. But this is a first step. I've rarely apologized in my life!"

"That's for sure," Violet said. "Hey, we of course forgive you—you're our sister. You don't seem okay, though. How can we help? Can you get counseling? Do you still have that therapist?"

Roxanna shook her head, not even sure who Violet was talking about. "I'm grateful for your forgiveness." She looked at her younger sisters, each of whom looked appalled in her own way.

"Yeah, I forgive you too," Haylee said. "You have always been my favorite and I'm just sad this is happening, though I really hope this doesn't involve us all."

Roxanna nodded. "Me too. It shouldn't. I'll make sure to figure out the apology and the confession."

"You're gonna tell the world about this too, right? After apologizing for the other stuff?" Mina asked.

"I mean, the N-word and Blackfishing—that stuff is pretty major so I just need to focus on that—"

"You haven't made any other bigoted comments? No other nasty tweets?" Mina glared at her.

Roxanna shrugged. "I mean, probably! I haven't searched. I probably should."

Mina nodded. "Yeah, you probably should. Knowing you, there might be some other stuff."

"Mina, be gentle," Violet said under her breath.

But that was it. "I gotta go." Mina suddenly got up. "I don't know if I forgive you, to be honest, Roxanna. You have a way of thinking only about yourself and hurting so many people. I hope this has made you realize that, and I hope you will actually change."

Roxanna sniffled, nodding. "I'm gonna do my best. This has been my worst nightmare."

Violet got up and gave Roxanna a big hug, which made Roxanna cry even harder. Haylee gave her a pat on the shoulder and joined Mina on their way back to the house.

"What the fuck," Haylee whispered as they made their way up the stairs to their respective rooms.

"She's a mess," Mina whispered back.

"I mean, yes, but, like, holy shit." Haylee's whisper grew to a mumble.

"Well, take it as a cautionary tale and make sure this kind of thing never happens to you," Mina said as they parted.

Haylee nodded slowly, all the way to her room. She was Roxanna's mini-me—everyone knew that. But she could never be that messy, she thought. Especially not after this year, not after waking up. She looked out the window, and Roxanna and Violet were still there in an embrace. The sky was unusually clear, perfect twilight indigo, for Los Angeles. The pandemic had cleared much of the city's smog, they said—pretty much every big city had reported this. But Haylee these days saw other problems, the kind only some knew to point out, though she never did publicly. But there they were again: she could make out one, two, three white streaks that were suspect, which had to on some level explain why everyone was acting so out of character these days.

Damon came over for the first time in nearly four months the next day. Roxanna had sent him a cryptic text that he was sure meant a breakup awaited him. He never felt that safe with Roxanna, and he questioned at times if that was part of it—the chase, the constant pursuit of this girl he'd been dating for so many years.

Damon Damiano had had a crush on Roxanna-Vanna Milani since they were in elementary school. Back then, her hair was its natural dark brown and curly and she was a bit of a class clown, beating everyone to jokes and always making the teachers look like fools. He was much shyer and admired how extroverted she was. He knew he was mostly invisible to her—he was so awkward back then, already way too tall for his grade, a bit of a loner. It wasn't until middle school, when he grew into his looks and his height became a bonus, and he became at least mid-range popular, that he got the guts to ask Roxanna to dance during a social. Roxanna had acted like she didn't know who he was, though later she told him she thought he had been cute from a distance. She had a thing for basketball players. They had occasionally hung out after school, and Damon invited her to his birthday party. Roxanna was impressed by the Damiano mansion, and so when, in ninth grade, Damon asked Roxanna to *go out,* she was ready. She had been asked out many times before, but Damon just made the most sense to her. She never imagined it would go on for years and years.

One of their most memorable outings was the Halloween when Damon dressed up as Mario and she as Princess Peach. Damon pointed out they were an Italian couple, and Roxanna shifted the attention to how funny it was that Damon decided to be a short guy for Halloween. But other than that, they just never spoke about their ethnicities, their heritage, their families, or anything. They were just a normal teenage couple.

Often when Roxanna felt the urge to lie to Damon, that would be her sign that they needed an off-period. She might hook up with another guy she had a crush on, but often—like this time—she barely even knew why she had asked for a break. Damon could be boring, and that was the biggest difference between them. Roxanna was anything but boring—Damon often wished she was a bit more boring, actually. But Roxanna was addicted to drama the way Damon was allergic to it and so maybe it was, as the saying went, a case of opposites attracting.

Who knew, but Roxanna was very aware that she needed all the allies in the world at that moment. She was a bit irked by Mina's reaction, but otherwise, confessing to her sisters had gone better than she'd imagined. She found the courage that night to text Damon and ask him over the next day. As cringey as it was, it felt right to do it in person. Somehow in her heart she knew Damon would forgive her, but she was still so stressed about it.

Damon, meanwhile, was rattled by her formality. He freaked, thinking this would be the real, once-and-for-all breakup he had dreaded for years. He tried to pick out an outfit she would love—a Brooks Brothers dress shirt and Armani slacks, a bit too dressy, but he wanted her to know that after this long separation, it was a big deal to him to see her. He picked up some red tulips at a corner boutique, and he pulled up in his red Tesla Model S.

He could see her long legs dangling on a chaise by the pool. She was wearing a white silk robe and little makeup. The minute she saw him, her eyes filled with tears, and she ran up to him and hugged him so tight. She could almost hear Mina's voice going on about *social distancing* but she couldn't bring herself to care. She hadn't expected to have missed him that much. His body felt warm and receptive and she could feel it on him that he had missed her too.

"Hi, my baby," he whispered in her ear. "God, I missed you so much, Roxi."

She cried into his chest, as far as she got up to him even with

Balenciaga platforms. "I miss you too, babe—god, I miss you too!"

He put the tulips in between them. "I got you these."

She cried even harder. She wished they were roses, but she was too upset to even let that thought simmer too long. She didn't even deserve tulips. "I, like, do not deserve anything! I am a monster, Damon, I really am! I don't deserve this, you, anything!"

He looked at her, so perplexed. This wasn't going to be a breakup, or if it was, it was because she had done something. Maybe she had cheated on him again, but he never recalled her crying so hard about all that. In fact, he'd never seen her crying so hard at all.

"Roxi, what's going on, baby?" he said, wiping her tears with his thumb on her cheek. She looked strangely beautiful all puffy like that.

"Have a seat," she said and then promptly sat right on his lap before getting up and sitting across from him. This was no time to be sexy or cute. "I, like, don't even know where to start! I told my sisters last night."

He was confused.

"Okay, just give me a second," she said, breathing deeply with her eyes closed, as if doing some yogic meditation exercise. She was muttering what sounded like prayers under her breath and he realized he had never seen Roxanna pray either. It was supremely weird and extremely beautiful.

She was taking longer than he expected, but he didn't want to interrupt the beauty of the moment, so he joined her. It shocked him to do it, but he thought, *Why not?* The pandemic was a strange time and maybe prayer made sense for everyone. He didn't really know what to pray to or how it should sound, but he found himself whispering in a loop: *Dear God, let everything be okay, let everything that can be okay be okay, let me and Roxi and my parents and all our friends and all the good people find their way and let this pandemic be over soon and let everything right stay right and everything wrong turn right and everything lost be found again . . .*

He suddenly felt something warm and soft at his shins, as if it were probing under his slacks, something a bit light and airy and soft, between feathery and furry, and he opened his eyes. It was Pari nudging herself at him. He chuckled to himself—he had missed her.

When Roxanna opened her eyes, her eyes were too full of tears to understand what that white blob that Damon was cradling was. It took her a second to register the big Persian cat in his arms as the house cat they'd been searching for.

"Oh my god, Perry is back," she whispered. It was almost a miracle, an omen. She couldn't wait to tell everyone—especially that it was Damon, of all people, who had summoned her back.

Damon nuzzled the cat's mounds of shaggy hair. She smelled like rain and flowers and dirt. "What do you mean, 'back'?"

Roxanna laughed softly through her tears. "A long story—or I mean one I don't know well. But it's just . . . this lockdown time, Damon. We lost so much."

Damon nodded slowly, though he wasn't sure what she meant. She moved in to hug him again and Pari leaped out of his arms and out of their sight, into the Milani mansion, bounding up the stairs and into Mina's room as she was walking out to gather the pots and pans for her seven o'clock ritual.

She was embracing Pari with more tears in her eyes than she could have imagined when her cell went off. Roxanna had notified their group chat: *PERRY IS BACK, BITCHES!!!!!*

Book II

~~The War~~
~~The Pandemic~~
The Party

11

Production

"None of them feel . . . usable?" The producer was searching for the right word in the production meeting and that was all he could come up with.

"What do you mean? Is the quality off?"

"No, of course these girls can afford the best tech, but the stuff they say in these video journals—it's just not good TV, you know?"

The other producers looked at one another glumly. "Whose is the best?" one asked.

"Well, I would have thought Roxanna-Vanna's would top everyone's but she barely remembers to do them and when she does—I think she's on a bunch of drugs? Violet's are just boring, very pretty, but boring. Haylee's lately are almost good in that they are so nuts, but maybe too nuts? And Mina's have the opposite problem: they're too sane. She's a normal smart person. I actually think Al's have the most potential—oh, and Homa hasn't done a single one." The producer looked exhausted.

"Maybe we can see some of the ones that are strongest? I'm not ready to give up on this show yet," another producer said.

"No one said give up," the producer insisted. "It's just . . . we need to talk to them."

"It's a pandemic, you know. What are they supposed to be sending us?" another offered.

Still another producer chimed in. "When we really begin to shoot, we'll have the best material, I am sure—the show can't ride on confessionals. No show does. Plus, it's all in the editing."

The producer shrugged and began to pull up files on his laptop, which he had wired to play on their big screen. "Let's just get Haylee's over with." He pulled up a file and immediately there was Haylee, looking very serious, wide-eyed and alert, her white-blond bob perfectly glossed. She was wearing a peach velour hoodie and matching sweatpants, workout clothes, it seemed, the luxury kind.

"Okay, I think this thing is on. Sorry I haven't updated in a while. A lot has been happening, and I mean a lot. Where to begin? Well, I wonder how many people know about the depopulation agenda and how it correlates to the virus. In China, the convenient line has been about the Wuhan wet markets but what if I told you those bats were not real bats—"

"Let's skip that one," one of the other producers sighed.

"Agree," another one piped up.

"See what I mean?" the producer said. He couldn't even laugh. "Let's try Mina. Opposite vibe—here you go."

The camera zoomed in on Mina, who was trying to find a good angle. Mina looked chic, in jeans and a T-shirt featuring a K-pop group.

She smiled and waved. "Hi, production team! It's me, Mina. Anyway, what to report? It's been a time, we might say! This pandemic has really tested us all. Mom and Dad are their usual, mostly, although I don't think they imagined how awful it would be to be stuck with all of us all the time. Violet is doing okay— she was having some issues with food but she's better now. Roxanna is a mess and I really don't even want to talk about her. Haylee has become a conspiracy theorist and maybe even a low-key white supremacist? Yeah, I don't know. Randy got COVID but recovered—their family is okay. Oh, Pari—our cat—went missing but returned. Let's see . . . I don't talk to anyone else,

really, except my friend Ian in Ohio. I mean, we mainly text.
Oh—I know—have I mentioned how at seven each day I go out
on the balcony and bang on pans? I even played a horn once! It's
a ritual, worldwide, where we honor rescue efforts. I think most
of my family hates it, but I will keep doing it. In K-pop news,
well, it's pretty sad—all my favorite groups had to stop touring
this spring even though South Korea's rates are so much lower
than ours—and only about four or five idols have tested positive
so far—"

The producer stopped the tape. "Well, you see, it just goes on
like that. Stunningly boring. Like, you tell me what we could
clip there?"

Everyone just blinked.

"Let's move on to Violet. . . ." He pulled hers up. Immediately, the image was way more professionally produced, with a
ring-light glow and some kind of filter. Violet's hair was in one
long braid and she wore perfect makeup that went elegantly
with her floral dress. She was smiling shyly. In her hand, she held
something that looked like a bouquet of cake pops.

"Here we are again. It's me, Banafsheh, more popularly
known as Violet. Well, I wanted to go by my real name but all
my sisters—even Mina, amazingly—thought it would be a bad
idea. I thought it would be worse when we were going to war
but that seems to be on pause? Funny how war can be, no? You
can just hit pause. Like, if it's so easy to say time-out on war, why
have it, anyway? It makes me think, maybe they can just put it
off forever? Anyway, I was so sure I was sick the other day but
then Mom pointed out I'd only had cupcake batter and frosting
all day. I really am trying to eat a bit better. I had an episode a
while ago where I tried to throw up—and I did—and it was just
so bad. What a cliché for a model. Roxi seemed to think it was
almost cool, but we know she has eating issues. Anyway, I'm
not doing that anymore. I've started to think plus-size modeling might be a better fit for me anyway. I hate to exercise and

just can't get myself to take up Haylee's offers at the gym, even though everyone says it would be good for me. So if I can't do that and I just want to eat like this all the time, eventually I will get bigger. So why not commit to the plus-size life? We're really in a dawn of positivity these days—"

He shut it off. "Sorry—she goes on and on. Modeling shit. But she's really gorgeous, that's for sure."

Everyone nodded blankly.

"And then there's Roxanna-Vanna." He pulled up what he thought might be her most usable confessional, a more recent one.

At first she appeared as a blur but then she backed up and they could see her face: teary, puffy, streaked with mascara and smudged lipstick. Numerous gold chains hung around her neck, almost blending with her wiry, damaged honey-blond hair and copper tube top. "Hi, world," she began, slurring. "This has been the worst week of my life but maybe also it has been for the best? I'm not making sense already, goddammit. I had a few drinks and a few smokes and a few pills." She laughed off into the distance and proceeded to cry. In the background, some generic hip-hop played. "So like I told everyone—well, the sissies. Not Mom and Dad, 'cause whatever, or, like, all of social media. But I had to. I got canceled. Bound to happen. They tried before. But this time was like big-time. I thought I was gonna die. And so I told them and I guess now I am telling the producer—hi—which is weird, I know, 'cause I thought I could call you, but here I am. So it's kind of a big deal, and something I made up ages ago. I just never thought I'd live in, like, a world where I'd be, like, famous and I'd owe a public the truth. But here we are! Like, what a mess. Anyway, I don't lie this much usually, so don't think that, but yeah, I did tell a big lie and one that has went on for years. Ugh, I do not want to talk about it, but these confessionals might be the best place—somehow easier than making an IG post or something. Anyway, I lied about us . . . about

me. About who I, like, am. I mean, not entirely who I am, but
where I am from. Like, I said I am from Italy when really it's
another I-country, which, duh, you producers know well. And
you would not get it—you probably don't know Iranians have
passed for Italians for ages and I wasn't the first person to come
up with this idea. But it just seemed like the right thing to do at
school and they always, like, think my last name is Italian anyway
and plus Dad doing the Pizzabomme thing—why not. Anyway,
I decided to come clean. Because of all y'all! Like, the show did
this to me. I had no choice. The show is all about us being the
first big Iranian reality TV family and so how could I even be
Italian? Anyway, it was all cringe and yes I am cringe, and what
else is new. It's over now, though, like, dealing with the school
and the public—I mean, it's possible the public knows, but Dad
always made sure we never dwelled too much on ethnicity in
our public profiles, you know? So there's not much you can dig
up about us and Iran. But now with the show—anyway! I am a
mess. I am doing too many drugs too so that will be a hoot. But
I am gonna get more clean and change my ways, I swear. Okay,
logging off, ugh, like, peace, bitches!"

The production team looked transfixed suddenly, to the shock
of the producer. Maybe he had just watched it too many times.
But somehow Roxanna's tape had them.

"I love it," one of them said. "She's the one. A star. Isn't she
our star, anyway?"

"She is," the producer said slowly. "You don't think she's . . .
a mess?"

"Of course she is," another said. "But this is reality TV—we
are in the business of messes!"

"It's amazing—her confession is a scoop, no? Who pretends
to be an ethnicity they are not their whole life? Trainwreck
city!"

"Isn't she the one who legally changed her birthday so she'd
have a different zodiac sign?!"

"I love it—I can't wait to see what happens next!"

"And can we just say, even with the drugs and crying and whatever, Roxanna-Vanna looks increds?"

The producer sighed. Frozen on the screen was Roxanna, making a peace sign with her tongue sticking out to the side in the wacky way influencers all seemed to do these days. He hadn't thought to worry about this. For months now, a part of him had wished the show would just get dropped.

"I can't wait to see if her crazy ass will change her ways for real!" one of the producers was saying.

"Do you really believe that?" The producer was a bit stunned. Maybe the pandemic had them all rusty. "Do you believe this girl here will actually for real change her ways?"

But he couldn't kill their mood. Roxanna was, as usual, as they were about to understand, in spite of herself, even, in spite of all of them, somehow too powerful.

Roxanna really did believe she had changed on some level. In the weeks to come, she started to meditate a bit (thanks to Haylee) before her exercise sessions, though she would duck out once the actual exercising began. She started a journal. She decided she might one day write her own memoir, and that she could even become a writer, if she had to have a real job, though being a writer sounded far from having a real job. She decided to be a better girlfriend to Damon and a better sister to her sisters. She had also gotten back in touch with her crew who she had ditched somewhat at the start of the pandemic. She also decided she would do less drugs—she was going to keep to the prescribed dose of Adderall and the Xanax, and use weed only on the weekends—and she was going to drink White Claw and champagne only.

All of these changes had started to make her feel like a new person, so much so that she had almost forgotten about her crisis, about being canceled. It was around that time, between self-forgiveness and complete, vapid forgetfulness, that Roxanna returned to her party idea.

Maybe it could be a Persian coming-out party, although that might be weird for the people she went to school with, but maybe only some could know. Maybe it could just be a big, regular party, like the kind they used to have.

They had all been through so much; a party was just what they needed.

Roxanna decided to go to her parents again. If they gave the okay, then no one else would be able to override that decision, and she was pretty sure she could work her charm on Al. He was into parties and he probably had his own people he wanted over—that could be the compromise.

They could even pretend the pandemic was over. If there was one thing Roxanna had learned in the past weeks it was that mindset was everything, and part of being okay was just telling yourself you were okay. The rest would fall into place somehow, wouldn't it.

She gave a long speech to Homa and Al.

". . . and I will bet the producers will love it and maybe this is where the actual production could start! You know, like if the network can okay that, if, like, the virus numbers go down or whatever. I just think it's time for this and we could all, like, use it, and why not? We've been suffering, like, so much."

It was hard to read their faces. Homa was squinting as if reading fine print and chewing on her bottom lip, glancing at Al every few sentences; Al seemed preoccupied, but snapped out of it every so often enough to smile and nod.

"Well, I think—and this is not just my decision—that it would be fun!" Al finally said. "Don't you, Homa?"

Homa shrugged. "You all know I was never a party person," Homa began carefully. "And I think it can be dangerous. Don't forget what happened to Randy. They say the vaccines will be here soon enough, no? Maybe we should wait?"

Al shrugged. "That makes sense to me too. What's the rush, Roxi?"

Roxi groaned. "I don't know—I just wasn't built for nothing to happen! I am getting restless. Everywhere is closed. People are, like, so bored. We keep doing these video confessionals but there is nothing to tell. I used to go to like several parties a week!"

"No one is having any parties right now," Homa said. "This is a global emergency."

"Yeah, it could be bad publicity, Roxanna," Al said gently. "Especially after what happened a while ago. Do we want more bad press?"

The sisters had eventually filled Al in on how Roxanna had been canceled, and he had been very relieved it had not affected his own business.

Roxanna sulked at her parents. It was hard to argue with that.

"You just can't have life without *events,*" she said. "Events like your pearl anniversary, remember that? Remember life events?!"

"We *have* events!" Homa said. "The event is the pandemic."

Roxanna groaned. "You don't get it. I'm the Main Character. I've always been the Main Character. Like, what do I do now?"

Al and Homa looked at her helplessly.

"What if it never even ends," she said with a whimper on her way out.

They were both relieved when she was gone, because they didn't have an answer.

The producers set up a video conference with the sisters the next week. They all gathered in Al's conference room, eager to hear what the staff had to say about their confessionals.

"Well, I just want to say we are all so pleased to have you all and it was such a delight to receive your confessionals," the main producer said. "So, please just take all we have to say with a grain of salt—this isn't meant to be criticism, it's just what we thought our viewers may also think of. But remember you are our stars and you should do what you want. Does that make sense?"

They all nodded, with varying degrees of enthusiasm.

"Okay, let's start with Roxanna-Vanna," the main producer said, looking at his notes. "Roxanna, you're a hit. No one has much to say other than what you've done is amazing. It's fabulous, perfection. We are all in. Just give us more of the same, okay? You've been really raw and honest and it's having big payoffs."

Roxanna grinned. "Thanks. I was sort of born for this!" She laughed, rolling her eyes. "So you don't think I've been too, like, I don't know, too messy?"

The main producer paused. "Well, you have, but that's perfect—we want that. For you. It's great. Keep it up!"

Roxanna laughed again. "Wow, okay then. That's the first time no one has talked me out of a mess!"

"Okay, Violet, let's look at your notes," the main producer went on, trying to figure out how to put what he was going to say. "Violet, you look absolutely to die for. Great outfits. On aesthetics you are a ten. You are a model, of course. Anyway, we love it. Just wondering if maybe you could be a little less technical in your anecdotes?"

Violet's expression went from beam to frown. "Technical? How do you mean?"

The main producer froze a bit. "It's just—it gets a bit bogged down, all the details. A bit slow."

"He's saying you're snoozy, Vivs! Spice it up!" Roxanna interjected.

Violet looked wounded. "Really?"

The main producer wasn't sure what to say when that was

the truth. "I mean, it's not boring, but you just need to keep it moving for our viewers. Short attention spans, you know! Just move it along!"

Violet tilted her head, a bit confused. She turned to Roxanna and in a lowered voice asked, "Can you show me?"

Roxanna grabbed her hand, nodding confidently.

"Okay, let's move on to Mina," the main producer said. "Mina, the feedback is the same. You're a joy, we really love having you—you are so very stabilizing, relatable, smart, centered. We love that anchor. So wise beyond your years! But maybe it gets a bit slow or just kind of a tad, you know, too normal?"

Mina turned red. She hated this so much. "I mean, I'm just being myself. Are we supposed to act some part?" she muttered. She didn't want to sound rude, but she found it so insulting. She could not imagine a test where Roxanna passed and she failed.

"Oh, Mina, don't get me wrong—we absolutely love you, can't get enough of you!" the main producer exclaimed. "Just maybe bring in whatever wild or unpredictable or weird thing you got going on? Just for the viewers—they really are like children, gotta keep them fed!"

Mina nodded slowly, trying to suppress an eye roll. Violet glanced at her sympathetically.

"And finally, Haylee," the main producer said, dreading this one. Where to start, and she was the youngest too. He had to be careful. "Haylee, we adore you too. Such spicy stuff, interesting, mind-blowing. The viewers are not bored one bit! Really riveting. But maybe . . ." He really was at a loss at how to say this.

"Too far out? Too weird? Conspiracy stuff?" Haylee offered. She had predicted this, knowing very well her entries would stand out from her sisters'.

"Well . . . yes!" The main producer was grateful, surprised by her self-awareness. "I mean, some of it does get a bit scary, which is fine for us, but it could make the audience, I don't know, confused!"

"Not everyone is ready for the truth—I get it," Haylee said coldly.

"That's it, right," the main producer said. "So, do you think we could tone it down? The virus, apocalypse, government stuff?"

"I don't want to be, like, censored," Haylee said, again as if she had rehearsed it.

"You know, Haylee, do what you need to do! We are not censoring. If this is you right now, then so be it. Go for it." He really just wanted this conversation to be over.

"I can help you, Hayles." Roxanna winked at her.

"All in all, you're all doing great!" the main producer said.

"But what if we don't have much to say? I mean, my career has been at such a pause. Nothing is happening. Every day is the same," Violet said.

"Well, and that's very understandable," the main producer said. "You guys could always do something some of our other shows do and you could create content for the confessionals. You know what I mean? Instead of just going on about your day, you can write something to read for the camera about any topic."

"Oh my god, like a school essay?" Roxanna was horrified.

"Oh, wow, I could do an essay!" Mina said.

"Well, no and yes!" The main producer chuckled nervously, trying to make sure everyone was appeased. "You *could* make it like an essay or you could not! Roxanna, you really just do what you did before. No changes there, hon. But the rest of you, yeah, you could think of a topic you like and riff on that. You could write an essay, but just keep it lively and entertaining!"

"I mean, they all go to school, so it should not be hard," Violet pointed out. "And I'd prefer that, actually."

"Me too," Mina said.

"Me too—it's a perfect way for me to share all the critical information I've been gathering, as long as my freedom of speech is not threatened," Haylee said.

"Of course not," the producer said gently. He could not stand Haylee. There was no way around it. "Anyway, see what you come up with! That's all I wanted to share today. Things are obviously on pause with the pandemic but we still hope to tape soon!"

"Thanks so much again!" Roxanna smiled, taking the lead. "It's an honor to be doing this, and I am sure my sisters agree. We're gonna give you lots of good stuff. I will, like, totally help them. We are gonna be like the top-rated show for sure!"

Roxanna's sisters looked at her like she was crazy, but she didn't care. She had already gotten her approval where it mattered most. They saw her star power. Soon the world would too.

No one could stop it—the party was not something that could be stopped. Homa and Al never officially said no, Roxanna felt, so she used that to ask the producers. At first they expressed the usual hesitation—the pandemic, lockdown, possible bad press, and so on—but by the end of the call, they were convinced. Roxanna agreed to pay for her own film crew, and they agreed it could make for a good opening episode. Fun, a bit high-risk, definitely messy—it was Roxanna's brand.

Roxanna was already making lists and debating arrangements by the time the producers called Al to tell them it was a go.

Al went to see Roxanna that evening in her room. It was seven and they could hear Mina's banging and cheering on the balcony.

"Roxi, I don't know how your mother and sisters are going to feel about this," he began.

"Haylee is in and Violet can be won over and whatever about Mina. We've been putting up with her daily craziness every day!" She motioned to the upstairs balcony. "I can win them all over. Can you win Mom?"

Al sighed. "*Aziz,* you know I love a party. You have my genes. And I can win over your mother, of course, but right now, in private, we can be very honest together. Let's go over the what-ifs. That's part of my job, how I run my business. I do risk assessment. Okay?"

Roxanna shrugged. "Sure, but what's the worst that happens? It gets reported online and people cancel me again? I just survived that and I barely even had to use any publicists!"

Al sighed again. "No, I think a worst-case scenario is everyone getting the virus. What then?"

Roxanna rolled her eyes. "Then they get better! Aren't we all gonna get this thing until there's a vaccine? I mean, no one dies of this, or barely any people, right? I mean, not people like us— not people like my party guests."

"It can kill anyone."

"How many, like, legit rich people have, like, died of this, Dad?" Roxanna challenged. "They get sick, they get the best health care in the world, and done. I feel sorry for poor people— it really is not fair. But what can you do? We were blessed! Even Randy totally recovered!"

Al found, as he often did in these kinds of discussions with his second-oldest daughter, that he both disagreed and agreed with her. Roxanna often had a point, but how she went about it? It was messy.

"They are calling these parties superspreaders. With all the bad press on Iran, can we really be 'superspreaders'?"

Roxanna's eyes flashed excitedly—an idea had popped in her head. "Oh, oh, I got it! Everyone, like, has to have, like, a doctor's note from that day or the day before. A negative test and, like, a clean bill of health. We could have special maids use disinfecting agents all through the night."

Al paused. On the one hand, this daughter was screeching at him for a big party in the middle of the pandemic; on the other hand, another daughter was thanklessly making a symbolic gesture every night on the balcony to recognize the collective suffering and sacrifice this pandemic had brought about. It was hard to resist Roxanna, especially when he wanted this too, but he knew it could be a major mistake.

"Okay, Roxi, very carefully and cautiously and all that, we can go ahead, but I really need you and everyone on top of every detail," he finally said. "I don't want this to be bad for business."

Roxanna cheered as if watching a favorite concert. "Thank you, thank you, thank you, Dad!" She noticed that his eyes looked sadder than she wished they would. "I promise I will do this right and nothing bad will happen! Promise."

Al nodded. "I just want you to keep in mind, though, that I have a bad feeling about this. I just have to tell you that."

Roxanna turned around to glare at him mockingly. "Oh, Dad, didn't you have the same bad feeling about Pizzabomme?"

Al was amazed she remembered that anecdote. A year into his business, he had been plagued by this feeling that it would all be a disaster. Then things took a big turn up. Since then, he had learned to doubt his instincts. After all, his first instinct about Homa had been wrong too—she had stayed with him.

"You have a point," he murmured and got up to leave.

"I always do!" she said with a laugh in her singsongy Roxanna-Vanna way.

The bad feeling never quite left Al, not until long after the party and, some could argue, the pandemic. He thought about stopping her, about giving Roxanna a few more concrete warnings, but she was already somewhere else. God had taken the wheel, whether he liked it or not.

Roxanna was on the phone with her old stylist, laughing as she rolled a joint and dreamed up her many outfits. "Anything, anything! Pull absolutely whatever you can and then some! And I don't want to look girlish—like, I want to be a woman! Like,

old, yesss! Like, the lady of the house or something—like, someone who is over it, you know? Old! Like, I don't know . . . *old
old,* like, maybe just off the top of my head . . . twenty-six?"

The Hervé Léger Bandage Dress
by Roxanna Milani

*the hervé léger bandage dress here we are ok so it has only been
in production from 1989-1997 and from 2008-present, but it
would be no exaggeration to consider them the most iconic dress in
modern history. truly 'body-con' would not be in our vocabularies
if it were not for this perfect creation.*

*hervé léger's dresses became the it-dress slowly in the early
1990s. who is hervé léger, you may ask? he was born as hervé
peugnet on may 30 1957 in northern france and died on october 6
2017. he studied sculpture and shortly after became a hairstylist.
from there, he began designing hats and bags. he soon tried dresses.
in 1980, he met lagerfeld and three days later, he was hired to
work as lagerfeld's assistant, at fendi and then at chanel. hervé
peugnet became léger at the suggestion of lagerfeld. when max
azria took over the brand in the late '90s, léger used the last name
leroux for the new label he started in 2000 but honestly all these
names are getting confusing and all you need to know is he was
the hervé léger of the bandage dresses (of which I have 4, my older
sister has 3, and I think even my mom has 1).*

*at age 28, he began working for himself, the hervé léger line. he
also worked as a freelance haute couture designer at lanvin. and he
worked at diane von furstenberg and swarovski.*

*his first take on the first bandage dress was the finale look of
hervé léger's 1989 runway show originally called "bender dress,"
it became an instant hit. (the dress was called "bender" because it
bended the body into the ideal feminine form). he went as far as*

having mannequins created based on the exact measurements of his client which like wow.

what exactly is a bandage dress, you might ask? (how can you not know lol) anyway it's simply a tight-fitting dress that appears to be made from multiple thin strips of cloth sewn together, with the individual strips shaped like bandages. while it is most closely associated with the designer hervé léger, it is important to note the "king of cling" azzedine alaïa was the designer of the dress. (king of cling!!!) so he included bandage dresses in his collections in the mid-1980s; in fact, legendary performer grace jones was wearing a bandage dress from azzedine alaïa's spring/summer 1986 collection as she accompanied him onstage to accept his "designer of the year" award at the 1985 oscars de la mode. Iconique!

anyway a bunch of weird business stuff i don't really understand happened and then it was relaunched in 2008 under bcbg max azria hervé léger. that's when it reached a much larger audience. after bcbg max azria released a capsule collection of the hervé léger dress in 2007 bandage dresses were all over the red carpet through the early 2010s but today many insiders even still do not realize that hervé léger dresses were around before 2008. sorry this part is so boring but I just don't know what people know these days, only a few people it seems really get fashion . . .

anyway the point is this dress is just everything and everyone has always known it. even now in 2020, as the 20-tens and 20-teens come back into style, you can see fashion's top insiders and hollywood's biggest stars bringing back this look in such a way that you have to ask, was it ever even gone? you can't miss a bitch that never leaves! and I mean please: kate moss, saweetie, beyoncé, olivia rodrigo, kim kardashian west, jlo, and roxanna-vanna milani can't all be wrong—

Oh, yikes, my bad—can we, like, cross out Olivia Rodrigo? Don't mention this—

Sure? Is there a beef there or something?

Oh, no—I don't know her.

Then . . . ?

I just—there only needs to be one Gen Z on there! I'm plenty!

The sisters were all mired in mixed emotions but Mina was ready to flip out, to flood their group chat with some choice words for her older sister. But she knew it was hopeless—Al and Homa were already on board with the party, and so were the producers. It was done. She should have tried to thwart Roxanna's plans earlier, but now it was too late. And what difference did any of it really make? Things were so hopeless. The pandemic was not ending. Mina told no one that she had grown sick of performing her seven o'clock ritual. Celebrities were getting canceled for traveling during the pandemic and throwing parties, but none of it really mattered. Nothing mattered in the pandemic. People would just move on from one horrible topic to the next—no one's defamation even felt like such a big deal, as none of it compared to the scale of atrocity around them. Let Roxanna have her party, let it blow up in her face, and let them all move on, Mina thought. It was just another meaningless, awful thing in a meaningless, awful period.

Mina decided she would try to be away during the night of the party, which was to be a "Midsummer Night's Maskerade." Roxanna had thought it was a clever way to get people to remember to wear masks and to feel festive about it. She wanted to keep the attention on that and not the fact that it would be the day of her pre-zodiac-reassignment nineteenth birthday (*Gemini life is, like, bye-bye!*). She'd openly and properly celebrate nineteen in November—hopefully the pandemic would be history—though it was an afterthought at best, as nineteen felt like such a nothing year after the officially adult glamour of eighteen had passed.

Of course she sets it on her real birthday so no one can bear to actually cancel it—such a monster! Mina kept thinking. *Not gonna go.* But then it occurred to Mina she had nowhere to go. All her friends, like Ian, were spread around the country or, in the case of some of her K-pop friends, around the world. She would just hide in her room. She'd pull down the blackout curtains, put in earplugs. She could just ignore it.

It wasn't until Roxanna started to tease the party on social media that Mina really lost it. People were starting to, for one thing, make the connection that they were sisters. Another moderator of a prominent K-pop Instagram account wrote her, concerned: *Is Roxanna-Vanna your sister? And are you okay with this stunt she is pulling? Who has a party in a pandemic? Can you say something to her? Sorry if this is weird.* Variations of that message came flooding in. She didn't know what to say, so she ignored them. She knew that eventually the messages were going to reach some boiling point and she would have to come up with a line. She worried that if she publicly spoke out against Roxanna, the producers could use the drama as a plot point for the show. She didn't want that.

But it irked her to see Roxanna's popularity skyrocket from the social media party promotion. Flocks of gay men from all over the world were on her IG. Maybe it was the more over-the-top hair and makeup she was presenting? Maybe it was how she was suddenly adding lots of new followers, the optics of transcendent popularity? Maybe it was the gay talent she had hired, from drag queens to a beauty team that would offer makeovers on the spot? Maybe it was the A-list crowd she had invited? It was hard to know, but when she saw a headline that called her sister QUEER ICON ROXANNA-VANNA MILANI, Mina felt like she had been repeatedly punched in the head. How could this happen? Mina had never wanted to be famous—it wasn't that she wanted to be known as a "queer icon." But her sister? She just could not be the one known out there for her queerness. This was a new level of pandemic madness, and Mina was reaching her limit.

Queer icon wtf Roxi, she wrote in a text to her sister.

Isn't that cute? Love being an ally!

How are you anywhere close to an ally? You never do or say a thing?

Mina, I get that this is your lane, but you get the lesbs and non-binaries and the trans. These are gay men. What on earth would you offer them?

Mina's blood boiled. *Okay, but what are you doing to get this reputation? How are you overnight this queer-loving sensation? I just don't get it.*

Oh, Mina! You know how it works. There's like a bad neighborhood, then the gays move in, then everyone wants in. That's what me and my team decided. Let's get it hyped with the gays first! That's why we have the drag queens—a bunch of RuPaul's Drag Race *faves!—and stuff like that! And we were right, then everyone got like so excited!*

The most annoying thing about Roxanna—or one of the most annoying things about her—was that she was kind of smart.

So manipulative, Roxi.

Roxanna typed a bunch of crazy-smiley-face emojis just to drive home the point that she was totally unbothered. *Maybe you can like be involved? Don't you think it's time for you to come out? To not just us but to the world? I mean, it's 2020!*

Mina froze. She was not ready to go there, and she hated Roxanna's confidence in going there with her. *I am not discussing that with you.*

Oooh did not deny! No prob, girl. Like I accept you. Anyway there's gonna be lots of hot girls and Haylee already said we could use her pole to put in the basement as a stripper pole. So I was thinking we could get some, you know, special dancers too! I am sure Dad would not object!

Mina was still stuck on *I accept you.* That was the thing. Out of all her family members, Mina went back and forth on just how accepting Roxanna could be—her communities were often way more queer than any of theirs, but she never seemed like a safe person. Haylee, she knew, would continue to be so weird about it, and Violet was definitely more traditional than people thought—she'd probably just be awkward about it, and alarmed. Al and Homa—who could be sure? But with Roxanna, in spite of the awful tweets, there was always a surprising degree of hope within the hopelessness. She knew Roxanna found being queer trendy and flashy, cool. She probably thought it was a major plus for her look to have a queer sister.

The idea of the stripper pole turned Mina red. She was astounded Roxanna thought she would be into that. How mortifying. She really would have to hide.

A party of this magnitude, your whole rep could be diff once back at school and like who knows when that is. But you could even find true love or something—we're thinking 500+ people. There'll be so many people and maybe you can get out of your weird nun state!

Mina was livid. *No one thinks of me as a nun but you. I'm a teenager! So are you.*

Oh, girl, all you do all day is play video games and pine after kpop stars who will never breathe the same air as you. Don't you want to actually exist?????!!

That last line would haunt her for a long while. She did not exist, not at home, at school, online, anywhere. It was scary how Roxanna could read her.

And then die of the virus, I guess? Whatever, at this rate, I don't even care what happens to anyone—this pandemic is never ending. Mina added a bunch of weird-alien-head emojis just to throw her off.

We will survive, Mini, that's the thing, we always do. Especially folks like us. We might as well live it up for all the people who can't.

'Cause they're dead?

No no, cuz they're poor.

After confronting Mina, Roxanna felt she could now plan her party in peace. But she did not predict that Haylee would cause her problems too.

"It can't all be liberals, Rox," Haylee said to her. "I really need a good look at the guest list. Like, I get that it will be mostly a bunch of druggy trans radical left communists or whatever, but some of my people need to be there too. I'm just getting to know them but I really want to have them be part of my world."

Roxanna tried to hide her disgust—it had become so hard tolerating this side of Haylee lately, but she had to try, as alienating her main supporter in the household was not going to win her favors. "We're all allowed to have some of our own guests and then there's the general people—like the people we don't know as well, but who just need to be there, the A-list, of course. And I mean, I can't control their politics, Hayles. Like, sorry, MAGAland is not in style right now."

"It *is* in style—you are just in your liberal bubble," Haylee said. Her smile was cold steel. "I don't want to argue with you. You just know by now the stakes are high here. This party can ruin each of us. You could get canceled again, Dad could get in trouble and it could look bad for business, Violet's agency could freak out. I know I'm young but you guys have not paid attention to how much I personally do have at stake too. I've been building my network for months."

Roxanna was working so hard to suppress an eye roll. She tried to tell herself what Violet had reminded her of, that Haylee was young and this was a phase. "Okay, like, your network can come. I mean, this is a big estate! Hundreds can come! This is a summer party—it will be, like, indoors and outdoors! Tons of room for whatever freaks you want!"

"My people will be the only non-freaks," Haylee said coolly.

"Oh, sure, whatever, Haylee!" Roxanna just laughed it off. "Anyway, it will be, like, so fun! I love how, like, the theme—"

"Oh, that's another thing—my people don't wear masks," Haylee said.

Roxanna almost lost it. "Oh my god, Haylee, why on earth? This is to add some semblance of safety and to still make it cute! 'Mask-erade'—get it? When life hands you masks, make mask-erade! Anyway what is your problem with masks? Are you an anti-masker now for real?"

Haylee just kept her stony glare on Roxanna. "I am not anti-anything but lies," she said. "There is no scientific evidence masks work. In fact, there is some evidence they make you sicker—you breathe in the virus through that covering even worse. And not being able to see people's facial expressions? Hiding their faces from each other? Don't you see how our governments are trying to control us? Taking away our basic humanity? They say young children's brains cannot develop if they are deprived from their mother's facial expressions. Also it's just another paranoid nod to the fallacy of this pandemic. Bowing down to—"

"Haylee, please stop," Roxanna said, so alarmed at Haylee's conviction. "This is just, like, too much. You've really been going too far with all this. It's so uncool, Hayles!"

"No, there's a whole world, actually, that finds you and your world uncool," Haylee responded, with the same measured iciness. "They don't care what you think. They live in service of the truth. You'll all see when the truth comes out. They are on the right and they are good, honest, intelligent Americans who are fighting for their rights."

"Yeah, just a bunch of crazy white supremacists!" Roxanna shot back.

"God, you are so brainwashed, Roxanna," Haylee said. "White supremacists. So now I guess you think it's wrong to be white?"

Roxanna rolled her eyes. "I don't have anything to say about white people in this context. Please stop, Haylee—"

"You are white—we are white," Haylee said. This was the first time Roxanna had heard Haylee say it. It was chilling.

"We're, like, totally brown," Roxanna said softly.

"Please! Look at us!" Haylee put her bare arm next to Roxanna's. And then she knew exactly what to say to really get at her sister. "How else do you think you were able to pull that one off, anyway, if we aren't white?"

"Pull off what?" Roxanna asked, though she knew what was coming.

"Italiana?" Haylee said, grinning defiantly. "Blackfishing one moment, whitefishing the next. Must be nice, Roxanna-Vanna! I'm surprised your friends don't have you checking your privilege."

Roxanna looked at her sister uneasily. There was something about this new Haylee that was legit scary. She suddenly seemed very old, and not in the glamorous-older-woman way. Haylee had always been her favorite sister but now there was this chasm between them.

She could not believe what nightmares her younger sisters were all being, and over a party, of all things.

All About 5G
by Haylee Milani

You've probably seen those ads everywhere—on billboards, in magazines, all over the internet. They're talking about 5G, the super-fast wireless technology. But what's the real deal behind it? Let's break it down.

Back in 2019, the U.S. wanted to be the best in the 5G game. They felt like they were falling behind China in the tech race. So, they kicked off some of the first 5G networks that year—that's where this all starts.

Now, 5G has some folks worried, and for a reason. Some people even think the big flu outbreak in 1918 happened because of far-reaching radio waves. Governments don't always tell us every-

thing, so folks come up with different ideas. One thing we know is that they tested 5G in Wuhan, where the pandemic began. Some say the crisis was made on purpose so that 5G tech could be set up everywhere while we stayed home. Others think 5G radiation weakens our bodies, making us more likely to get sick. Some even go as far as saying 5G spreads the virus. There are other ideas too, like the virus being made as a weapon, maybe by China. Then there's another one where powerful people like Bill Gates and George Soros are teaming up with Big Pharma to force everyone to get shots and put tracking chips in us—and 5G makes the chips work. Plus, people remember times when the U.S. played around with mind control stuff and secret military projects.

Oh, and back in the 1990s, there was this thing called HAARP—it's like a radio thing the U.S. military had in Alaska. It did experiments with radio waves in the air and some people thought it was making weird weather and messing with people's minds. They finally shut it down in 2015, but the rumors stuck around.

People who are worried about this 5G stuff are taking action. Some folks have set fire to phone towers to show they're not happy. It's not the first time people freaked out about this—in 2018, a guy climbed a lamppost to take down what he thought was a 5G thing. There's even a video from Hong Kong where protesters knocked over a fancy streetlight.

And then there are the birds. Yeah, birds have been dying around those 5G towers. Like, in The Hague, almost 300 birds just dropped dead in a park in 2018. Same thing in North Wales in 2019. No one really knows why, though.

Finally, there's a bunch of smart folks in lab coats who say that 5G waves can mess with water, like heating it up and stuff. They even say these waves could lead to cancer and mess with our minds. And honestly, the list just keeps going on and on.

So, what can we actually do about it? Sometimes when we bring up these ideas, people look at us like we're wearing tin-

*foil hats. Our friends, family, coworkers—they might call us con-
spiracy theorists. But how are we supposed to make things better
if we're being told we're nuts? It's like the world's turned upside
down. But guess what? There's proof all around us. We're being
made to feel weird for eating organic, drinking fancy water, doing
detox diets, practicing yoga and meditation, or turning to natural
remedies. Instead, we're called strange while others treat technology like their new religion, popping pills from Big Pharma for
their messed-up heads, breathing in air that's full of cancer-causing
fumes. It's like they worship money more than their own souls. It's
pretty freaky out there, but here's the deal: we've got time on our
side. Stay strong, have hope, do your own reading and research,
trust your gut, and pay attention to the signs. You know where
the real truth lies. You know where the real truth lies. You know
where the real truth lies. You know where the real truth lies. You
know where the real truth lies. You know where the real truth lies.
You know where the real truth lies. You know where the real truth
lies. You know where the real truth lies. You know where the real
truth lies. You know where the real truth lies. You know where
the real truth lies. You know where the real truth lies. You know
where the real truth lies. . . .*

12

Shifts and Revelations

It all started with a dream—an unlikely one for Al. He had not dreamed of Iran once since he left. He preferred to not even talk about Iran, if he was being completely honest. He was an American now, and not since accent-elimination class, really, had he felt he had to prove it. By the time he was at the Los Angeles Federal Court for his naturalization ceremony—thanks to a steep expedited lawyer's fee, as all the wealthiest Tehrangelenos he knew advised—he saw himself as very distinct from all the other immigrants in that courtroom. He sang "America the Beautiful" without having to look at the lyrics projected on the screen and he already had a large America-themed ceremony planned at a ballroom downtown. His favorite holiday was the Fourth of July and he rarely called himself "Iranian American." He preferred "Persian" if he had to elaborate but he made it very clear that he preferred nothing more than "American." Only around other Persians did he mention his previous life in Iran; among Americans he rarely acknowledged a past at all.

But this dream pulled him in. He was a high school student, a teenager, at least, somewhere in the vicinity of his girls' median ages. He looked as he had when he was young: too thin, tan, unfashionable in every way. The dream was set in the present day, so he was wearing one of those surgical masks. His mask was dirty. In his family home, the situation was worse than he remembered—the house more slovenly, and barren and dark. His mother was on a mat in the corner of the living room, rocking back and forth in tears. The vision snapped young Ali out of his smile. She was saying a prayer he grew up with and he no longer knew. In her hand she held beads and a photo of his father. In the dream he knew that his father had died of the virus. Young Ali wondered just then where his five older siblings were, and it became clear to him he was the only one apart from his mother who had survived. The virus had claimed them all. He went to bring his mother tea and saw that in the kitchen there was a giant pot of clothing boiling on the range—to disinfect, presumably. The kitchen smelled like chemicals and also something rotten, like it was beyond cleaning. Faintly he could smell the familiar spices of his youth, fenugreek and sumac and turmeric. He looked down at his bare feet, which were bandaged. They were in trouble, he could tell. He brought his mother her tea with a shaking hand and she turned to him and wailed, *They don't care about us, son. Never forget they do not care about us. They let us die. They made our home a tomb.* Ali tried to console her but she shook her head. *Keep yourself clean. It is time for your chemical bath. Don't use all the water.* In the next scene, he was naked, in their awful bathroom, with the mold spots on the ceiling, the water coming out in an ice-cold trickle. He knew what to do: he lathered himself in a toxic blue liquid the consistency of honey. It smelled like it could kill him. The bandages came undone in the water and blood filled the tub. What had happened to his feet? He heard his mother call to not waste water and he turned off the tap and turned to the rags that were his towel and saw the fresh roll of bandage. He applied it expertly to his feet, which he could not bear to look at. He had nothing but his old clothes to put on, and so he did and went to the living room, where his mother had a meal waiting for him: scraps of burnt lavash bread and a few mint leaves, plus a quarter of an onion. They ate with their hands, silently, until she said, *America did this. Whatever you do, promise me, no America.* He watched with horror, this young alternate self of his, nod earnestly and promise to his mother, whatever it meant, *No America.*

And then he woke up.

The dream felt so real, he reflexively checked his feet. They were fine.

It was just before dawn and Homa was in her other room, so he slowly made his way into his office and decided to tune in through BBC Persian's website and the other Iranian news sites he very rarely watched. Just in case, he thought, when he did.

There was so little happening and so much news, it felt like. Black Lives Matters protests ongoing, DNC news, more shootings in the U.S., a fuel spill in Russia, a Boko Haram attack in Nigeria, a humanitarian crisis in Yemen, mass graves in Libya, worsening tensions between China and India, and protests in Lebanon. And Iran was back in crisis, still with some of the highest numbers of virus cases.

He felt a strong sense of alarm. He remembered that when he left, he already knew he would never return to Iran. And many months ago, when war seemed likely, he was more determined than ever that they would never return—there would be no Muslim camp, no deportations, even as rumors began to circulate about lists of naturalized citizens. He would find a way to buy himself out of it. He knew the former Persian American Beverly Hills mayor, Jimmy Delshad, pretty well. He was among the top five richest Persians in America, last he checked, at least. He was never going to go back, no matter what it cost or whether other Iranians would have to.

But he had no idea why that one early dawn that strange nightmare had brought feelings for his old country back in him. It was more than nostalgia, not quite yearning. He didn't want to be there, exactly, but he did care. He felt he should at least check on his homeland, perhaps spend some money there, help the people, maybe even save some lives in this crisis. That would get him recognized as a hero.

People knew of him in Iran, after all. That had become clear a few years ago, when Voice of America had interviewed him. The response from viewers had been awful. The segment had low ratings because Pizzabomme meant little to Persians. Then he found out that they resented him—his American patriotism, his phony Los Angeles airs, his condescension toward Iran. *Iran is my past, America my present and future—I am not happy for the Revolution and the war, but I have to say, in terms of my life, it was a blessing, because I am right where I belong. And I hope every Persian can experience that feeling. You know how the Beach Boys said, "I wish they all could be California girls"—that's how I feel about Persians, "I wish they all could be Americans." But they can't, and so hopefully they have pride in me and see that me and my family and our legacy represents them well: we are majestic, proud, fierce, lovable, and unstoppable. We are true Tehrangeles royals!* He had said this after having worked with a speechwriter, and it had been quoted widely in Persian publications, and, of course, violently derided. They had called him a "low-budget Bijan" and "American-ass-kisser-in-chief Ali Milani," and there had been a couple of rude cartoons drawn about him. He had decided after that he wouldn't do any more press in Iran—not that he was asked often. Still, he was a well-known public figure there. Other Persians were bitter and jealous, no doubt, that he had fled and not just survived but thrived to an extent they could not imagine possible.

He had everything they wanted and now he had the ultimate privilege: health. *Health + wealth = unstoppable!*

Maybe it was guilt? That was not a feeling Al knew well. Or was it just a complicated kind of concern? He wondered if it was time to dial his old therapist again. Typically, he would find a way to drop a load of money as a donation and then forget about whatever he was feeling, but there was no easy way to donate to Iran. It was like trying to donate to North Korea. You could not work with a country when your present country had no diplomatic ties with it. He felt helpless, and he did not like feeling helpless.

The strange emotions from that dream stayed with him that whole day. He periodically checked his feet. He tried to explain that plot point to himself: maybe they had no place to go, nowhere to run to, the soles of his feet literally scorched by stagnation. He wondered if that was what it felt like to be there, and he was sad he had no one to ask. The few people he could dial there, he imagined had no time for his questions.

As dinnertime approached, he grew increasingly agitated. He wondered if the idea that he kept trying to push out of his mind was such a bad one, after all. What had he to lose? He could make it a short trip—it could be great press too, after all. He could wait for the vaccine they said would be coming soon and book a flight for, say, a week, and have photos taken of him doing humanitarian work. He could maybe even meet with government officials—if he could guarantee he would not be imprisoned and kept for bail. Maybe he could preemptively bribe them? Persians could be bought. And sanctions had grown so bad that people were desperate, he assumed. That was it, he thought. What if there was a way for him to singlehandedly off-set sanctions with his own capital?

He looked at his wife, who was flipping through a shopping catalog on a window seat in the living room. Would she come? Would she want to? In a way, he thought, she would be more game than he was. Homa would have been the one to suggest aid in the first place. She didn't need the alarming nightmares to prompt her, like he apparently did.

He hesitated. If he spoke to her about it, it would become real. She would jump at it. His daughters would surely protest, and his assistants and managers would be horrified. The producers of the show might like it for dramatic potential—there could be video journals taken in Iran, of course, and his do-gooding would be a boost for his image, something more than the cheap thrills that were promised by the show. But as he opened his mouth and stepped over to his wife, he decided to stop himself. If Homa agreed, they would be on their way to Iran, and then what?

He swore he felt the back of his foot heat up as he backed up and out of the room.

The History of Hot Pockets and Cinnabon
by Al Milani

To really understand what Pizzabomme is in essence, you have to know a bit about its predecessors. You can think of them as the mom and pop of Pizzabomme—Hot Pockets and Cinnabon. When I first came to America, I was so inspired by these two. I kept thinking about them, and I developed Pizzabomme.

Let's begin with Hot Pockets. I was shocked to discover that two Iranian men founded Hot Pockets. Paul and David Merage were two Iranian Jewish brothers. They came to America in the 1960s to attend university. Paul got an MBA. When the Merages were in Europe during the '70s on business, they were first introduced to Belgian waffles and subsequently tested countless recipes to create an easy-to-make frozen version for the States. In 1977 in Chatsworth, LA, they founded Chef America, Inc., and their waffles became a big hit among restaurants and cafés. This paved the way for Hot Pockets. The brothers knew the desire for portable meals was growing in America and they decided to shift their focus to lunch and dinner meals that could replicate the success of their waffles. Microwaves were all the rage and Hot Pockets were made for them. In 1980, they released the Tastywich, which was renamed three years later as the "Hot Pocket." Chef America was sold to Nestlé in 2002 for $2.6 billion and the Merage brothers, *who were very rich by this point, went on to work in real estate. (The Merage family was at one point the 139th richest family in America.) In 2015, the recipe was revamped into a healthier version with less sodium, artificial flavors, etc. There is so much mythology around this American food but there is also horrific true crime. In 2016, a Georgia man was so upset that a local convenience store was sold out of Hot Pockets that he shot his sister's boyfriend, who had been sent out to buy the Hot Pockets and reported they were out. He's serving a life in prison sentence: homicide over a Hot Pocket. On the other hand, Hot Pockets are what helped Jason Segel gain 40 pounds for his 2015 film* <u>The End of the Tour</u>. *He had to portray an out-of-shape famous person I've never heard of named David Foster Wallace.*

Let's move on to Cinnabon, another legendary American creation: Cinnabon overlaps with Hot Pockets. It launched just two years later, in 1985. A staple in malls around the country these days, the first Cinnabon opened in Seattle. In 1984 restauranteur Rich Komen was told of a very popular shop in a shopping center in Kansas City called T.J. Cinnamon's, which specialized in giant cinnamon rolls. He decided to approach them for a franchise deal in Washington. The deal fell apart, but he had already acquired the space for his store and he even had an agreement with Seattle's Sea Tac Mall to open a cinnamon roll shop. He decided to develop his own concept. He called Jerilyn Brusseau, a chef he knew in Seattle, to help with the recipe. She was known for her cinnamon rolls, which she made from a recipe her grandmother gave her. Apparently more than 200 recipes were tried out before they settled on one. By somehow striking the perfect balance of dough, cinnamon, margarine, brown sugar, and frosting, they created an iconic treat. They needed it to be worth the $1.25 it would cost and they needed it to cook fast. It was very successful, even in our health-food-obsessed culture. With 880 calories and 59 grams of sugar and 37 grams of fat, it is not an everyday food. But its sales have never lagged. Cinnabon sells 8,000 rolls an hour nation-

wide. One of their tricks is to place their ovens in the front of their stores, so customers are drawn in by the smell. When the ovens were placed in the back of the stores, sales figures were dramatically lower. They heated up sheets of sugar and cinnamon to keep the smell in the air. They now sell blended beverages and coffee drinks at their locations and, in retail, the brand has expanded even to vodka.

When I developed Pizzabomme, it was my own idea but as I made it better and better, it was made in homage to these iconic snacks that were still so very new in America at the time. I had no idea I would be building an empire on these other empires and improving upon them. Pizzabomme takes the savory hot sleeve concept of Hot Pockets and merges it with the form and shape and gooey indulgence of the Cinnabon. If "pizza had sex with a cinnamon roll," some might say (me)! It's a truly unique treat that takes the best from all those that came before it. You should buy some today! www.pizzabommeusa.com

Around the time of Al's nightmare, something happened to Pari again. Violet, who spent the most time with the cat (Mina was almost tied with her), noticed it first: she was refusing to eat. Violet immediately called the family vet, who refused to come for a house call. Rose ended up taking Pari and reported back that the vet couldn't find any problems. There was bloodwork, X-rays, a CT scan, even. In the end, the vet felt the issue had to be psychological.

"Has she been under any stress?" the vet asked.

"No, I don't think so," Rose said. "Well, she ran away a while back. But she was normal after that. She always ate. Too much, even."

The vet shrugged. "We can give her something to try to stimulate her appetite, but really you'd be best off trying that yourselves. Try offering new snacks, new foods, maybe some extra toys for exercise. Change it up. Older cats can get into funks like all of us do as we get older."

In the coming days, Violet bought every kind of cat food she could online. She ordered what was known as the world's best feline kibble from Germany, then another highly rated brand from Japan. She even hired a Montana hunter to ship her a variety of freshly killed wild specimens of every local kind they had on hand. Violet finally resorted to putting her newfound kitchen skills to work with Rose's help, looking up special cat food recipes to try out. But every creation she concocted went to waste. Pari only nibbled here and there, the bare minimum just to stay alive.

Pari had started to look skinnier, her bones visible through her lush coat.

"She looks kind of chic, to be honest!" Roxanna tried to joke.

"Ugh, Rox," Mina groaned. "This is definitely worrying. I wonder if the pandemic got to her too. Who knows what these cats can sense? I mean, maybe she thinks we are off. Are we off?"

Silence.

"I really think the pet psychic I suggested a while back is the way to go," Haylee said. "I have the number handy. He's done wonders. I just think we can try it. The guy specializes in telling people what their pets are thinking, especially cats."

"At the very least, wouldn't it be kinda freaky and cool to know what this weird cat thinks of all of us?" Roxanna seemed way too amused.

This time, Violet looked Haylee deep in the eyes and nodded. It might be worth a shot. She had tried literally everything else and after nearly losing Pari not that long ago, they could not lose her for real.

"Can you go ahead and make an appointment, Haylee? Have him come over later in the week?" Violet asked.

"Are you serious—" Mina started.

"Have, like, an open mind, Mins," Roxanna snapped.

"You don't even care about this cat!" Mina snapped back.

"You guys, please, no stress around Pari," Violet said gently. "Please."

"Mina is basic and can't think outside the box," Haylee said, glaring. "Like so much of the Radical Left, she lacks the imagination needed to survive."

Mina rolled her eyes and stormed off. She had started feeling allergic to Haylee these days.

Haylee smiled at Violet in a way that made her nervous. She prayed the psychic was not a MAGA conspiracy-theorist type. Given what Haylee was like these days, he probably was. But she knew she had to put the cat before politics.

"Crazier things have happened than a pet psychic," Haylee said, her smile widening. "Look around you, the world!"

Violet nodded, eyeing Roxanna, who looked equally assured. "Let's hope. Let's hope for Pari. Let's hope for absolutely everything to just go back to normal again."

The pet psychic was Haylee's friend Marci's stepdad, and sadly they all soon remembered that one detail Haylee had mentioned earlier: they were big Republican donors. Apparently Marci's family owned a yoga studio and their own line of yoga mats. Usually Jasper—that was the psychic's name—worked over Zoom, but based on the situation, he was willing to do more. In this case, given the severity of Pari's case, and given that he ultimately could charge them anything—Haylee had mentioned to Marci on the phone that her family was quite rich, *I'm never sure if people know*—Jasper decided it was best for him to come over.

"I know there's a pandemic and all," Haylee began, not sure if she needed to reassure him that they weren't sick.

"We don't worry about that stuff!" Jasper had said, chuckling.

Violet was there to greet him, and the sisters soon assembled, eager to see what would happen. Pari sat stationed a suspicious distance away, under one of the couches. Jasper was an unusually tall, sandy-haired, tan surfer–looking guy. Jeans, white T-shirt, Ray-Bans. The kind of guy who'd be in an ad for orange juice. Not quite what anyone imagined a psychic to look like. Mina was immediately suspicious of his boy-next-door demeanor, Roxanna thought he was kind of cute for an older dude, Haylee was relieved he looked normal, and Violet was so desperate she could barely register him or the way his eyes lingered on her chest.

"So very pleased to meet you all! Marci says such nice things about Haylee!" He was making it up on the spot, grinning. He very theatrically surveyed the living room. "And wow, gorgeous home here. I have a few other clients around here. Really nice. I can't imagine a dog would object to this kind of life!"

"It's a cat," Mina immediately corrected him. "Do you want a mask? I have some—"

"Nah! I'm not a fear guy!"

Mina sighed. "It's a cat, anyway."

"No big diff for me. They are all *spirits*," he said. Big smile bigger. "Like us."

"Do you work with people too?" Roxanna asked.

"Nope," he said. "Just animals. Mainly dogs and cats and horses, but sometimes pigs and turtles and ferrets and goats and cows, and I had an amazing session with a boa constrictor last week. So much going on in their brains. I mean, wow!"

Silence.

"Okay, so where is this little guy—or little girl!" he said, clapping his hands eagerly. "What's the name again—Larry, was it?"

"Pari," Violet corrected him nervously. She hated how much felt off so far, but she reminded herself they were doing this because they had run out of options. "Please have a seat on the couch and she'll come right out—I'll hold her."

As if on cue, Pari cautiously crept into their view.

Pari tended to be more suspicious around men. It was clear Pari did not have any interest in this man. Violet gathered her slowly into her lap.

"What a beauty," he said, smiling at her. "So here's the deal. I'm gonna hold her and then I'm gonna just start speaking nonstop for as long as she'll go, basically. But I'm not gonna be me— I'm gonna be her. I'm just channeling her and her thoughts. She'll say things I won't understand. She'll say things maybe you or I or all of us won't like—I can't help that. She's in command here, and I'm just the vessel. It's just important no one interrupts or else the spell gets messed up—that's the best way I can put it for you all. And I can't explain my process. To be honest, I don't even understand *how* I channel these spirits. It's just what I do, what I always have done. I can't give you insights. I can just . . . well, be your pet and tell you what she says. So go ahead and let me know what your questions are."

They looked at one another.

"Well," Violet began. " 'Why are you not eating, Pari?' That's probably the big one, the main one."

He nodded, smiling.

"And then maybe, like, 'Are you sad? Are you understanding all the craziness in the world right now? The fake news—' " Haylee began.

"That's enough, Hayles, but yeah, stuff about how she's been feeling," Mina said.

"Maybe, like, stuff about us? Like what she thinks about all of us?" Roxanna asked, giggling.

Everyone looked at her, a bit confused, except Jasper.

"Hey, that's a legit question! Everyone wants to know that," Jasper said, grinning at Roxanna. "Okay, well, I can work with all that and maybe the cat will say some stuff that we didn't ask about. That sometimes comes out. Sometimes the quietest animals have the most to say—you just never know. I really can't say a word about her until I begin my process and that will usually kick off a minute into me holding her."

Violet very gingerly gave Pari a sweet air-kiss and then regathered the abundant mass of long, shaggy white fur in her arms and reluctantly passed her over to the tan arms of this strange man.

Jasper cuddled Pari like a dog, which was exactly not how to touch her, and Pari let him know with a weird, guttural growl. They all watched in shock at how he gruffly snapped her out of it, locking her up tighter in his arms, so that she could barely move. He went from affable to controlling in seconds. Suddenly his goofy smile was gone and there was a tension in his jaw. He closed his eyes.

"Okay, everyone, I'm gonna just get right into it, so please just let me do my thing and no interrupting at all for any reason, got it?" he said, his eyes still closed. He took a very theatrical, presumably yogic deep breath.

Everyone muttered their agreement, and Jasper gave a thumbs-up, eyes still shut. Pari's classic glacier-blue eyes were wide and her entire body looked awkwardly paralyzed in his arms, her Persian cat hairs standing on end. Pari had not signed up for this. Violet wanted to cry, it looked so uncomfortable for her, but it was too late. She just wanted it to be over. She wondered if Jasper had made up his expertise or if he only specialized in dogs—a cat person would know never to hold a cat this way. She glanced over at Haylee, who looked so proud she had brought this strange man into their space, this man who was apparently going to give them the definitive window into their cat's self-destruction.

Another deep breath. For some reason Haylee shut her eyes, but Violet, Roxanna, and Mina all glanced at one another nervously. Pari just glared at them all, still petrified and frozen as Jasper's big breaths fell on her.

"Sisters, hello," Jasper said in a huskier, lower voice than the voice he had been speaking in.

Mina put her hand over her mouth to make sure not to laugh as Roxanna mouthed, *Sisters?* Is that what Pari knew them as? Violet shrugged to herself; in a way it actually made sense.

"Sisters, thank you for taking this step in trying to understand me. It is unusual, they say, for humankind to try this, but you are not ordinary sisters, of course. First, forgive my state: I will explain. I have not been myself and that is why I left a while ago and that is why I am not up to eating these days. . . ."

Mina rolled her eyes, while Violet's eyes pleaded with her to cooperate.

"It's not an easy time for humans, I know, but know it's not an easy time for felines either. We sense what is off in the universe. We are dependent on you and you all seem like you are falling apart: divided, fighting, panicking, ailing, deluding each other. Where is the stability? You were also on thin ice, as they say." Jasper paused, chuckling, in that same husky rasp. It was a strange theater.

"Okay, let me go around. Let's just say, our parents, the Milani Sir and Ma'am, I will leave out of this, as you don't really recognize me anyway. Let's be clear that I am not your daughter while I am your sister. We all know this. But let me go around, one by one. First of all, Haylee, thank you for bringing this medium to me. You are a wise girl, wiser than the rest give you credit for, and your beliefs may be far more sound than they know. But, Haylee, why do you only change when all is nearly lost? Why did it take my almost-destruction to really pay me mind? Am I not your sister? You claim to love me, to want to heal me, but why is it I cannot recall our last time together? And yet, Haylee, you possess so many feline qualities, qualities I admire—you are a bit aloof, narcissistic, self-satisfied, independent, strange, seeking. Dangerous? Dangerous. We could do so well together. We can plot. And that means staying off your phone and taking a break from all the exercise and simply being a cat-sister for a second. I believe in you, Haylee, I want you to believe in me too. . . ."

Haylee looked a bit shocked, a bit moved, and just generally weirded out. Her purple eyes were wide and locked with Pari's.

"Mina, the next youngest, well, you and I are very different. We know this. You know the saying *opposites attract,* of course, and maybe it can be our guiding light. Mina, you are so smart, a real foundation for your sisters and family in general, but where is your heart? I am not sure, Mina, if you have ever put that heart of yours to use—have you ever loved anyone deeply? Sure, you love your sisters and parents, but I am talking about a more profound love. I offer myself as practice, dear Mina. I know what you're thinking: 'That is so perverse—who would practice a sort of romantic love on a cat?' But, Mina, you have a way to go before you're even ready for romantic love. The love I mean might be pre-romantic. You are different from your sisters. In a house of strong feminine energy, you pose a threat. I don't know why you fear your own heart, but once you let it go, there will be room for us too. I'm asking you to meet me where it could also perhaps benefit you too, and give up the key to the most sacred chambers of your heart."

It was hard to convey Mina's facial expression—Roxanna nearly lost it looking at her. Mina went from eye rolls to disgust to horror to numb apathy. She was convinced that Jasper was a con artist—that wasn't going to change—but it did touch her a bit that he was not so wrong about her. She wondered how he did that. Still, there was something to it—it was at least entertaining, like fortune tellers could be when they managed to just barely skim at the truth through some twists and turns of speculation.

Jasper went on: "Next is Roxanna-Vanna. Oh, what to say to you? You barely know me. I mean, you like the idea of animals—

Siegfried and Roy's tigers in Las Vegas, Britney's yellow python in her 'I'm a Slave 4 U' VMA performance, the borzois of old Russian aristocracy. But the reality of cat ownership feels so onerous to you. You have never touched a litter box, never filled a water bowl, or tended to my food dish; you wouldn't even know what a cat toy looks like. I am not sure you have ever really held me in your arms or whether you know how. I think a part of you fears me. Because I am so much of what you are not and never can be: I am mysterious and I don't have to say a word and still people worship me and care for me. I don't have to demand attention, I don't need the spotlight. I can just be. I trust in the universe in a way you cannot. I have to admit you rub me the wrong way, especially these last months. You can't relax and you want to control everything. But even if you can't be a cat person, perhaps it's time to see me as an ally. Have you ever imagined putting me in one of those many popular photos of you? Don't you think your audience will love it? Perhaps they will see another side of you? I could be a boon for you. It would soften your image. I once heard a human say dogs are boys and cats are girls and I have to agree—not just because I am one. I could so be your brand. The bad blood between us doesn't have to be good—it could just be *not-bad*."

Roxanna had a huge grin on her face. She was nodding at Haylee, who proudly smiled back. This felt like a reading. And Roxanna was amazed. She really should use Pari in a shoot, especially post-cancellation, when she was still trying to make good with her public. She winked and blew a kiss to Pari, who was looking around with less horror but with the same confused expression she'd worn before: expectant and indifferent at once.

"And finally, Violet. Violet, my soul. Violet, beautiful girl, have I told you how much I love you? You intuit it because of course I never have. If I belonged to anyone, it would be you. I love everything about you—your kindness, your warmth, your sweetness, your gentleness, how you care for me. Also, you are so beautiful—to have a mother, a sister, but also kind of like a mother, who is a model, wow. What a dream. But, Violet, as the oldest, you are the one your younger sisters rely on. You try your best to keep things cool. But you too have your cares and your anxieties. Your big fear has become things going back to normal, as this break has given you an opportunity to stall. Violet, for this reason, I worry about you. Who will you be when this crisis ends? Will you be a better version of yourself, the one you dreamed of? I want a life with you on the other side. I need you to fear that less, like your sister Roxanna, take solace in your mind, as your sister Mina does, I need you to put yourself first, the way Haylee does. What if we made it the Violet and Pari show? I thrive when you thrive. You are my emotional support animal. Please tend to your wounds."

Violet was looking down, tears streaming down her cheeks. She had heard versions of this—a mix of what therapists and astrologers and psychics and shamans and healers had told her over the years. She wondered if Pari knew about her short stint with bulimia, if she had an inkling of her desire to leave modeling if the plus-size thing fell through—and, god knew, a part of her wanted that so badly. She looked up at Pari. Haylee gave her a mimed head-butt nudge from across the room that asked, *You okay?* and she nodded. She had not expected to be grateful to Haylee for Jasper.

"You're all gonna do well, sisters. Just remember that we must band together. Man and animal, flesh and spirit. We have to become one." Pari's pitch was sounding higher when suddenly Jasper said, "That part was just me. Well, that's it. Looks like Pari wanted to psychoanalyze you all individually a bit, huh? They do that sometimes. A lifetime of silence and observation!"

They were all stunned by the abrupt end and even more stunned by Pari suddenly using the opportunity of Jasper's slightly loosened grip to run out of his lap and back under the couch.

"She wants out, don't we all? Out of this crazy beautiful planet, right?" He laughed at the ceiling and then paused to look at his phone. A change in tone: "Because I know Haylee, we can do a deal. That'll be seventeen hundred and forty-five dollars."

Violet slowly went to get her pocketbook while everyone else stared at their laps. It didn't sound like the right price, but they had never negotiated prices in their life.

"That was amazing, Jasper," Haylee said. "So worth it."

"It wasn't me! That's all Pari steering the ship—I just help out, is how I see it," he said, laughing.

"It was, like, really cool," Roxanna said. "You should maybe do people?"

"Oh, no, animals are already so much—I get at people that way anyway, as you see!" he said. He looked over at Mina, who was already on her phone. "Mina, did you enjoy it? You're a hard sell, I'd think."

Mina nodded slowly. "Actually, it was better than I thought. You did your research."

"Pari gave me the keys," he said and chuckled clumsily as Violet came back with the check.

"Thanks again," she said. "Maybe we can use you in the future."

"Absolutely, girls! Have a blessed day!" he said and then left.

As Jasper walked out, Pari peered at them from under the couch.

"Hey, baby, come out," Violet cooed, but Pari was suspicious.

It was a lot for her to have had her mind spoken for like that. The sisters were too much too often.

"It's cool that the cat doesn't hate us," Roxanna said into the weird silence.

"Well, she hates some of us more than others," Haylee said

with a giggle. "But it's cool to know that a cat has so many thoughts. The world really is so much more than we imagine. A lot to stay open to, you know?"

"So if we just work on ourselves, magically Pari eats? That was why he charged us almost two thousand dollars?" Mina asked.

"Shut up, Mina," Haylee groaned.

"Well, maybe," Violet said. "I think if we work on ourselves, a lot can change for the better. We have time and space to do that. So why aren't we doing it?"

They sat in silence for what felt like ages, until one by one, they fell off again back into the world of their phones and pre-occupations. When they were gone, Pari slowly got out from under the couch and slid into the kitchen. She sat by her always-filled and always-refreshed bowl of dry food.

By the time Roxanna's black fur Gucci bikini came in the mail, after she ordered feline makeup and a Persian kitty blow-out from the hairstylist who made house calls—she wore a mask, a bedazzled mask, and charged triple because "risking my life, babes"—and once she did her "My Persian kitty & me: a RoXXXanna-Vanna Exclusive <3" photo shoot . . . Pari was back to eating. It was as if she would do anything to just make them all leave her alone again.

They were all going to feel nostalgia for the worst parts of lockdown, Pari could tell that they were slowly realizing. They just didn't know where in the story they were, Pari knew, though they were pretty sure the answer was what it always was: some-where in the middle.

Blackpink: Icons in Every Area
by Mina Milani
Girl groups have always been popular around the world—
particularly quartets of women with unique traits—and K-pop

has also registered this winning formula for ultimate girl power! In 2016, one of the greatest K-pop acts in recent history debuted, Blackpink. They were four parts perfect: extra-cute, a little bit tough and courageous, a little bit soft and goofy, 100 percent ultra-mesmerizing They performed monster ballads, EDM bangers, hip-hop hits, and pop anthems. They became stars not just in South Korea, but all over the world, where they continue to have legions of fans. The four members make it look easy, but it's definitely worth taking a closer look at who they are and how they got here.

Jisoo is the oldest member in the group. She is an original in every sense, known for her offbeat humor and her unique mix of introversion and extroversion. Jisoo is a vocalist but she also enjoys hosting and acting—she's starred in a number of music videos and commercials in her pre-Blackpink years. Jisoo is trilingual, able to speak Korean, Japanese, and Chinese—however, she is the only member of the group who does not speak English fluently. Jennie is the rapper of the group. She is fluent in English (in addition to Korean and Japanese), as she lived in New Zealand for a number of years before moving back to South Korea in 2010. She's also been a solo artist, with a track called "SOLO," which established her as a fashion icon: she wore more than twenty outfits in that one video. Then there is Rosé, the group's primary vocalist, who was born in New Zealand and raised in Australia, and thus is fluent in English too. Rosé also plays the guitar and often does acoustic covers of modern hits. She is known for her love of food while maintaining a very skinny frame. Finally, there is the youngest (or the "maknae" in Korean), Lisa, the primary dancer and also a rapper. Lisa is Thai. She moved to South Korea in 2011—and she speaks Thai, Korean, Japanese, Chinese, and English. She has a very fun personality and funky aesthetic, and she often puts out videos of her dance routines to hit songs. She is the most popular female K-pop artist on Instagram, with more than 67 million followers. Being a multilingual international quartet like this already sets Blackpink apart in an industry so often criticized for its homogeneity.

Blackpink debuted with the album Square One, *which consisted of only two songs, "Whistle" and "Boombayah," both of which grabbed the attention of the world. They were the first girl group in seven years to come from YG Entertainment, a major company, home to powerhouse groups like BIGBANG and 2NE1. "Boombayah" made the group the fastest musical act at the time to hit No. 1 on Billboard's World Digital Songs chart. They also became the first female K-pop group to play at the Coachella music festival. This amazing group accomplished many firsts.*

In 2018, Blackpink became the highest-charting K-pop girl group with the single "Ddu-Du Ddu-Du." "Ddu-Du Ddu-Du" climbed as high as No. 55 on the Billboard Hot 100 ("Ddu-Du Ddu-Du" is currently the most-watched music video by a K-pop group on YouTube, boasting 730 million views). Shortly after, Blackpink collaborated with Dua Lipa on "Kiss and Make Up," a bilingual song that expanded their audience even further. They signed with Interscope Records and Universal Music Group. Soon they made their debut on U.S. TV with a performance on The Late Show with Stephen Colbert *and then* Good Morning America.

Their fandom—called "BLINKs," a portmanteau (like Tehrangeles!) of "black" and "pink"—remains extremely devoted and loyal. And I should know—I am the West Coast North American social media manager of the most popular source for Blackpink news, Twitter's BLINKINYOURAREA account. We can only imagine what the future, hopefully a better future, has in store for this extremely talented, legendary group.

13

Party Time

There was no escaping it: The Party was going to happen and that was that.

And that was what Roxanna had decided to call it: *The Party.* Roxanna had texted the group chat: *I need an iconic name because this is THE event and to be honest who the fuck knows when we are gonna be able to do this again? No Mask-erade please, wrong vibe! Any objections to The Party, bitches?*

That wasn't the part anyone objected to. Mina contemplated moving out for the few days before, the day of, and the days after—the setup and aftermath were sure to be chaos too—but Roxanna assured her that her room would be off-limits and she—and her friends, if she wanted!—could create her own little haven, undisturbed. Roxanna would even pay for insulation for her room, if Mina's chronic illnesses made it so she needed to be fully sheltered from everything that would be going on, but even the way she said *chronic illnesses* made Mina think this was going to be hopeless. Nothing was going to get in the way of The Party.

Haylee insisted on her own guest list—no one was going to interfere with who she invited *or their politics, thank you very much*—so she was happy. And Violet was assured it would be good for networking because, let's face it, her industry was suffering. Her agent could come, and Roxanna mentioned that maybe people at some competing agencies could too, and of course there would be lots of A- and B-list celebrities. She would go to C-list (some would consider the Milanis C-list), but The Party was there for them to overshoot, not compromise.

Al and Homa appeased themselves by treating it as their own party too—they could invite all sorts of Iranian and non-Iranian luminaries they'd been lax about seeing for ages.

There were going to be several rotating DJs, four performances (one belly dancer, a rapper, a rookie pop star, and an emerging girl group), a magician, a fire-breather, a snake charmer, a face-painting stand, a tattoo station, three photo sets, an ayahuasca ritual hub in the garden, four dance floors (one each for ballroom: hip-hop, electronic, and acid jazz/yacht rock for Al), and a boutique where each guest could pick out their choice of three complimentary gift bags. There would also be exotic animals: in addition to the snakes, there would be peacocks and flamingos, llamas, a couple of Akhal-Teke golden horses, and one white tiger they were hoping could just lounge by the garden water-fall without disturbing the koi pond. In the end, the producers decided they would participate too. They were sending over camera crews, on top of the camera crew the Milanis said they'd finance, but a friend of a friend of Roxanna's would be there too, filming for a documentary on affluent Angelenos.

It was almost too easy for Roxanna. She'd been daydreaming about it all lockdown, so when the final okay was given, all she had to do was make a list and check some boxes. The only big decisions she had to make was what she would wear—Marc Jacobs? Louis Vuitton? Versace? Gucci? Balenciaga?—and what shade of blond she should go (platinum, alabaster, light ash, but-ter, strawberry, cherry, copper, bronze, honey, rose gold?). She also had to figure out which elite drug dealers to add to the guest list.

She nixed other suggestions. Mina wasn't going to get a

virus-testing station where people could have their temperatures taken, Haylee wouldn't be able to put up an "information
booth" from which to hand out pamphlets on what was really
going on in the world, and there would be no life-size chocolate
sculpture garden for Violet. It would definitely melt in the L.A.
heat, so they settled on life-size crystal-candy swans they could
float in the koi-less koi pond.

Somehow Roxanna felt The Party would make up for the
lockdown and the pandemic, even. It would tell the world—or
those who mattered—that the Milanis, and especially Roxanna, were still in the game. Everyone had felt so invisible for
months—and this thing wasn't over yet—so they might as well
make an explosive, anomalous memory that would announce
to everyone that they were able to conquer at least one amazing
night.

Roxanna had never quite known what she would be when
she grew up—she never really had to—but on the off chance
this virus or something else should cause some untimely death,
at least she could say her legacy was The Party.

*We are like pizza-snack heiresses! Please, don't you dare tell me I
can't be known for the biggest party of the pandemic!*

Under the couch, Pari shuddered. A long night, many long
nights still up ahead.

Invites went out shortly after the date was set, and publicists
were hired to talk it up—as if normal people or even D-listers
could even have a chance at getting in. It had been a real con-
sideration whether they should hire publicists to hype the event
in advance. Homa, especially, had worried that it would seem
tacky to publicize a *mehmooni* like this, because what if the virus
news grew grimmer and they got pressured to call it off? They

had already spent, literally, millions. But the City of Los Angeles and the LAPD were cooperating with them on it, so it was no secret anyway.

"We have to, like, stop thinking without pessimism! What is wrong with you all? You've forgotten your joy! That's the virus! You've all let it infect you!" Roxanna had learned a few things from Haylee. "Just let's pretend for once that everything will go totally right! And it will!"

"How are you always so sure?" Mina said.

"Because I know as well as you do, though you pretend not to, that once you have enough money, there's a solution for everything!" Roxanna said. "Dad taught us that, and he is right! If you're rich—like, really *rich* rich, like us—it's in the bag."

Al shrugged with a smile. He was looking forward to The Party, actually, his worries about it fading as his excitement grew.

"I have a not-great feeling," Mina said, though the truth was she was mostly saying that to deflate Roxanna.

"Can someone make sure Pari will be okay?" Violet brought up suddenly. "That's been my one worry. Mina, if you're gonna be in your room, maybe we can keep her there with you or at least in that wing? She's gonna be petrified. Especially with all those weird exotic animals roaming around."

Mina nodded. "Poor Pari, just when she was getting over whatever she was getting over."

"I'll get a special pet sitter for the cat and anyone else who wants to bring a pet," Roxanna assured them. "There's, like, already a team of babysitters and a designated playroom for any-one bringing kids, the, like, horror!"

They were all a little bit impressed with how much Rox-anna had worked out. She seemed to have thought of absolutely everything.

"We're paying Randy and Rose and the girls double, right?" Violet asked Homa.

"Triple! I worked it out." Roxanna grinned.

The day was like a wedding day—or what Roxanna imagined a wedding day might be like. She had stylists, hair and makeup, gardeners, landscapers, maintenance workers, and the interior decorating team all there at dawn. There was a special group of cooks and cleaners set to work with Randy and Rose. The party photographers—there were a half dozen—got there early too so they could capture the premises unsullied.

The colors for the evening were peach and gold, Roxanna's favorites. The flowers were all Juliet roses from Napa, white hydrangeas from Hydra, gardenias from Yorkshire, lilies of the valley from Provence, arum lilies from Cape Town, phalaenopsis orchids from Bangkok, and peonies from Bangor. There was gold ribbon everywhere: gold silk, gold satin, gold velvet, all from some special ribbon maker in London. Roxanna had a perfumer, the same fragrance architect who helmed scents at L'Artisan, design a house scent for the night and called it The Party. Guests would receive samples of it in their gift bags: a mix of tuberose, panna cotta, saffron, canned peaches, pink champagne, and cannabis.

Even Mina had to admit—from afar, masked—that the undertaking was stunning. How had it all come together so immaculately? Answer: money, always money. If that dazzle hadn't entered her consciousness, then disgust would have entirely overwhelmed her.

Roxanna had begged her sisters to dress to the theme and her designer specifications. She had decided to wear vintage Tom Ford Gucci from 1998—a slinky gold body-con dress made of real gold flakes—plus gold fishnets made of real gold thread, topped with a vintage crème Halston shawl she could throw over her bony shoulders in case it got cold. She also had on real gold-and-diamond Jimmy Choos—the same style worn by the Queen of Jordan at Beyoncé's wedding, her stylist told her. Her hair was a mix of alabaster-blond and rose-gold highlights, blown out to vintage-bombshell proportions, and her makeup was "cokehead lioness," as she had envisioned, a mix of orange-and-gold contours and shimmers.

Violet wore exactly what Roxanna had ordered—their fashion tastes were not always compatible but Violet knew how to be the model without upstaging Roxanna. She had on vintage pink-and-gold suede Vivienne Westwood from the 1980s— a long-sleeved, shoulder-padded blazer dress, which was a far cry from her usual floral sundresses and Zac Posen formals. This was much more edgy. She was going bare-legged with Michael Kors gold shimmer on her legs, topped with gold vinyl stiletto Versace booties. Her hair was slicked back and straightened and she let Roxanna convince her to add clip-in peach chunks. Gold hoop earrings and a gold manicure, and Violet looked more runway-ready than she ever had, she felt.

Haylee had also cooperated with Roxanna's vision. She decided on vintage too, and wore a Bill Blass sweetheart dress that was a rose-gold-and-peach jacquard floral—it had ruffles and puffy sleeves—and Haylee topped her platinum bob with a glittering gold beret Roxanna's stylist had found in a junk shop in Rome. She had on gold velvet Marc Jacobs Mary Janes with pink sheer tights. Haylee looked sweeter than she was, and Roxanna was so relieved she'd talked her out of the jockish Jeremy Scott tank dress she'd wanted to wear with her new Nike Ambush Dunks.

Roxanna had tried very hard to talk Mina into a Christian Dior summer dress (also vintage) that wasn't overly feminine, but as she predicted, Mina nixed it instantly. Mina reminded her she'd barely be visible—she'd be hiding the whole night, but they all knew there was a chance she'd peek in or at least step out to get some food. They compromised on a unisex vintage gold Gaultier tunic that Mina could wear with an oversize Rick Owens brown linen scarf. Roxanna begged her to wear a pair of Givenchy floral tights, but Mina insisted on trousers. Roxanna managed to find some crème Chanel slacks that at least gave off the semblance of her trying. Mina refused to do her hair and insisted on just wearing a cap, so Roxanna offered her two choices: an off-white leather Margiela or a gold-bedazzled late-1990s Von Dutch. (Mina chose the Margiela.)

Homa she put in a classic gold Valentino two-piece suit from that season—by far, the priciest outfit, but it gave off the heavy elegance the woman of the house required. Homa also draped a loosely tied Carolina Herrera soft orange scarf around her shoulders. She wore lots of gold jewelry from Iran—Roxanna begged her to say the pieces were from Italy. And Roxanna found her the perfect tan Prada pumps. She was all set.

For Al, Roxanna asked him to break from the Bijan suits he wore without mentioning to him that she didn't want to tip off people to her secret. She got him to wear an Oscar de la Renta classic tuxedo with a vintage Yves Saint Laurent gold bow tie. He wore some great Ferragamo alligator shoes, and he looked perfect.

Roxanna was so proud of her household. Even Randy and Rose and the waitstaff were wearing Ralph Lauren uniforms. They all took several sets of photos on the grand staircase— Roxanna could not wait to put them up on social media.

The night had success written all over it. Roxanna could not be more pleased.

There was a rumor Britney Spears and her Persian boyfriend were coming. It was said they never left their mansion, so this was a big deal, but Roxanna was trying not to get her own hopes up too high. The assistants of Kim Kardashian West and Khloé Kardashian had promised to stop by, and a friend of a friend was very likely bringing Doja Cat, although she could probably stay only a half hour at most. On the maybe list were also Lil Nas X, Kim Petras, Winnie Harlow, Bella and Gigi Hadid, Tyler the Creator, Timothée Chalamet, Solange, Steve Aoki, Becky G, and Jojo Siwa. Plus lots of other older people Roxanna was not totally in the know about, but the party planners assured would be major gets.

She rushed to her room and did the first of many lines of the "good coke"—she was told Tom Ford's Santa Fe chef's best friend's cousin's dealer had brought it to the homecoming game's after-party last year—and she took one last look at herself in the mirror. Star power: she had it written all over her.

She knew it was inevitable that with an operation this big, something would go wrong. But she promised herself right then and there to give no fucks about it. *Or a few fucks, like, at most,* she said. *When you throw The Party, the fucks have to be few and far between.* She felt like someone famous had to have said that. She shrugged and blew herself a kiss and told herself to stay with the self-love.

The guests started to arrive earlier than she expected. Raised by Persian parents, she always assumed that if it said 8 p.m. on the invite, no one of import or good manners really would come before 10 p.m. But maybe because it said "8 p.m.–?" the open-endedness inspired people to play it safe. Or maybe it was because everyone was out of practice—this was, after all, most people's first party since the pandemic had struck. *Popping the pandemic's cherry!* Roxanna had been cackling to friends over text for weeks, and now she got to say it in person. In fact, she was convinced the few noes and no-shows they got were because people were being cautious—or as Haylee would put it, *ultra-paranoid and programmed by their government.*

Early was no problem because things were, for the most part, going right. One of the crystal-candy swans' necks had snapped in the pond minutes into installation, which was a shame, and two of the cooks had to go home early, as they were running low-grade fevers, and Violet's bootie heel broke twenty minutes into the night, forcing her to wear black-patent leather Manolos that sort of ruined her outfit. The tiger was a no-show. They were told the possibility of Britney showing was extremely unlikely, though her boyfriend, Sam, sent his regards to Al, of all people. The main downer was that Mina was sitting tight in her room. Hopefully Pari was with her or with the pet sitter, who had only an elderly tobacco's heiresses's giant, ancient apricot-colored poodle to watch in her pen. Homa lost one of her contacts and the goat-cheese ballet-dancer sculpture got impaled by someone's acrylic nails, but still all was going exceptionally well.

"The vibes are just, like, correct, you know?" Roxanna shouted, hoping she sounded less coked up than she felt to Violet, who was sipping at her Moët rainbow-sherbet float, slowly taking it all in while also keeping an eye out for industry folks.

"I think it could be a good night," Violet shouted back. She eyed the cupcake tower longingly and wondered how bad it would look for her to eat some of it. She wasn't sure who would be watching. She wasn't even sure if a lot of people knew who they were, whose party this was. The place was packed, but she recognized almost no one. "Do you know who these people are, Roxi?"

Roxanna performatively scanned the crowds. "I recognize that guy from a cereal commercial, I think, and I am almost positive she's an influencer. Isn't that one of Haylee's friends over there? I think Dad's people are pretty much everywhere too. I don't know . . . No, I don't know too many of these people. My people always show up late, anyway. I'm not expecting a soul before midnight." She waved at a pair of exhausted llamas in the garden, pretending she had spotted old friends.

Violet nodded. "It's weird to be in our own house and know no one." She smiled shyly. "Do I really look okay? This isn't too much?"

Roxanna rolled her eyes. "Violet, please. We've had parties

before. And you look perfect." She paused. "Do you want any of my drugs? I have a bump in my purse here."

Violet always refused Roxanna's drugs, almost as a rule, not because she didn't like drugs—and she didn't like drugs, to be clear—but she found it a real violation of her role as the older sister. But this time, she thought about it for a second. Coke, which she had done only a few times, seemed like it might actually help her get through this, but so could the alcohol in her hand. She knew at some point she was likely to be taking care of Roxanna and maybe even Haylee. She declined. "It's gonna be a long night—better pace myself."

"I'll offer you some later," Roxanna said and then she tilted her head toward the door. "I think that's Addison Rae. The girl from TikTok. Wow, she's a lot shorter in person. Wait, maybe it's not her. Or maybe it is? Whatever."

Someone on the patio was throwing a gold basketball at a group of albino peacocks. "Is Damon coming?" Violet asked.

Roxanna looked low-key outraged. "Is he coming? Why would he not? Everyone, all my people, are coming. Like, where the fuck do you think people are? All we've been doing for months now is absolutely nothing. People are here because A) it's us, but also because, like, where the fuck else would they be, anyway? At, like, home? Again?"

Mina wasn't just hiding from The Party; in fact, in a way, she was at its control deck. From afar, it looked like she was having just another Mina night—though in a formal party costume, of sorts—with her headset on, sitting at her PC, playing *Overwatch* or *Fortnite* and scanning social media. But tonight she was monitoring posts on Twitter and Instagram and Snapchat and TikTok. Roxanna had created a couple of hashtags for the night, #RoxannaVannasTheParty and #TheMilanisTheParty. Mina had been skeptical about them being used but they were not only used, they even trended at moments. With a guest list of nearly six hundred people, it made sense, Mina thought, but she wanted to keep track of what people were saying.

The truth was that Mina lived to watch Roxanna's bubbles burst and she could foresee a backlash. While Roxanna was pretty oblivious to any criticism about her, blocking and muting all of it almost instantly, Mina read it all carefully. The pandemic was still raging and vaccines were still a ways away. The term "superspreader" and "superspreader gatherings" had become a common tag of admonishment, and she quickly saw it applied to The Party on Twitter.

Superspreader event at the House of Pizzabomme, say it ain't so

The virus IS RoxannaVanna Milani lmao

Where are the masks—I see three in these photos and one is just some bedazzled netting?

Not the Milanis doing a pandemic party for absolutely no reason

"Of-fucking-course," she muttered at her computer. "You see this, Pari?" Pari was hiding behind her desk, horrified by the sounds coming from the other rooms. "We knew this would happen."

Mina had another monitor set up that operated like a secondary security camera. She could see several rooms of The Party on that screen, like she was working security. It was hilarious to watch—and also boring.

"God, they look so much less cool than they think." She almost laughed, watching Roxanna and Violet in the corner surveying the audience. Violet was sipping at some kind of milky drink and Roxanna was fidgeting and twitching and gesticulating and rolling her eyes theatrically. No one was speaking to them.

"Lonely at their own house," Mina said. "Couldn't be me."

Then she noticed over by the doughnut jungle-gym thing (hard to explain), a group of kids who for a moment looked like her friends. Or maybe like what her friends would look like

in the future, as they were much older than she was. They had
to be queer. Mina felt herself blush to no one but herself. That
had to be why she had noticed them. They were probably the
weirdest-dressed of The Party.

There was one person she took particular note of. She couldn't
tell if it was just the camera playing tricks on her, but Mina was
suddenly convinced she was looking at one of the most beautiful human beings she had ever seen. She had a shaved head and
what looked like a tattoo—or else a very dramatic birthmark—
just above her ear. She was wearing a worn brown leather jacket
on top of a simple, flowy white dress that looked like it was
made of paper, over what looked like classic Doc Martens. No
makeup, no jewelry, from what Mina could tell. Her friends
were laughing and having fun, it seemed, but she was silent, her
eyes possibly fixed on a lone flamingo next to what looked like
a snow machine.

She texted Violet, who could probably see her from where
she was standing.

*Hey V, just watching The Party from the camera, I'm in my room,
but hey who is that girl, over by the doughnuts, shaved head, long white
dress, leather jacket?*

She watched Violet get the text and look around until it
seemed her gaze landed on the girl. Violet looked confused,
scoping her out, and so she nudged Roxanna, to ask her, apparently. Roxanna looked over and shrugged.

*No clue. Roxi doesn't know either and says the party list got out of
hand and these are just people's friends of friends. But she kind of looks
like . . . a model? V tall.*

Mina tried to zoom in for a better look. Her height was sort
of unclear from the angle—it also seemed like she was slouch-
ing. She wondered why this person looked so dazed and bored
and then realized she herself would be looking just like that too.

Thx Violet, no reason, she texted and then realized Violet had
not even asked why.

You should come out and hang for a sec. It's not as bad as I thought.
Ppl seem to be happy. It's chill.

Mina paused. There was something about that girl that made
her want to go out there. Not that she'd know what to say. Normally she would have stayed where she was—she would not have
even been tempted. But there was something about that girl.

Mina had never really actively explored her interest in women,
and she could not imagine Roxanna's party being where she
started. *A hideous origin story,* she told herself.

She looked away from the screen, grabbed Pari's laser pointer
toy, sitting idly on her desk, and tried to play with Pari, but Pari
would not budge.

Go to The Party, silly, she imagined Pari saying to her.

Why? What is there for me there? she argued back. She looked
down at her outfit. The fact that she had agreed to get out of her
hoodie-and-jeans uniform already meant she was halfway there.
She glanced at the screen again and there was that girl, still in
the same spot, still no expression, though she seemed to have a
beverage in her hand now. Her friends were all having fun, it
seemed, and sort of ignoring her. The flamingo had disappeared.
She imagined this girl had been dragged out to The Party.

In the bathroom, Mina washed her face and put on some
moisturizer. She thought about adding on this berry stain that
Violet had lent her, but she didn't want to do too much. Plus,
she wasn't sure she was going to take off her N95 mask. She had
thought about covering it in stickers, but now she was happy
she hadn't. Maybe this had to be an exception, the one time in a
crowd she could risk it—for the sake of the girl seeing her face,
of course. She felt embarrassed that she could cave so easily but
she reminded herself that she wasn't committing to The Party
just yet. She was just poking her head in, saying a few obligatory
hellos, making sure her sisters knew she had tried, maybe just
attempting eye contact with a beautiful girl.

It looked from the screen as if Roxanna was now playing

hostess, darting from one party corner to another, while Violet mainly stayed where she was. She could at least hang out with her. Violet was an empath: she'd note her younger sister's discomfort and stick near her. Roxanna, meanwhile, had bigger and better people to seek out and entertain than her.

She looked at Pari, who was looking away. Worst-case scenario, she had a place to run to: her room was just a long corridor away. She could come back, turn off the lights and turn on the white-noise machine, and go to sleep whenever she wanted.

She ventured outside her door and immediately she was shocked by how intense the sound was. Her room was decked out with special insulation and special air purifiers whirred 24/7. She'd never heard their home louder. It seemed like every inch of the house was covered in people, conflicting DJs playing at every corner, and she could even hear a few hollering animals that were hard for her to identify. She knew she would not last long.

She walked right over to Violet, who was still standing where she had been, shyly gazing at all the activity. She seemed very relieved when Mina approached.

"Hey, Mins, so glad you decided to come!" she said with a half hug. "It's crazy, isn't it? When Roxi plans something, my god . . ."

Mina was overwhelmed. The Weeknd's "Starboy" was playing, which added to the extremely intense everything of the entire everything. She contemplated getting food but doubted she could even chew, with all the layers of pounding bass. She knew where she wanted to look but she was also afraid to.

"That girl is still right there," Violet said, reading her mind. "I love her outfit—so simple, so edgy, but hard to pull off. She really might be a model."

Mina had no choice but to look. She turned in her direction—it had been so much easier with that screen in her room. But in person, the girl was even more breathtaking. She was far paler than she had looked on the camera and also taller—probably six feet. She had a bottle of beer in her hand and looked every bit as bored as she had on the screen.

Immediately Mina realized talking to her would be near impossible for her. She was the least approachable person she had ever seen.

"She's tall," Mina said, her voice a dry rasp. Violet nodded.

"Why did you notice her? Does she look familiar? Everyone looks familiar to me at this party and I guess a lot of them are famous. I wish I was better at knowing who everyone is, like Roxanna."

Mina shrugged. She hoped Violet was not registering her fixation, and she was even more hopeful that the girl—or the nonbinary person; who knew?—was not noticing it either. Mina was counting on the general party havoc to camouflage her interest—she would normally never be so bold.

"Do you want to go talk to her?" Violet asked.

Mina nearly choked at the idea. "No. Do you?"

Violet shrugged. "I don't know. If she's a model, that would be good for me, the contacts. I was thinking that before The Party, that fashion people would be important for me to talk to. Roxi says that too." Violet looked a bit embarrassed. "I don't know—doesn't her crew look like fashion people?"

Mina almost corrected her with what she really thought, but it was close enough, she realized. "In a way," she said. "I really hope she's not a fashion person. No offense."

Violet smiled. "I know, it's not for you. But, well, we could go talk to her. Or really anyone. This *is* our party."

Mina blinked blankly. *Our party.* It was so hard to understand that. Mina would never have a party. And if she did, it would be a small gathering, a simple dinner, maybe, possibly outdoors, somewhere pretty. Not this. She imagined going up to that beautiful person and telling her this was her party. It gave her chills.

"What would we say? She's a stranger. Like, just say that we think she looks cool or something?" Mina muttered.

Violet shrugged. "She's drinking. Everyone is. It never really matters what you say at a party. But if you don't say anything to anyone, then you're not even really at a party. We have a long night ahead—what could go wrong? It's our house."

Our house. Even that was hard for Mina to grasp. The place was so transformed that she almost could not recall what it had looked like in its natural state.

At that moment, a couple of very drunk men came over, no doubt to ogle Violet. They looked vaguely Iranian. "Are you one of the daughters, baby?" one of them slurred, as the other held him up, barely. They were wearing awful shiny suits, giving off booze and cologne in such heavy measure, Mina actually gagged.

"We have to go—our friend is waiting for us." Mina pulled on Violet's arm, worried she'd get stuck talking to them out of politeness.

And just like that, they were walking over to that beautiful person, who, unsuspecting, was still standing there, a bit hunched, beer bottle in hand.

"Thanks," Violet whispered. "Ugh, it's gonna be a long night of that!"

"It doesn't have to be," Mina grumbled. Suddenly she froze. She was a foot away from that person and she had no plan at all. What was she doing? She looked to Violet.

Violet got it immediately. "Hi there, I'm one of the Milani sisters," she said awkwardly to the person who looked a bit flustered at their invasion of her space.

"Who?" she said.

Mina wanted to die. She probably had no idea who they were or why they were talking to her.

"Oh, I'm Violet Milani and this is my sister Mina—we live here." Violet smiled awkwardly. "We're just saying hi to people."

Mina's stomach did flips. It was such an awful line. She decided to focus on her feet—the girl's steel-toed Docs.

"Oh, I'm sorry, yes, hi," she said quickly. Awkwardness met awkwardness. "So nice to meet you. Great party." She said it in a tone that made Mina feel like she was lying. "I'm Lila."

Lila. The name made Mina feel a bit light-headed. It was beautiful. She didn't want to look up, but she couldn't help but notice that she was gorgeous up close. Flawless, really.

"Hello," Mina decided to finally mumble, still looking down.

"My friend Roz knows Roxanna, I think," Lila said. "Roxanna is your sister, right? You three?"

"We have another sister too," Violet said. "The youngest. I am the oldest."

Mina slowly looked up to see Lila smile politely, a tiny, tight smile. Her emotional range, like Mina's, seemed rather narrow, which felt relieving in that room of hyper-animated people.

"Are you a model, maybe?" Violet asked.

Mina wanted to die at Violet's sudden audacity.

Lila shook her head. "Yeah, people ask 'cause I'm tall," she said. "But nope."

"Oh, I'm not even as tall as you, but I am one," Violet said.

"How cool," Lila said, again in a tone that made it seem like she didn't actually think it was that cool. "I do art—I'm an artist."

Of course, Mina thought. It made so much sense.

"How great! I think there are a lot of artists here tonight," Violet said.

Lila's eyes focused on Mina. "What about you?" she asked Mina.

Mina froze. What to say. "I'm a . . . student," she said. What else could she say. "I like the arts. But also other stuff."

"Oh, I'm a student too," she said. "I go to Beverly."

Mina nodded. She could not place her age. But she was just a bit older. "Saint Michael's." She immediately looked to her eyes to see if there was judgment, for going to the most expensive private school in the state, but then again, she was seeing her home, so it should not have been a shocker.

"I wish I went there," Lila said. "I hate Beverly."

Mina nodded. "Saint Michael's is bad too. It's all bad."

"Are you in college?" Lila asked Violet.

Violet turned red. "I haven't quite gone to college. I did modeling instead." It was a sore subject for her, but it came up often. "Do you want another beer? Or any food?" she said, changing the subject.

"I barely drink," Lila said, tapping her mostly full bottle. "I just didn't know what else to do."

"It's boring," Mina quickly said for her.

Lila smiled. "I didn't mean that—there's so much happening, but yeah, I just . . . my friends know a lot more people."

"Well, now you know us!" Violet said, beaming.

Lila nodded shyly. "I like the animals here, that flamingo."

At that moment, Roxanna swooped in out of nowhere like a bird of prey, out of breath. "The ayahuasca guy, is he one of your friends' friends or Haylee's?"

"Um, no way is he one of mine—sounds like Haylee's!" Violet backed away from Roxanna, who smelled strongly of booze and weed.

Roxanna had a very 4 a.m. way about her and it was barely 11 p.m.

"Shit," she snapped. "There's two of them, luckily, but one has to go. My friend Lisa says he was recently canceled for low-key raping a girl in surf camp in Costa Rica."

"Oh my god," Violet muttered. "We should find him and get him out of here. There's Haylee—let's go ask her!"

"What's *low-key* rape?" Mina sneered.

Mina wasn't sure if she was meant to run along with them in their panic, but she found she couldn't move away, and suddenly it was just her and Lila, still points in a manically buzzing room.

"That's so terrible," Lila was saying.

"Which thing?" Mina asked, alarmed.

"Rape?" Lila said.

Mina sighed, nodding. She was blowing this, but then again she wasn't even sure what she was blowing. Lila barely seemed to register her, and yet what was she even supposed to register? She suddenly felt very dizzy, like she was swaying, and she looked for a seat where there was absolutely none. "I'm sorry—I have to sit down. I have health issues."

"Oh, I understand—so do I," Lila said quickly. She looked around for a chair, but Mina was already stumbling to a stool in a dark corner, just outside the kitchen.

There were fewer people there, and immediately Mina worried that what she'd done looked like a ploy. She banished the thought from her mind; she was highly preoccupied with not passing out.

"I'm okay—I just feel weird," she was saying, even though no one was asking. She wondered what it was—her blood pressure? Her blood sugar?

"Have you eaten? Can I bring you something?" Lila asked, and Mina melted at the sweetness.

She refused, of course, shaking her head. "No, it's okay. Also, I am allergic to everything and this is not our usual, you know."

Lila nodded. "It must be so weird, hundreds of people descending on your space like this," she said. "And then you can't even get to your food. . . . Should I get your sister?"

Mina shook her head. "It will pass. You can go to your friends if you want—I'll be fine. Sorry." She worried that sounded super weird, like she was playing at being some kind of victim or implying that Lila was attending to her in some odd way.

Lila shook her head. "No way. I've been there. I have lupus and a bunch of other issues. I know how it is. I wouldn't leave you."

I wouldn't leave you. The intimacy of it struck Mina hard. No one had ever said that to her. She knew she was overblowing the context, but still. She tried to think of something other than Lila's beauty.

"I hate being chronically ill," Mina said. "It's just so much to worry about."

Lila nodded. "Oh, yeah. It's something. And in this ableist society. And when you already have so many boxes checked."

Mina gulped. She wondered if she was about to ask or to announce it. What other boxes?

"Yeah, I have a few too," Mina said quietly.

"Queer Jewish chronically ill woman," Lila mumbled. "It's a lot. Actually, the woman part might be nonbinary."

Mina nodded, hoping it was a cool nod. "Me too, maybe."

"Cool."

Mina suddenly felt a few notches bolder. "I mean, I haven't come out. But no one would be surprised. Are you using *they* pronouns?"

"No," Lila said. "Not yet. I'm not sure."

"Same," Mina said. "I am sometimes online, though."

Lila nodded. "That makes sense."

The two just sat there, as Mina's dizziness faded and—for reasons she could not understand later that night nor the next day nor even months down the line—they ended up in Mina's room for the rest of the party, which meant that out of the Milani sisters, by far, against all odds, Mina Milani had the best night.

"He *is* a doctor!" Haylee screamed at a group of men. They were sitting in one of the adjacent dens. Haylee had just met them that night, each of them except Damon, who had just arrived and, in his search for Roxanna, somehow had found himself in Haylee's corner.

"A doctor of Oriental medicine," a tall, bald man corrected her. "And, I have a BA in nutrition."

"That's fine. But it's enough to tell us this is a hoax," she snapped.

"Well, let's just put it this way," he said, lowering his voice. "There's no reason to believe this is a real virus and not, say, electro smog or one of the numerous other pollutants that manifest as free radicals in our bodies."

"I'm with you, but what's the solution?" another guy asked. He looked vaguely like an actor in an eighties sitcom.

"Ozone," the nutritionist declared. "It's O_3 and it's very easy to access. You can get ozonated olive-oil capsules at Lassens, I believe. Ozone can be transmitted orally, anally, vaginally, or topically—even via IV, which is the method I prefer. You can do everything from injections to major autohemotherapy. They used it in Africa for Ebola, and I have a second cousin who is a resident in Taiwan who said you can find it in some clinics there. But with the FDA and the CDC, we stand no real chance. So while you can go to, say, an IV clinic and get a supermodel drip or a Myer's cocktail for your hangover or whatnot, conventional medicine still has a ways to go. . . ."

"Why isn't this something we're hearing about on the news if it cured Ebola?" Damon asked.

"Oh my god, even I can answer this—the media, Damon?" Haylee snapped. "Please! It's all fake news. It's all controlled. They're the real ones behind this virus—them and Big Pharma and Big Tech. The perfect trio. That's why we don't stand a chance with things as they are now—"

"Now, we actually do stand a chance," a businessman-looking guy piped up. "But it's a matter of winning elections at this point. The Democrats, as you can see with abortion, would rather billions of children die for their own sense of justice. Meanwhile, they manufacture a whole disease with the plan to kill off half the planet, and then they call us problematic? I tell you, if the Democrats win the presidency this fall, we're doomed. The stock market is already primed for trouble. I'm telling you, we're gonna all be working for the Chinese—"

Just then Roxanna and Violet burst into the inner circle, breathlessly.

"Hi, sorry to butt in, everyone, but this is urgent. Um, can we talk to you, Hayles?" Violet said, as Roxanna looked ready to pass out.

"No, you can say it right here, in front of everyone. There are no secrets in my world!" Haylee said proudly, if nonsensically.

"Hayles, do you, like, know the rapist—" Roxanna blurted out.

"Roxi, where have you been, babe—are you okay?" Damon quickly gave her a back hug.

"Wait, what rapist? What's going on?" Haylee cried.

"Roxanna means the ayahuasca instructor—or I think one of them? One of them has, um, allegations against him," Violet tried to explain.

"I didn't invite the ayahuasca guy!" Haylee said, looking indignant. And then she paused—did she? She wasn't sure. "What's his name?"

"Either Dave or Dan?" Roxanna managed to say. "Please, he has to, like, go!"

"Wait, I think I know him!" the nutritionist butted in, or maybe he was looking for an excuse to leave the group he had found himself in. "I saw him outside by the face painters? I can show you!"

Violet quickly linked arms with him. "Thank you—let's do it. We've got to get rid of him!"

They ran out and made their way through the crowds, past a camera crew milling around by the champagne station. "Is that Roxanna-Vanna?" they heard one of the crew say.

"We'll be back!" Violet shouted into the crowd.

Meanwhile, another camera crew member had taken the seat of the nutritionist, over by Haylee. "So you're Roxanna-Vanna's youngest sister?" he asked her, with a big grin. "Are you the sporty one?"

Haylee rolled her eyes. "I am into health and wellness."

"She's a virus conspiracy theorist!" a woman in a red sequin dress suddenly yelled.

"Excuse me?" Haylee stood up and glared at her.

"Try me, bitch." The woman and her red sparkles bristled. "Do you know who I am here with?" She pointed to a woman in a black dress, who had her back to them as she was taking photos.

"Who is that?" Haylee whispered to one of the guys by her.

"Haylee, that's Doja Cat!"

Haylee's eyes widened. "Doja Cat?" she said a bit too loudly.

A woman who was definitely not Doja Cat turned around, hearing her name, and flashed a big smile at the crowd. Her hair was honey-colored and bobbed. She blended in way too much to be a major celebrity. "Who's calling me?"

"It's the lady of the house, Haylee Milani!" someone said.

"That little bitch lives here?" the red-sequined-dress woman sneered.

"That girl? She looks twelve!" Doja laughed, waving at Haylee.

"I'm fourteen," Haylee said, lifting her champagne glass, as if the sophistication of the move made up for her lack of years.

"Yikes!" Doja said. She turned to her handlers. "I'm hungry—can we get to the main hall?"

Haylee stood there stunned, as Fake Doja Cat walked away and disappeared into the crowd. She hoped Roxanna was sober enough to notice she wasn't the real deal.

Haylee sank back into the giant peach velvet couch. She

checked her phone. She had tons of notifications, as she expected, but many were just tagged tweets, calling the Milani party a "superspreader" event and denouncing Al and his daughters.

"Superspreading? What the hell?" she said.

"Superspreading." An older woman laughed. "Definition: what we are doing right now!"

Haylee squinted at her. "Like spreading the virus?"

The woman nodded drunkenly. "Who the hell cares!"

Haylee got up, disgusted. "There is no virus, lady."

Roxanna and Violet never succeeded in finding the ayahuasca shaman/alleged rapist, but Roxanna did get stopped by some media.

"Roxanna-Vanna Milani, how does it feel to be throwing *the* party of the pandemic?" asked the interviewer, inexplicably wearing a plaid suit.

Roxanna was blinded by the camera lights.

"Well, hopefully, we're sending it off," she said, laughing. "Kissing it goodbye or whatever!"

"Do you think this is the official end of the virus?"

Roxanna paused. "Who can say, but for our sake, for tonight's sake, sure, like, why the fuck not?"

"Roxanna-Vanna, can you tell us a little bit about who is here?"

"Well, they say, um, Doja Cat and Lil Nas X and I think the Hadids? Some of the Kardashians and their people are supposed to come too," she said, looking around.

"We hear Cardi B is here!" the interviewer declared.

"Where? Wow, I didn't know! To be honest . . . the guest list got crazy, I have, like, no clue. I guess everyone needed a party after what we've been through!"

"Are you worried about the absence of masks and potential for The Party to be a superspreader?"

"Do I look like I'm worried about anything?" Roxanna flashed the popular TikTok tongue-wag square at the camera. "Let's not be a buzzkill, okay? It's too late for that! When life gives you masks, throw a mask-erade!"

"Got it. Well, can you tell us a bit about the show?"

"Oh, yeah, sure," Roxanna said, stalling. She wasn't sure what to say and she couldn't recall what the publicist had advised. "We're the Milanis. It'll be about all of us, our everyday lives. And you're living it right now!"

"We hear the Kardashians may be ending their hit reality show. . . ."

Roxanna rolled her eyes. "Is that even confirmed?"

"Some worry it will be the death knell for reality television!"

Roxanna shrugged. "I highly doubt that! Things have gotten way too real for us to be sick of reality, like, you know what I mean?" She paused. "Is Khloé here or not?"

"Final question: So you just turned eighteen years old and—"

Roxanna made a disapproving noise. "No, no, let's not age me! My birthday's in November, love! Scorpi-ess here, thank you!"

"Guess we got that wrong—thanks for clarifying! Well, thank you, Roxanna-Vanna. Have a wonderful night—this has certainly been a party to remember, and we look forward to seeing you on television soon!"

As the man disappeared, Roxanna flashed one of those immaculate winks she'd practiced in front of the bathroom mirror.

Suddenly Violet popped back in, as if she'd split to stay away from the camera. "I think I see Cardi B!" she said, excited.

"What? Where?" Roxanna's heart was racing. She loved Cardi.

Violet was pointing to the kitchen, where a group was huddling around someone. It looked like someone was readjusting her dress and a team of assistants was helping her reassemble it. It was a mess of feathers and rhinestones and gauze—just the thing you'd imagine Cardi pulling off.

Roxanna grabbed Violet's hand, and they rushed over. "It's so great when it's your own party, and you can just do shameless things like this—like we can act any whatever way, since this is our house!" Roxanna laughed into the crowd as they bumped and nudged and pushed their way into the kitchen.

"Roxanna, they are claiming Turkish Delight kicked a child!" Rose suddenly rushed at her.

"Who is that? Like, a drag queen?"

"One of the golden horses!" Rose looked way too upset for Roxanna to deal with, so she snapped her head to the room's focal point.

And there she was, waving her bangled arms with a raspy but high-pitched, booming twang, ordering a couple of assistants to tie her straps tighter, shrieking every time they were too tight.

"Oh my god, I just want to say hi, I'm such a huge fan!" Roxanna gushed into the cluster of people around Cardi.

Cardi rolled her eyes with an amused smile. "That's what they all say! Who the fuck are you?"

Roxanna rolled her eyes back, mirroring her by accident. "I, like, own this place, bitch!" she said, laughing, the alcohol and drugs in her allowing that *bitch* to come out just perfect.

Cardi looked surprised. "This kid owns the place?"

"Her daddy does," one of her assistants said.

"No way! Okay, girl! You Puerto Rican?" she said, looking Roxanna up and down.

"She's Persian!" one of the other assistants yelled.

Roxanna froze. How did they know? Some people, of course, had to know, as Al's crowd was here too, and there were only so many in Hollywood one could keep a secret like that from, but Roxanna was still shocked.

"Italian," Roxanna said in a low tenor, unsure of who could be listening, and added, for realism, "mixed. Kind of. Long story!"

"I gotchu!" Cardi grinned and squealed as her assistants wrapped her in a ropelike layer of ribbons.

Rose again appeared at Roxanna's ear. "Hey, Roxanna, they say there's a man who's been puking really intensely in your room upstairs—they have him lying down. Shall we call the paramedics? I can't find Al or Homa."

Roxanna turned red with rage and squared herself, so she was staring Rose straight in the eye. "Ew, not my room! And are you, like, fucking crazy, Rose? Are you kidding me?"

Rose shook her head. She looked panicked.

"Rose, are you, like, out of your mind? Do you see this all? Cardi right here, all the models and rappers and NBA players and media and everything? There will be no fucking cops or firefighters or ambulance—you got that?"

"But what do we do about that man?" Rose asked. She looked helpless, and very sober.

Roxanna rolled her eyes and shrugged. "Do we, like, know him?"

Rose shook her head.

"Then it's not, like, our fucking problem! People are, like, apparently getting sick everywhere every second these days! It's like a fucking pandemic—a good time to, like, play that card? I mean, maybe, like, tell him we can't have COVID here and his whole pukey things feels sus and COVID-y! Anyway, get him outta here, thanksies!" She waved her arms frantically, hoping Cardi had heard none of this, and excused herself to find more drugs, as the night was still young.

Al had thought the whole thing was Roxanna's party, mainly, so he was surprised by just how many people recognized him. He was enjoying The Party, enjoying so much, including, for once, not being the only man in that huge house of his. Finally he felt in his natural element. Homa kept locking herself in different guest bathrooms to take little naps until someone knocked—

probably needing it to do drugs. Al was happy that he was mostly left to himself to entertain.

A famous tennis player (that's who Randy told him he was) and a social media comedian were asking him about Pizza-bomme. Apparently, they were the only two people at The Party who had never tried one.

"You know, it's very funny you are all asking this, because I thought about having some Pizzabomme here for The Party!" he admitted. It had been a short-lived argument between him and Roxanna, Al insisting that their Holiday Pizzabomme was an upscale version of the original. They could even serve the organic version or the Japanese versions that featured ume and miso? He was fine with a compromise, but Roxanna wouldn't hear of it. He even appealed to her sense of irony: *It could be kitschy, Roxi—isn't that what you guys call it?* But she kept remind-ing him this was an upscale, A-list party. *No offense, Dad, but we may be, like, junk-food heiresses but we don't need to hang out with the junk in front of people. It's not like we even eat it!* Points had been made, and Al dropped it.

But of course, the house was supplied with lots of boxes of Pizzabomme. They had a whole extra freezer in the basement, next to the wine cellar, with pretty much every flavor possible, rock solid on ice. No one really touched the stuff, but it was important to Al somehow that it be there.

"Well, can we try one? Or a few?" the comedian kept asking. "I've seen the commercials!"

"Yeah, same here, but I just want to know—is it like a Hot Pocket?" the tennis player asked.

"We do not discuss the competition in this house." Al chuckled.

He sent Rose down for an assortment of Pizzabomme and she came up with a platter, freshly microwaved. She had left them plainly on their wax-paper wrapping, a few oozing and crum-bling. There was no way to dress them up.

Al theatrically made jazz hands, as they were placed on the counter. Several people took photos with their cell phones.

"Okay, okay, moment of truth—let's try a bite!" the comedian called out.

"Say no more," Al said a bit proudly, as he approached the platter with a steak knife. He had an uncanny ability, even after not having Pizzabomme for years, for knowing just which one was which, without slicing in. There were subtle differences in the shade and texture of the dough that were invisible to most, but not to Al.

He chose an Independence Day–themed Pizzabomme, their latest offering, just in time for the upcoming holiday. There were swirls of red and white on the pastry shell, meant to resemble the stripes of the flag, with gray blobs for stars. Al was very proud of this limited-edition option, as it featured the best flavors of the cookout: hamburger, barbecue sauce, corn, potato chips. The reviews had just come in, and they were excellent.

He also chose a Classic Original Pizzabomme for contrast. He carefully sliced the two options into several bite-size pieces, speared them with toothpicks, and gestured to his guests. "Please! Help yourself and enjoy! Careful, it might be hot!"

The tennis player and the comedian were now flanked by others craning their necks, as if this were a stand with samples in a suburban discount megastore. More people than he initially thought had not tried his Pizzabomme, or else they were putting on a show.

The smell of cheap, generic cheese, low-grade tomato paste, and plasticky dough filled the air as if Barbie-doll food had melted on a radiator.

"Well, well, well!" the comedian said, applauding. "I think I have had these before! How could I forget! My compliments to the chef!"

Al beamed, even though he registered the hyperbole.

"Hmmm, not bad, not bad," the tennis player was saying,

while feeding a woman in a tight iridescent dress who looked way too pleased.

"You know, it's not rocket science—I just saw a need out here and we made it! I was new to the country, and I had no fear," Al said, and suddenly he remembered he did not talk about the old country with others.

"Pizza is universal!" someone in the crowd called, saving him.

"Yes, we even have pizza in Iran," one of his Iranian friends said from the back, without outing him entirely. "We top them with stews sometimes. Delicious!"

"We have an international line, yes!" Al said and launched into a speech about his company's history.

Roxanna was on her way to the back door of the house to meet a drug dealer when she passed her dad and the crowd and picked up the unmistakable stench of that cursed "food" of his.

She rushed to his side and hissed in his ear, "Dad, what the fuck is this? You promised!"

"Roxi, baby, they asked about it—they're in our house! They probably wonder what the House of Milani is all about!"

"We begged him!" the comedian said. "Wow, is that Roxanna-Vanna?" he asked a young woman at his side, who nodded with wide eyes.

"It smells disgusting—please make it go away, Rose, after they have their quick little sideshow or whatever this, like, freak gathering is!" Roxanna waved her arms as she walked away.

Al watched his daughter storm off, and smiled at the platter. Only a few samples were left. "Kids are never proud of you the way you are of them!" he said. "None of this would be possible without my little Pizzabomme."

"The end of the pandemic, brought to you by Pizzabomme!" the comedian howled, and everyone laughed way too loud and for far too long.

◆

By 1 a.m., The Party was getting out of hand. There had been a bomb threat and the snake charmer lost a baby snake and the woman everyone thought was Cardi B turned out to just be a Cardi B impersonator named Caridee Bree. The rest of the celebrities were real, Roxanna was assured. She had dragged Damon into her room with a few choice friends to do lines of a new psychedelic drug from Eastern Europe, and Homa was attempting to sleep in her own bedroom, but it was just impossible with every wall vibrating with the bass and cackles and fireworks and car alarms too. The police had stopped by several times, always to be greeted by Al. He knew the police chief well, and slipped hundreds into the cops' palms while offering selfies.

The quietest place in the house was Mina's room, just not for the reasons she had imagined. Mina was still there with Lila. They had stepped out only to fill their plates with food and refresh drinks, but each time they rushed back. It turned out they shared a mutual love of K-pop, and Mina had quite the collection on her computer, something, to her relief, that would take hours and hours to get through showing off.

Lila sat on the edge of Mina's bed—which Mina tried to ignore, it was so thrilling and terrifying—while Mina sat in her desk chair, navigating her computer and messing with her speakers.

"I really hope Ateez tours next year—I can't believe how many shows they had to cancel. I had really good floor seats for their Berlin show," Lila said.

"Yeah, that's like me with Red Velvet and NCT," Mina said, putting on an Ateez B side. "Who's your Ateez bias, anyway?"

Lila smiled and rolled her eyes at herself. "Definitely San bias with Wooyoung bias-wrecking but sometimes Yunho gets me too," she said. "And I think I just kind of want to be Seonghwa."

Mina nodded. "I'm Yunho with San bias wreck," she said. "I think everyone wants to be Seonghwa, though."

"Queer girls, for sure," Lila said, staring hard at the side of

Mina's head. Mina could not turn her head and meet Lila's eyes. She was so scared that she would kiss Lila—she never imagined she would have her first kiss before going to college, but suddenly it was all she could think of. She kept trying to push the thought away and then something Lila would do would make the feeling impossible to ignore again.

Meanwhile, Pari had become social, darting between their ankles, back and forth, little cat figure eights, with her tail raised, alert and bold.

"Pari is such a flirt," Mina mumbled, hoping she didn't sound like a flirt for saying that.

"We have three Siamese cats—Belle, Ariel, and Jasmine, for the Disney princesses," Lila said. "Cats are the best. I trust cat people."

Mina nodded. "Same." She thought about telling Lila the story of the pet psychic and everything that had happened, but decided it was maybe still too early for that one. She felt like she had to ration anecdotes through the night. She had no idea when Lila was going to leave. In a way she hoped it would be soon so they could end on a high note. She kept worrying she would do something disastrous and Lila would vanish to dust, turning out to be just another anxiety dream of hers.

"I can't wait to leave Tehrangeles," Lila said suddenly.

"What?"

"I can't wait to leave Los Angeles," Lila repeated.

"Oh," Mina said. "That too."

Lila looked flustered, suddenly. "Sorry, I'm not used to conversation and talking to people with lockdown and all. I think I forgot how normal talking works. It just popped into my head."

Mina turned to look at her, concerned. "I hate this party too."

Lila laughed, shaking her head. "I don't mean this party! I mean the city, I swear!" She paused, shyly. "I am actually having such a nice time at this party, surprisingly. I didn't expect to. I thought I would have left hours ago."

Mina matched her fluster. "Oh." She revised, as that sounded weird. "Yeah, I was supposed to be asleep by now."

"Oh, I am so sorry for keeping you up!" Lila said. "I actually could go. It's really late. I can just call an Uber—I don't live that far."

Mina suddenly felt her stomach drop like a roller coaster in free fall. "Please don't go!" she heard herself almost whine. She was mortified. "Sorry—I think I forgot how to speak normally too. This is probably the longest lockdown conversation I've had with anyone outside my family."

Lila nodded. "I was gonna tell you that, but I didn't want it to sound weird, even though I keep sounding weird."

Mina smiled tensely. "It doesn't sound weird," she said quietly, not knowing quite what to say.

"I am really happy we met," Lila said, leaning in a bit.

Maybe she was imagining the lean, Mina thought.

"You are really cool," Lila added.

Mina wanted to die. That moment was enough. She wished it could stop, while at the same time, she wished she could live inside this single moment forever.

"You are too," Mina nearly whispered. She realized her hands were sweating hard, her heart beating so fast.

Lila suddenly got up, as if to walk to the door. Mina reflexively darted up just a second later, presumably to . . . stop her? she wondered. What was she doing? Mina was struggling to recognize herself. Was she in some Wattpad fan fiction, facing her dream girl?

And like clockwork, the situation escalated, as they both guessed it could. Itzy was playing ecstatically in the background, which felt right, somehow. Lila reached out her hand first, but Mina could have sworn her hand was moving too. Like magnets they attached, both hands sweaty, though Mina thought Lila looked so relaxed and ready, her eyes firmly on Mina's. Mina wanted so badly to look away but it was too late. *Ain't nobody like you, I like you!* Itzy cheered. The thing was about to happen, the thing she had dreamed of forever and took comfort in thinking would never happen. *Now I want you bad, I can't lose!*

It was hard to say who leaned in first, but Mina was willing to bet it was Lila, especially as she towered over her so majestically and Mina felt the shadow of her beautiful shaved head looming over her face.

Mina had no idea how this was to be done, though she'd looked it up before, of course, just in case. This was her first kiss. And as Lila's lips met hers, she was stunned by how natural it felt, how soft and subtle it was at first, only growing more gradually assured and even forceful, as if a dial were turning up in even increments.

Nobody like youuuu, Itzy kept gushing as Pari gave a soft growl and disappeared behind the desk again. Just as they gently bowed down to sit on Mina's bed . . .

It astounded Mina, thinking of her night later, that she had Roxanna and her awful party—which she had fought against so fiercely—to thank for her first kiss.

After the cop's fourth "routine" visit—to appease the neighbors and the calls and to give the general sense they were doing their job—Al had convinced the police officers not to come anymore. He assured them that The Party would definitely wrap up soon. It was 3 a.m. The Party, in reality, was going quite strong, and by this point, Al was more drunk than he realized. He was relieved Homa had turned in early, though he had no idea how she could sleep with all the noise. Still, he felt he was the man of the house and he could call the shots. Violet and Haylee seemed to be attending to their own very different corners of guests while Roxanna had disappeared to her room with some friends and

Damon, and Mina had been missing for hours, as he'd expected she would be. Food and drink were still plentiful, and there was an intriguing rotation of drugs popping up here and there. He had done a couple bumps of coke in between tequila shots with his old electrical-engineer friend Asgar, though he had promised himself that would be it—heart problems ran in his family and he did not want to tempt fate. There were other options. There was even a Persian corner, where people appeared to be passing around opium pipes to classical sitar music.

He stepped outside to take in the scene there. It was wilder than he'd imagined. On the main dance floor, the DJ was playing electronic music and a group of girls around his daughters' age were dancing topless. It was starting to appear like an orgy, and he decided it was bad form for him to look. In another corner, it seemed like people were taking some kind of yoga lesson: they were sitting in full lotus, eyes closed, gazing into the starlight peacefully. He thought it might be nice to join them. Haylee had recently started teaching him yoga poses and he had enjoyed the stretches. Suddenly, a couple in the back began writhing and vomiting violently. There was a bucket next to them—in fact, there were buckets all about the area, and no one seemed to notice, or if they did, they did not care. A few moments later, a thin girl, all by herself, began vomiting too, calmly taking a bucket to barf into.

"Batshit, right?" Randy suddenly piped up, next to him. "And doing this while there is a virus going around!"

Al was relieved Randy was there or he would have sworn he had hallucinated the bizarre scene.

"What kind of yoga makes you throw up like that? Are they just drunk?" Al asked him. "So weird. What could be the benefit? Cleansing?"

Randy chuckled. "Oh, that's not yoga," he said. "Or maybe it is, kind of, but it's actually an ayahuasca ceremony. I mean,

my girls told me about it—I had no idea, but when Roxi told
me about the vomit and how that area needed to be particularly
tended to with sanitation concerns and all, I looked it up."

Al tilted his head at him, confused. "What the hell are you
talking about?"

Randy explained what he could, but eventually he just took
his cell phone out, Googled it, and showed Al:

*Ayahuasca—also known as the tea, the vine, and la purga—is
a brew made from the leaves of the Psychotria viridis shrub along
with the stalks of the Banisteriopsis caapi vine, though other
plants and ingredients can be added as well. This drink was used
for spiritual and religious purposes by ancient Amazonian tribes
and is still used as a sacred beverage by some religious communities in Brazil and North America, including the Santo Daime.
Traditionally, a shaman or curandero—an experienced healer who
leads Ayahuasca ceremonies—prepares the brew by boiling torn
leaves of the Psychotria viridis shrub and stalks of the Banisteriopsis caapi vine in water. A highly concentrated liquid is produced.
It's strongly recommended that Ayahuasca only be taken when
supervised by an experienced shaman, as those who take it need
to be looked after carefully. Before partaking in an Ayahuasca
ceremony, it's recommended that participants abstain from cigarettes, drugs, alcohol, sex, and caffeine to purify their bodies. It's
also often suggested to follow various diets, such as vegetarianism
or veganism, for two to four weeks prior to the experience. This
is believed to free the body of toxins. Ayahuasca ceremonies are
usually held at night and last until the effects of Ayahuasca have
worn off. After consuming the Ayahuasca, most people start to
feel its effects within twenty to sixty minutes. The effects are dose-
dependent, and the trip can last two to six hours. Those who take
Ayahuasca can experience symptoms like vomiting, diarrhea, feelings of euphoria, strong visual and auditory hallucinations, mind-
altering psychedelic effects, fear, and paranoia. It should be noted*

that some of the adverse effects, such as vomiting and diarrhea,
are considered a normal part of the cleansing experience. It's not
uncommon for those taking Ayahuasca to experience both positive
and negative effects from the brew.

"So, yeah, it's pretty batshit!" Randy laughed.

Al looked over his shoulder with the wide-eyed look of a kid on Christmas. "Not batshit—it sounds amazing!" he cried. "Wow, no one told me about this!"

Randy shrugged. "Why would they? The girls probably were worried you wouldn't want it here."

Al was shocked. "What? Why would I not? This sounds like the most incredible thing happening here tonight!"

Randy didn't know what to say.

"In fact, why don't we join them?" Al knew the alcohol was talking—and so did Randy—but he didn't care. He had taken mushrooms once at a party in his early years in America, and while it had been a bit terrifying, he had loved it too. His business partners and friends always only had coke, which he never found to be that fun. But this drug and this ritual, this seemed not just fun, but profound.

"Al, I don't think this is a good idea," Randy mumbled, smiling nervously, as another woman began to hurl. Randy pointed to the group. "They're in a trance, waking up to throw up violently. Does that look fun to you?"

Al realized he had a point, but he was so intrigued. He knew he would not have a wild night like this again. He walked over to the shaman, a thin, shirtless man in a baseball cap, wearing a long skirt with peace signs over it. He was peering out into the group, nodding occasionally at the vomiters, as if to say, *You got this.*

Randy considered stopping Al, but thought he better just disappear, lest he get roped into this fiasco. Al would certainly have forgotten he was on the clock.

"Hi, sir—how do I join this?" Al asked with a big smile.

The shaman looked him up and down. "It's a bit late, friend. These guys got started a while ago."

Al sighed. "Okay, I know, but I really want to be part of this. I want your magic!" He said it, he hoped, charmingly.

The shaman shook his head gingerly.

Al never took well to being told no. Especially not at his house. "Hey, listen to me, buddy, this is my party that you are at. I call the orders here, not you. If I want to participate in some ceremony on my grounds, I can—got it?"

The shaman looked taken aback, less by Al's rage than by his being the host of The Party. "Oh, dude, my bad, I did not realize this was your party. Very sorry!" He put out his hand. "I used to sell pills to Roxi back in the day."

Al nodded, relieved. "I wish she were here getting enlightened too!"

The shaman nodded. "Yeah, I tried to tell her. I thought she would be into it, but she gets antsy. She said she had a lot to tend to tonight. The other shaman was a rapist, they say. Amazing party, by the way."

Al beamed. "It's been pretty good. Rapist? Anyway, does this thing conflict with booze and some coke?"

The shaman paused. "Well, officially yes, but we're doing things different tonight. The thing is being chill and along for the ride. You know?"

Al gave him a thumbs-up, and the shaman escorted him over to a seat cushion. Next to it was one of those buckets. He crouched by Al as he sat and said simply, "Okay, I want you to think about what you want to know about yourself after tonight. If you can't think of anything specific, most people start with *Reveal to me who I am.*"

Al gave another thumbs-up and, seemingly out of midair, the shaman brought him a cup made out of some sort of eco-friendly bamboo. In it was tea. "It's gonna take around a half hour to kick in," the shaman said. "Some people like to say, *Drink, don't think.* But whatever works for you. Just try not to fight it."

Al decided to not even look at the tea and take a big swig: it tasted awful, like molasses with vinegar and gasoline and some vague herby essence that gave it a somehow more pleasant aftertaste.

"Great job, Amir," the shaman said. Al didn't bother to correct him. He was trying to be at peace.

The shaman walked away, and suddenly Al noticed Randy wasn't with him. Typical. He looked around, and the crowd was composed mainly of young women. Not all of them had their eyes closed, but many did. One older woman started screaming into the ground until the shaman appeared by her side. She started to cry.

"Oh, yeah, you might cry," the shaman whispered down to Al as he made his rounds after tending to her.

Al decided to just give another thumbs-up. As the clock ticked on, he grew more and more excited, and then, just as if perfectly on time, around the half-hour point, Al started seeing strange swirls in the sky, as if the stars and moon were in a blender. The Party and its sounds were closing in on themselves and everything was growing much louder and then much softer.

It was happening.

He saw the shaman's face suddenly come close to his, wearing a big grin, his hand giving Al's a high five. "You got this," the shaman said.

"I sure do!" Al said, laughing, and his laughter sounded like breaking glass, like a roaring subway, like a very large earthquake. He felt powerful.

And then all sorts of memories came flooding to him. His daughters at various ages, past employees in different offices, Homa at a café or at a restaurant or at a benefit or just at home relaxing. He saw his parents. His relatives.

And he saw, most vividly of all, Iran.

His brain was flooded with prayers, nursery rhymes, pop songs, TV commercials, protest slogans, everything in Farsi, everything he'd once known so well.

He thought, *Please don't take me there, not back to Iran,* and just as he struggled in the tangles of that thought, he felt vomit forcefully push up through his insides burning his throat, until he let it out into the bucket. The shaman handed him a roll of toilet paper, gesturing to his chin.

It was too late to be at The Party, to be present there. The tea transported him somewhere else, somewhere he had long tried to escape. He was going back to Iran. Actually, it was less that he was going back than Iran was coming to him. Meeting him on his soil, on his domain, at his very home. *Reveal to me who I am,* the shaman had said, and here he was, with a much stronger sense of it than he had wanted: he was Iranian. And he was in Tehrangeles.

He could taste it—sumac, saffron, rosewater—and he could hear it, the sitar and santur and tabla and all kinds of other ancient instruments. All the most beautiful things of his culture. And then the unfortunate ones too: the notorious prison where cousins and friends who were left behind had died, the horrible pollution weighing down the skyline, the old murals and monu-ments removed and replaced with harsh, authoritarian slogans, grim factories and government buildings where there were once palaces and ballrooms and discos and bars. He saw Iran, the Iran of today, in black and white. He learned he was not surprised by all the women in hijab and chador but by their expressions of acceptance. He saw only their disapproval when their eyes met his, as if he were the one who was wrong, the outsider who had the wrong story. Somehow the narrative was twisting and turn-ing beyond his control, and he realized he was learning a lesson, that this was the reason this mass of people was sitting in his yard praying to the heavens and vomiting up their hors d'oeuvres and booze.

Please, I don't want to stay in Iran, he heard himself cry, but it was in the voice he had had when he was a child. It startled him how it sounded so realistic, until it hit him that this voice had existed in him all along, that he could have accessed it all these years, if only he weren't so . . . so something.

Please, I just want to go back to Tehrangeles, he said. *I belong there now—this isn't my homeland.*

But he knew that was a lie. Iran was a part of him.

I don't need to prove I'm American—look at my house, my mansion, look at all these people, these Americans. They don't doubt or question me. I belong! he was now sobbing into his own lawn.

The shaman tapped him on the shoulder, mouthing, *Are you okay?*

Not really! Al said, crying, and the shaman motioned to a young barefoot woman wearing a ratty peasant dress. She waved at him to come inside his own home.

He didn't question it—he was a child—and before he knew it, he was in a dark room, one of his own guest rooms, full of mats, where half a dozen people were in various degrees of sleep or rest. One man was snoring loudly and a woman moaning.

Al started laughing at the absurdity of feeling like a stranger in his own home, but soon he was crying again, knowing his trip was far from over. He was stuck with his memories. He had never been done with Iran.

Reveal to me who I am, he kept hearing himself think, over and over, until the words bent around themselves and he heard them in Farsi. His feet were burning terribly.

When he crawled into bed with Homa two hours later, at dawn, Homa annoyed he had chosen to share a bed that night of all nights, he began muttering to her in Persian.

She darted up, staring at him in his pathetic state. She looked at him with pure awe. It wasn't that he was high—she expected booze and worse. Rather, it was the first time she had heard Al speak that much Persian in years—or, maybe, ever.

When the sun rose, they were both crying in each other's arms for reasons neither of them quite understood.

Homa knew; Homa remembered.

زیبایی طبیعی ایران
نگارش هما میلانی

من مطمئن نیستم که در اینجا به چه چیزی فکر کنم، بنابراین در مورد.
چیزی که دلم برایش تنگ شده است خواهم نوشت: ایران و طبیعت

یکی از چیزهای ایران که دلم برایش تنگ شده طبیعت است. مردم.
متوجه نیستند که ایران کشوری بسیار زیبا و پر از شکوه طبیعی است

بیابان خالی نیست. در حالی که ما چند صحرای معروف داریم، من
دوست ندارم در این مورد تاکید کنم

زیرا این کلیشه ایران و کل خاورمیانه است. در ایران چیزهای بیشتری .
برای لذت بردن وجود دارد

یکی از جا های مورد علاقه من برای بازدید کوه دماوند بود. خیلی ها.
نمی دانند که این بلند ترین نقطه ایران و در واقع غرب آسیا است

جزو رشته کوه البرز و نزدیک دریای خزر است.

درباره کوه دماوند در اساطیر، شعر، موسیقی و هنرهای تجسمی ایرانی.
بسیار گفته شده است

همچنین این یک آتشفشان با چشمه های آب گرم معدنی است. در نزدیکی.
چشمه ها گرمابه های عمومی وجود دارد

و برخی معتقدند بیماران را می توان با آب آن درمان کرد

قزل آلای قهوه ای آن معروف است. شقایق سرخ، درختان پسته، .
درختان بید، درختان بلوط و بسیاری گیاهان دیگر دارد

در یک روز صاف می توانید آن را از تهران ببینید. در تمام طول سال.
پوشیده از برف است

من از افراد زیادی را نمی شناسم که به آن صعود کرده باشند. شما باید در،
فرم بدنی عالی باشید. روزهای زیادی طول می کشد

و به تجهیزات خاصی نیاز دارید. (دایی من می خواست آن را امتحان کند
تا به کمک آن برای صعود به قله اورست تمرین کند

اما وضعیت سلامتی خوبی نداشت.)

من از رفتن به گیلان هم لذت می بردم، جایی که برخی می گویند بستگان
دور من از آنجا هستند. از تهران به آنجا مسیری طولانی است

اما به هشت ساعت یا بیشتر می ارزد. شما میتوانید به جنگل ماسال که به
زیبایی معروف است بروید

این یک جای عالی برای پیاده روی است. روستا های منحصر به فرد و
جالب زیادی در این منطقه پراکنده هستند

سپس آبشار لاتون است که بسیار زیباست. بلندترین آبشار ایران است..
شما می توانید در آن یک پیک نیک داشته باشید و برخی حتی در آن شنا
میکنند

جایی که هرگز نرفته ام اما امیدوارم روزی که به ایران برگردیم از آن
دیدن کنم جنگل ابر در منطقه ی هیرکانی خزردر استان سمنان
است

آنجا به دلیل ارتفاع و نحوه قرارگیری کوه ها به نظر می رسد که پوشیده
از ابر است و شما می توانید چیزی شبیه راه رفتن روی

ابرها را تجربه کنید. وقتی نوجوان بودم آرزوی زندگی در آنجا را داشتم
و پدرم به من میگفت که فقط حیوانات وحشی بسیار عجیب و غریب

در آنجا زندگی می کنند و بنابراین فکرمیکردم شاید آن موقع آنجا بمیرم!!
هنوز خیلی دیر نشده

به هر حال من معتقدم مردم باید بیشتر روی طبیعت ایران تمرکز کنند.
این موضوعی است که به ندرت مورد بحث قرار می گیرد

زیرا مردم به شدت به سیاست و مذهب و نفت و همه اینها توجه دارند. اما
اگر زیبایی های طبیعی ایران را در نظر نگیرید، چیزهای

زیادی را از دست می دهید.این هرگز از ذهن من خارج نشده و مطمئن
هستم که روزی دوباره آن را کشف خواهم کرد

14

The Aftermath

In spite of a temporary cancellation campaign on social media, The Party was deemed a success by all who attended. Roxanna was so stunned to see a friend of Khloé Kardashian's post a selfie with the Cirque du Soleil performers, and Rico Nasty's cousin tweeted, "Pandemic or not, parties still lit #MilaniMansion," with three purple smiling-devil emojis. A bunch of people she didn't know also tweeted about it and Damon, on his rarely used Instagram, put up a selfie of himself and a very drunk-looking Roxanna. She decided she wouldn't ask him to delete it because of how skinny she looked. She had made three outfit changes that night, which made Violet say, *It's like it's your wedding, Roxi!* to which Roxanna had said, *It might as well be.* And when Al got the final tally for the cost of the thing, he had to agree.

"We made history—you can't put a price tag on that!" Roxanna declared.

No one asked how it was that they made history, but it was clear that to Roxanna—and maybe to others—it was *the* party of the pandemic. No lockdown event could top it. And maybe the irony of that made it extra delicious. Roxanna knew it wasn't going to happen again.

Randy and Rose were still cleaning, long after two sets of cleaning crews left, when the sisters gathered on their favorite poolside perches to debrief. Roxanna had made sure there was a special hangover menu set—a jumbo margarita for her and deviled eggs and pancake bites and gold-dusted doughnut holes for her sisters.

Haylee was wearing her extra-oversize Tom Ford butterfly sunglasses that covered half her face. She looked either ill or angry, but definitely not social. She was buried in her phone and had nothing to contribute.

Violet looked cheerful, relieved it was finally over, as she polished off doughnut after doughnut and licked the gold flakes off her fingers. She had mastered making hot-chocolate bombs and was deeply engaged in the chocolate globe erupting into a bouquet of tiny marshmallows in her hot oat milk.

Mina . . . well, Mina looked surprising. Roxanna had never seen a glow like that on her sister. She looked engaged, happy to be there, even refreshed. She was sunning in a shimmery black bandeau Roxanna had never seen her wear, though she also had an old flannel thrown over it and wore ratty jean shorts. She was still Mina.

"Well, how did we do?" Roxanna asked, peering more into her phone than at her sisters. "I mean, like, I know how, but humor me! I feel like hell, but it was so worth it!"

"I can't believe Dad did ayahuasca." Violet giggled.

"I thought Randy was joking but I saw Dad for a second and he looked like he had been crying!" Roxanna laughed. "The ayahuascers seemed to have a good night, all in all, though the shaman kind of creeped me out. Glad the rapist one split, though!"

"Mom doesn't know what to do with him today," Violet said, shaking her head.

"I wish Britney had made it," Roxanna said, sighing into her phone. "Can you imagine the headlines we'd be seeing today? It would have been so beyond!"

"I'm surprised they didn't send an impersonator like that awful one who was supposed to be Cardi B," Haylee grumbled.

"Oh, Hayles! You okay? You were rolling with some, like, weirdos," Roxanna said pointedly.

Haylee shrugged, closing her eyes behind her sunglasses. She wasn't about to get into it with Roxanna, not today.

"Okay, but can we say, Mina, like what the fucking fuck?" Roxanna dramatically gushed. "Like, what were you even doing last night? I didn't see you once. Maybe once, but barely! But you look amazing and like you are acting so sus, Mins!"

Mina blushed. She didn't want to spoil it. And she also didn't know how much they could handle. She hadn't totally gotten over those homophobic tweets of Roxanna's.

"She cat-sat Pari, of course!" Violet winked at Mina, but Mina wasn't sure why. Violet had definitely seen her and Lila chatting, but did she know they spent all those hours in her room?

"I did, indeed." Mina smiled. "Pari did well. And, well, I did come out and I did make some friends, so that was a surprise!"

"Holy shit, could this be Mina enjoying a party? One of my parties? *The* Party? Mina, who opposed the thing with all her heart and soul, who thought, like, this night would destroy us?"

"Well, you did get canceled again," Mina said. "But, yeah, I'm not too proud to say, it had some high points, and I'm glad I was there."

Roxanna applauded into the sunlight. Winning Mina over felt like a strangely satisfying triumph.

"That girl seemed really cool, Mina," Violet said gently.

Mina met her eyes searchingly. She couldn't tell what she knew. Violet was so damn discreet. She sat back and texted Violet, *What are you referring to? What do you know? Did you see something?*

Violet slowly typed, *I was with you when you met but yep I saw her leave your room really late and you guys holding hands, sooooo cute!*

Mina's eyes widened and she glanced up at Violet, who was smiling into her phone.

"What girl?" Roxanna asked. Of course, she had noticed that something was up immediately.

"A friend I made," Mina said. "This girl Lila, who lives not that far from here."

"Lila? What did she look like?"

Mina tried to be careful not to blush. "She was very tall with a shaved head, in this long white dress and biker jacket."

"Like a model, basically," Violet said almost in unison. "Very striking. Giving nineties Sinéad in a really fashion way."

"Oh, weird, I think I remember! She was with those gay kids, right? I think they were friends with Lil Nas X's backup dancers?"

Mina shrugged. "I couldn't say. We didn't really talk to anyone else."

"Huh," Roxanna said, gears shifting in her head. She gave Mina one more good look, taking it all in. She had a suspicion, but she didn't want to chip into everyone's good—or decent—moods.

Meanwhile, Lila had been texting Mina all morning—at first to thank her for The Party and say what a good time she had, but then to also mention being a bit worried about their physical contact, given the virus.

I know I know I thought about that too but . . . I can't say I regretted it. We all got tested the day before and we were all clear but I'll get tested tomorrow again, Mina wrote.

Yeah, I definitely do not regret it either. It was just a surprise. I did not expect to at that party. I didn't expect YOU, Lila typed back.

Mina's heart felt like it was literally melting—she could not believe her luck. In less than twenty-four hours, her life had been turned upside down. Here she was, after her first kiss, worrying if she had contracted a virus because of it. It was the best kind of concern, the anxiety of someone who was finally really alive.

"Well, we'll have another one when this crazy fucking thing is over!" Roxanna said, beaming.

"The government and the media will never let it be over— just watch," Haylee muttered.

They had all learned to ignore those kinds of statements from Haylee.

"Let's manifest it, my babes!" Roxanna said, clapping at no one but herself.

It was only a little over a week after the party—The Party, rather—that Violet started to feel strange. She was spending the afternoon on one of her baking projects, a double-fudge snickerdoodle cake with caramel-apple frosting, when suddenly something was very off. It took her a second to register what it was. As she spooned blobs of batter into her mouth with the spatula—her favorite part—she suddenly realized the batter tasted like . . . nothing. Or, rather, she could not taste it at all. She increased the sugar and cinnamon and added a shot of maple syrup, thinking she must have messed up the flavoring. That wasn't it. She paused and reached for the fridge—her beloved Dr Pepper & Cream Soda was in full stock, so she opened one can and took a big sip. Again: nothing. Her heart began to race—what the hell was this? Did she accidentally take one of Roxi's drugs? Was she tripping? How could this be possible? She cracked open the jar of cardamom on the counter—one of her favorite smells—and nothing. She went to the tube of vanilla extract—another favorite—and, again, nothing.

She started to panic.

This was like a children's fairy tale gone horribly wrong: Was she being punished for a lifetime of gluttony? Would she have to limit her intake of food? Was this going to teach her a lesson? And how would she tell people about this, and could it please, oh please, be restored?

She had another thought. She put her head under the opening of her blouse, sniffing at her armpits, which should have smelled like sweat and lavender deodorant. But again: nothing. How could she not even smell herself?

She was starting to feel frantic. She went over to one of Pari's litter boxes and inhaled: nothing again. In a comic version of this same scenario, she'd be thinking this could have some benefits—a world without shit, farts, and burp smells!—but she was far too distressed.

Rose, who was cleaning the pantry, caught Violet in her frenzied state. Violet was always serene, so the sight of her pacing around the kitchen, grabbing jars and inhaling and slamming them down, upset, was hard to watch.

"Violet, are you okay?" Rose asked gently.

Tears were streaming down Violet's face. "No, I am not, Rose!" she said, trying to choke back bawls. "Something is very wrong. Can you tell me something—can you smell this?" She put the bowl of batter under Rose's nose.

Rose nodded. "It smells delicious, Violet."

Violet looked even more agonized and grabbed Rose's cleaning spray. Rose was alarmed—what was she up to?—but Violet unscrewed it and took a big whiff. "What the fuck? What is this supposed to smell like? Anything?"

Rose shrugged. "Ammonia?"

Violet's eyes grew huge. "Ammonia?! Oh my god, I can't smell ammonia?"

"What's going on, Violet?"

Violet sat on a counter stool and put her head on her arms, bursting into full sobs. "I can't smell or taste, as crazy as that sounds!"

Suddenly Rose understood. She had gone through this with Randy—the doctors had asked him over and over if his sense of taste and smell was compromised. And they had just had that party that the whole internet was calling a "superspreader event."

"Oh, no, Violet," Rose said, backing away from her instinctually.

Violet barely registered Rose's retreat, she was so overwhelmed.

"It's so creepy! Like, how can you explain this? Maybe it's a type of migraine? I guess I could ask Mina—she would know. But it felt so sudden—like, I was so excited to bake and suddenly I realized I couldn't taste or smell the cake! Like, literally how?"

Rose took her hand and cleared her throat, snapping out of her own desire to get far away from Violet. She would disinfect and if she hadn't caught it when Randy had it, maybe she was somehow immune anyway. "Violet, I think I have some bad news. Not sure, but I think no smell and no taste is a sign of the virus."

Violet's head darted up and she looked at Rose, horrified. "What on earth? But I don't feel sick!"

Rose shrugged. "But you might be. Best to call the doctor, I think. I'm sorry to say this. Randy went through it."

Violet's face went ghostly pale. Maybe she was sick, and she hadn't noticed? But how? And then she realized. "The Party. The fucking party."

Rose nodded. "It's very possible. Hundreds of people were just here."

Violet shook her head in denial. "I can't believe this! Is anyone else sick?"

Rose shrugged. "No one has said anything."

Violet ran up to her room and immediately texted her whole family. *You guys, I can't smell or taste. Like it's very intense, not subtle. Rose says it could be the virus. I can't believe it got me. Are you guys okay?*

Slowly each member got the message. Roxanna was driving through the canyons with Damon blasting Frank Ocean, and it was Damon who read her the text. "Oh, shit, I can't be dealing with this right now—she needs to get a grip and see a doc. Like, I can't do this!" Roxanna hollered, ignoring it.

Mina was in her room, tending to a K-pop forum dispute. *Oh my god, I heard about this symptom. Yikes. Take your temp and let's call Dr. Beheshti.*

Haylee was running in the paths behind their home and

paused in her tracks, snorting at the text. *Here we go. There is no virus, sheep. Try some allergy medicine—I have some herbal ones in my room.*

Homa in the garden: *Oh, no, Violet. Gonna call Dr. Beheshti right now.*

Al on a Zoom call: *What sort of illness is no taste and smell? Yeah, call the doc, I guess, but maybe you just need more sleep, baby?*

Meanwhile, Violet decided she would stay in her room to isolate herself from her family, just in case. But the more she looked it up online, the more it seemed like it had to be the virus. Apparently no one knew why people became "anosmic," but it seemed that the virus would attack cells that supported sensory neurons in the nose. The olfactory bulb in the brain was unharmed but the support cells were affected. Most people improved in a month or so, but for some the effects were long-lasting. She read about a woman in Japan who had contracted the virus early and still hadn't recovered her sense of smell and taste; she simply relied on memory to know what the foods she ate tasted like. Doctors weren't sure what it would take for the woman to recover, but they simply tracked her progress, as they did everyone's.

Violet was horrified. What if this was going to be her life? This amazing life she'd lived, with candy and dessert and pastries and pies and cakes and jellies and jams—all of it could already be gone without her even having the chance to say goodbye. On some level she knew it was a silly thought when her life was at stake, but somehow it was easier to fixate on that than to confront that her life might be in danger.

She cried herself to a thick, murky, viscous sleep, and when she woke up, she could feel Dr. Beheshti's hot breath on her face, even through his paper mask. She could see from his eyes that he was smiling at her, and he was so close, she almost worried he could kiss her face. Once again, for a split second, she experienced comic relief at not being able to smell and taste.

"Not Banafsheh being the one down!" he was saying, almost laughing.

"Dr. Beheshti, am I going to go back to normal?" she said softly. She could see Homa pacing in the background, Mina at her side.

"Yes, of course!" he said, going into his bag and fishing out piles of paperwork. "I mean, who knows—we don't understand a lot about this virus—but I highly doubt this is how your story ends, my girl!"

In the days to come, Violet went from having no symptoms but the loss of taste and smell to feeling like she had a mild cold to feeling like she had the flu. Homa called in a special nurse to tend to her, so the rest of them would not get sick. Dr. Beheshti mentioned there was an experimental vaccine in China that was coming but it would still be months until the U.S. had one approved. They had to be cautious, so they stuck to group texts, and the nurse—who specialized in caretaking during this pandemic and swore she had seen many patients through with no one dying on her—wore something that resembled a slightly more fashionable hazmat suit.

Violet felt the days blend into each other, and after the first week she wondered if there was a chance she could die. Was this really how it would go for her? A few years of modeling fame and then the virus would wipe her out? She thought of all the desserts she was missing out on, but she could barely summon the imagination to re-create their taste. A long series of lifeless broths and smoothies and teas were brought to her every day, and they all tasted like air in different textures.

The only person in the family who visited her ended up being, of all people, Haylee. At first everyone assumed that was because of what she reminded them of so often: she didn't believe in the virus, it was fake news, the pandemic was a conspiracy. Homa and Al chastised her and demanded she wear an Israeli Army surplus gas mask that they, for some reason, had on hand in storage, but Haylee refused. She went into Violet's room one afternoon when she knew Violet was up without a mask, even—the truth was no one had seen Haylee in a mask at all this whole time; it was also something she did not believe in. The minute Violet saw Haylee, she was filled with dread. What could be worse than suffering with an illness and then being faced with some fanatical nonbeliever who was there just to challenge you or to somehow prove you were an agent of some grand hoax?

"Please, not now, Haylee," Violet said, her voice sounding like muffled gravel. "I can't argue with you now. I'm sick and it doesn't matter if you don't believe—"

"Who said that?" Haylee said with uncharacteristic gentleness. There was a sober elegance in her demeanor. She took a seat near Violet's bed.

Violet thought she was hallucinating. She saw genuine concern in her sister's face. Haylee's eyes were searching Violet's, but not out of spite, disbelief, scorn, or annoyance. Haylee looked like someone rattled, a war widow who was trying to keep some composure at a memorial. Now Violet was even more scared than she had been before.

"What is it, Hayles? Did they tell you something?" Violet asked. "Am I okay?"

Haylee fought the urge to reach out to her older sister. "No one said anything. And I have no idea—I think you are still stable, like they said? Do you still have a fever?"

Violet nodded. They took her temperature every four hours or so and recorded it on a log. "It's so weird this happened to me."

Haylee nodded. "I know. I wouldn't have thought you." She paused, looking down, and for a moment Violet worried she was going to cry. "I always thought it would be Mina."

Violet thought about it and had to agree. "Yeah, with all her chronic illnesses and her crippled immune system. I hope she stays okay—we have to watch out for her."

Haylee nodded and then clarified her point. "No, I mean there's that, but it's more like she's . . . Beth."

Violet was not following. "Beth? Who is Beth?" For a second, she thought it was her own fevered brain that was missing something obvious.

"*Little Women*, remember?" Haylee said. "I am Amy, you are Meg, Roxi is Jo, and Mina is, obviously, Beth."

It took Violet a second, but then she remembered the book. They had read it to one another one winter break after watching two movie adaptations full of starlets they were all into. The book was mostly skimmed but none of them had liked the movies much either—*old-fashioned is not our vibe ever,* she recalled Roxanna saying. What was nice was that they had noticed their ages and roles lined up rather directly with the girls in the films. Of course, they were much richer and probably more beautiful and they led far more exciting lives, but there were similarities. The setting was depressing, the parents unrelatable, the love interests boring—but the one thing that really stuck with all of them was the dead-sister plotline. Beth had left a big impact on them.

Wait, what if one of us dies? Haylee remembered asking her older sisters.

It is a terrible fear, of course, Violet had said.

Why would we die? People don't die of scarlet fever anymore! Roxanna had told her.

I guess it would be me since I am sick all the time, Mina had said.

Yeah, you're definitely Beth, Haylee had said.

Stop it! None of us are those frumpy girls! Roxanna had snapped. *I mean, I could write a memoir, but I am definitely not some annoying writer girl who is gonna give it up for some guy with a girl's name. Plus, by the time we're older, people will probably live, like, forever!*

"Yeah, I remember—yikes," Violet said. "It was such a sad story."

"I think it was mostly happy," Haylee said. "But that one part was sad. I do remember praying extra hard for a while that Mina would be okay."

"Oh, that's so sweet, Haylee," Violet cooed. It was so unusual to see Haylee like this, so caring and vulnerable and selfless.

"I probably should have prayed more for you," Haylee mumbled, and there it came: the purple eyes, full of tears threatening to overflow. This time, though, it felt real.

"Oh god, Haylee, I am going to be okay! I promise!" Violet tried to laugh, which triggered a chorus of coughs. "I really will. But wait, didn't you not even believe in this?"

Haylee looked at her lap silently. Big single tears, like ones drawn in cartoons, fell into her lap.

"Haylee, answer me. Come on, stop crying. I will be okay! But you've spent months saying this is all a hoax or something!"

Haylee nodded remorsefully. "I don't know. Yeah. Maybe it is. A hoax can still make you sick."

Violet had no idea what to say to that. "You need to leave and go wear a mask, please. Maybe you believe in it now?"

Haylee shrugged, tears still rolling down her face. Suddenly she began heaving in a way that made it seem like she was having a coughing fit too. It took a second for Haylee to recognize it: a panic attack. Mina had had panic disorder all her life and so all the girls knew how to spot it. Once, after an early shoot, Violet had had a mini panic attack too. She had to be convinced not to go to an ER, she was so sure she was dying.

Violet helplessly watched her sister shaking, her eyes growing wider and wider, her face growing paler and paler, her arms flailing like she was trying to fan out a fire. Finally, Haylee got up and began pacing, ranting under her breath: a full breakdown.

"Haylee, Haylee, calm down," Violet was saying, but it was no use.

Hey everyone, Hayles is having a full-on breakdown in my room, can someone get her please, sorry to ask, Violet quickly wrote the family group chat.

Mina popped up at the door, double-masked and in surgical gloves. She went right up to Haylee and held her by the shoulders. "What on earth, Haylee? Why are you here?"

Haylee just continued sobbing.

"She was worried about me, and I guess she believes in it now?" Violet said.

Mina nodded, trying to suppress an eye roll. "Come on—let's get out of here and calm you down in your room. Violet needs to rest."

"Oh my god, what if you get it too—now you are exposed!" Haylee cried.

"What on earth—" Mina had no idea what was going on.

Haylee hugged Mina tightly. "Not Beth!" she kept bawling.

"Oh god, she's calling you Beth because of *Little Women*," Violet said, trying not to laugh, mostly because she did not want to cough.

"Why Beth?" Mina was confused as she tried to wrestle out of Haylee's strong grip.

"Beth dies, I guess?" Violet said.

"Oh," Mina said, remembering. "And I'm most like Beth's character?"

Haylee said something that was muffled into Mina's now-soggy hoodie.

"No one's dying," Violet moaned.

"Violet's going to be okay and so am I!" Mina said to her younger sister.

They were both taken aback by how like a baby Haylee seemed. And it hit them both. They rarely remembered Haylee was still a young teenager.

Mina gathered her out and closed Violet's door after a quick wave. She walked Haylee slowly to her room and sat with her on her bed as she continued to cry. She could not remember the last time she saw Haylee cry like this.

"Did you believe it the whole time and were you just trying to convince yourself it wasn't real?" Mina knew it wasn't quite the time or place, but knowing Haylee, she'd snap back to normal by the next day and pretend this episode never happened.

Haylee sniffled into the air and shrugged at Mina.

"I'm so scared, Mina," she said. "I've been scared. Are we all gonna die? Be honest."

Mina suddenly felt tears burning in her eyes too. She had rarely had a chance to be afraid this whole time, and there was something about her least-vulnerable sister losing it that gave her permission to really be afraid too.

"I'm scared too," Mina said. "And I don't know. No one knows. I don't think so?"

The answer was not good enough for Haylee, who exploded into more sobs. "It's so crazy that we die at all!"

Mina nodded. She had to agree.

"It's weird that being rich can't, like, buy you out of death!" Haylee cried.

Mina wanted to laugh, but it came out as a sob too. She had to admit she knew what Haylee meant. This virus. Just as they were coming of age. She had just had her first kiss.

"Why don't we just tell ourselves we're gonna survive?" Mina said. "We can't lose hope."

Haylee seemed unconvinced but she nodded slowly. "What if the world just grows scarier and scarier?"

Mina didn't know what to say. She thought about *Little Women*. "I think in the real story, Louisa May Alcott's sister gets scarlet fever but then gets better. People do get sick and get better, you know. Dr. Beheshti was not that worried about Violet—young people do okay."

Haylee tried to smile. Later that night, Mina had a mini panic attack of her own, imagining Haylee's state and then worrying about Violet, and it all just came crashing down on her. She tried to distract herself by reading about Louisa May Alcott. She read about Beth, who indeed was based on the author's sister Lizzie. Her heart didn't even sink, she was so passed the point of being distraught, when she saw that Lizzie had died and died young, not unlike Beth. Louisa May Alcott had had a chance to change the story in her novel but she chose not to.

The History of Candy Land
by Violet Milani

In these troubled times, when the sweetness of the world might be escaping us more than we know, let's go back to a question of happier times: Who doesn't love Candy Land? Cupcake Commons, Licorice Lagoon, Molasses Swamp, Lollypop Woods, Peppermint Forest, Gumdrop Mountains! But does everyone know why we all even have a Candy Land to love in the first place? But where this sweet game came from may surprise you, as the story is less sweet than you'd think.

Since the 1950s Candy Land has been incredibly popular, at home and school. The game is like <u>Willy Wonka & the Chocolate Factory</u> *come to life. Children are transported into a mythic kingdom of all things sugar and the game is as easy as pie. But the origins are not quite as appetizing: the game was invented to entertain children in polio wards. The creator of Candy Land was a teacher named Eleanor Abbott, who had had polio herself. She had spent time in a San Diego polio ward, where she learned about the harsh realities of the illness. She wondered how to keep the children who might be there for weeks and months occupied and entertained. Could one actually bring joy to a polio ward? And what could unify all kinds of kids anyway?*

One word: candy.

Let's back up. The first half of the 20th century was plagued by a poliomyelitis virus epidemic. Many cases were presenting in children. It seemed like the virus targeted children. Testing was still not very advanced and the public panicked trying to decipher who was at risk and who wasn't. Polio could refer to "abortive polio" or to "paralytic polio," which could cause the loss of muscle function in one or both legs. The lungs were also targeted by the virus, requiring some to use an "iron lung" to breathe for years.

Since medication was limited and viruses have no known cures, there was little that could be offered apart from physical therapy. Patients could either learn to live with paralysis or learn to walk again after a period of inactivity, depending on how severe their illness was and the level of care they received. Recovery took a long time and so polio wards were set up in many cities across the country. But the polio wards were not always near residential areas and it was not uncommon for patients to spend days there alone and without visitors. This of course would be extra devastating for children who were stuck there.

Abbott came up with an idea: what about a game that centered around something all children loved and with rules so simple that even the sickest kids could understand them? Candy Land was designed to be lengthy so the kids could play for hours and hours on end, to occupy them and also to give their nurses a break. Once the game made its way to the general public, it also helped keep people at home and indoors, and not outside, where they were more likely to be infected, it was believed.

You can even see, in the early illustrations of the game, a boy and girl racing on a path, with the boy wearing a leg brace like polio patients often did.

Eventually Abbott sold the game to Milton Bradley. It released widely in 1949. She reportedly donated most of her earnings from the game to be used for the purchase of supplies and equipment for local schools. Now the game is owned by Hasbro, and it's become one of the most successful games of all time; it sells a million copies a year.

And in 2014, Gamesformotion created a Belgian chocolate version of the game that featured chocolate cards wrapped in paper. Once they are played, they can be eaten, which makes a game like this a bargain! Not a great idea for a polio ward, but perhaps better for us, although we do have a virus of our own now. :/

It took less time than their imaginations all feared for Violet to recover. Slowly her body aches and fever waned. She started walking more and sleeping less. Her sore throat, cough, and congestion cleared up. But the most disconcerting symptom of all—for Violet, that is—her loss of taste and smell, lingered for weeks.

"Oh, come on—that's nothing, given what you have been through! People die of this thing! And you're a model, anyway—isn't this a benefit? Easier to lose weight this way, no?" Dr. Beheshti said, laughing over on the phone.

Violet didn't say anything. She found herself praying every day. She would test out her senses each day with sour gummies and black licorice and Jolly Ranchers—the most flavorful candies she could think of. But, at best, she'd only sense the memory of their tang. She still ate her sweets as if to egg the deficiency on somehow. She needed to be patient.

Meanwhile, Violet's infection affected Haylee the most. Suddenly N95 and KN95 masks were appearing in bulk at their door. Everyone assumed Mina had ordered them. They were wrong. Haylee began wearing the masks indoors, even long after Violet was better. The conspiracy theories she had so fervently believed in had lost their allure for her. She no longer thought the virus was a hoax and she began to distance herself from those who did. All that was left of the old Haylee was a desire to exercise and eat healthy, even more so than before.

Roxanna clung to her usual foolhardy optimism. She had

believed Violet would be fine from day one, but the truth was that she was not well either. Since The Party, she hadn't been the same. She had heard of something called "post-party syndrome," the feeling once the high of a party had worn off. There was nothing for her to look forward to. All that lay ahead for her was something she could not quite understand anymore: normalcy. There would be school to go to again, her friends, her dates with Damon, the usual stuff.

Al was convinced Roxanna's mood had first soured when the producers stopped returning their calls. After The Party, the show kept being pushed back. Roxanna couldn't tell if it was the result of her being canceled a few times or what, but when she checked in, she was told *We will definitely get back to you when there is more news.* But the news didn't come. Meanwhile, other new shows were being advertised. One about a very Scandinavian-looking family of survivalists who had spent the pandemic on a deserted island. Another about a group of nuns who had spent the pandemic months out in the world finding "sinners" and helping them find the right road again. Another—the one that made Roxanna most angry—was called *Bad Girls Gone Good.* It was all about the lifestyle makeovers of famous party girls—all kinds of socialites Roxanna knew well, actually—who had reformed their old ways and become "good girls."

It was hard to miss the message. A family of filthy-rich, decadent Iranians, whose biggest contribution to a global pandemic was a superspreader event, had maybe not the same allure. Plus, the show had been plugged as being about "affluent Iranian sisters at a time of war with Iran," and it looked like the war wasn't going to happen anytime soon.

"But come on, Iran is always in the news!" Roxanna argued to her dad, who was walking her through the possible explanations. "Like, has it ever been a good time to be from Iran in this country? In this world, even? We're always hot, if even in a bad way!"

"True, but times have changed, my Roxi." Al smiled at his

mini-me. "People maybe want a different—what do you guys
call it—a different vibe? All these new shows are not the usual
reality TV stuff. They are maybe more meaningful, more sin-
cere, more good, in a way?"

Roxanna made a gag face. "Who wants to watch that?!"

Al shrugged. "A world where people are dying, maybe," he
muttered.

"I had Violet do a few video journals during her virus!" Roxanna said. "We have those on tape! So we even have the illness
stuff! They can even make that look like worse than it is."

Al sighed. "And you told the producers that. It's all up to
them now, my girl. No matter what, though, we'll be fine. We
don't need to do this show. We're doing fine in the big picture—
we're not like those desperate people who need to do reality TV
to make a few dollars."

Roxanna tilted her head at him, confused. "Like, I've never
been worried about money a day in my life," she said, her voice
shaking. "It's not about that. It's about something much bigger.
Don't you think about how you'll be remembered, Dad?"

Al paused. He thought about it a lot. But it came down
mostly to *rich*. "Sure. Everyone does, maybe."

"I mean, do you really want to be known as some pizza-snack
junk-food tycoon?!" Roxanna was almost screaming. "Like, you
came all the way from Iran just to make Americans diabetic
and heart-diseased for some shitty product you won't even eat
yourself!"

He was about to argue, but he patiently let her continue.

"It's such a joke! No one cares about Pizzabomme! It doesn't,
like, matter in the scheme of the world! Sure, you've got chari-
ties and nonprofits you help out for your tax write-off, but,
seriously, this can't be, like, your legacy. And it can't be ours:
Pizzabomme heiresses?! No way."

"Roxi, you have your whole life to make something of
yourself."

"No, I don't—I'll always be known as that! But this show was an opportunity, a gateway to other things! It was a way in for me! It was a way to show who I am, who we all are! It wasn't all this bullshit nonsense, this fake crap—it was, like, reality! We were literally going to be our real selves! For the world to see! Do you know how many people dream of that?"

Al had an answer for that that he just let go.

"I'm an influencer, but what is my influence? Like, seriously? In a world where people ask kids what they want to be when they grow up when they are in kindergarten, this could have been the answer. We were given a shortcut to being ourselves and being recognized for being ourselves, and now it's, like, gone!"

"It might not be gone, baby," Al said, trying to hug her as she wriggled away.

"It might not be, but it looks like it might be!" Roxanna insisted, with tears in her eyes. "I don't know what I'm going to do—I have nothing to look forward to. And fuck living in the present! There is no present! The entire world is just sick, like, in every way! I had goals and dreams and now I have to do it all again? And money can't solve that, Dad! That stuff isn't material! It's imagination! And I'm depressed—"

"Oh, my dear R—"

"And the thing I've noticed about depression is that the first thing to go is imagination! So here we are. I have no schemes. Like, nothing! It's like Violet without her sense of smell and taste, how she can't imagine continuing without her sweets and all that. Well, this is my drama! It's a mess. I really feel like my life is over!"

Al let his daughter cry herself into a ball on his sofa, until she grew even bored of that, wiped her face, and walked off to the garden, where Homa was napping in her silk hammock.

"Hey, sorry," Roxanna said softly.

"Come here, Roxi," her mom said, sitting up as if she'd been waiting for her. She was too alert and fresh-faced to have been sleeping as deeply as Roxanna thought she was.

"Do you fake sleep a lot?" Roxanna asked as she cuddled up in the seemingly infinite folds of the plush hammock next to Homa. She didn't know why she never did this; she also didn't know why it felt so strange for her to lie down next to her mother. She realized she had virtually no memories of ever doing it. She must have slept in her arms constantly as a baby, and yet.

"I don't know if I would call it 'fake,'" Homa said, smiling at the clouds. "I try to sleep but it doesn't always come. Then I realize it is so nice to shut the world out."

"It must be nice." Roxanna felt her throat get raspy. Something about lying next to her mother like this made her want to cry again. "We never shut a thing out. Like, your era, you guys could just be without, like, being on for everyone. I can't even understand what that could be like."

Homa had thought that many times, of course. These generations of young people, hooked to their phones, treating their social media like jobs, performing themselves endlessly. How would she have coped if she had that back then? Homa didn't think she could have. She could not stand it now—she imagined how much worse it would have been when she was young and even more insecure, perhaps without AI to help draw her out of her shell.

"Well, we let ourselves not exist," Homa said softly. "Which maybe sounds so bad to you all. But it was a kind of freedom."

"I wish I was free like that. I hate all this shit," Roxanna grumbled. "Did people get along more?"

Homa thought about it for a few moments. She let images of her childhood, snapshots against tidbits of memory, float by through her mind's eye. She was amazed at how much felt so fresh. She could smell Iran—that was what wounded her the most.

"People getting along more? No." Homa could always be counted on to answer honestly. "We still fought and had enemies and were jealous. Maybe it was even worse. It was maybe harder to meet people and make friends."

Roxanna was surprised to hear this. "Then what made it better?"

Homa looked at her, perplexed. "Why do you keep assuming it was better?"

"I know all of you from past eras look at us and think we are so doomed, and we know it too! Everything is dying, failing, everything is, like, going to be trash. Your time had to be better!"

Homa laughed softly. There was something so sweet about having Roxanna alongside her, in an almost embrace. And there was something so special in hearing Roxanna like this, like *herself*. Homa realized that maybe she also was rarely herself with Roxanna.

"I don't know about better, but I think we had more times like this. Downtimes. Do you like moments like this?"

Roxanna had rarely in her life been asked to evaluate her present state—only ever in therapy. Her mother's question startled her a bit. She didn't know the answer. She shrugged.

"It's okay." Homa pulled Roxanna's head in for an embrace, a kiss on her forehead. She felt tears well up in her eyes, all because of how rare a simple moment like this was in their lives. "You don't have to know everything, not even how you feel. Do you know that?"

Roxanna wrinkled her nose at the question. "I don't know that I don't need to know! Is that it?" A few stray laughs tumbled out of her. "I hate how hard it is to be a human, but I hope I can have more quiet moments. I hate . . . content. I don't want to be content."

Homa squinted at her. "I don't even know how you'd think

of yourself that way. But I don't think of you like that. You are more than all that. You are real. Our very real baby."

At that, Roxanna's laugh got the best of her, and soon she was in a fit, tears in her eyes. "Sometimes I am totally out of touch with all that stuff. Like reality. God, I am so fucking nuts."

Homa hushed her. "You are fine. And we are very lucky. Not because of all this, but because of all of us." She had one hand on Roxanna's heart.

Roxanna broke down into sobs, a long-swallowed sorrow gripping her. Her mother soothed her with an embrace that Roxanna had to fight to think of as real. She wanted to imagine it as a hug in a movie between a mother and a daughter. But it was real. She was real.

That night she put a selfie on Instagram with the caption: "Time to get real: I cry too. I feel too. I hurt too. I need to come clean and show you all the real me, which is not clean. I have a long way to go. How do you help your heart? Comment below with a black heart if you are in your feelz too." The photo was a barely filtered one of her just after she had cried, her face makeup-streaked and puffy and red. It was unlike her in every way, but it got her more likes and comments than she had ever had before.

Bad Girls Gone Good. It made her sick what the public was turning to—what she was turning into too.

Love you sis was the first comment she got, from Mina, to her surprise. No black heart. Mina was the only one out of all of them who seemed okay that season. What a strange reversal of normal life.

Are you ok, Violet immediately texted Roxanna, without commenting on her post.

No of course not, you saw the post, Roxanna wrote back.

Well, I didn't know if it was for the 'gram or whatever lol, Violet wrote back. *What happened tho?*

Nothing, just the same old, Roxanna wrote back. *I mean, the show could be gone and that sucks.*

Oh Roxi, we'll all be fine, there will be more stuff for us, I know it.

Ugh whatever. So much for my needing to tell everyone the truth about my Secret lol sigh.

It never hurts to do good, Roxi.

Hey why is Mina so happy these days? She NEVER comments on my IG and there she was suddenly.

Oh wow I just saw it lol.

Yeah so weird. Maybe she got the virus and it went to her head.

Oh, I think it's something else.

What is it? What do you know?

It's really important you not tell her I told you or anyone really. Please, Rox.

Oh god, I am deep in depression, I'm not out here gossiping about my most boring sister, V.

ROX.

Ok, what is it tho?

I think she's in love 😱

In love? WTF? With who? How?

Your party!

Oh god. She is the one out of all of us who found someone there?

Ha, it's crazy, right? And it's kind of great that it's, you know

Know what?

PLEASE do not say a word, Roxi. Srsly.

Oh god, I know she's a lesbian.

She might be more nonbinary or gender-fluid or something, not sure what she's calling it. Anyway, let's be careful not to say much.

Roxanna laughed to herself. Smoggy sunshine was bursting through the window blinds, against her will. She closed them tighter. *It really is end-times if Mina is the one in love, but hey like whatever happy 4 her, happy 4 like someone's fucking shit to go right in this fucking endless apocalypse!*

15

Roxanna-Vanna Soraya Milani

NO because he never did a thing like that before not of all times the sunday before school began again the fucking fuck of it all starting again like we did all this for nothing like what even was this and now they say or Mina says at least there's gonna be what-do-you-call-it mutations or variants or something and they say the vaccines won't even cover it or maybe they will goddamn apocalypse all i know is haylee is already freaking about the fucking vaccines though but like thank god she's not as fucking nuts as she was a few months back and yeah mina's in love with her lesbo lover, that whatever bald model girl, which like i'm happy for her, but like the truth is we're all teens and our hearts were made to be broken like what do you think that's gonna turn into some real love your very first love like i can't even remember my first love wait like actually i can because it was him damon of course though he was not the last because of course not and it wasn't cheating you can't cheat if it's on-and-off and i always said to everyone who asked he's my on-and-off which some budget-angelina cool girl said in a movie so just let's say anytime i felt like that could even remotely like even happen i knew to call things off like yup baby need a break and then i could like freely do my thing and well that first time i definitely did not waste time there cuz with ricky i really thought i was in love with him cuz of course he was a dj and like my first dj and so our whole life was clubs until i realized what being a dj's girl really was and like him making out with me in the dj booth when i was high as a kite was just a way to temporarily shut me up because hey what do they say i might as well take a ticket with those dj boys and you'd think i would learn a lesson because he was not my last there was also that guy emerald whose real name i never learned and i think no one really knows though wait there was some rando dude named john before him but he was just another athlete and my god he had a hot body even though there wasn't a whole lot going on upstairs and frankly he wasn't rich enough anyway after emerald there was tj who was a drug dealer not like weed drug but you know a level up and like i think he did something else but i didn't stick around long enough to figure it out and then there was cristian who was gay and frankly what a waste but wow anyway i gotta thank violet for getting me through that and then there was that half persian guy who went by rusty but i think was named rustom lol i can't even get into the disaster there but i did have dad meet him so at least he knew i tried at least once even though ol' al was not impressed either when rusty said he hoped to teach math in inner city schools or whatever and like then there was takeo who was a tattoo artist and from one of japan's richest families but like really had no ambitions and frankly just wanted to get back to that other city that's not tokyo sorry i spaced when he said it and oof then there was that like old guy who had worked with dad before i think he was like forty or forty-five and i swear his name was like herman or something like i have no idea what happened there i think that could have been roofies but i did love that he said he'd try to kill that one ex–substitute teacher from our high school mr. leonard who was always massaging my shoulders whenever i was in anything sleeveless anyway he doesn't count but i could have ew just thought and like ok now i am totally out of order but did i get to lamar oh he was so cute and i think i'm still in love with him but he actually punched damon and that was like a lot to deal with especially when damon was like you're barely taking my side and i couldn't be like well lamar is kinda like my boo tho of course damon would figure all of them out eventually because the thing with damon is that he's not dumb at all tho you probably can't tell at first he's just very different in how he expressed himself from me and my family which honestly surprised me because i thought we acted more italian than he did and no one really batted an eye and not even him so anyway when he said that thing about talking on sunday i was like this is what it's going to be about because when i asked him for a hint he was like *it was something you said at the party* and i was like what party and then i realized like damon is still talking about my party months ago like that party had such an impact like it was everyone's first and maybe even last of the pandemic like i heard violet was not the only one who got sick and someone in fake doja's entourage had brought the virus to the party and so a few other people tested positive but like everyone was fine i mean i would have heard if someone had died or some shit right i mean this goes back to my theory about rich people and how they survive shit and how ok maybe this is bad to say but this virus really got the poors and not us tho i know violet got it but like have you seen how that bitch eats like yikes but she's really been improving yep we've got mina in love and haylee's head straight and now violet taking care of herself and also what trips me out is she's considering applying to college next year which like whoa what the hell and when i asked her about modeling she was like yeah no it's just not a priority or whatever but like if i do it it will be plus-size only which like bitch what are you talking about, if you eat better now after the virus you won't have to be plus-size but i guess count on violet to be extreme about consuming cause i think the bitch is doing healthy fats a bit too much like she's picking avocados off our tree and making batch after batch of guacamole like that is so much fat and she's been putting raw eggs in her smoothies you just can't fix a bitch so like whatever i guess enjoy plus-size modeling which i know we're in the body positivity™ era but like kill me these millennials will do anything for clout how is this shit going to last no one wants to be fat and when i look at these photos of these big girls i'm just like ok what about girls like me like is body positivity™ gonna go full circle and then we need justice for skinny bitches eventually you see what i mean like not to be all maga but this is like the woke shit that just reads as crazy which sorry to say crazy cuz some bitch probably mina will like say that's ableist but you know what whatever i know who i am i am roxanna-vanna milani roxanna-vanna soraya milani and i am problematic as fuck like how many times did i get canceled during the lockdown period alone like so many bitches and what did it do well some minor damage here and there but nothing that publicists and some social media magic and a phoned-in apology and a hot follow-up ig post and basically just money could not fix you know?

11:11 make a wish god I love the angel chimes okay new wish same old wish Scorpio season is almost here but did I tell you about the time I first learned that but I remembered it as *9:11 make a wish* and then like I accidentally said it and that was the first time I worried they would know what we were I was born just a few months before it all went down but still I was told still I know enough to know people like me don't get to make jet fuel steel beams or whatever jokes no I'll stick to *7:11 make a wish* if it comes to that

did i mention my new thing is shitting glitter lol i am not even kidding like tmi whatever i don't want to give away all my secrets but this is a real thing like anyone can hook the fuck up like i found this vendor in tokyo that sells these little pills these little capsules full of food grade gold glitter and you just swallow on an empty stomach preferably i think and a few hours later when you have to shit it's like gold poo like how perfect is that like that is just so my brand and if our show had happened i swear that would have been the first episode not that i want to show my actual shit on tv but we would be talking about it like that kardashians episode where they are all discussing their pussy juice and then it turns into a pussy juice competition between the sisters where they are drinking pineapple juice nonstop for days and then they have a taste test which yeah cringe but then of course it turns out kim has the best pussy juice of course lol i can't believe that was aired anyway we are so like 2.0 anyway if they can air that they can air me announcing i shit gold lol how classic how iconic would that have been anyway yeah it's sad the kardashians are over i mean they are not over but the show is over they just made it official 14 years last season ending 2021 season 20 so crazy another casualty of the pandemic like i don't know i just feel like in addition to human lives lost or whatever there was a real loss of the culture you know like people couldn't handle laughing and just like vibing and tuning themselves out which like could not be me if you ask anyone including my family ask the fucking milanis if there was one person who handled all this well who was it and they will tell you roxi fucking milani 100 percent i was that bitch and i gotta be honest there were entire days where my life was no different which is another reason why it's such fucking trash that our show got canned though dad says it could still happen but the producers are saying indefinite and i don't keep my hopes up high for anyone or anything like i know a bum deal and a cold shoulder when i see one and they went from being so psyched to being all weird and i kinda feel like we should blame haylee tbh tho not because of what you think because like ok that phase of hers was america too y'know no but i mean the cat psychic that was like a real low for me even tho the dude whatever his name was was actually not wrong about all of us or should i say the cat or whatever but like if you'll believe it haylee actually called him again i guess cause after her illness violet wanted a check-in or whatever and then he was at it again with perry looking all possessed like the weird household milani god perry is and saying all

kinds of shit about us like the show was over and that was why
he or she i can't even remember what perry is anyway that was
why perry was happier because we could just go back to being
normal whatever normal is if you could even say a family like
us knows normal we are the milanis after all this is tehrangeles
after all anyway the cat basically said a lot of what he said last
time which was like yeah everyone hang out with me more or
whatever and like work on yourselves bitches or whatever but
one thing did stick out and it really kind of upset me and it was
just know the world does not stop for you and like the troubles
will not be over anytime soon which like what lol i guess they
meant the pandemic and lockdown which yeah duh we get it
there's gonna be new strains or whatever but all of us but violet
are teens our worldview is already fucked like i know gen z has
grown up faster than the others and people forget we're minors
and sometimes we do too tbh but like we are only prepared for
the worst and accept nothing but the worst news always like
who are you even kidding like bring it on the virus sucks but
life already sucked anyway which is why someone like me i fill
it with shit like the party and drugs tho yes i have cut down and
i've already set 2024 as the date i will begin my adderall wean
and i only take xanax one or twice a week and i promise i am
staying away from angel dust anyway i fill life with all this crazy
shit like shitting gold for example lmao anyway just don't talk
to me about troubles tho going there took me back to the party
and what damon wanted to say and let's just say it was heavier
than heavy it was like concrete batter from hell heavy

he looked like he was like crying but then he swore it was
allergies tho he said he hadn't slept much lately because he was
worrying about a lot of things like his parents' business and the
virus and his cousin and of course his dead aunt and then this
whole thing with me which i was like bitch like just tell me
what it is but of course a part of me was like please do not tell
me can we just avoid this shit altogether like this is the part

where me suddenly being a scorpio after a lifetime of gemini means nothing like i am avoidant as shit and when people need to talk to me and they say talk in that voice where i am just like ok shit like this is gonna be some important shit about me i guess and i probably won't like it or whatever anyway damon was being so dramatic like he's never been good with words but like wow the drama of the pause and his puffy face and everyone knows i can't stand silence like i began humming some lana del rey song like just to fill in the tension or whatever it was and then he was like roxanna-vanna which already i'm like oop ok what's this like he never calls me by my full name like that like no one really does anymore anyway he's all like roxanna-vanna i've heard some things for a while and i just didn't know what to make of them because they didn't make sense because you and i have been together forever and i can honestly say no one knows me better than you and i thought the same for me with you but now i really don't know because this was just so weird and i'm like flipping through my brain like a rolodex like this can't be the cheating because that was always allowed like wtf is this then the bitch looks so fucking plagued but then he just says it all awkward and kinda crazy-like he goes so i've been hearing you're like iranian or persian or whichever you say but like you've always been telling me you're italian which made sense to me because i am and i really am by the way so i just never thought to doubt it because who would lie about a thing like that and actually you've been accused of blackfishing so it's like why would you go the other direction because pretty sure italian is more white than persian but anyway i feel so stupid because how would i as your boyfriend not even know this like your last name even sounds so italian and you all have these american sounding names and i never heard you speak whatever the persian language is or whatever like how could your family hide this and well there you fucking had it my worst nightmare like i know i've tried to tell him for ages and i've told my sisters and i knew i would have to tell the whole school with the show but honestly when the show went bust or looked like it was going to i was like ok this is the one godsend because like it's one thing to explain to your sisters who think you're fucking crazy anyway but to set the record straight with everyone else like it would just be too crazy because like damon said who would even do that and honestly the most cringe thing of all was the idea of telling damon partially because he was italian and partially because well love tho i hate saying love with us because we're too young for love tbh i think i will always be too young for love and hopefully damon will be my last boyfriend because i am just not cut out for this which is what i was thinking after he said it and it was more silence and like i was thinking ok this is it this is the perfect exit this is actually the excuse i've been looking for because i can't do this i was not cut out for this and how am i going to fix this anyway like sorry damon i lied and yes damon like i am crazy and yes damon i make up toxic lies that no one would dare make up like ok bye anyway like there is no better exit moment than this one so i'm just sitting in the silence trying to gather my words like how do you dump a guy who'd gotten the balls to confront you on the fact that your life has been a lie or whatever and i'm humming that line from "born to die" where lana says "you like your girls insane" when he suddenly says because roxi this changes nothing i want you to know that i will love you always and i still want to spend my life together with you forever and ever and i'm thinking my god this has somehow driven him to more commitment like who is even the crazy one like why would you want to spend your life with someone who lied to you in the most cringe way imaginable but like honestly i don't know who damon would end up with because while he's hot and rich he has little game and not many friends and most of his personality he really borrows from me so i am kinda shocked now like did this somehow give me some edge like why would he need to reassure me like why is he all loving on me like what

i did was fucking disgusting and then he goes on and roxi i tried
to read about it online and i read about the history of discrimi-
nation against people from iran in america and it was really awful
and so it makes sense to me why you needed to do it and somehow that truth just becomes way too much for me because like
why of all things is he talking sense now i suddenly get up and
try to get out and he suddenly i don't see where they came from
he has this big thing of pink and red roses the forever flower kind
that never die and i think cost a lot anyway he never really did
the flower thing except those tulips that one time after that long
break and i don't know how he read my mind but i wanted roses
not tulips anyway it kind of feels like a movie but not a movie i
star in and every time he opens his mouth it gets worse and
worse and there he goes again roxi the part that bugged me honestly was the part where you lied to me and i just want you to
know i forgive you and also that it is never necessary there is
nothing you can't tell me i know you get misunderstood by lots
of people roxi but i really see you and i know the true good and
beauty that is there so please don't lie can i just ask you for that
one commitment that we have a life of no lies and i'm like i'm
stuck on the life part like what the hell is going on if this was
someone else i would have thought i was being pranked honestly because i know mina found love and haylee found sanity
and violet found health and all of them got their happy ending
or whatever and then there's me just being me shitting gold lol
so the temptation is to somehow to fix me here too but like i
was not about this at all like the thing with me is while i know i
need to change i don't want to change like honestly the biggest
change i have had in the last few years was the change from
gemini to scorpio and that was like dramatic bitches so do not
come to me for more changes i am not that bitch like this is not
the moment where the fairy waves a wand and i go from italian
to iranian in front of my prince charming or whatever and like i
must have looked disgusted because he was like suddenly so

alarmed and his hand was at my face all soothing or whatever his thumb rubbing my cheek his thumb somehow wet with something and i was like ew damon what is that was the first thing i said to him after all that tbh and he looked confused and he was like what is what babe and i was like why is your hand wet ew gross and he was like even more confused and was like roxi babe those are your tears and i was like what and like i guess that was the truth because i got up and suddenly saw my makeup was smeared and streaked and my eyes were all watery and i will be honest i come from a family of crybaby sisters and i am not someone who what wait the hell am i saying i was gonna say i am not someone who cries but how many times did they did you did everyone see me cry jfc but like still seeing me like that was like a horror film of someone else plus like i don't cry cute like lana said "don't make me sad, don't make me cry" and suddenly i was like this just has to stop so i was like maybe i can talk about something else and i was like damon i think i am gonna book a flight to hawaii for a while which might have seemed like a random thing to say but i was pretty sure i could convince homa or even violet though of course he had to be like roxi school starts tomorrow to which i had nothing to say because tbh i had forgotten and like honestly who can remember anyway we've been in this weird lockdown world too long and suddenly that reality also hit me like school yikes the real world just waiting for me there in not months not weeks not days but like hours yikes and that's when i really start to cry to which he says don't worry babe i won't be telling anyone and if anyone asks me i'll just say i have no idea what they are talking about or we can consult your publicist or whatever assuming she knows or whatever you want babe we'll make it okay and i'm so disgusted because like of course everything is going to be okay like it always is and maybe that's the problem and i swear for a second i have a feeling like i don't want to exist and it has nothing absolutely nothing to do with the lie but i don't want to be here or there or anywhere like what i wanted was to be in reality like a reality star not a person in reality like lol what is this hell and then he just keeps saying the main thing is you and i are okay that's all i want to know that i can count on us that we will be together forever and okay through this all i'm just feeling so dizzy hearing but pls like i don't get sick ever and i don't even want to say it because i know where everyone's brains will go like she has the virus or something or whatever but i truly feel sick no lie and like i need to get out of there asap even tho it's my room but like i got to get out of my room and my house and like maybe even tehrangeles tbh but he's just looking at me with those eyes but no i just want to get out and get back to normal or just getting out is fine no i just have to get out and back to myself or back to some better self and i mean tbh it was a nightmare no are you hearing me but no there's suddenly a crunch i hear underneath me like bones and it's the forever roses not so forever i guess and like now the smell their smell is just fake some spray rose scent no i swear i am sick no i think it's my heart but my heart what heart what is there to break but his no damon i can't do this no and he's like do what i love you baby and i'm trying to think how i said it before how did i ask for a break and how can i do it again but damon is telling me over and over i love you i forgive you and then i need you to love yourself no and i'm like this song is too corny where's lana "feet don't fail me now, take me to the finish line" but isn't this the moment i was waiting for isn't this the forever the true the real love then why does it feel so no i don't love you damon but i don't tell him that because maybe i'm not sure what do i know but i do know i love myself that after all we've been through this planet this time i love myself do i love myself i love my good my bad my lies i love when they hated me i love when they hated me more i loved when they loved me back i am all love don't you no i don't know no i feel sick what is wrong with him what is wrong with us what is wrong with this place and he's asking baby i am wor-

ried baby are you okay no one thing i know is no i swear on my
everyfuckingthing on gold and glitter and tehrangeles no and i
wanted to go but something made me put my arm around him
and i drew him down so he could feel my vintage versace corset
boob armor and nothing else but instead i felt it like i heard it
this time it was his heart just his heart was going like a bomb i'll
spare you the bomb joke it's not an italian thing anyway his heart
this boy who was my everything and his heart the way it's going
it's scaring me worse and he's asking again and i'm saying baby
when have i ever been okay baby no i said never i said baby just
let me be never forever no

Acknowledgments

This novel started as a joke back in 2011—*I know I know:* let me explain . . .

All my life I have been haunted by my extreme dislike of the book *Little Women*—a book I thought, as a child, I was supposed to love and could not love. It turns out its beloved author, Louisa May Alcott, was her own hater too! This mattered to me because this third novel of mine was a book I was determined to hate-write my way through. When the idea for *Tehrangeles* came to me, I was still trying to sell the dreaded "sophomore effort"—my very weird fabulist second novel, *The Last Illusion*. After a host of editors, mostly male, said they wished I'd written a more realist story with more women characters—it was about a bird boy (long story!)—in a moment of perhaps ill-advised rebellion, I started writing what I thought was a pretty funny parody of their requests. I landed on writing a book with an all-female cast (except a dad and a boyfriend—even the cat is female!). What I didn't know at the time was that this mirrored Alcott's experience. *Little Women* got its start when Alcott asked her publisher, Thomas Niles, to publish a collection of short stories. Instead, under pressure from Niles and her father, Amos Bronson Alcott, she consented reluctantly to write the tale of the March sisters after Niles insisted it was time for a book about girls that would have widespread appeal. "So I plod away, though I don't enjoy this sort of thing," she wrote. "Never liked girls or knew many, except my sisters; but our queer plays and experiences may prove interesting, though I doubt it." She was wrong—it was a hit! And she wrote it in under three years— more than I can say for this book, which took thirteen-plus years!

If this is my way of thanking Alcott, let's thank the other authors that made this possible: most of all I thank Kevin Kwan, whose Crazy Rich Asians trilogy—masterpieces!—made me realize I could have a Crazy Rich West Asians on my hand. Bret Easton Ellis's *American Psycho* and *Glamorama* poisoned my brain properly in my youth and so I returned to them for some style-over-substance, devil-on-my-shoulder courage. Of course, I also could not have written the final chapter without James Joyce's *Ulysses;* for a long time, the very prospect of rewriting the Molly Bloom chapter in Valley Girl stream-of-consciousness fueled this whole endeavor.

Many drafts came and went but this recent one gelled in the pandemic, among so much loss. Gone are several extraordinary women: Alanna, Shanna, Mona, Kassandra, Jess, Voyce, Ariel, Deena. I also always think of Marsha Mehran, who died ten years ago, and who I wish were here to discuss women's fiction with me. The only thing I gained during this pandemic was this book (but I'd rather have my friends).

This book's lifespan was over the hardest years of my life, so I have to thank a core group of friends (some first readers), who encouraged me and this project on this journey, at some point or another: Candice Tang, Alex Chee, Ben Moser, Cal Morgan, Joseph Caceres, William Berry, Amina AlTai, Steve Judd, Ariel Tonkel, and Brett Baldridge.

Most of all I owe everything to Danzy Senna and Victoria Redel, mentors and dearest friends and brilliant writers, who have known me since the late nineties; what a blessing to have known these women for over half my life.

A big thanks to the entire Pantheon family and the team

that supported it there. Thank you to the late great Dan Frank, who had first seen my work in 2006 with some encouraging words and had urged Pantheon to buy this on proposal back in 2018 as a two-book deal with *Brown Album;* thank you to Lisa Lucas for gloriously building on Pantheon's tremendous legacy. Thank you to my legend-of-an-agent Susan Golomb, for not just loving this but for giving me renewed hope as an author in this strange (middle-aged!) moment in my life. Thank you, my brilliant editor Maria Goldverg, for your great eye, sharp brain, patience, and kindness; we've been together for two books, and her reassurances still feel like magic to me. I am so grateful to her genius assistant Lisa Kwan as well—they were an invaluable part of this, especially as my dream target audience. Thank you to Naomi Gibbs, Julianne Clancy, Josefine Kals, Amy Hagedorn, Natalia Berry, Bianca Ducasse, Melissa Yoon, Philip Pascuzzo, and truly everyone at Pantheon whose efforts made this book come together with so much grace, confidence, and joy. Thanks also to my speaking agent, Leslie Shipman, for not being just an agent but a wonderful friend. Thank you finally to Sylvie Rabineau, my film/TV agent, at William Morris Endeavor—Sylvie's vision of my novel's potential threw me back into another honeymoon phase with it.

Thank you to the great Gen Z muse-of-muses writer/model/actress Helya Salarvand, my half-Mina, who not just gave me a way to imagine my favorite character, but who became family along the way. Thank you to our older brother and dad, fashion icon Hushi Mortezaie, to whom this book is dedicated, for *everything* plus bringing us together whether in our forever group chat or at L.A.'s Tehran-Ro, Pardis, Raffi, and more, for sustaining us back when #WomenLifeFreedom left us spiritually invigorated and depleted at once, in the way only all things Iran can.

Thank you to all the obscenely wealthy Iranians of Tehrangeles who alienated this San Gabriel Valley kid of the rickety dingbat hills. Thank you, Tehrangelenos, who came into the Rodeo

Drive boutique I was a shopgirl at and made it known you felt so sorry for me. As I smiled and nodded and showed you five-figure handbags, I thought to myself one day, *I will write about you*. I never thought that through the exercise I would come to feel for you. (Take that, Louisa May Alcott!)

I am also very grateful to the *New York Times* Arts and Leisure section, where the mentions first appeared; in a 2011 and 2012 essay I mentioned working on this book to hold myself account-able to do it. ". . . I decided to embark on a novel about two of my worst nightmares: the first Iranian-American reality televi-sion family and war with Iran."

Thank you to the Ucross Foundation, South Pasadena Pub-lic Library, the Beverly Centre, Marcus Garvey NYPL branch library in Harlem and the Flushing QPL branch, Residence Inn by Marriott New York JFK Airport in Jamaica, Queens, Hotel Fauchère in Milford, Pennsylvania, various other hotels in L.A. and N.Y., the places where so much of this was written.

Thank you also to my Evergreen Review family: editing among you all has been the honor of a lifetime!

Most of all, thank you to my beloved partner, Bing Guan. Such bliss when someone you love looks at something you made with so much love! Bing read this so many times from the first month we began dating, all the way to doing all-nighters with me to years later in edits. He saw me cry, fret, give up, try again, love, hate, and everything-in-between with this book. He also did time with me in Tehrangeles over much kabob, ghormeh sabzi, and doogh! I love you with all my heart, angel floof.

Thanks to our child, fluffy icon Cosmo, who was a baby dog the first time I printed this out and made it to an elder of eleven by the time it was done. He passed away during my last pass, but this book truly would not have existed without his constant love.

Oodles of gratitude and big love, *sepas, tashakor, mamnun, and merci,* loves/dears/*azizes*/*joons!* <3

A Note About the Author

Porochista Khakpour was born in Tehran and raised in the greater Los Angeles area. She is the critically acclaimed author of two previous novels, *Sons and Other Flammable Objects* and *The Last Illusion;* a memoir, *Sick;* and a collection of essays, *Brown Album.* Her writing has appeared in *The New York Times, The Washington Post,* the *Los Angeles Times, The Wall Street Journal, Bookforum, Elle,* and many other publications. She lives in New York City.

A Note on the Type

This book was set in a version of the well-known Monotype face Bembo. This letter was cut for the celebrated Venetian printer Aldus Manutius by Francesco Griffo, and first used in Pietro Cardinal Bembo's *De Aetna* of 1495.

Typeset by Scribe,
Philadelphia, Pennsylvania

Printed by LSC Communications,
Harrisonburg, Virginia

Designed by Michael Collica